Prize Stories
1988
THE O. HENRY AWARDS

Prize Stories
1988

=== THE ===

O. HENRY
AWARDS

Edited and with
an Introduction
by William Abrahams

⚓

890099

Doubleday

NEW YORK

1988

SC
HEN
1988

The Library of Congress has cataloged this work as follows:
Prize stories. 1947–
Garden City, N.Y., Doubleday.
v. 22 cm.
Annual
The O. Henry awards.
None published 1952–53
Continues: O. Henry memorial award prize stories.
Key title: Prize stories, ISSN 0079-5453.
1. Short stories, American—Collected works.
PZ1.011   813'.01'08—dc19   21-9372
MARC-S
Library of Congress   [8402r83]rev4
ISBN 0-385-24183-6

Contents

Publisher's Note

This volume is the sixty-eighth in the O. Henry Memorial Award series.

In 1918, the Society of Arts and Sciences met to vote upon a monument to the master of the short story, O. Henry. They decided that this memorial should be in the form of two prizes for the best short stories published by American authors in American magazines during the year 1919. From this beginning, the memorial developed into an annual anthology of outstanding short stories by American authors, published, with the exception of the years 1952 and 1953, by Doubleday & Company, Inc.

Blanche Colton Williams, one of the founders of the awards, was editor from 1919 to 1932; Harry Hansen from 1933 to 1940; Herschel Brickell from 1941 to 1951. The annual collection did not appear in 1952 and 1953, when the continuity of the series was interrupted by the death of Herschel Brickell. Paul Engle was editor from 1954 to 1959 with Hanson Martin co-editor in the years 1954 to 1960; Mary Stegner in 1960; Richard Poirier from 1961 to 1966, with assistance from and co-editorship with William Abrahams from 1964 to 1966. William Abrahams became editor of the series in 1967.

In 1970 Doubleday published under Mr. Abrahams' editorship *Fifty Years of the American Short Story,* and in 1981, *Prize Stories of the Seventies.* Both are collections of stories selected from this series.

The stories chosen for this volume were published in the period from the summer of 1986 to the summer of 1987. A list of the magazines consulted appears at the back of the book. The choice of stories and the selection of prize winners are exclusively the responsibility of the editor. Biographical material is based on information provided by the contributors and obtained from standard works of reference.

Introduction

With the publication of *Prize Stories 1988: The O. Henry Awards,* we are chronologically within hailing distance of the year 2000. Whatever else the new century may bring, one can anticipate much looking back, retrospective summaries, surveys, and reevaluations: the twentieth century will become history. Yet even now, twelve years before the significant date, I don't think it too reckless to suggest that the modern short story will prove to be one of the enduring literary achievements of the twentieth century. Nor do I doubt that in the twelve years ahead new writers will emerge to join the ranks of those who have made their individual contributions to the art, and I trust that many of them will be welcomed with O. Henry Awards. It has always been my intention, in the twenty-two years that I have served as editor for this series, to recognize new writers—as for example, in the present volume, Richard Currey, Sheila Kohler, Philip Deaver, and Richard Plant, who are represented with their first published stories.

It is gratifying to come upon such writers in the early stages of their careers, when the voice is being heard for the first time. But it is equally gratifying, if in a different fashion, to watch the unfolding of a career and to know that the allegiance to the story by established writers has not dimmed, may indeed have deepened and strengthened. In 1970 the series introduced as a mark of recognition, a Special Award for Continuing Achievement. That award has been given to Joyce Carol Oates (1970), to John Updike (1976), to Alice Adams (1982), and again to Joyce Carol Oates (1986). All three writers are present this year; familiarity has not diminished their power, and I should further point out that fourteen of the contributors to this volume have appeared here in the past. The evidence of continuity is not unimportant. I am always saddened when a promising beginning is followed by a long, and in some cases, unbroken silence. Of course one is grateful for the story one has been given, yet one hopes for more.

"More," as it happens, is precisely the word to describe the situation of the story at the present time. More stories are being published; more magazines that welcome the story have come into existence—I note that the list of Magazines Consulted this year has been expanded by twenty-nine new magazines to a total of 158; more annual collections are being offered to readers; more attention is being paid to the story by reviewers and in bookshops. It is reassuring to discover that all this plenty has not led to a dilution of quality. As has happened with the O. Henry Awards in previous years, the repeated siftings have brought the number of possible stories to the neighborhood of one hundred.

I think it only fair to add that among the stories that have been reluctantly let go are several whose excellence is not in dispute, and I expect to reacquaint myself with them in one or another of the annual anthologies. Questions of personal preference and subjective response do, after all, figure in a final selection.

As before, there is a remarkable variety among the stories—each has its excellence. What seems more noticeable, however, is the ancestral presence of that great master of the story, Anton Chekhov. It becomes increasingly clear that his has been the dominating spirit in the twentieth-century story, in its authenticity, its humane concerns, and its openness to experience. Consciously or not, for he has been with us so long that he can be taken for granted, we are all in his debt.

Raymond Carver's "Errand," this year's First Prize story, is a beautiful and affecting acknowledgment of that debt. Carver has been too easily pigeonholed as the leader of the new (so-called) "Minimalist" school, a distinction he has not sought and which does him a disservice. Certainly "Errand" has been written with an openness and range that is, I would think, remote from the minimal. Admittedly, the story does begin with a sentence of one word. But the word is "Chekhov." And how that word illuminates our lives, how much resonance it gives off, simply by being there, telling us of a life that is in itself an exemplary story and that, in fiction, will be Carver's story for us. Let me dispose of an irrelevancy: that Chekhov was a "real person" and there-

fore a story in which he appears can't be fiction. The biographical
details around which the story has been composed will be found in any
biography. But almost at once Carver strikes a note of his own, as
though one were engaged in a conversation. He will tell us about
"this" Chekhov, who "went to dinner in Moscow with his friend and
confidant Alexei Suvorin. This Suvorin was a very rich newspaper and
book publisher. . . ."

In its quiet conversational way the story moves forward from 1897
to the last night of Chekhov's life, July 2, 1904, achieving a perfect
verisimilitude. Indeed, the details are so vividly chosen—the moth
flying into the room, the cork popping from the champagne bottle—
that I consulted Henri Troyat's biography, wondering if perhaps they
had been invented. But even as this scene occurred in life, recorded
later by Chekhov's wife in a memoir, so it reappears in Carver's story
but with subtle, hardly noticeable alternatives—the alternatives of art.
For it is precisely at this point that Carver's story glides across a
threshold, so to speak, into fiction. The young tousled waiter who
brings the champagne to the Chekhovs' hotel suite now becomes the
central figure in what is, in effect, a second story. Madame Chekhov,
an actress of great renown, later would write about the death: "There
were no human voices, no everyday sounds. There was only beauty,
peace, and the grandeur of death." But art reveals to us that there was
more. The second story is signaled by a very slight change in tone:
"She stayed with Chekhov until daybreak, when thrushes began to
call from the garden below. Then came the sound of tables and chairs
being moved about down there. Before long, voices carried up to her.
It was then a knock sounded at the door."

We are entering into the world of fiction, and Carver is writing a
kind of Chekhovian story. Now, we understand why the first story
pretends to be no more than a retelling of biographical fact. One life
has gone, another life enters. Earlier, Carver remarks of Chekhov's
doctor, Schwörher: "He picked up his bag and left the room and, for
that matter, history." Now it is the young waiter—one feels that Chekhov might have written about himself—who enters the room. Carver
has brought him before us: art has remembered him as though he had
actually existed. Perhaps he did.

"Errand" recalls to us how Chekhov "once told someone that he lacked 'a political, religious, and philosophical world view. I change it every month, so I'll have to limit myself to the description of how my heroes love, marry, give birth, die, and how they speak.' " This is much too modest, of course. Characteristically, it makes no allowance for the genius that was his. And yet is it not a statement that any writer of any quality would find comprehensible and inspiring? Does it not remind us of what so often we find at the heart of the twentieth-century American story?

—William Abrahams

Prize Stories
1988
THE O. HENRY AWARDS

Errand

•

RAYMOND CARVER

Raymond Carver is the author of Where I'm Calling From: New and
Selected Stories, *published in 1988 by Atlantic Monthly Press, and
recently, two books of poems:* Ultramarine *(1986) and* Where Water
Comes Together with Other Water *(1985), published by Random
House. His work has been translated into more than twenty lan-
guages. He was born in Clatskanie, Oregon.*

Chekhov. On the evening of March 22, 1897, he went to dinner in
Moscow with his friend and confidant Alexei Suvorin. This Suvorin
was a very rich newspaper and book publisher, a reactionary, a self-
made man whose father was a private at the battle of Borodino. Like
Chekhov, he was the grandson of a serf. They had that in common:
each had peasant's blood in his veins. Otherwise, politically and tem-
peramentally, they were miles apart. Nevertheless, Suvorin was one of
Chekhov's few intimates, and Chekhov enjoyed his company.

Naturally, they went to the best restaurant in the city, a former
town house called the Hermitage—a place where it could take hours,
half the night even, to get through a ten-course meal that would, of
course, include several wines, liqueurs, and coffee. Chekhov was im-
peccably dressed, as always—a dark suit and waistcoat, his usual
pince-nez. He looked that night very much as he looks in the photographs taken of him during this period. He was relaxed, jovial. He
shook hands with the maître d', and with a glance took in the large
dining room. It was brilliantly illuminated by ornate chandeliers, the
tables occupied by elegantly dressed men and women. Waiters came

and went ceaselessly. He had just been seated across the table from
Suvorin when suddenly, without warning, blood began gushing from
his mouth. Suvorin and two waiters helped him to the gentlemen's
room and tried to stanch the flow of blood with ice packs. Suvorin saw
him back to his own hotel and had a bed prepared for Chekhov in one
of the rooms of the suite. Later, after another hemorrhage, Chekhov
allowed himself to be moved to a clinic that specialized in the treatment of tuberculosis and related respiratory infections. When Suvorin
visited him there, Chekhov apologized for the "scandal" at the restaurant three nights earlier but continued to insist there was nothing
seriously wrong. "He laughed and jested as usual," Suvorin noted in
his diary, "while spitting blood into a large vessel."

Maria Chekhov, his younger sister, visited Chekhov in the clinic
during the last days of March. The weather was miserable; a sleet
storm was in progress, and frozen heaps of snow lay everywhere. It
was hard for her to wave down a carriage to take her to the hospital.
By the time she arrived she was filled with dread and anxiety.

"Anton Pavlovich lay on his back," Maria wrote in her "Memoirs."
"He was not allowed to speak. After greeting him, I went over to the
table to hide my emotions." There, among bottles of champagne, jars
of caviar, bouquets of flowers from well-wishers, she saw something
that terrified her: a freehand drawing, obviously done by a specialist in
these matters, of Chekhov's lungs. It was the kind of sketch a doctor
often makes in order to show his patient what he thinks is taking
place. The lungs were outlined in blue, but the upper parts were filled
in with red. "I realized they were diseased," Maria wrote.

Leo Tolstoy was another visitor. The hospital staff were awed to
find themselves in the presence of the country's greatest writer. The
most famous man in Russia? Of course they had to let him in to see
Chekhov, even though "nonessential" visitors were forbidden. With
much obsequiousness on the part of the nurses and resident doctors,
the bearded, fierce-looking old man was shown into Chekhov's room.
Despite his low opinion of Chekhov's abilities as a playwright (Tolstoy
felt the plays were static and lacking in any moral vision. "Where do
your characters take you?" he once demanded of Chekhov. "From the
sofa to the junk room and back"), Tolstoy liked Chekhov's short sto-

ries. Furthermore, and quite simply, he loved the man. He told Gorky, "What a beautiful, magnificent man: modest and quiet, like a girl. He even walks like a girl. He's simply wonderful." And Tolstoy wrote in his journal (everyone kept a journal or a diary in those days), "I am glad I love . . . Chekhov."

Tolstoy removed his woollen scarf and bearskin coat, then lowered himself into a chair next to Chekhov's bed. Never mind that Chekhov was taking medication and not permitted to talk, much less carry on a conversation. He had to listen, amazedly, as the Count began to discourse on his theories of the immortality of the soul. Concerning that visit, Chekhov later wrote, "Tolstoy assumes that all of us (humans and animals alike) will live on in a principle (such as reason or love) the essence and goals of which are a mystery to us. . . . I have no use for that kind of immortality. I don't understand it, and Lev Nikolayevich was astonished I didn't."

Nevertheless, Chekhov was impressed with the solicitude shown by Tolstoy's visit. But, unlike Tolstoy, Chekhov didn't believe in an afterlife and never had. He didn't believe in anything that couldn't be apprehended by one or more of his five senses. And as far as his outlook on life and writing went, he once told someone that he lacked "a political, religious, and philosophical world view. I change it every month, so I'll have to limit myself to the description of how my heroes love, marry, give birth, die, and how they speak."

Earlier, before his t.b. was diagnosed, Chekhov had remarked, "When a peasant has consumption, he says, 'There's nothing I can do. I'll go off in the spring with the melting of the snows.'" (Chekhov himself died in the summer, during a heat wave.) But once Chekhov's own tuberculosis was discovered he continually tried to minimize the seriousness of his condition. To all appearances, it was as if he felt, right up to the end, that he might be able to throw off the disease as he would a lingering catarrh. Well into his final days, he spoke with seeming conviction of the possibility of an improvement. In fact, in a letter written shortly before his end, he went so far as to tell his sister that he was "putting on a bit of flesh" and felt much better now that he was in Badenweiler.

Badenweiler is a spa and resort city in the western area of the Black Forest, not far from Basel. The Vosges are visible from nearly anywhere in the city, and in those days the air was pure and invigorating. Russians had been going there for years to soak in the hot mineral baths and promenade on the boulevards. In June, 1904, Chekhov went there to die.

Earlier that month, he'd made a difficult journey by train from Moscow to Berlin. He travelled with his wife, the actress Olga Knipper, a woman he'd met in 1898 during rehearsals for "The Seagull." Her contemporaries describe her as an excellent actress. She was talented, pretty, and almost ten years younger than the playwright. Chekhov had been immediately attracted to her, but was slow to act on his feelings. As always, he preferred a flirtation to marriage. Finally, after a three-year courtship involving many separations, letters, and the inevitable misunderstandings, they were at last married, in a private ceremony in Moscow, on May 25, 1901. Chekhov was enormously happy. He called Olga his "pony," and sometimes "dog" or "puppy." He was also fond of addressing her as "little turkey" or simply as "my joy."

In Berlin, Chekhov consulted with a renowned specialist in pulmonary disorders, a Dr. Karl Ewald. But, according to an eyewitness, after the doctor examined Chekhov he threw up his hands and left the room without a word. Chekhov was too far gone for help: this Dr. Ewald was furious with himself for not being able to work miracles, and with Chekhov for being so ill.

A Russian journalist happened to visit the Chekhovs at their hotel and sent back this dispatch to his editor: "Chekhov's days are numbered. He seems mortally ill, is terribly thin, coughs all the time, gasps for breath at the slightest movement, and is running a high temperature." This same journalist saw the Chekhovs off at Potsdam Station when they boarded their train for Badenweiler. According to his account, "Chekhov had trouble making his way up the small staircase at the station. He had to sit down for several minutes to catch his breath." In fact, it was painful for Chekhov to move: his legs ached continually and his insides hurt. The disease had attacked his intestines and spinal cord. At this point he had less than a month to live.

When Chekhov spoke of his condition now, it was, according to Olga, "with an almost reckless indifference."

Dr. Schwöhrer was one of the many Badenweiler physicians who earned a good living by treating the well-to-do who came to the spa seeking relief from various maladies. Some of his patients were ill and infirm, others simply old and hypochondriacal. But Chekhov's was a special case: he was clearly beyond help and in his last days. He was also very famous. Even Dr. Schwöhrer knew his name: he'd read some of Chekhov's stories in a German magazine. When he examined the writer early in June, he voiced his appreciation of Chekhov's art but kept his medical opinions to himself. Instead, he prescribed a diet of cocoa, oatmeal drenched in butter, and strawberry tea. This last was supposed to help Chekhov sleep at night.

On June 13th, less than three weeks before he died, Chekhov wrote a letter to his mother in which he told her his health was on the mend. In it he said, "It's likely that I'll be completely cured in a week." Who knows why he said this? What could he have been thinking? He was a doctor himself, and he knew better. He was dying, it was as simple and as unavoidable as that. Nevertheless, he sat out on the balcony of his hotel room and read railway timetables. He asked for information on sailings of boats bound for Odessa from Marseilles. But he *knew*. At this stage he had to have known. Yet in one of the last letters he ever wrote he told his sister he was growing stronger by the day.

He no longer had any appetite for literary work, and hadn't for a long time. In fact, he had very nearly failed to complete "The Cherry Orchard" the year before. Writing that play was the hardest thing he'd ever done in his life. Toward the end, he was able to manage only six or seven lines a day. "I've started losing heart," he wrote Olga. "I feel I'm finished as a writer, and every sentence strikes me as worthless and of no use whatever." But he didn't stop. He finished his play in October, 1903. It was the last thing he ever wrote, except for letters and a few entries in his notebook.

A little after midnight on July 2, 1904, Olga sent someone to fetch Dr. Schwöhrer. It was an emergency: Chekhov was delirious. Two young Russians on holiday happened to have the adjacent room, and Olga hurried next door to explain what was happening. One of the youths was in his bed asleep, but the other was still awake, smoking and reading. He left the hotel at a run to find Dr. Schwöhrer. "I can still hear the sound of the gravel under his shoes in the silence of that stifling July night," Olga wrote later on in her memoirs. Chekhov was hallucinating, talking about sailors, and there were snatches of something about the Japanese. "You don't put ice on an empty stomach," he said when she tried to place an ice pack on his chest.

Dr. Schwöhrer arrived and unpacked his bag, all the while keeping his gaze fastened on Chekhov, who lay gasping in the bed. The sick man's pupils were dilated and his temples glistened with sweat. Dr. Schwöhrer's face didn't register anything. He was not an emotional man, but he knew Chekhov's end was near. Still, he was a doctor, sworn to do his utmost, and Chekhov held on to life, however tenuously. Dr. Schwöhrer prepared a hypodermic and administered an injection of camphor, something that was supposed to speed up the heart. But the injection didn't help—nothing, of course, could have helped. Nevertheless, the doctor made known to Olga his intention of sending for oxygen. Suddenly, Chekhov roused himself, became lucid, and said quietly, "What's the use? Before it arrives I'll be a corpse."

Dr. Schwöhrer pulled on his big mustache and stared at Chekhov. The writer's cheeks were sunken and gray, his complexion waxen; his breath was raspy. Dr. Schwöhrer knew the time could be reckoned in minutes. Without a word, without conferring with Olga, he went over to an alcove where there was a telephone on the wall. He read the instructions for using the device. If he activated it by holding his finger on a button and turning a handle on the side of the phone, he could reach the lower regions of the hotel—the kitchen. He picked up the receiver, held it to his ear, and did as the instructions told him. When someone finally answered, Dr. Schwöhrer ordered a bottle of the hotel's best champagne. "How many glasses?" he was asked. "Three glasses!" the doctor shouted into the mouthpiece. "And hurry, do you hear?" It was one of those rare moments of inspiration that can easily enough be overlooked later on, because the action is so entirely appropriate it seems inevitable.

The champagne was brought to the door by a tired-looking young man whose blond hair was standing up. The trousers of his uniform were wrinkled, the creases gone, and in his haste he'd missed a loop while buttoning his jacket. His appearance was that of someone who'd been resting (slumped in a chair, say, dozing a little), when off in the distance the phone had clamored in the early-morning hours—great God in Heaven!—and the next thing he knew he was being shaken awake by a superior and told to deliver a bottle of Moët to Room 211. "And hurry, do you hear?"

The young man entered the room carrying a silver ice bucket with the champagne in it and a silver tray with three cut-crystal glasses. He found a place on the table for the bucket and glasses, all the while craning his neck, trying to see into the other room, where someone panted ferociously for breath. It was a dreadful, harrowing sound, and the young man lowered his chin into his collar and turned away as the ratchety breathing worsened. Forgetting himself, he stared out the open window toward the darkened city. Then this big imposing man with a thick mustache pressed some coins into his hand—a large tip, by the feel of it—and suddenly the young man saw the door open. He took some steps and found himself on the landing, where he opened his hand and looked at the coins in amazement.

Methodically, the way he did everything, the doctor went about the business of working the cork out of the bottle. He did it in such a way as to minimize, as much as possible, the festive explosion. He poured three glasses and, out of habit, pushed the cork back into the neck of the bottle. He then took the glasses of champagne over to the bed. Olga momentarily released her grip on Chekhov's hand—a hand, she said later, that burned her fingers. She arranged another pillow behind his head. Then she put the cool glass of champagne against Chekhov's palm and made sure his fingers closed around the stem. They exchanged looks—Chekhov, Olga, Dr. Schwöhrer. They didn't touch glasses. There was no toast. What on earth was there to drink to? To death? Chekhov summoned his remaining strength and said, "It's been so long since I've had champagne." He brought the glass to his lips and drank. In a minute or two Olga took the empty glass from his hand and set it on the nightstand. Then Chekhov turned onto his side. He closed his eyes and sighed. A minute later, his breathing stopped.

Dr. Schwöhrer picked up Chekhov's hand from the bedsheet. He held his fingers to Chekhov's wrist and drew a gold watch from his vest pocket, opening the lid of the watch as he did so. The second hand on the watch moved slowly, very slowly. He let it move around the face of the watch three times while he waited for signs of a pulse. It was three o'clock in the morning and still sultry in the room. Badenweiler was in the grip of its worst heat wave in years. All the windows in both rooms stood open, but there was no sign of a breeze. A large, black-winged moth flew through a window and banged wildly against the electric lamp. Dr. Schwöhrer let go of Chekhov's wrist. "It's over," he said. He closed the lid of his watch and returned it to his vest pocket.

At once Olga dried her eyes and set about composing herself. She thanked the doctor for coming. He asked if she wanted some medication—laudanum, perhaps, or a few drops of valerian. She shook her head. She did have one request, though: before the authorities were notified and the newspapers found out, before the time came when Chekhov was no longer in her keeping, she wanted to be alone with him for a while. Could the doctor help with this? Could he withhold, for a while anyway, news of what had just occurred?

Dr. Schwöhrer stroked his mustache with the back of a finger. Why not? After all, what difference would it make to anyone whether this matter became known now or a few hours from now? The only detail that remained was to fill out a death certificate, and this could be done at his office later on in the morning, after he'd slept a few hours. Dr. Schwöhrer nodded his agreement and prepared to leave. He murmured a few words of condolence. Olga inclined her head. "An honor," Dr. Schwöhrer said. He picked up his bag and left the room and, for that matter, history.

It was at this moment that the cork popped out of the champagne bottle; foam spilled down onto the table. Olga went back to Chekhov's bedside. She sat on a footstool, holding his hand, from time to time stroking his face. "There were no human voices, no everyday sounds," she wrote. "There was only beauty, peace, and the grandeur of death."

She stayed with Chekhov until daybreak, when thrushes began to call from the garden below. Then came the sound of tables and chairs being moved about down there. Before long, voices carried up to her. It was then a knock sounded at the door. Of course she thought it must be an official of some sort—the medical examiner, say, or someone from the police who had questions to ask and forms for her to fill out, or maybe, just maybe, it could be Dr. Schwöhrer returning with a mortician to render assistance in embalming and transporting Chekhov's remains back to Russia.

But, instead, it was the same blond young man who'd brought the champagne a few hours earlier. This time, however, his uniform trousers were neatly pressed, with stiff creases in front, and every button on his snug green jacket was fastened. He seemed quite another person. Not only was he wide awake but his plump cheeks were smooth-shaven, his hair was in place, and he appeared anxious to please. He was holding a porcelain vase with three long-stemmed yellow roses. He presented these to Olga with a smart click of his heels. She stepped back and let him into the room. He was there, he said, to collect the glasses, ice bucket, and tray, yes. But he also wanted to say that, because of the extreme heat, breakfast would be served in the garden this morning. He hoped this weather wasn't too bothersome; he apologized for it.

The woman seemed distracted. While he talked, she turned her eyes away and looked down at something in the carpet. She crossed her arms and held her elbows. Meanwhile, still holding his vase, waiting for a sign, the young man took in the details of the room. Bright sunlight flooded through the open windows. The room was tidy and seemed undisturbed, almost untouched. No garments were flung over chairs, no shoes, stockings, braces, or stays were in evidence, no open suitcases. In short, there was no clutter, nothing but the usual heavy pieces of hotel-room furniture. Then, because the woman was still looking down, he looked down, too, and at once spied a cork near the toe of his shoe. The woman did not see it—she was looking somewhere else. The young man wanted to bend over and pick up the cork, but he was still holding the roses and was afraid of seeming to intrude even more by drawing any further attention to himself. Reluctantly, he left the cork where it was and raised his eyes. Everything was in order except for the uncorked, half-empty bottle of champagne that stood alongside two crystal glasses over on the little table. He cast his gaze about once more. Through an open door he saw that the third glass was in the bedroom, on the nightstand. But someone still occupied the bed! He couldn't see a face, but the figure under the covers lay perfectly motionless and quiet. He noted the figure and looked elsewhere. Then, for a reason he couldn't understand, a feeling of uneasiness took hold of him. He cleared his throat and moved his weight to the other leg. The woman still didn't look up or break her silence. The young man felt his cheeks grow warm. It occurred to him, quite without his having thought it through, that he should perhaps suggest an alternative to breakfast in the garden. He coughed, hoping to focus the woman's attention, but she didn't look at him. The distinguished foreign guests could, he said, take breakfast in their rooms this morning if they wished. The young man (his name hasn't survived, and it's likely he perished in the Great War) said he would be happy to bring up a tray. Two trays, he added, glancing uncertainly once again in the direction of the bedroom.

He fell silent and ran a finger around the inside of his collar. He didn't understand. He wasn't even sure the woman had been listening. He didn't know what else to do now; he was still holding the vase. The sweet odor of the roses filled his nostrils and inexplicably caused a pang of regret. The entire time he'd been waiting, the woman had apparently been lost in thought. It was as if all the while he'd been standing there, talking, shifting his weight, holding his flowers, she had been someplace else, somewhere far from Badenweiler. But now she came back to herself, and her face assumed another expression. She raised her eyes, looked at him, and then shook her head. She seemed to be struggling to understand what on earth this young man could be doing there in the room holding a vase with three yellow roses. Flowers? She hadn't ordered flowers.

The moment passed. She went over to her handbag and scooped up some coins. She drew out a number of banknotes as well. The young man touched his lips with his tongue; another large tip was forthcom-

ing, but for what? What did she want him to do? He'd never before
waited on such guests. He cleared his throat once more.

No breakfast, the woman said. Not yet, at any rate. Breakfast
wasn't the important thing this morning. She required something else.
She needed him to go out and bring back a mortician. Did he understand her? Herr Chekhov was dead, you see. *Comprenez-vous?* Young
man? Anton Chekhov was dead. Now listen carefully to me, she said.
She wanted him to go downstairs and ask someone at the front desk
where he could go to find the most respected mortician in the city.
Someone reliable, who took great pains in his work and whose manner
was appropriately reserved. A mortician, in short, worthy of a great
artist. Here, she said, and pressed the money on him. Tell them downstairs that I have specifically requested you to perform this duty for
me. Are you listening? Do you understand what I'm saying to you?

The young man grappled to take in what she was saying. He chose
not to look again in the direction of the other room. He had sensed
that something was not right. He became aware of his heart beating
rapidly under his jacket, and he felt perspiration break out on his
forehead. He didn't know where he should turn his eyes. He wanted to
put the vase down.

Please do this for me, the woman said. I'll remember you with
gratitude. Tell them downstairs that I insist. Say that. But don't call
any unnecessary attention to yourself or to the situation. Just say that
this is necessary, that I request it—and that's all. Do you hear me?
Nod if you understand. Above all, don't raise an alarm. Everything
else, all the rest, the commotion—that'll come soon enough. The
worst is over. Do we understand each other?

The young man's face had grown pale. He stood rigid, clasping the
vase. He managed to nod his head.

After securing permission to leave the hotel he was to proceed quietly and resolutely, though without any unbecoming haste, to the mortician's. He was to behave exactly as if he were engaged on a very
important errand, nothing more. He *was* engaged on an important
errand, she said. And if it would help keep his movements purposeful
he should imagine himself as someone moving down the busy sidewalk
carrying in his arms a porcelain vase of roses that he had to deliver to

an important man. (She spoke quietly, almost confidentially, as if to a relative or a friend.) He could even tell himself that the man he was going to see was expecting him, was perhaps impatient for him to arrive with his flowers. Nevertheless, the young man was not to become excited and run, or otherwise break his stride. Remember the vase he was carrying! He was to walk briskly, comporting himself at all times in as dignified a manner as possible. He should keep walking until he came to the mortician's house and stood before the door. He would then raise the brass knocker and let it fall, once, twice, three times. In a minute the mortician himself would answer.

This mortician would be in his forties, no doubt, or maybe early fifties—bald, solidly built, wearing steel-frame spectacles set very low on his nose. He would be modest, unassuming, a man who would ask only the most direct and necessary questions. An apron. Probably he would be wearing an apron. He might even be wiping his hands on a dark towel while he listened to what was being said. There'd be a faint whiff of formaldehyde on his clothes. But it was all right, and the young man shouldn't worry. He was nearly a grownup now and shouldn't be frightened or repelled by any of this. The mortician would hear him out. He was a man of restraint and bearing, this mortician, someone who could help allay people's fears in this situation, not increase them. Long ago he'd acquainted himself with death in all its various guises and forms; death held no surprises for him any longer, no hidden secrets. It was this man whose services were required this morning.

The mortician takes the vase of roses. Only once while the young man is speaking does the mortician betray the least flicker of interest, or indicate that he'd heard anything out of the ordinary. But the one time the young man mentions the name of the deceased, the mortician's eyebrows rise just a little. Chekhov, you say? Just a minute, and I'll be with you.

Do you understand what I'm saying, Olga said to the young man. Leave the glasses. Don't worry about them. Forget about crystal wineglasses and such. Leave the room as it is. Everything is ready now. We're ready. Will you go?

But at that moment the young man was thinking of the cork still resting near the toe of his shoe. To retrieve it he would have to bend over, still gripping the vase. He would do this. He leaned over. Without looking down, he reached out and closed it into his hand.

Ocracoke Island

•

================ ALICE ADAMS ================

Alice Adams grew up in Chapel Hill, North Carolina, and graduated from Radcliffe; since then she has lived mostly in San Francisco. Her most recent collection of stories, Return Trips, *was published in 1985, and a new novel,* Second Chances, *will be appearing from Knopf this spring.*

Tall and too thin, sometimes stooped but now bent bravely forward into the wind, old Duncan Elliott heads southward in Central Park, down a steep and cindery path—his scattered, shamed and tormented mind still alert to the avoidance of dangerously large steel baby carriages, and runners (he must not be run down by babies or by runners, he cautions himself), but most of his thoughts are concentrated on the question of comparative evils: of all that has befallen him lately, and particularly today, what is worse—or rather, which is worst of all? To have been abandoned by one's fourth and one had hoped final wife, or to have made a total fool of one's self discussing that event, even trying as it were to explain it away.

Duncan is a distinguished professor, now an emeritus at a large midwestern university (for all the good that is doing him now); his wife Cath left the month before, in hot September; disconsolately travelling to New York, in part to cheer himself up, along with some publishing business, Duncan forgot the possibility of chill late October breezes.

Or—he continues his plaintive litany—is the worst thing of all to have broken off and lost an old, much filled and refilled tooth, leaving what must be a conspicuously ugly black hole in the forefront of one's mouth? Oh, what matter which is worse! thinks Duncan then. All of these things have happened (the most recent being the tooth, which only came to his attention out here in the cold) and he can stand none of them.

The runners that Duncan encounters along his way are grim-faced, red and sweaty, and the young mothers pushing those carriages are scruffy, sloppily dressed; and the babies are, well, babies. Where are the handsome, glamorous pairs of lovers that one used to glimpse in New York, in Central Park? Duncan asks this wistful question of himself, and then he answers (insanely!): On Ocracoke Island. For it is to Ocracoke that Cath has run off with her poet, and in his mind Duncan has just seen the two of them, Cath and Brennan O'Donahue (of all corny, phoney, false-literary names), Brennan as handsome and fair as Cath herself is—he sees Brennan and Cath and scores of other couples, all young and blond, all healthy and beautiful, and running, running like horses, on a wild and endless beach.

Cath's gesture—if you call running off to an island with a poet a gesture—was made even less bearable for Duncan by the publicity it drew; she had to choose a famous poet, a Pulitzer Prize-winning, brawling media hero of a poet. A small item in *Newsweek* (Newsmakers) described O'Donahue as having run off to Ocracoke Island "like a pirate, a professor's wife his plunder." Very poetic for a news magazine, Duncan thought: perhaps Brennan himself had written the item? In any case a lot of people seemed to know whose wife was meant.

At times Duncan feels literally murderous: he will go there to Ocracoke and shoot them both, and then himself. He has found the place on a map, and it looks as though you had to take a ferry from a town called Swansquarter. *Swansquarter?* But surely murder would be a more respectable, even a nobler act than a lot of talk, so deeply embarrassing, so sickly humiliating to recall.

Nearing his hotel, and the promise of some comfort, Duncan begins though to dread the coming night. He is to dine with Emily, his second wife: his briefest marriage, that to Emily, and perhaps for that reason they have stayed in touch, have remained almost friends. Emily and Cath have even met, Duncan now recalls, on a trip to New York that he and Cath took, just before their marriage. Emily is a painter, beginning to be quite successful. She is, as they all have been, considerably younger than Duncan.

(Younger and in one way or another very talented, all of them, Duncan reflects. More talented than he? That was surely a problem with Jessica, the first wife, a poet who took a very low view of criticism. Less so with Emily, perhaps because painting is, well, not literary, and they were not together very long. The worst was Janice, herself a professor, a literary critic. Undoubtedly Janice in her way was responsible for Cath, who is talentless, a born appreciator.)

But: unless he exercises the utmost caution, for which he feels himself much too tired, devoid of resources, Duncan fears that he will simply repeat the follies of the day, with Emily, tonight. He will talk again—perhaps even more ridiculously—about Cath; obviously he will do so, since she and Emily have met. Emily by now is probably—is undoubtedly a feminist; she could finish him off entirely.

At the hotel desk Duncan looks longingly toward the cubbyholes of messages. If only there were a pink phone slip from Emily, cancelling, for whatever reason. (Or: a slip saying Cath had called?) But there is nothing, and heavily now Duncan walks over to the elevator. He rings, ascends.

This making a fool of himself began for Duncan at breakfast, in the somewhat dingy diningroom of his hotel, as he talked (or tried to explain) to Jasper Wilkes, a former student, and began to babble: "In point of fact I actually encouraged her to have an affair—or affairs; one can't say I wasn't generous. Ironically enough, she could be said to be doing just what I told her to do. In a sense."

Jasper repeated, "In a sense," with perhaps too much relish. A highly successful advertising executive since abandoning *academe*, Jasper is a prematurely, quite shiningly bald young man, with clever, hooded eyes.

"After all," Duncan continued, long fingers playing with his croissant's cold buttery remains, "I'm very busy. And besides." He smiled briefly, sadly, implying much.

"Of course." Jasper's eyes closed, but his voice had an agreeing sound.

Gulping at strong lukewarm coffee—he had just sent back for fresh —Duncan had a nervously exhilarated sense that this was not how men talked to each other, or, not usually. Or perhaps these days they do? They are 'open' with each other, as women have always been? In any case he hoped that he had not got out of his depth, with Jasper. The coffee had made him feel a little drunk.

And at the word 'depth' his mind stopped, totally, and replayed, *depth, depth*. He had suddenly, involuntarily seen Atlantic waves, brilliant and mountainous, quite possibly fatal. He had imagined Ocracoke Island. Again.

But could Jasper be in a hurry? Off somewhere? Duncan was conscious of wanting to prolong (oh! all day) this relieving, if highly unusual conversation. "Precisely," he hastened to agree with what he imagined Jasper just had said. "I intended something discreet and, I suppose I also hoped, something minor. A dalliance more or less along my own lines. My old lines, I suppose I should say." He attempted a modest laugh, but the sound was bleak.

"Right," Jasper agreed. "Something to take up a certain amount of her time and energy. Rather like going to a gym."

"Oh, precisely."

The two men exchanged looks in which there was expressed some shock at their complicitous cynicism, but more pure pleasure—or so Duncan for the moment believed.

The coffee arrived, at which Jasper frowned, conclusively proving to Duncan that he was after all in a hurry; he did not even want more coffee.

"The point is," said Jasper, in a summing-up way, "whether or not you want her back. One. And, two, if you do, how to get her."

Unprepared for this *précis*, Duncan felt quite dizzied.

Nor was he prepared for what came next, which was Jasper's efficient departure: a smooth rise to his feet, and a firm, sincere handshake. Lots of eye contact. Murmurs of friendship. And then Jasper was gone, last glimpsed as a narrow, animated back departing through the door that led out to the lobby.

Quite disconcerted, and alone with his hot, unconsoling coffee, Duncan looked around. This room had got uglier, he thought, trying to recall what he used to like about it. Surely not the pictures, the big bright oils which all looked like copies of famous works, giving the room a spurious look of 'taste'? Never the pictures, he concluded, and surely not the inferior coffee, and fake croissants. Dismally he reminded himself that he had always chosen this hotel for reasons of economy, never for charm.

Now everything seemed to disturb him, though: the room with its awful art, the bad coffee, and particularly his just-ended conversation with Jasper Wilkes. And why? Rerunning that conversation, he succeeded in finding nothing truly objectionable. (Unless: that crack about going to gyms—would that have been a 'put-on'?) Bright Jasper, though. All agreement, stating and restating Duncan's own views in a clear succinct way. But perhaps that very succinctness was the problem? Especially at the end, just before Jasper hurried off to wherever?

Leaning back into the once-pneumatic banquette, for reassurance Duncan stroked his hair, now white but still gratifyingly thick and fine. How Jasper must envy his hair! That in itself could explain quite a lot.

Duncan thought then of the old days, when Jasper as a student came petitioning with his poetry. In conference with Jasper, Duncan might sneak a quick look at his large grandfather clock, while pretending to allow his gaze to wander. And apprised of the time, he, Duncan, might then too brusquely sum up his view of Jasper's poem, or poems: Jasper had been all too prolific. And, as Jasper at last got up reluctantly to leave, the also departing Duncan, a man in early middle age, might well be off to visit some pert-breasted, ambitious literary girl, for something 'discreet,' and 'minor.'

As though Jasper had encouraged him, seduced him, even, into all that talk about Cath, Duncan felt a pained resentment. Especially he resented Jasper's just getting up and leaving him like that—all at sea, almost drowned in ungovernable feelings.

But, at lunchtime, Duncan could be said to have done it again.

"It was really the way she left that I so much minded," he remarked to his lunch companion, Marcus Thistlethwaite, an English critic, a very old friend. They were seated in a corner of a pretty new Upper West Side restaurant, banks of fall flowers in the windows, filtered sunshine. "I would have given a maid more notice," Duncan added, and then reflected that his analogy had been slightly confused: just whom did he mean was whose maid, and who gave notice? He hoped that Marcus had not observed this, but naturally no such luck.

"I'm not sure just who was whose maid," said Marcus, with his rachety, cropped-off laugh. "But I believe I rather catch your drift, as it were." And then, "Is this quite the proper thing to do with lobster claws?"

"Oh yes, you just crack them like nuts," instructed Duncan, who had just wondered why on earth he had ordered something he had never much liked, and that was at best quite difficult to eat. (And that reminded him inevitably of the sea-coast.)

Marcus's hair is thin and silvery, like tinsel; draped across his bright impressive skull, it ornamented his head. Duncan has always been somewhat in awe of Marcus, of his erudition and his cool, uncluttered, passionless judgements. And so why on earth did he have to make that silly remark about Cath, and the dismissal of maids? "Say what you like about New York," he then attempted, striving for an even tone despite a certain pressure in his chest, "the autumns here are wonderful. You know I walked up through the park from my hotel, and the air—so brisk! And the color of sky, and those flowers."

Marcus just perceptibly inclined his head, acknowledging flowers, and weather. And then he launched into one of the mini-speeches to which he is given. "An interesting fact, and one that I've made note of—" (to those who know Marcus, a familiar beginning, very likely boding no good to his audience, be it plural or singular)—"and of which you, my dear Duncan, have just furnished further proof, in any case so interesting, is the human tendency in times of distress at some ill-treatment by a fellow human to complain of the method of treatment, the form it took, rather than the actuality. The cruel event itself is not mentioned, even. A man who is fired from his job invariably sounds as though a little more tact would have made it perfectly acceptable. And a fellow whose mistress has taken off—well, I'm sure you quite see what I mean."

"In my own case I do think even some slight warning might have been in order," Duncan bravely if weakly managed to say. "And she was not my mistress—my *wife*. We'd been married for almost three years."

"My dear fellow, naturally I was speaking in a general way, and you know how I tend to run on. Well, I don't think I much care for these lobsters of yours. What's our next course? I seem already to have forgotten."

What an old bore Marcus has become, so opinionated, so—so insensitive, thought Duncan, once they parted and he began his walk. However, irritation soon gave way to the sound of darker voices, which asked if he himself was not almost as old, and as boring. And perhaps Marcus was less insensitive than he, Duncan was hyper-sensitive, an open wound.

At which point he made—or rather, his probing tongue made the most unwelcome discovery about his missing tooth.

Back at last in his hotel room, that cold and perilous park walk done with, behind him, Duncan picks up the phone and almost instantly he succeeds (the day's first small piece of luck) in reaching his dentist. Who is reassuring. Nothing to worry about, the dentist tells Duncan, happens all the time. He adds that it probably does not look as unsightly as Duncan thinks it does; and gives him an appointment for the following week.

The bathroom mirror informs Duncan that his missing tooth, his 'black hole' is unsightly only when he very broadly grins, which he can surely see no reason for doing at any foreseeable time.

Lying at last across his oversized bed, eyes closed, Duncan attempts to generalize about his situation; particulars are what finally do you in, he has found—and so he will not think about Cath's pretty shoulders, nor her odd harsh mountain consonants. He strives instead for abstraction, beginning some mental notes on jealousy in an older person, as opposed to what is experienced by the young.

When one is young, he thinks the emotion of jealousy is wracking, torturous, but at the same time very arousing (he has to admit), an almost delicious pain. Whereas when one is older, and jealous, there is only deep, irremovable sadness, deprivation, hopelessness.

(So much for notes.)

Cath: just a pallid, slightly gangling, easily blushing, mild-tempered girl from the land of the Great Smokey Mountains, from whence those consonants, those vowels. But a girl with an amazing ear for poetry, and a passion for it. Cath was (she *is,* oh, surely she still is) literally crazy about the verse of Andrew Marvell, Herrick, Donne. Wallace Stevens (Duncan's own particular enthusiasm) and more recently some women with curious names: Levertov? Pollitt? Clampton? And most recently of all, Mr. Brennan O'Donahue.

Though at first she did not even want to go to his reading. "It's too hot to go anywhere," she complained.

"But you're crazy about O'Donahue," Duncan (oh irony!) reminded her, and he added, "He's just back from Nicaragua, remember? Besides, I do think one of us should go." Duncan sniffed to emphasize the bad summer cold from which he was suffering (and he now remembers that self-pitying, self-justifying sniff with such shame, such regret). "I'm sure the Taylors would come by for you," he added, naming a younger, obsequious colleague, with a silly wife.

Cath sighed. "Oh, I'll go by myself. That way I can come home early. And Bipsy Taylor is such a nerd." Another sigh. "If I can work out what to wear in this weather."

It was an especially hot September, everything limp and drooping, or fallen to the ground. Bleached rose petals on yellow lawns, and out in the woods where Duncan liked to walk the silence was thick and heavy, as though even the birds were prostrate, drugged with heat.

Cath chose to wear her barest dress that night, which seemed sensible, if slightly inappropriate for a poetry reading. But Duncan felt that it would not do to object: he was making her go there, was he not? And so she went out alone, bare armed and bra-less, in her loose black cotton; her sun-bleached hair loosely falling, her small round shoulders lightly tanned.

You look almost beautiful, is what Duncan thought of saying, and fortunately or not forebore; too often he said things to Cath that he later lived to regret. His suggestion—half joking, actually—that she could have an affair had aroused real rage. An obscene suggestion, she seemed to take it as; clear evidence of lack of love. Whereas he was not even really serious (God knows he was not). And so as she left that night Duncan only said, "I hope it won't be too dull for you, my love."

"Oh no, don't worry. But you take care of your cold, now. I put the bottle of C pills right next to your bed."

She came home very late, explaining at breakfast that there had been a party at the Taylors' who lived out of town. She had not wanted to wake Duncan with a phone call. She had driven O'Donahue back to the Hilton, where he was staying. The reading was good. He was nice. She thought she would go downtown to do some shopping. Would probably not be back before Duncan's afternoon seminar.

And Duncan returned late that afternoon, after the seminar that included a sherry hour, to find her note. Gone off to Ocracoke Island, with Brennan O'Donahue.

The Village restaurant in which Duncan meets Emily for dinner is a comforting surprise, however; a most unfashionable homey old-Bohemian decor, checkered tablecloths and multi-colored candles in fat dark green wine bottles, a look dearly familiar to Duncan, who spent feckless youthful years in this neighborhood. Then he was a handsome young man, very easy with women—with a great deal to say about literature, he thought.

Emily at least at first seems determinedly nice. "It's wonderfully corny, don't you think?" she says, of the restaurant. "But with our luck this look will come back and be madly fashionable. Oh dear, do you suppose it has, and we're the last to know?" And she laughs, companionably. "I'm taking you to dinner," she tells him. "We're celebrating a grant I just got."

"You look splendid, my dear, you really do," Duncan tells her gratefully, as they are seated; he has never been taken to dinner by a woman before, and he rather enjoys the sensation. This is feminism? And it is true that Emily in early middle age, or wherever she is, has never looked better. A tall woman, she has put on a little weight, in her case very becoming (but can you say that to a woman?) Short curled gray hair, gray eyes, and very white teeth. She looks strong, and immensely healthy. "You look so—so very *fit*," Duncan says to her. "Do you, er, jog, or something?"

Emily laughs again. "Well, I have, but I didn't like it much. Now I just walk a lot."

"Well, I must say, I'm glad to hear that. I find runners such a grim group, they quite scare me," Duncan confesses.

"Oh, me too, they never smile. But dear Duncan, why are you smiling in that somewhat odd way?"

"I've lost a tooth."

"Well, we all do," Emily tells him. "But you don't have to twist your mouth that way. It's only a gap."

Quite amiably then she talks about her work: painting, teaching, a summer workshop in Provincetown—until Duncan suspects that she is being quite consciously nice to him, that she is purposefully not mentioning Cath—(whom he himself has determined not to talk about).

Well, if that is the case he surely does not mind; nice is perfectly okay with him, Duncan decides, and then he wonders, *Are* women after all really nicer than men are? (He does not voice this question, however, not just then wanting to hear Emily too-strongly agree.)

But Emily does at last bring up the subject of Cath, though gently. "I am sorry about Cath," she says. "That must be rough for you."

"Well yes, it is. But it's nice of you to say so." Which it was.

"I'm sure your literary friends have been enormously comforting though," Emily in a changed tone goes on, her irony so heavy that Duncan is quite taken aback until he remembers just how much she disliked his 'literary' friends, especially Jasper Wilkes, who was still a poet when Emily knew him.

Duncan can only be straight-forward with her now. "You're right," he says. "The friends I've talked to have succeeded in making me feel much worse. I had it coming, seems to be the general view."

Emily smiles, her eyes bright. "Oh, you could say that to almost anyone, I think. It's even said to cancer patients. But it really doesn't seem to me that you've been any worse than most men are."

Grasping at even this dubious compliment, Duncan smiles, and then he further complains, "You know, even well-deserved pain is painful."

"Of course it is."

Why did he ever leave Emily, who is as intelligent as she is kind—and attractive? But he did not leave Emily, Duncan then recalls; Emily left him, with sensible remarks about not being cut out for marriage, either of them. Which did not stop her from marrying an Indian painter a few years later, and a sculptor soon after that—nor did it stop Duncan from marrying Janice, and then Cath.

In any case, kind or not, right or wrong, Emily is far better to talk to than Jasper or Marcus. Duncan feels safe with Emily—which leads him to yet another confession. "I did one really dumb thing though. At some point I told Cath that she should have an affair. Of course I spoke in jest, but can she have taken me seriously?"

Emily frowns. "Well, jesting or not, that's really worse than dumb. That's cruel. It's what men say to wives they want to get rid of."

"Oh, but I surely didn't mean—" Crestfallen Duncan.

Fortunately just at that moment the food arrives, and it is after some silence between them that Emily asks, "You do know that she'll be back?"

"Oh no, no, of course I don't know that at all." Duncan feels dizzy.

"Well, she will. She's basically very sensible, I think. She'll see that Brennan O'Donahue is no one to live with. Running off with poets is just something young women do. Or some of them do."

"Oh? They do?"

"She'll come back, and if you want her to stick around you'd better be very kind. Just remember, a lot of women have been really nice to you. Be understanding. Sensitive. You're good at that."

He is? Entirely flustered, Duncan gulps at wine, hitherto untouched in his swirled dark blue glass. "I find it extremely hard to believe that you're right," he tells Emily, "that she's coming back."

"You just wait." She gives a confident flash of her regular, somewhat large teeth, and then she frowns. "The real problem may be whether or not you really want her back."

"Oh, that's more or less what Jasper said."

Emily's frown becomes a scowl. "*That* expert. Well, probably you shouldn't listen to anyone, really. Just see what happens, and then see what you feel like doing about it. But I'll bet she does come back. And quite soon, I'd imagine."

Once more picking up his key at the hotel desk, as he notes the absence of any phone message, nothing pink, Duncan's tremulous, wavering heart informs him that he has actually feared as much as he has been hoping for a message from Cath. He is so tired, so extraordinarily tired; he has neither the stamina for Cath's return nor for her continued absence. Which is worse? Oh, everything is worse!

In his room, in bed (so depressing, the great size of hotel beds, when you travel alone), feeling weakened rather than tipsy from the moderate amount of wine that he has drunk, nevertheless Duncan's imagination begins to wander quite wildly, and he thinks again of assaulting Ocracoke—oh, the whole bloody island, all those couples, the tall blond lovers, all racing around. As waves crash, as winds hurl sheets of sand, maybe even a hurricane.

Sleepless, disoriented, Duncan feels the sharp anguish of someone very young—of a young man whose beautiful wife has been stolen away. The forsaken merman.

He feels in fact as though he had been forsaken by everyone—by Jasper and by Marcus, even by Emily, with her great superior health and all her hoards of female wisdom. By Cath especially of course, and by Brennan O'Donahue. By all the people on Ocracoke Island— that most beautiful, isolated and imperilled scrap of ground, the one place to which he can never, ever go—and for which Duncan's whole tormented landlocked soul now longs.

Blessings

•

======== **ANDRE DUBUS** ========

*Andre Dubus lives in Haverhill, Massachusetts, with his wife, Peggy
Rambach, and their two young daughters. He is a retired teacher and
has four adult children and a grandson.*

Early in the morning on the first anniversary of the day her family
survived, the mother woke. At first she thought it was the birds. In the
trees near the cabin their songs in the early twilight were too sharp,
more a sound of intrusion or alarm than the peace she and Cal had
rented for two weeks on this New Hampshire lake. She had never
liked to wake early, and on most days she woke before she was ready
and needed coffee and a cigarette at once, and as she pushed and
pulled the circling handle of the coffee grinder she felt that she toiled,
while upstairs in their home in Massachusetts Cal's brisk walk to
bathroom to bedroom to closet grated so against her dull mind that
she needed more than during any other moments of a normal day the
cigarette that as a ritual of discipline she had always denied herself
until, seated, she drank her first hot sip of coffee.

But in this early morning, in the grey beginning of light, she was
awake and alert as though in evening, when her body was most vi-
brant, when she and Cal drank their two martinis, sometimes three,
and she told him of the birds and animals she had seen that day and
whom she had seen and what she had heard, and the questions and
answers or attempts at them she had stored up in her silent mono-
logues with herself and with Cal. Cal would often interrupt her, smiling, watching her, and ask: *What did I say to that?* To her wondering

whether families and America were worse now than when she and Cal were children, or even when their own daughter and son were children, or why those women, certainly with good intentions, were trying to stop a supervised hunt to kill some of the weak among too many deer in a small state-protected woods in a neighboring town. Why didn't they know that, having killed or run off for buildings and asphalt the deer's natural predators, people had to perform the function of coyotes and wolves? She also, on those evenings, entertained Cal, made him laugh at her anecdotes about the supermarket, or traffic, or phone calls from friends. Her name was Rusty. It had been Margaret until Cal Williams met and courted her when she was 21 and he was 23; he had called her Rusty because of her hair, because he was in love with her, and it had become her name.

He was sleeping on his right side now, his face toward her, his left hand resting on her stomach. Below his hand her legs were tensed to spring from the bed, to run not from but at an intruder in the room, while her hand grabbed whatever weapon it could to swing at his face; beneath Cal's hand her stomach rose and dropped with her accelerated breath, and she felt her heart beating with that adrenaline they now said could kill you, if you were sedentary, if your heart were accustomed to a soft cushion of quotidian calm. Hers was not; but even if it were, she knew the thought of a heart attack would still be as distant as their home among the pines and poplars and maples and copper beeches on the long wide hill. For she knew it was not the birds that had alerted the muscles in her legs and arms and the one beating beneath her ribs, ready to fight the intruder her body was gathered for, the intruder she had known when she first woke was not there; it was the day itself that woke her: the 14th of July.

It had waked her before, while Cal slept as he did now, as he did on that night one year ago when the day ended and she and Cal and Gina and Ryan had showered the saltwater and perhaps some of the terror from their bodies, had eaten even, for they were very hungry, and their bodies were frail, too, with a weakness that food alone could not strengthen, and in the restaurant in Christiansted they had drunk a lot, all of them, before and during and after dinner. Then Gina had gone to her room in the hotel and Ryan to his, and she and Cal had

gone to bed, and soon Cal was asleep while she smoked and listened to
Gina and Ryan settling in their rooms on either side of hers, and she
knew Cal slept so easily not because he was oblivious but because his
body was more in harmony with itself and life, and death, than hers.
His family had survived. The young captain and mate were dead, the
captain at least ashore now to lie beneath a monument marking his
passage on earth and his possession of his final six feet of it, while the
mate was forever in the Caribbean, swallowed by its creatures, parts of
him—some bones, perhaps even flesh (where was his head, his face?)
—left to sink, to become parts of the bottom of the sea, parts of the sea
itself. Cal's body and mind and heart had endured that, demanded of
him, as hers could not or would not, that he sleep.

For a long time that night a year ago she did not sleep. Once she
heard Gina flush the toilet and she looked at her traveling clock and it
glowed 2:15 at her; at 3:20 Ryan flushed his toilet. And both times she
heard the children drop heavily into their beds and the sleep their
bladders had barely disturbed; and each time she quietly and briefly
wept, for their sounds recalled to her the nights of Gina's and Ryan's
growing up when she woke hearing them walking down the hall to
their rooms, their light footsteps audible only when the flushing that
woke her had ceased and she could hear the moving weight of their
small warm bodies above the faint sound of water filling the tank. Her
weeping that night in the hotel at St. Croix was soundless, her tears so
few they did not even leave her eyes, and it was neither joyful nor
frightened nor relieved: it simply came, as milk had once come from
her breasts.

Some time after 3:20 she slept. They stayed one more week on the
island, to answer questions and sign statements, to attend the captain's
funeral, a young blond man from California whose young blond
tanned woman wore a white dress and sat with his family in the front
pew—a father and mother and two older brothers, who arrived in
three different planes from the United States and wore black—and all
through the service the young woman stared at the casket, her face
still lax with the disbelief that for others becomes in moments a truth
they must bear all their lives. Then at the grave, as the brothers at her
sides turned her tall strong body away from the open hole where the

captain lay under flowers, the young woman, having plucked the first from a wreath and dropped it onto the casket, collapsed, and the two brothers strained to hold her as, doubled over, her lowered face covered by the long blond hair fallen forward and down, she keened.

Rusty and Cal and Gina and Ryan attended the memorial service for the mate, who was from Rhode Island. Rusty sensed that the mate had not had a lover on the day of his death, but there were two young women, one in blue, one in grey, in the pew behind the family, and something about the way they entered together, and sat close, and glanced from time to time at each other, and lowered their faces to cry made Rusty believe they had at one time, separately but probably in quick succession, been the mate's lovers; and whether the one in blue had taken the place of the one in grey in the mate's heart, or the other way around, they were joined for at least these minutes, in the church, somehow united as sisters are, even sisters who dislike each other but despite that are bound anyway because they will never again see or hear or touch someone they both loved. The memorial service was the day after the captain's funeral, and the questions and answers and signing of statements for the Coast Guard lieutenant from Puerto Rico were done, but the family stayed for the remainder of the week, because they had planned to.

They had planned those 14 days while eating dinner in Massachusetts, when the thermometer outside Rusty's kitchen window was at 12 degrees and there was a wind from the north and Cal had said: *If we wait till the off-season I can pay for the whole thing. For everybody.* Gina and Ryan, both working, renting apartments, buying cars, had happily, gratefully, protested; and agreed when Cal said: *Or we can all go Dutch this week.* During those final days at St. Croix they swam in the small pool at the hotel, but none of them went into the sea, whose breakers struck a reef a short distance from the beach, a natural shield against both depth and sharks, so that only a tepid shallow pool with the motion of a lake reached the sand at the hotel. One evening, from the outdoor bar, Rusty watched Gina standing with a tall sunset-colored rum drink on the beach, near the water; she stepped toward it once and stopped paces from where it touched the sand. Then she stepped back and finished her drink, looking beyond the reef at the

blue water and the half-disc of red sun at its horizon. Rusty watched
the sun until it was gone, and green balls rose from the spot where it
sank; they seemed shot into the sky like fireworks, and she thought of
the mate scattered in the sea.

That 14th of July had waked Rusty on nights in the final months of
last year's New England summer, and in the autumn when she could
smell the changes in the cooler air coming through the windows: a
near absence of living plants and trees, the air beginning to have the
aroma of itself alone, as it did in winter when still she woke, not every
night or even every week, and lay in the room with the windows
closed and frosted, her face pleasantly cold, and listened to the basement furnace, its thermostat lowered for the night, pushing heated air
through the grates in the house. In that first spring she woke in the
dark and breathed air tinged with the growth of buds and leaves and
grass beyond her windows. Now it was the anniversary of the day
itself, and she and Cal and Gina and Ryan had decided, again in
winter, again eating dinner on a Sunday night, not to let it pass as
though it were any other day, any set of two numerals on the calendar,
but to gather, either at home or wherever she and Cal chose to be in
the middle of July.

She left the bed, and by that simple motion of pushing away sheet
and summer blanket and swinging her feet to the floor, her breath and
heart and muscles eased, and softly she left the bedroom and went
down the hall and into the kitchen, everything visible though not
distinct in this last of darkness her eyes had adjusted to while in bed
she listened to birds and saw the fins of sharks.

She still did, standing at the sink in her white gown and looking
through the window screen at dark pines, and she heard the mate's
scream just after he tied the knot lashing together the two orange life
preservers and she had looked up from buckling her life jacket, looked
at his scream and saw a face she had never seen before and now would
always see: his eyes and mouth widened in final horror and the absolute loss of hope that caused it, then he was gone, as though propelled
downward, and his orange life jacket he had waited to put on, had
held by one strap in his teeth as he wrapped the lines down through
the water and up over the sides of the life preservers, floated on the

calm blue surface. She saw, too, in her memory that moved into the
space of lawn and grey air between her and the pines, the young blond
captain bobbing in his jacket in the churning water beneath the helicopter blades. He helped Gina first onto the ladder; Rusty, holding the
swinging ropes, watched Gina's legs, glistening brown in the sun,
climbing fast, above the water; then the captain lifted Rusty and
pushed her legs to the rung they were reaching for, and then Ryan and
then Cal; and Cal's wet hair blew down and out from his head. Rusty
was aboard then, on her hands and knees on the vibrating deck of the
helicopter, calling louder it seemed than the engine, calling to Cal to
hurry, hurry, climb, then she saw the shark's fin and in front of it the
rising blue back and head, its blank and staring eyes, then its mouth as
the captain reached for the ladder but only his left arm rose as she
screamed his name so loudly she did not hear the engine but heard the
bite as she saw it and blood spurting into the air, onto the roiled water
while the captain's right shoulder still moved upward as though it or
the captain still believed it was attached to an arm.

Cal heard her scream. He looked down over his shoulder then
sprang backward into the water and then she could not scream, or
hear the engine, or feel the deck's quick throb against her knees and
palms: she could only see Cal's feet hit the water and his legs sink into
it, before the jacket stopped and lifted him, one arm straight upward,
his hand gripping a rung. With the other he reached underwater and
pushed the captain up and held him while the captain moved his left
hand up the vertical rope to the next rung. Then Cal lifted him again
and the captain's hand moved up the next rung and pulled, the sun-
burn gone now from his face more pale than his sun-bleached hair,
and blood fell on Cal and spurted on the water where a fin came with
the insouciant speed of nature and her remorseless killing. Cal was
looking only at the captain's back above him; he straightened his leg
and the other ascended from the water as quickly, it seemed, as it had
entered. Below him the eyes and head rose from blown waves then
went under, and the fin moved round the bound orange preservers
turning and rocking and rising and falling in the water. The loud
circling of the huge blades above her made Rusty feel contained from

all other time and space save these moments and feet of rope that both separated her from Cal and joined her to him.

Then quickly and firmly yet not roughly a man removed her from the hatch—pushed her maybe; lifted and set her down maybe—and went backward down the ladder. She crawled to the hatch's side: Cal stood behind the captain, his head near the middle of the captain's back, his right hand holding the vertical rope beneath the slowing spurt of blood, his left pulling the captain's hand from a rung, pushing it to the one above; then the man descending stopped and held onto the swinging ladder with the crook of his elbow, and hung out over the water and the fins—four now: five—and lowered a white line to Cal, then tied it around his waist and held the captain's wrist while Cal knotted the line beneath the orange jacket and the face that now was so white she knew the captain would die. But her heart did not: it urged the three men up as Cal with his body held the captain on the ladder and pushed his hand up to a rung, then lifted his left leg to one, then his right, and followed him up while the crewman, with the line around his waist, slowly climbed until he reached the hatch and leaned through it, his chest on the deck, and Gina and Ryan each took an arm and pulled, and Rusty worked her hands under his web belt at his back, and on her knees she pulled until he was inside, kneeling then standing and turning seaward, to look down the ladder and tighten the rope and say to any of them behind him: *First aid kit.*

Hand over hand he pulled the rope, looking down the ladder at his work, keeping his pull steady but slow, too, holding the captain on the ladder and between it and Cal. Then at the bottom edge of the hatch, against a background of blue sky and water, the captain's face appeared; then the jacket, and the shoulder she could not look away from but she saw the other one, too, and his left arm that did not reach into the helicopter but simply fell forward and lay still. The crewman stepped back, leaning against the rope around his waist, pulling it faster now but smoothly, and though she could not see Cal she saw the effort of his push as the captain rose and dropped to the deck. She bent over his back, gripped his belt at both sides, and threw herself backward and he slid forward as she fell on her rump and sat

beside him, on the spot where his right arm would have been, and she felt his blood through her wet jeans.

The blood did not spurt now. It flowed, and Cal was aboard, crawling in it, before Rusty or Gina or Ryan could move around the captain to hold out a hand; blood was in Cal's dark brown hair, flecks and smears among the grey streaks and the grey above his ears and in his short sideburns, and on his hands and sleeves and jacket and face. But what Rusty saw in a grateful instant that released her into time and space again was Cal's own blood, pumping within his body, coloring his face a deep, living red.

The helicopter veered and climbed and the crewman rolled the captain onto his back and, without looking, reached up for the compress Gina had removed from the first aid kit. Rusty looked at her hand, holding the compress as limply as with guilt, then Rusty looked up at the tearless futility of her daughter's face. The compress did not change hands. The crewman was looking at the captain's face and then he lowered his arm and placed his fingers on the captain's throat. Rusty knew from the crewman's eyes, and from the captain's face while he was still on the ladder, that this touch of the pulse was no more than a gesture. Her legs lay straight in front of her, and she bent them and with her palms she pushed herself up, stumbling into the imbalance of the helicopter's flight, rising from the captain's blood, and wiping it from her palms onto the legs of her jeans.

"And it was his own fault," she said at the kitchen sink, surprised that she had spoken aloud, in a voice softly hoarse, after the silence of sleep. She cleared her throat but it was dry, so she left the sink and the window and the images between her and the pines of the dead captain in the helicopter, and the first fin—the second: no one had seen the shark that came up under the mate—and poured a glass of orange juice and drank it in one long swallow, her hand still holding open the refrigerator door. She stood looking at the turkey, covered with plastic wrapping. Last night she had removed the shelf above it to make room for the turkey's breast. She had put in the ice chest the random assortment of food from the shelf that leaned now against one side of the refrigerator. Some of the food she had thrown away: a peach and two oranges molding at the rear of the shelf, a tomato so soft her fingers pierced it—and was angry again at her incompetence, after all these years, at maintaining order in a refrigerator, at even knowing what on a given day it contained. She saw Gina's long bare legs beside hers in the water, bending then kicking the soles of her sneakers against the noses of sharks.

It was what the captain had told them to do—had shouted at them to do—and for 47 minutes (according to the Coast Guard) Rusty had kicked. Her arms were behind her, down through the life preserver, her hands underwater holding the bottom of its rim. Gina, holding the same preserver, was to her right. Rusty could glance to her left and see Cal's back, his head, and his arms going down through that preserver; Ryan and the captain were behind her. She wore jeans, tight and heavy with water, and when a fin came toward her she drew in her legs then kicked between the eyes as they surfaced, those eyes that seemed to want her without seeing her. Later when she told the story to friends at home, she said the eyes were like those of an utterly drunken man trying to pick you up in a bar: all but a glimmer of sentience and motive invisible beneath the glaze of drunkenness, so that he did not truly see you, but only woman, bar, night. Each time she kicked, and while she readied herself for the next shark, she waited for her blue-jeaned legs to disappear in a crunch and tearing of teeth through her flesh and bones. But more than her own legs she had watched Gina's, or had been aware of them as though she never stopped watching, for while her memory was of Gina's legs and her waiting to see them severed, memory told her, too, that she could not have looked at them as often or for as long as she believed. She had to watch the water in front of her; even to hope for a fin there, because she waited for a shark to come straight up beneath her, to kill her before she even saw it. So she had glimpsed Gina's legs, had sometimes looked directly at them when Gina kicked and kicked until the shark turned; but always she had felt those legs, more even than her own; and she had not felt—or had she? and would she ever know?— Cal's legs or body, or Ryan's, though she had called to them, every minute or so it seemed now: *Cal? Are you all right? Ryan?* She had not felt the captain at all.

She closed the refrigerator, thought of making coffee and starting this day. But it was too early. She wanted the day to be over, wanted tomorrow to come, Monday, the day that since she was a little girl had asserted itself on her life, as an end to weekends, an affirmation of their transitory ease.

The linoleum floor chilled her bare feet. She went quietly to the bedroom, stood on its carpet and looked once with loving envy, nearly pride, at Cal sleeping; then she stepped into her slippers and put on her robe and dropped her cigarettes and lighter into a pocket and went out into the hall, where on the wood floor the skidding and slapping of her slippers made her halt and for an instant hold her breath. Then lifting and lowering her feet in a slow creeping walk she went to the bathroom, knowing for the first time since the day woke her that she wanted Cal asleep, she wanted to be alone. She eased open the medicine cabinet and lowered a sleeping pill into the pocket of her robe.

In the kitchen she filled a glass with ice from the chest that held beer, jarred food, and a carton of milk, and pulled a Coke from under ice, and went through the living room and unlatched the screen door. She sat on the old porch swing hanging by chains from the ceiling and looked at the lake; in the faint light it was dark blue and smooth. On both sides of her were trees, so she could not see the cabins that flanked theirs nor, at this hour, hear the voices and music that later would come through the woods, and around them, too, as though carried by the lake's surface. She poured Coke fizzing over ice and when the foam settled she poured again. She pinched the pill out of her pocket, blew off aqua lint, then holding it at her mouth she paused. She would sleep till noon. Then she placed it on her tongue and drank.

Soon she would feel it: the dullness in her legs and arms and behind her eyes, so they would see then only what they looked at, objects and doors and rooms and hall; free of sharks and blood, they would steer her to bed, where she would wake a second time to the 14th of July, a day in history she had memorized in school; but a year ago, in a sea as tranquil as this lake, that date had molted the prison and the revolution. As when Vietnam had disappeared in 1968, burned up in Gina's fever when she was nine and had pneumonia. Then Rusty's passive sorrow and anger about the war, harder to bear because they were passive, so on some nights awake in bed she saw herself pouring her blood on draft files, going to jail; and all the pictures of the war her heart received from television and newspapers and magazines; and her imagined visions of wounded and dying, and the suffering of those alive, first the Vietnamese children, then all Vietnamese and those American boys who were lost in false fervor or drafted and forced to be soldiers so they could survive; all were cold ashes in her mind and heart while for three days Gina, her first-born, lay on the hospital bed with a needle in her vein and every six hours a nurse added an antibiotic to the fluid, and every four took Gina's temperature. Rusty stayed in the room, watched Gina, read, fell asleep in the chair, ate at the hospital cafeteria; when Cal got home from work he and Ryan came and sat with Gina, while Rusty went home to shower and change clothes, then she returned to spend the night sleeping in the leather arm chair.

On the fourth day Gina's fever was down and Rusty brought her home, to her bed with fresh sheets Rusty had tucked and folded, and for the next ten days she ministered to her, sat and talked with her, gave her socks and slippers and helped her into her robe when Gina wanted to watch television from the living room couch, where she lay on her side and Rusty covered her with a blanket and sat at the couch's end, with Gina's feet touching her leg, and did not smoke. For those ten days the foolishness Gina watched was not foolishness; their watching it was ceremonial. During these days Rusty's life drew her back into it: she became married again, she cooked meals, and received the praise of Cal and Ryan, who gave it to her by joking about their cereal and sandwiches and Chinese dinners while she was at the hospital. Three times she and Cal made love, and she guided him to long tenderness before she opened herself to him, and did not tell him that his lover's slow kissing and touching were exorcising the vapor of death above their bed, stirring her passion until it consumed her, and left no space in the room or bed or her body for the death of Gina. As Gina became strong and cheerful and finally restless, the Vietnam War seeped back into Rusty's days and nights and she began reading the *Boston Globe* again and watching the news on television and, within the first week of Gina's return to school, her old thwarted sorrow and anger distracted her quietude, and rose in her conversations with her friends and her family.

She felt the pill in her legs now, and her fingers as she lit her last cigarette before the walk she would have to control to the bedroom. Near the shore in front of the house a mallard swam. In the still air the lake was as calm as the Caribbean on Bastille Day when they fished for marlin. As they headed out to sea in the 32-foot wooden boat, Gina had said: *Let them eat hooks.* Rusty killed fish every summer and sometimes, with Cal, pheasants in the fall. She had given up trying to explain to her friends who did not hunt, both women and men, the thrill of the flushing bird and her gun coming to her shoulder and its muzzle and bead sight swinging up to the shape and colors, the thrill of firing only once and seeing it fall, and her fear as she ran to it and, above all, the third feeling: sacredness, a joy subdued by sorrow not for the dead bird, or even for her killing it, but for something she knew in her heart yet could not name, something universal and as old as the earth and the first breath of plants. Those same friends who did not understand her hunting were puzzled when she told them that catching even a mackerel, small and plentiful as they were, or a cod that she reeled up from the bottom of the sea onto boats they chartered in New Hampshire, gave her that same feeling when she unhooked them and placed them in the ice chest. She never mentioned to those friends what she felt when she caught a bluefish. They fought as if they were a heavy cod with the vigor of a mackerel, and the fish's struggle for life wearied her as she reeled. When she brought it alongside and Cal or Gina or Ryan gaffed it and lifted it onto the deck, she put on thick cotton working gloves and pushed one hand into a gill while with pliers in the other she pulled and twisted and worked out the hook, watching the eye looking at hers, and telling her as clearly as if it were human: *I'm going to bite off your finger, you bitch.* She had never shot any game but pheasants or an occasional rabbit, had never caught anything larger than a bluefish. She did not know whether or not she wanted to catch a marlin; she did not know whether she wanted any of her family to. So when Gina made the joke about hooks, Rusty had quickly turned to her, a scolding sentence taking shape; but she said nothing. For Gina, seeing Rusty's face, had

blushed and said: *I just remembered what day it is. That's all.* Ryan
stepped beside Gina at the gunwale and kissed her cheek and said:
Aristocrat. Or maybe a royal asshole. Cal said: *Did somebody call?*

An hour or two later, some time before noon, the boat sank. It
struck nothing. The engine stopped but there was no sound of wooden
bow or hull hitting a reef or up-turned sunken boat or whale. There
was no shock, no force to make them fall to the deck, or to lurch and
reach for each other's bodies for balance. There was only the captain's
voice: not even a cry, but a low clear sentence so weighted with the
absolute knowledge of what had happened that to Rusty it was more
frightening than a scream: *We have to go overboard; she's sinking.* Then
he said to the mate, Zack Chaffee, dark and small and muscular,
already running forward the few strides from stern to fo'c'sle, and
minutes away from his own death: *Get the preservers and jackets.*
Rusty went forward, too, and felt her family behind and beside her as
she halted midway to the fo'c'sle and looked at the water rising in it,
covering the bunks. A cushion and two life jackets floated. Chaffee
went down the ladder and was in water to his waist. He tossed the two
floating jackets out to the deck and saw Rusty and her family, and he
was looking at her face when he waved his arm toward the boat's port
side and either said or mouthed: *Go.* Cal picked up the jackets and
gave them to Gina and Ryan, then took her arm and led her to the
side. As he lifted her to the gunwale she heard the captain's voice
repeating MAYDAY and the digits of their location and she looked over
her shoulder at him before she jumped. Then all of them were in the
water, swimming away from the boat, Zack pushing the preservers in
front of him, holding his jacket's strap in his teeth, a coil of line
around one shoulder; and the captain rising in the water to throw
jackets ahead of her and Cal.

Holding a preserver while Zack lashed at them, she watched the
boat sinking, then looked past Zack at the captain's profile and saw
what his first knowledge had been, what she had heard in his voice
when he spoke to them on the boat: not of drowning; they were floating and already help was coming from everywhere within range of his
radio. He had known why they were sinking, and she knew it was
something he had done or had not done, and it should not have hap-

pened, should not have been allowed to happen, and she was about to accuse him but could not, for his face was like that of landed codfish, resigned to sunlight and air and death, as if they accepted that they had destroyed themselves, feeding on the dark bottom, taking the clam and the barb with it, and that was why they fought so little, if at all, while she reeled them up, why they were simply weight on the end of her line.

The captain's name was Lenny Walters. Watching his face with its look of being caught in a trap that he had set, she forgave him. He looked at his boat until it was gone, and still he stared at the water where it had been as if the gentle waves were a chorus, their peaceful sound of moving water coming to his ears as hue and cry. In the water beside her Gina and Ryan, 25 and 23 then, were building a bridge of jokes and laughter over their fear. Cal was asking Zack, but quietly, what the goddamn hell had happened. Zack was silently tying together the preservers. Rusty looked at his face lowered over the knot, but lowered as well from Cal's voice and eyes. So he knew, too. She looked up at the sky for respite, then pushed her arms through the holes in her life jacket and looked down to buckle the straps and Zack screamed.

We can never know for sure, the Coast Guard lieutenant had said. *But that's the only thing that makes sense. I've got four intelligent adults here. And they tell me you were all a lot calmer than people ought to have to be. With what you went through. No panic. Working together in the water, even this fellow*—he nodded toward Cal, smoking in a chair near a window—*going back in to help the captain up when he got it. So I believe the boat didn't hit anything. So I'm going to report that, in my professional opinion, that's exactly what it was. And I want to thank all of you for your time and your courtesy. There's not one thousandth of one percent of the whole human race that's been through what you good people did.* He paused. *Not on a fishing trip anyway. It was probably the first shark that brought the rest, got them feeding. And most times that first shark wouldn't have hit either. By and large, they're just big fish that leave people alone. So you had a whole lot of bad luck, and a whole lot of good luck to get out of it alive. If there's anything I can do—.* But Rusty said: *It wasn't bad luck.*

He turned to her, placed his arms on the desk, and leaned over them.

Beg pardon? he said. He was a tall man, not broad, and his stomach was widening. Lenny Walters was a very large man, not tall and not fat, but strong; she had only noticed his size when she watched Cal pushing him up the ladder and holding him on it and then the crewman climbing against the pull of the rope around his waist, and at the end when she had gripped Lenny Walters' belt and thrown herself backward onto the deck. Cal was five feet eight inches tall and weighed 165 pounds, three inches taller and 30 pounds heavier than she, yet for 35 years she had seen him as bigger and stronger than everything she feared. Maybe she had not seen the 200-odd pounds of Lenny Walters until he was dying on the ladder because there was something about him that was small, indolent.

It wasn't bad luck, she said. *The sharks, yes. But not the boat sinking. It wasn't an accident either. Maybe the first shark was an accident. Maybe he didn't even want Zack. Maybe he wanted something better.*

The lieutenant's blue eyes did not move from hers. They looked at her as one sailor's eyes to another, curious, interested, ready to receive a truth about the unpredictable and mysterious sea they shared. She said: *It was—what's the word?*

Electrolysis.

Yes. Of the sea cock. He knew. He knew he hadn't done his maintenance. It was in his voice. When he told us we had to go overboard. I can still hear him. It was in his voice: there was no surprise, you see. Not even excitement. It was like something had been on his mind for a while—.

A good while, the lieutenant said. *Excuse me.*

—so that brass fitting snapped off and the boat filled under the water line and he still didn't know it. Then the water burst through the bulkhead into the fo'c'sle and what he had been putting off doing came in on him. And he knew it. It was in his voice, and it was in his face when he was watching his boat go down. It was in Zack's face, too, right up to the moment the shark came.

The lieutenant nodded.

I believe you, he said. He looked at Cal across the room from Rusty.

Cal was watching her. The red in his cheeks deepened, and he said: *Maybe that's why he was so good in the water. He was a goddamned captain in that water. He put Gina up the ladder first. I don't believe he was thinking women and children first either. He knew there was just us four in the family. I think he picked her first because she can still have babies.* Cal's eyes did not shift to Gina, or to Ryan when he said: *Then Ryan. Same reason, I suppose. He can't have them but he can get them started. Then the mother. Then the old bastard that's paid his dues and his insurance premiums, too. Then the poor son of a bitch paid all his dues at once.*

The deeper color was still in his cheeks and she saw in his eyes the dampness of tears, but his hands did not rise to them either; he let them glisten there, for her. To her left Gina sniffled. Still watching Cal, her face warmed by his, she reached to Gina, who with two hands took hers and tightened and stroked, and Rusty saw those lovely brown legs in the blue water. Had a shark's jaws opened for one she would have triumphantly thrust her own leg into its mouth. Yet Cal, without even a pause to look for another way to get Lenny Walters onto the ladder, had leaped backward into the sea, among the sharks whose number they would never know. Looking at him across the small room she felt no shame or envy. She saw only Cal, and in his face she saw only herself, and though she felt bodiless, too, out of the room, as though her spirit and Cal's had left their bodies and were moving side by side, above time, above mortality. Then she was in her body again, in the room and the cool of the trade winds coming through the window behind Cal, and she was aware again of the tall lieutenant. She looked at him, then at Ryan, then at Gina. They were all watching her, as they might if she had beautifully sung an aria, and they could not yet speak, suspended in that instant of purity before their hands would move to clap, and their legs would push them out of their chairs, to their feet.

On the porch swing she carefully lowered the glass with its melting ice to the floor. She had a few minutes still to sit and watch the lake, time even for another cigarette, though her fingers were slow and heavy with it, and her mind was moving back through the house, into bed and sleep, its path cluttered with images it tried to skirt: a large codfish staring straight ahead at air as she gently removed the hook; a bluefish pressed down by her knee, flopping and twisting against her gloved hand in its gill, biting the shank of the hook and glaring at her; the strange eyes of sharks driven from feeding by kicking feet. But the pill neither distorted nor quieted her heart. Its beat was not as rapid as when it woke her; but it was strong, so eager now for the day that she was glad she had taken the pill, for excitement would have kept her awake as it does a child.

She saw motion to her right: not a thing or a creature, but only its movement. She sat very still, moved her eyes toward it, and saw a doe drinking at the lake: her graceful and exposed neck lowered to the water. Then behind the doe, at the edge of the woods, the antlers and head and shoulders of a buck seemed to separate themselves from the trees. Then it stopped. Quietly Rusty breathed the smell of pines and water. The buck lifted its head. Then he stepped forward once, swung his head in an arc that started up the lake and ended with her. She stared at his nose and eyes and antlers, and did not move. Rusty saw the length of his body emerge from the woods, as if it were growing out of the trees. At the lake he stopped, his head up, listening. Then he drank. Rusty tossed her cigarette to the lawn and watched him drinking, and the doe turning back to the woods, then disappearing into it. She waited until the buck finished drinking and vanished, too.

She pushed herself up from the swing and at the sound of its chains she stopped and listened for the running deer, but heard only water lapping at the shore. She had not been drunk for over ten years, and in her sleepy happiness she smiled at her walk through the cabin, no more than two steps in a straight line before she swerved, slowly and heavily. She kept her palms on both walls till she reached the door and Cal's breathing. She stood in the doorway, aiming herself at her side of the bed, the far side. Then she moved, weaving, her arms up and out for balance. *Like dancing,* she thought, and felt like twirling but knew she would fall. When she turned the corner of the foot of the bed she did fall: she simply let go all control of herself and landed on the mattress and laughed with a sound as soft as Cal's breath. He rolled toward her, then opened his eyes. They were calm, like Gina's and Ryan's were when they quietly woke in their cradles then cribs on mornings when they were neither hungry or uncomfortably wet, only awake. She kissed both of his eyes shut and with her thickened tongue said, "I took a pill. But wake me up anyway. With coffee. Okay?"

"A pill," he said, as sleep drew him away from her. Then he opened his eyes. "Why?"

"I couldn't sleep."

"I know. But why?"

"Today."

Her eyes closed and she was asleep but trying to return, and she forced open her lids.

"I was on the porch. Remembering all of it. You." She lay her hand on his sides, pressed his ribs. "It was the worst day our family's ever had."

"It was the worst day most families have ever had."

Her eyes closed.

"But it was the best, too," she said, her voice detached from her body, coming from a throat somewhere above her. She felt his voice close to her face but she heard one word at a time then it drifted away from her and the next word and the next were alone and meant nothing.

"Do you understand?" she said.

Then his mouth was at her ear, and she heard: "I said yes."

"Good. Make the coffee strong."

His hand was smoothing her hair back from her forehead, he was talking, and his voice was gentle. She heard only her name, then was asleep.

The Business Venture

•

====== **ELIZABETH SPENCER** ======

Elizabeth Spencer was born and brought up in Carrollton, Mississippi. She attended Vanderbilt University in Nashville, and taught at the University of Mississippi until going to Italy, where she lived from 1953 to 1958. She lived a number of years in Montreal, but has recently moved to Chapel Hill, North Carolina, where she is a member of the creative writing staff at the University of North Carolina. She received the Award of Merit medal of the American Academy of Arts and Letters in 1983, for the short story, and in 1985 was elected to the American Academy/Institute's Department of Literature. Her latest book, The Salt Line, *a novel, was published by Doubleday in 1984.*

We were down at the river that night. Pete Owens was there with his young wife Hope (his name for her was Jezzie, after Jezebel in the Bible), and Charlie and me, and both the Houston boys, one with his wife and the other with the latest in a string of new girl friends. But Nelle Townshend, his steady girl, wasn't there.

We talked and watched the water flow. It was different from those nights we used to go up to the club and dance, because we were older and hadn't bothered to dress, just wore slacks and shorts. It was a clear night but no moon.

Even five years married to him, I was in love with Charlie more than ever, and took his hand to rub the reddish hairs around his wrist. I held his hand under water and watched the flow around it, and later when the others went up to the highway for more whisky, we kissed like two high school kids and then waded out laughing and splashed water on each other.

The next day Pete Owens looked me up at the office when my boss, Mr. McGinnis, was gone to lunch. "Charlie's never quit, you know, Eileen. He's still passing favors out."

My heart dropped. I could guess it, but wasn't letting myself know I really knew it. I put my hard mask on. "What's the matter? Isn't Hope getting enough from you?"

"Oh, I'm the one for Jezzie. You're the main one for Charlie. I just mean, don't kid yourself he's ever stopped."

"When did any of us ever stop?"

"You have. You like him that much. But don't think you're home free. The funny thing is nobody's ever took a shotgun to Charlie. So far's I know, nobody's ever even punched him in the jaw."

"It is odd," I said, sarcastic, but he didn't notice.

"It's downright peculiar," said Pete. "But then I guess we're a special sort of bunch, Eileen."

I went back to typing and wished he'd go. He'd be asking me next. We'd dated and done a few things, but that was so long ago, it didn't count now. It never really mattered. I never thought much about it.

"What I wonder is, Eileen, is everybody else like us, or so different from us they don't know what we're like at all?"

"The world's changing," I said. "They're all getting like us."

"You mean it?"

I nodded. "The word got out," I said. "You told somebody, and they told somebody else, and now everybody is like us."

"Or soon will be," he said.

"That's right," I said.

I kept on typing letters, reeling them on and off the platen and working on my electric machine the whole time he was talking, turning his hat over and picking at a straw or two off the synthetic weave. I had a headache that got worse after he was gone.

Also at the picnic that night was Grey Houston, one of the Houston brothers, who was always with a different girl. His former steady girl friend, Nelle Townshend, kept a cleaning and pressing shop on her

own premises. Her mother had been a stay-at-home lady for years.
They had one of these beautiful old Victorian-type houses—it just
missed being a photographer's and tourist attraction, being about
twenty years too late and having the wooden trim too ornate for the
connoisseurs to call it the real classical style. Nelle had been enterpris-
ing enough to turn one wing of the house where nobody went anymore
into a cleaning shop because she needed to make some money and felt
she had to be near her mother. She had working for them off and on a
Negro back from the Vietnam War who had used his veterans' educa-
tional benefits to train as a dry cleaner. She picked up the idea when
her mother happened to remark one night after she had paid him for
some carpenter work, "Ain't that a dumb nigger, learning dry cleaning with nothing to dry-clean."

Now when Mrs. Townshend said "nigger," it wasn't as if one of us
had said it. She went back through the centuries for her words, back
to when "ain't" was good grammar. "Nigger" for her just meant
"black." But it was assuming Robin had done something dumb that
was the mistake. Because he wasn't dumb, and Nelle knew it. He told
her he'd applied for jobs all around, but they didn't offer much and he
might have to go to Biloxi or Hattiesburg or Gulfport to get one. The
trouble was he owned a house here. Nelle said, "Maybe you could
work for me."

He told her about a whole dry cleaning plant up in Magee that had
folded up recently due to the old man who ran it dying on his feet one
day. They drove up there together and she bought it. Her mother
didn't like it much when she moved the equipment in, but Nelle did it
anyway. "I never get the smell out of my hair," she would say, "but if
it can just make money I'll get used to it." She was dating Grey at the
time, and I thought that's what gave her that much nerve.

Grey was a darling man. He was divorced from a New Orleans
woman, somebody with a lot of class and money. She'd been crazy
about Grey, as who wouldn't be, but he didn't "fit in," was her complaint. "Why do I have to fit in with her?" he kept asking. "Why
shouldn't she fit in with us?" "She was okay with us," I said. "Not
quite," he said. "Y'all never did relax. You never felt easy. That's why
Charlie kept working at her, flirting and all. She maybe ought to have

gone ahead with Charlie. Then she'd have been one of us. But she acted serious about it. I said, 'Whatever you decide about Charlie, just don't tell me.' She was too serious."

"Anybody takes it seriously ought to be me," I said.

"Oh-oh," said Grey, breaking out with fun, the way he could do—in the depths one minute, up and laughing the next. "You can't afford that, Eileen."

That time I raised a storm at Charlie. "What did you want to get married for? You're nothing but a goddam stud!"

"What's news about it?" Charlie wanted to know. "You're just getting worked up over nothing."

"Nothing! Is what we do just nothing?"

"That's right. When it's done with, it's nothing. What I think of you —now, that's something." He had had some problem with a new car at the garage—he had the GM agency then—and he smelled of clean lubricating products and new upholstery and the rough soap where the mechanics cleaned up. He was big and gleaming, the all-over male. Oh hell, I thought, what can I do? Then, suddenly curious, I asked: *"Did* you make out with Grey's wife?"

He laughed out loud and gave me a sidelong kiss. "Now that's more like it."

Because he'd never tell me. He'd never tell me who he made out with. "Honey," he'd say, late at night in the dark, lying straight out beside me, occasionally tangling his toes in mine or reaching for his cigarettes, "if I'd say I never had another woman outside you, would you believe it?"

I couldn't say No from sheer astonishment.

"Because it just might be true," he went on in the dark, serious as a judge. Then I would start laughing, couldn't help it. Because there are few things in the world which you know are true. You don't know (not anymore: our mamas knew) if there's a God or not, much less if He so loved the world. You don't know what your own native land is up to, or the true meaning of freedom, or the real cost of gasoline and cigarettes, or whether your insurance company will pay up. But one thing I personally know that is *not* true is that Charlie Waybridge has had only one woman. Looked at that way, it can be a comfort, one thing to be sure of.

It was soon after the picnic on the river that Grey Houston came by to see me at the office. You'd think I had nothing to do but stop and talk. What he came about was Nelle.

"She won't date me anymore," he complained. "I thought we were doing fine, but she quit me just like that. Hell, I can't tell what's the trouble with her. I want to call up and say, 'Just tell me, Nelle. What's going on?' "

"Why don't you?" I asked.

Grey is always a little worried about things to do with people, especially since his divorce. We were glad when he started dating Nelle. She was hovering around thirty and didn't have anybody, and Grey was only a year or two younger.

"If I come right out and ask her, then she might just say, 'Let's decide to be good friends,' or something like that. Hell, I got enough friends."

"It's to be thought of," I agreed.

"What would you do?" he persisted.

"I'd rather know where I stand," I said, "but in this case I think I'd wait a while. Nelle's worrying over that business. Maybe she doesn't know herself."

"I might push her too soon. I thought that too."

"I ought to go around and see old Mrs. Townshend," I said. "She hardly gets out at all anymore. I mean to stop in and say hello."

"You're not going to repeat anything?"

See how he is? Skittery. "Of course not," I said. "But there's such a thing as keeping my eyes and ears open."

I went over to call on old Mrs. Townshend one Thursday afternoon when Mr. McGinnis' law office was closed anyway. The Townshend house is on a big lawn, a brick walk running up from the street to the front steps and a large round plot of elephant ears in the front yard. When away and thinking of home, I see right off the Townshend yard and the elephant ears.

I wasn't even to the steps before I smelled clothes just dry-cleaned. I don't guess it's so bad, though hardly what you'd think of living with. Nor would you particularly like to see the sign outside the porte-cochère, though way to the left of the walk and not visible from the front porch. Still, it was out there clearly, saying "TOWNSHEND DRY CLEANING: RAPID SERVICE." Better than a funeral parlor, but not much.

The Townshend house is stuffed with things. All these little Victorian tables on tall legs bowed outward, a small lower shelf, and the top covered katy-corner with a clean starched linen doily, tatting around the edge. All these chairs of various shapes, especially one that rocked squeaking on a walnut stand, and for every chair a doily at the head. Mrs. Townshend kept two bird cages, but no birds were in them. There never had been any as far as I knew. It wasn't a dark house, though. Nelle had taken out the stained glass way back when she graduated from college. That was soon after her older sister married, and her mama needed her. "If I'm going to live here," she had said, "that's got to go." So it went.

Mrs. Townshend never raised much of a fuss at Nelle. She was low to the ground because of a humpback, a rather placid old lady. The Townshends were the sort to keep everything just the way it was. Mrs. Townshend was a LeMoyne from over toward Natchez. She was an Episcopalian and had brought her daughters up in that church.

"I'm sorry about this smell," she said in her forthright way, coming in and offering me a Coke on a little tray with a folded linen napkin beside it. "Nelle told me I'd get used to it and she was right: I have. But at first I had headaches all the time. If you get one I'll get some aspirin for you."

"How's the business going?" I asked.

"Nelle will be in in a minute. She knows you're here. You can ask her." She never raised her voice. She had a soft little face and gray eyes back of her little gold-rimmed glasses. She hadn't got to the hearing aid stage yet, but you had to speak up. We went through the whole rigamarole of mine and Charlie's families. I had a feeling she was never much interested in all that, but around home you have to do it. Then I asked her what she was reading and she waked up. We got off the ground right away, and went strong about the president and

foreign affairs, the picture not being so bright but of great interest, and
about her books from the library always running out, and all the
things she had against book clubs—then Nelle walked in.

Nelle Townshend doesn't look like anybody else but herself. Her
face is like something done on purpose to use up all the fine skin,
drawing it evenly over the bones beneath, so that no matter at what
age, she always would look the same. But that day she had this
pinched look I'd never seen before, and her arms were splotched with
what must have been a reaction to the cleaning fluids. She rolled down
the sleeves of her blouse and sat in an old wicker rocker.

"I saw Grey the other day, Nelle," I said. "I think he misses you."

She didn't say anything outside of remarking she hadn't much time
to go out. Then she mentioned some sort of decorating at the church
she wanted to borrow some ferns for, from the florist. He's got some
he rents, in washtubs. "You can't get all those ferns in our little
church," Mrs. Townshend said, and Nelle said she thought two would
do. She'd send Robin, she said. Then the bell rang to announce another customer. Nelle had to go because Robin was at the "plant,"
actually the old cook's house in back of the property where they'd set
the machinery up.

I hadn't said all I had to say to Nelle, so when I got up to go, I said
to Mrs. Townshend that I'd go in the office a minute on the way out.
But Mrs. Townshend got to her feet, a surprise in itself. Her usual
words were, You'll excuse me if I don't get up. Of course, you would
excuse her and be too polite to ask why. Like a lot of old ladies, she
might have arthritis. But this time she stood.

"I wish you'd let Nelle alone. Nelle is all right now. She's the way
she wants to be. She's not the way you people are. She's just not a bit
that way!"

It may have been sheer surprise that kept me from telling Charlie all
this till the weekend. We were hurrying to get to Pete and Hope
Owens's place for a dinner they were having for some people from the
Delta, visitors.

"What did you say to that?" Charlie asked me.

"I was too surprised to open my mouth. I wouldn't have thought

Mrs. Townshend would express such a low opinion as that. And why does she have it in the first place? Nelle's always been part of our crowd. She grew up with us. I thought they liked us."

"Old ladies get notions. They talk on the phone too much."

To our surprise, Nelle was at the Owens's dinner, too. Hope told me in the kitchen that she'd asked her, and then asked Grey. But Grey had a date with the little Springer girl he'd brought to the picnic. Carole Springer. "If this keeps up," Hope said to me in the kitchen where I was helping her with a dip, "we're going to have a Springer in our crowd. I'm just not right ready for that." "Me either," I said. The Springers were from McComb, in lumber. They had money but they never were much fun.

"Did Nelle accept knowing you were going to ask Grey?" I asked.

"I couldn't tell that. She just said she'd love to and would come about seven."

It must have been seven, because Nelle walked in. "Can I help?"

"Your mama," I said, when Hope went out with the tray, "she sort of got upset with me the other day. I don't know why. If I said anything wrong, just tell her I'm sorry."

Nelle looked at her fresh nail polish. "Mama's a little peculiar now and then. Like everybody." So she wasn't about to open up.

"I've been feeling bad about Grey is all," I said. "You can think I'm meddling if you want to."

"Grey's all right," she said. "He's been going around with Carole Springer from McComb."

"All the more reason for feeling bad. Did you know they're coming tonight?"

She smiled a little distantly, and we went out to join the party. Charlie was already sitting up too close to the wife of the guest couple. I'd met them before. They have an antique shop. He is tall and nice, and she is short (wears spike heels) and nice. They are the sort you can't ever remember what their names are. If you get the first names right you're doing well. Shirley and Bob.

"Honey, you're just a doll," Charlie was saying (if he couldn't think of Shirley, Honey would do), and Pete said, "Watch out, Shirley, the next thing you know you'll be sitting on his lap."

"I almost went in for antiques myself," Nelle was saying to Bob, the husband. "I would have liked that better, of course, than a cleaning business, but I thought the turnover here would be too small. I do need to feel like I'm making money if I'm going to work at it. For a while, though, it was fun to go wandering around New Orleans and pick up good things cheap."

"I'd say they'd all been combed over down there," Bob objected.

"It's true about the best things," Nelle said. "I could hardly afford those anyway. But sometimes you see some pieces with really good design and you can see you might realize something on them. Real appreciation goes a long way."

"Bob has a jobber up in St. Louis," Shirley said. "We had enough of all this going around shaking the bushes. A few lucky finds was what got us started."

Nelle said, "I started thinking about it because I walked in the living room a few years back and there were some ladies I never saw before. They'd found the door open and walked in. They wanted to know the price of Mama's furniture. I said it wasn't for sale, but Mama was just coming in from the kitchen and heard them. You wouldn't believe how mad she got. 'I'm going straight and get out my pistol,' she said."

"You ought to just see her mama," said Hope. "This tiny little old lady."

"So what happened?" Shirley asked when she got through laughing.

"Nothing real bad," said Nelle. "They just got out the door as quick as they could."

"Yo' mama got a *pistol?*" Charlie asked, after a silence. We started to laugh again, the implication being plain that a Charlie Waybridge *needs* to know if a woman's mother has a pistol in the house.

"She does have one," said Nelle.

"So watch out, Charlie," said Pete.

Bob remarked, "Y'all certainly don't change much over here."

"Crazy as ever," Hope said proudly. It crossed my mind that Hope was always promoting herself, one way or the other.

Shirley said she thought it was just grand to be back, she wouldn't take anything for it, and after that Grey and Carole arrived. We had another drink and then went in to dinner. Everybody acted like every-thing was okay. After dinner, I went back in the kitchen for some water, and there was Charlie, kissing Shirley. She was so strained up on tiptoe, Charlie being over six feet, that I thought, in addition to being embarrassed, mad, and backing out before they saw me, What they need is a stepladder to do it right.

On the way home, I told Charlie about catching them. "I didn't know she was within a country mile," he said, ready with excuses. "She just plain grabbed me."

"I've been disgusted once too often," I said. "Tell it to Bob."

"If she wanted to do it right," he said, "she ought to get a steplad-der." So then I had to laugh. Even if our marriage wasn't ideal, we still had the same thoughts.

It sometimes seemed to me, in considering the crowd we were al-ways part of, from even before we went to school, straight on through, that we were all like one person, walking around different ways, but in some permanent way breathing together, feeling the same reactions, thinking each other's thoughts. What do you call that if not love? If asked, we'd all cry Yes! with one voice but then it's not our habit to ask anything serious. We're close to religious about keeping everything light and gay. Nelle Townshend knew that, all the above, but she was drawing back. A betrayer was what she was turning into. We felt weakened because of her. What did she think she was doing?

I had to drive Mr. McGinnis way back in the woods one day to serve a subpoena on a witness. He hadn't liked to drive since his heart attack, and his usual colored man was busy with Mrs. McGinnis' garden. In the course of that little trip, coming back into town, I saw Nelle Townshend's station wagon turn off onto a side road. I couldn't see who was with her, but somebody was, definitely.

I must add that this was spring and there were drifts of dogwood all mingled in the woods at different levels. Through those same woods, along the winding roads, the redbud, simultaneous, was spreading its wonderful pink haze. Mr. McGinnis sat beside me without saying much, his old knobby hands folded over a briefcase he held upright on his lap. "A trip like this just makes me think, Eileen, that everybody owes it to himself to get out in the woods this time of year. It's just

God's own garden," he said. About a mile back we had just crossed a wooden bridge over a pretty creek. That same creek, shallower, was crossed by a ford along the road that Nelle's car had taken. I know that little road, too, maybe the prettiest one of all.

Serpents have a taste for Eden, and in a small town, if they are busy elsewhere, lots of people are glad to fill in for them. It still upsets me to think of all the gossip that went on that year, and at the same time I have to blame Nelle Townshend for it, not so much for starting it, but for being so unconscious about it. She had stepped out of line and she didn't even bother to notice.

Once the business got going, the next thing she did was enroll in a class—a "seminar," she said—over at the university at Hattiesburg. It was something to do with art theory, she said, and she was thinking of going on from there to a degree, eventually, and get hold of a subject she could teach at the junior college right up the road. So settling in to be an old maid.

I said this last rather gloomily to Pete's wife, Hope, and Pete overheard and said, "There's all kinds of those." "You stop that," said Hope. "What's supposed to be going on?" I asked. (Some say, Don't ask, it's better not to, but I think you have to know if only to keep on guard.)

"Just that they're saying things about Nelle and that black Robin works for her."

"Well, they're in the same business," I said.

"Whatever it is people don't like it. They say she goes out to his house after dark. That they spend too much time over the books."

"Somebody ought to warn her," I said. "If Robin gets into trouble she won't find anybody to do that kind of work. He's the only one."

"Nelle's gotten too independent is the thing," said Pete. "She thinks she can live her own life."

"Maybe she can," said Hope.

Charlie was away that week. He had gone over to the Delta on business and Hope and Pete had dropped in to keep me company. Hope is ten years younger than Pete. (Pete used to date her sister, Mary Ruth, one of these beauty queen types, who had gone up to the Miss America pageant to represent Mississippi and come back first

runner-up. For the talent contest part of it, she had recited passages
from the Bible and Pete always said her trouble was she was too
religious but he hoped to get her over it. She used to try in a nice way
to get him into church work, and that embarrassed him. It's our common habit, as Mary Ruth well knew, to go to morning service, but
anything outside that is out. Anyway, around Mary Ruth's he used to
keep seeing the little sister Hope, and he'd say, "Mary Ruth, you
better start on that girl about church, she's growing up dynamite."
Mary Ruth got involved in a promotion trip, something about getting
right with America, and met a man on a plane trip to Dallas, and
before the seat belt sign went off they were in love. For Mary Ruth
that meant marriage. She was strict, a woman of faith, and I don't
think Pete would have been happy with her. But he had got the habit
of the house by then, and Mary Ruth's parents had got fond of him
and didn't want him drinking too much: they made him welcome. So
one day Hope turned seventeen and came out in a new flouncy dress
with heels on, and Pete saw the light.)

We had a saying by now that Pete had always been younger than
Hope, that she was older than any of us. Only twenty, she worked at
making their house look good and won gardening parties. She gave
grand parties, with attention to details.

"I stuck my neck out," I told Hope, "to keep Nelle dating Grey.
You remember her mama took a set at me like I never dreamed possible. Nelle's been doing us all funny, but she may have to come back
some day. We can't stop caring for her."

Hope thought it over. "Robin knows what it's like here, even if
Nelle may have temporarily forgotten. He's not going to tempt fate.
Anyway, somebody already spoke to Nelle."

"Who?"

"Grey, of course. He'll use any excuse to speak to her. She got mad
as a firecracker. She said, 'Don't you know this is nineteen seventy-*six!*
I've got a business to run. I've got a living to make!' But she quit going
out to his house at night. And Robin quit so much as answering the
phone, up at her office."

"You mean he's keeping one of those low profiles?" said Pete.

Soon after, I ran into Robin uptown in the grocery, and he said,

"How do you do, Mrs. Waybridge," like a schoolteacher or a foreigner, and I figured just from that, that he was on to everything and taking no chances. Nelle must have told him. I personally knew what not many people did, that he was a real partner with Nelle, not just her hired help. They had got Mr. McGinnis to draw up the papers. And they had plans for moving the plant uptown, to an empty store building, with some investment in more equipment. So maybe they'd get by till then. I felt a mellowness in my heart about Nelle's effort and all—a Townshend (LeMoyne on her mother's side) opening a dry cleaning business. I thought of Robin's effort, too—he had a sincere, intelligent look, reserved. What I hoped for them was something like a prayer.

Busying my thoughts about all this, I had been forgetting Charlie. That will never do.

For one thing, leaving aside women, Charlie's present way of life was very nearly wild. He'd got into oil leases two years before, and when something was going on, he'd drive like a demon over to East Texas by way of Shreveport and back through Pike and Amite counties. At one time he had to sit over Mr. McGinnis for a month getting him to study up on laws governing oil rights. In the end, Charlie got to know as much or more than Mr. McGinnis. He's in and out. The in-between times are when he gets restless. Drinks too much and starts simmering up about some new woman. One thing (except for me), with Charlie it's always a new woman. Once tried, soon dropped. Or so I like to believe. Then, truth to tell, there is really part of me that not only wants to believe but at unstated times does believe that I've been the only one for Charlie Waybridge. Not that I'd begrudge him a few times of having it off down in the hollow back of the gym with some girl who came in from the country, nor would I think anything about flings in New Orleans while he was in Tulane. But as for the outlandish reputation he's acquired now, sometimes I just want to say out loud to all and sundry, "There's not a word of truth in it. He's a big, attractive, friendly guy, okay. But he's not the town stud. He belongs to *me*."

All this before the evening along about first dark when Charlie was seen on the Townshend property by Nelle's mother, who went and got the pistol and shot at him.

"Christ, she could have killed me," Charlie said. He was too surprised about it even to shake. He was just dazed. Fixed a stiff drink and didn't want any supper. "She's gone off her rocker," he said. "That's all I could think."

I knew I had to ask it, sooner or later. "What were you doing up there, Charlie?"

"Nothing," he said. "I'd left the car at Wharton's garage to check why I'm burning too much oil. He's getting to it in the morning. It was a nice evening and I cut through the back alley and that led to a stroll through the Townshend pasture. That's all. I saw the little lady out on the back porch. I was too far off to holler at her. She scuttled off into the house and I was going past, when here she came out again with something black weighting her hand. You know what I thought? I thought she had a kitten by the neck. Next thing I knew there was a bullet smashing through the leaves not that far off." He put his hand out.

"Wonder if Nelle was home."

I was nervous as a monkey after I heard this, and nothing would do me but to call up Nelle.

She answered right away. "Nelle," I said, "is your little mama going in for target practice these days?"

She started laughing. "Did you hear that all the way to your place? She's mad 'cause the Johnsons' old cow keeps breaking down our fence. She took a shot in the air because she's tired complaining."

"Since when was Charlie Waybridge a cow?" I asked.

"Mercy, Eileen. You don't mean Charlie was back there?"

"You better load that thing with blanks," I said, "or hide it."

"Blanks is all it's got in it," said Nelle. "Mama doesn't tell that because she feels more protected not to."

"You certainly better check it out," I said. "Charlie says it was a bullet."

There was a pause. "You're not mad or anything, are you, Eileen?"

"Oh, no," I warbled. "We've been friends too long for that."

"Come over and see us," said Nelle. "Real soon."

I don't know who told it, but knowing this town like the back of my hand, I know *how* they told it. Charlie Waybridge was up at Nelle Townshend's and old Mrs. Townshend shot at him. Enough said. At the Garden Club Auxiliary tea, I came in and heard them giggling, and how they got quiet when I passed a plate of sandwiches. I went straight to the subject, which is the way I do. "Y'all off on Mrs. Townshend?" I asked. There was a silence, and then some little cross-eyed bride, new in town, piped up that there was just always something funny going on here, and Maud Varner, an old friend, said she thought Nelle ought to watch out for Mrs. Townshend, she was showing her age. "It's not such a funny goings-on when it almost kills somebody," I said. "Charlie came straight home and told me. He was glad to be alive, but I went and called Nelle. So she does know." There was another silence during which I could tell what everybody thought. The thing is not to get too distant or above it all. If you do, your friends will pull back, too, and you won't know anything. Gradually, you'll just turn into, "Poor Eileen, what does she think of all Charlie's carryings-on?"

Next, the injunction. Who brought it and why? I got the answer to the first before I guessed the second.

It was against the Townshend Cleaners because the chemicals used were a hazard to health and the smell they exuded a public nuisance. But the real reason wasn't this at all.

In order to speed up the deliveries, Nelle had taken to driving the station wagon herself, so that Robin could run in with the cleaning. Some people had begun to remark on this. Would it have been different if Nelle was married or had a brother, a father, a steady boy friend? I don't know. I used to hold my breath when they went by in the late afternoon together. Because sometimes when the back of the station wagon was full, Robin would be up on the front seat with her, and she with her head stuck in the air, driving carefully, her mind on nothing at all to do with other people. Once the cleaning load got lighter, Robin would usually sit on the backseat, as expected to do. But sometimes, busy talking to her, he wouldn't. He'd be up beside her, discussing business.

Then, suddenly, the business closed.

Nelle was beside herself. She came running to Mr. McGinnis. Her hair was every which way around her head and she was wearing an old checked shirt and no makeup.

She could hardly make herself sit still and visit with me while Mr. McGinnis got through with a client. "Now, Miss Nellie," he said, steering her through the door.

"Just when we were making a go of it!" I heard her say; then he closed the door.

I heard by way of the grapevine that very night that the person who had done it was John Houston, Grey's brother, whose wife's family lived on a property just below the Townshends. They claimed they couldn't sleep for the dry cleaning fumes and were getting violent attacks of nausea.

"Aren't they supposed to give warnings?" I asked.

We were all at John and Rose Houston's home, a real gathering of the bunch, only Nelle being absent, though she was the most present one of all. There was a silence after every statement, in itself unusual. Finally John Houston said, "Not in cases of extreme health hazard."

"That's a lot of you-know-what," I said. "Rose, your family's not dying."

Rose said: "They never claimed to be dying."

And Pete said: "Eileen, can't you sit right quiet and try to use your head?"

"In preference to running off at the mouth," said Charlie, which made me mad. I was refusing, I well knew, to see the point they all had in mind. But it seemed to me that was my privilege.

The thing to know about our crowd is that we never did go in for talking about the "Negro question." We talked about Negroes the way we always had, like people, one at the time. They were all around us, had always been, living around us, waiting on us, sharing our lives, brought up with us, nursing us, cooking for us, mourning and rejoicing with us, making us laugh, stealing from us, digging our graves. But when all the troubles started coming in on us after the Freedom Riders and the Ole Miss riots, we decided not to talk about it. I don't know but what we weren't afraid of getting nervous. We couldn't jump out of our own skins, nor those of our parents, grandparents, and those before them. "Nothing you can do about it," was Charlie's view. "Whatever you decide, you're going to act the same way tomorrow as you did today. Hoping you can get Alma to cook for you, and Peabody to clean the windows, and Bayman to cut the grass." "I'm not keeping anybody from voting—yellow, blue, or pink," said Hope, who had got her "ideas" straight from the first, she said. "I don't guess any of us is," said Pete, "them days is gone forever." "But wouldn't it just be wonderful," said Rose Houston, "to have a little colored gal to pick up your handkerchief and sew on your buttons and bring you cold lemonade and fan you when you're hot, and just love you to death?"

Rose was joking, of course, the way we all liked to do. But there are always one or two of them that we seriously insist we know—really *know*—that they love us. Would do anything for us, as we would for them. Otherwise, without that feeling, I guess we couldn't rest easy. You never can really know what they think, what they feel, so there's always the one chance it might be love.

So we—the we I'm always speaking of—decided not to talk about race relations because it spoiled things too much. We didn't like to consider any one of us really involved in any part of it. Then, in my mind's eye, I saw Nelle's car, that dogwood-laden day in the woods, headed off the road with somebody inside. Or such was my impression. I'd never mentioned it to anybody, and Mr. McGinnis hadn't, I think, seen. Was it Robin? Or maybe, I suddenly asked myself, Charlie? Mysteries multiplied.

"Nelle's got to make a living is the whole thing," said Pete, getting practical. "We can't not let her do that."

"Why doesn't somebody find her a job she'd like?" asked Grey.

"Why the hell," Charlie burst out, "don't you marry her, Grey? Women ought to get married," he announced in general. "You see what happens when they don't."

"Hell, I can't get near her," said Grey. "We dated for six months. I guess I wasn't the one," he added.

"She ought to relocate the plant uptown, then she could run the office in her house, one remove from it, acting like a lady."

"What about Robin?" said Hope.

"He could run back and forth," I said. "They do want to do that," I added, "but can't afford it yet."

"You'd think old Mrs. Townshend would have stopped it all."

"That lady's a mystery."

"If Nelle just had a brother."

"Or even an uncle."

Then the talk dwindled down to silence.

"John," said Pete, after a time, turning around to face him, "we all know it was you—not Rose's folks. Did you have to?"

John Houston was sitting quietly in his chair. He was a little older than the rest of us, turning gray, a little more settled and methodical, more like our uncle than an equal and friend. (Or was it just that he and Rose were the only ones so far to have children—what all our parents said we all ought to do, but couldn't quit having our good times.) He was sipping bourbon. He nodded slowly. "I had to." We didn't ask anymore.

"Let's just go quiet," John finally added. "Wait and see."

Now, all my life I'd been hearing first one person then another (and these, it would seem, appointed by silent consensus) say that things were to be taken care of in a certain way and no other. The person in this case who had this kind of appointment was evidently John Houston, from in our midst. But when did he get it? How did he get it? Where did it come from? There seemed to be no need to discuss it.

Rose Houston, who wore her long light hair in a sort of loose bun at the back and who sat straight up in her chair, adjusted a fallen strand, and Grey went off to fix another drink for himself and Pete and Hope. He sang on the way out, more or less to himself, "For the times they are a-changing . . ." and that, too, found reference in all our minds. Except I couldn't help but wonder whether anything had changed at all.

The hearing on the dry cleaning injunction was due to be held in two weeks. Nelle went off to the coast. She couldn't stand the tension, she told me, having come over to Mr. McGinnis' office to see him alone. "Thinking how we've worked and all," she said, "and how just before this came up the auditor was in and told us what good shape we were in. We were just about to buy a new condenser."

"What's that?" I asked.

"Makes use of the fumes," she said. "The very thing they're mad about. I could kill John Houston. Why couldn't he have come to me?"

I decided to be forthright. "Nelle, there's something you ought to evaluate . . . consider, I mean. Whatever word you want." I was shaking, surprising myself.

Nobody was around. Mr. McGinnis was in the next county.

Once when I was visiting a school friend up north, out from Philadelphia, a man at a party asked me if I would have sexual relations with a black. He wasn't black himself, so why was he curious? I said I'd never even thought about it. "It's a taboo, I think you call it," I said. "Girls like me get brainwashed early on. It's not that I'm against them," I added, feeling awkward. "Contrary to what you may think or may even believe," he told me, "you've probably thought a lot about it. You've suppressed your impulses, that's all." "Nobody can prove that," I said, "not even you," I added, thinking I was being amusing. But he only looked superior and walked away.

"It's you and Robin," I said. I could hear myself explaining to Charlie, somebody had to, sooner or later. "You won't find anybody really believing anything, I don't guess, but it's making people speculate."

Nelle Townshend never reacted the way you'd think she would. She didn't even get annoyed, much less hit the ceiling. She just gave a little sigh. "You start a business, you'll see. I've got no time for anything but worrying about customers and money."

I was wondering whether to tell her the latest. A woman named McCorkle from out in the country, who resembled Nelle so much from the back you'd think they were the same, got pushed off the sidewalk last Saturday and fell in the concrete gutter up near the drugstore. The person who did it, somebody from outside town, must have said something nobody heard but Mrs. McCorkle, because she jumped up with her skirt muddy and stockings torn and yelled out, "I ain't no nigger lover!"

But I didn't tell her. If she was anybody but a Townshend, I might have. Odd to think that, when the only Townshends left there were Nelle and her mother. In cases such as this, the absent are present and the dead are, too. Mr. Townshend had died so long ago you had to ask your parents what he was like. The answer was always the same, "Sid Townshend was a mighty good man." Nelle had had two sisters: one died in her twenties, the victim of a rare disease, and the other got married, and went to live on a place out from Helena, Arkansas. She had about six children and could be of no real help to the home branch.

"Come over to dinner," I coaxed. "You want me to ask Grey, I will. If you don't, I won't."

"Grey," she said, just blank, like that. He might have been somebody she met once a long time back. "She's a perpetual virgin," I heard Charlie say once. "Just because she won't cotton up to you," I said. But maybe he was right. Nelle and her mother lived up near the Episcopal Church. Since our little town could not support a full-time rector, it was they who kept the church linens and the chalice and saw that the robes were always cleaned and hung in their proper place in the little room off the chancel. Come to think of it, keeping those robes and surplices in order may have been one thing that started Nelle into dry cleaning.

Nelle got up suddenly, her face catching the light from our old window with the wobbly glass in the panes, and I thought, She's a grand-looking woman, sort of girlish and womanish both.

"I'm going to the coast," she said. "I'm taking some books and a sketch pad. I may look into some art courses. You have to have training to teach anything, that's the trouble."

"Look, Nelle, if it's money—Well, you do have friends, you know."

"Friends," she said, just the way she had said "Grey." I wondered just what Nelle was really like. None of us seemed to know.

"Have a good time," I said. After she left, I thought I heard the echo of that blank soft voice saying "Good time."

It was a week after Nelle had gone that old Mrs. Townshend rang up Mr. McGinnis at the office. Mr. McGinnis came out to tell me what it was all about.

"Mrs. Townshend says that last night somebody tore down the dry cleaning sign Nelle had put up out at the side. Some colored woman is staying with her at night, but neither one of them saw anybody. Now she can't find Robin to put it back. She's called his house but he's not there."

"Do they say he'll be back soon?"

"They say he's out of town."

"I'd get Charlie to go up and fix it, but you know what happened."

"I heard about it. Maybe in daylight the old lady won't shoot. I'll go around with our yardman after dinner." What we still mean by dinner is lunch. So they put the sign up and I sat in the empty office wondering about this and that, but mainly, Where was Robin Byers?

It's time to say that Robin Byers was not any Harry Belafonte calypso-singing sex-symbol of a "black." He was strong and thoughtful looking, not very tall, definitely chocolate, but not ebony. He wore his hair cropped short in an almost military fashion so that being thick it stuck straight up more often than not. From one side he could look positively frightening as he had a long white scar running down the side of his cheek. It was said that he got it in the army, in Vietnam, but the story of just how was not known. So maybe he had not gotten it in the war, but somewhere else. His folks had been in the county forever, his own house being not far out from town. He had a wife, two teenaged children, a telephone, and a TV set. The other side of Robin Byers' face was regular, smooth, and while not especially handsome it was good-humoured and likeable. All in all, he looked intelligent and conscientious, and that must have been how Nelle Townshend saw him, as he was.

I went to the hearing. I'd have had to, to keep Mr. McGinnis' notes straight, but I would have anyway, as all our crowd showed up, except Rose and John Houston. Rose's parents were there, having brought the complaint, and Rose's mama's doctor from over at Hattiesburg, to swear she'd had no end of allergies and migraines, and attacks of nausea, all brought on by the cleaning fumes. Sitting way in the back was Robin Byers, in a suit (a really nice suit) with a blue and white striped "city" shirt and a knit tie. He looked like an assistant university dean, except for the white scar. He also had the look of a specta-tor, very calm, I thought, not wanting to keep turning around and staring at him, but keeping the image in my mind like an all-day sucker, letting it slowly melt out its meaning. He was holding a certain surface. But he was scared. Half across the courtroom you could see his temple throbbing, and the sweat beads. He was that tense. The whole effect was amazing.

The complaint was read out and Mrs. Hammond, Rose's mother, testified and the doctor testified, and Mr. Hammond said they were both right. The way the Hammonds talk—big Presbyterians—you would think they had the Bible on their side, every minute, so natu-rally everybody else had to be mistaken. Friends and neighbors of the Townshends all these years, they now seemed to be speaking of people they knew only slightly. That is until Mrs. Hammond, a sort of dumplinglike woman with a practiced way of sounding accurate about whatever she said (she was a good gossip because she got all the details of everything), suddenly came down to a personal level and said, "Nelle, I just don't see why if you want to run that thing you don't move it into town," and Nelle said back right away just like they were in a living room instead of up at the courthouse, "Well, that's because of Mama, Miss Addie. This way I'm in and out with her." At that, everybody laughed, couldn't help it.

Then Mr. McGinnis got up and challenged that very much about Mrs. Hammond's headaches and allergies (he established her age, 52, which she didn't want to tell) had to do with the cleaning plant. If they had, somebody else would have such complaints, but in case we needed to go further into it, he would ask Miss Nelle to explain what he meant.

Nelle got up front and went about as far as she could concerning the type of equipment she used and how it was guaranteed against the very thing now being complained of, that it let very few vapors escape, but then she said she would rather call on Robin Byers to come and explain because he had had special training in the chemical processes and knew all their possible negative effects.

And he came. He walked down the aisle and sat in the chair and nobody had ever seen such composure. I think he was petrified, but so might an actor be who was doing a role to high perfection. And when he started to talk you'd think that dry cleaning was a text and that his God-appointed task was to preach a sermon on it. But it wasn't quite like that either. More modern. A professor giving a lecture to extremely ignorant students, with a good professor's accuracy, to the last degree. In the first place, he said, the cleaning fluid used was not varsol or carbon tetrachloride, which were known not only to give off harmful fumes but to damage fabrics, but something called "perluxe" or perchlorethylene (he paused to give the chemical composition), which was approved for commercial cleaning purposes in such and such a solution by federal and state bylaws, of certain numbers and codes, which Mr. McGinnis had listed in his records and would be glad to read aloud upon request. If an operator worked closely with "perluxe" for a certain number of hours a day, he might have headaches, it was true, but escaping vapor could scarcely be smelled at all more than a few feet from the exhaust pipes, and caused no harmful effects whatsoever, even to shrubs or "the leaves upon the trees." He said this last in such a lofty, rhythmic way that somebody giggled (I think it was Hope), and he stopped talking altogether.

"There might be smells down in those hollows back there," Nelle filled in from where she was sitting, "but it's not from my one little exhaust pipe."

"Then why," asked Mrs. Hammond right out, "do you keep on saying you need new equipment so you won't have any exhaust? Just answer me that."

"I'll let Robin explain," said Nelle.

"The fact is that 'perluxe' is an expensive product," Robin said. "At four dollars and twenty-five cents a gallon, using nearly thirty gallons each time the accumulation of the garments is put through the process, she can count on it that the overheads with two cleanings a week will run in the neighborhood of between two and three hundred dollars. So having the condenser machine would mean that the exhaust runs into it, and so converts the vapors back to the liquid, in order to use it once again."

"It's not for the neighbors," Nelle put in. "It's for me."

Everybody had spoken out of order by then, but what with the atmosphere having either declined or improved (depending on how you looked at it) to one of friendly inquiry among neighbors rather than a squabble in a court of law, the silence that finally descended was more meditative than not, having as its most impressive features, like high points in a landscape, Nelle, at some little distance down a front bench, but turned around so as to take everything in, her back straight and her Townshend head both superior and interested; and Robin Byers, who still had the chair by Judge Purvis' desk, collected and severe (he had forgotten the giggle), with testimony faultlessly delivered and nothing more he needed to say. (Would things have been any different if Charlie had been there? He was out of town.)

The judge cleared his throat and said he guessed the smells in the gullies around Tyler might be a nuisance, sure enough, but couldn't be said to be caused by dry cleaning, and he thought Miss Nelle could go on with her business. For a while, the white face and the black one seemed just the same, to be rising up quiet and superior above us all.

The judge asked, just out of curiosity, when Nelle planned to buy the condenser that was mentioned. She said whenever she could find one secondhand in good condition, they cost nearly two thousand dollars new, and Robin Byers put in that he had just been looking into one down in Biloxi, so it might not be too long. Biloxi is on the coast.

Judge Purvis said we'd adjourn now, and everybody stood up of one accord, except Mr. McGinnis, who had dozed off and was almost snoring.

Nelle, who was feeling friendly to the world, or seeming to (we all had clothes that got dirty, after all), said to all and sundry not to worry, "we plan to move the plant uptown one of these days before too long," and it was the "we" that came through again, a slip: she usually referred to the business as hers. It was just a reminder of what everybody wanted not to have to think about, and she probably hadn't intended to speak of it that way.

As if to smooth it well into the past, Judge Purvis remarked that these little towns ought to have zoning laws, but I sat there thinking there wouldn't be much support for that, not with the Gulf Oil station and garage right up on South Street between the Whitmans' and the Binghams', and the small appliance shop on the vacant lot where the old Marshall mansion had stood and the Tackett house, still elegant as you please, doing steady business as a funeral home. You can separate black from white but not business from nonbusiness. Not in our town.

Nelle came down and shook hands with Mr. McGinnis. "I don't know when I can afford to pay you." "Court costs go to them," he said. "Don't worry about the rest."

Back at the office, Mr. McGinnis closed the street door and said to me, "The fumes in this case have got nothing to do with dry cleaning. Has anybody talked to Miss Nelle?"

"They have," I said, "but she doesn't seem to pay any attention."

He said I could go home for the day and much obliged for my help at the courthouse. I powdered my nose and went out into the street. It wasn't but eleven-thirty.

Everything was still, and nobody around. The blue jays were having a good time on the courthouse yard, squalling and swooping from the lowest oak limbs, close to the ground, then mounting back up. There were some sparrows out near the old horse trough, which still ran water. They were splashing around. But except for somebody driving up for the mail at the post office, then driving off, there wasn't a soul around. I started walking, and just automatically I went by for the mail because as a rule Charlie didn't stop in for it till noon, even when in town. On the way I was mulling over the hearing and how Mrs. Hammond had said at the door of the courtroom to Nelle, "Aw right, Miss Nellie, you just wait." It wasn't said in any unpleasant way; in fact, it sounded right friendly. Except that she wasn't looking at Nelle, but past her, and except that being older, it wasn't the ordinary thing to call her "Miss," and except that Nelle is a pretty name but Nellie isn't. But Nelle in reply had suddenly laughed in that unexpected but delightful way she has, because something has struck her as really funny. "What am I supposed to wait *for*, Miss Addie?" Whatever else, Nelle wasn't scared. I looked for Robin Byers, but he had got sensible and gone off in that odd little blue German car he drives. I saw Nelle drive home alone.

Then, because the lay of my home direction was a short cut from the post office, and because the spring had been dry and the back lanes nice to walk in, I went through the same way Charlie had that time

Mrs. Townshend had about killed him, and enjoyed the way I had from childhood on, the soft fragrances of springtime, the brown wisps of spent jonquils withered on their stalks, the forsythia turned from yellow to green fronds, but the spirea still white as a bride's veil worked in blossoms, and the climbing roses mainly wild, just opening a delicate, simple pink bloom all along the back fence. I was crossing down that way when what I saw was a blue car.

It was stopped way back down the Townshend property on a little connecting road that made an entrance through to a lower town road, one that nobody used anymore. I stopped in the clump of bowdarc trees on the next property from the Townshends'. Then I saw Nelle, running down the hill. She still had that same laugh, honest and joyous, that she had shown the first of to Mrs. Hammond. And there coming to meet her was Robin, his teeth white as his scar. They grabbed each others' hands, black on white and white on black. They started whirling each other round, like two school children in a game, and I saw Nelle's mouth forming the words I could scarcely hear: "We won! We won!" And his, the same, a baritone underneath. It was pure joy. Washing the color out, saying that the dye didn't, this time, hold, they could have been brother and sister, happy at some good family news, or old lovers (Charlie and I sometimes meet like that, too happy at some piece of luck to really stop to talk about it, just dancing out our joy). But, my God, I thought, don't they know they're black and white and this is Tyler, Mississippi? Well, of course, they do, I thought next—that's more than half the joy—getting away with it! Dare and double-dare! Dumbfounded, I just stood, hidden, never seen by them at all, and let the image of black on white and white on black—those pale aristocratic Townshend hands and his strong square-cut black ones—linked perpetually now in my mind's eye—soak in.

It's going to stay with me forever, I thought, but what does it mean? I never told. I didn't think they were lovers. But they were into a triumph of the sort that lovers feel. They had acted as they pleased. They were above everything. They lived in another world because of a dry cleaning business. They had proved it when they had to. They knew it.

But nobody could be counted on to see it the way I did. It was too complicated for any two people to know about it.

Soon after this we got a call from Hope, Pete's wife. "I've got tired of all this foolishness," she said. "How did we ever get hung up on dry cleaning, of all things? Can you feature it? I'm going to give a party. Mary Foote Williams is coming home to see her folks and bringing Keith, so that's good enough for me. And don't kid yourself. I'm personally going to get Nelle Townshend to come, and Grey Houston is going to bring her. I'm getting good and ready for everybody to start acting normal again. I don't know what's been the matter with everybody, and furthermore I don't want to know."

Well, this is a kettle of fish, I thought, Hope the youngest taking us over. Of course, she did have the perspective to see everything whole.

I no sooner put down the phone than Pete called up from his office. "Jezzie's on the war path," he said. (He calls her Jezzie because she used to tell all kind of lies to some little high school boy she had crazy about her—her own age—just so she could go out with Pete and the older crowd. It was easy to see through that. She thought she might just be getting a short run with us and would have to fall back on her own bunch when we shoved her out, so she was keeping a foothold. Pete caught her at it, but all it did was make him like her better. Hope was pert. She had a sharp little chin she liked to stick up in the air, and a turned-up nose. "Both signs of meanness," said Mr. Owens, Pete's father, "especially the nose," and buried his own in the newspaper.)

"Well," I said doubtfully, "if you think it's a good idea—"

"No stopping her," said Pete, with the voice of a spectator at the game. "If anybody can swing it, she can."

So we finally said yes.

The morning of Hope's party there was some ugly weather, one nasty little black cloud after another and a lot of restless crosswinds. There was a tornado watch out for our county and two others, making you know it was a widespread weather system. I had promised to bring a platter of shrimp for the buffet table, and that meant a whole morning shucking them after driving out to pick up the order at the

Fish Shack. At times the lightning was popping so close I had to get out of the kitchen. I would go sit in the living room with the thunder blamming so hard I couldn't even read the paper. Looking out at my backyard through the picture window, the colors of the marigolds and pansies seemed to be electric bright, blazing, then shuddering in the wind.

I was bound to connect all this with the anxiety that had got into things about that party. Charlie's being over in Louisiana didn't help. Maybe all was calm and bright over there, but I doubted it.

However, along about two the sky did clear, and the sun came out. When I drove out to Hope and Pete's place with the shrimp—it's a little way north of town, reached by its own side road, on a hill— everything was wonderful. There was a warm buoyancy in the air that made you feel young and remember what it was like to skip home from school.

"It's cleared off," said Hope, as though in personal triumph over Nature.

Pete was behind her at the door, enveloped in a huge apron. "I feel like playing softball," he said.

"Me, too," I agreed. "If I could just hear from Charlie."

"Oh, he'll be back," said Pete. "Charlie miss a party? Never!"

Well, it was quite an affair. The effort was to get us all launched in a new and happy period and the method was the tried and true one of drinking and feasting, dancing, pranking, laughing, flirting, and having fun. I had a new knife-pleated silk skirt, ankle length, dark blue shot with green and cyclamen and a new off-the-shoulder blouse, and Mary Foote Williams, the visitor, wore a slit skirt, but Hope took the cake in her hoopskirts from her senior high school days, and her hair in a coarse gold net.

"The shrimp are gorgeous," she said. "Come look. I called Mama and requested prayer for good weather. It never fails."

"Charlie called," I said. "He said he'd be maybe thirty minutes late and would come on his own."

A car pulled up in the drive and there was Grey circling round and holding the door for Nelle herself. She had on a simple silk dress with her fine hair brushed loose and a pair of sexy new high-heeled sandals. It looked natural to see them together and I breathed easier without knowing I hadn't been doing it for quite a while. Hope was right, we'd had enough of all this foolishness.

"That just leaves John and Rose," said Hope, "and I have my own ideas about them."

"What?" I asked.

"Well, I shouldn't say. It's y'all's crowd." She was quick in her kitchen, clicking around with her skirts swaying. She had got a nice little colored girl, Perline, dressed up in black with a white ruffled apron. "I just think John's halfway to a stuffed shirt and Rose is going to get him all the way there."

So our crowd or not, she was going right ahead.

"I think this has to do with you-know-what," I said.

"We aren't going to mention you-know-what," said Hope. "From now on, honey, my only four-letter words are 'dry' and 'cleaning.' "

John and Rose didn't show up, but two new couples did, a pair from Hattiesburg and the Kellmans, new in town, but promising. Hope had let them in. Pete exercised himself at the bar and there was a strong punch as well. We strolled out to the pool and sat on white-painted iron chairs with cushions in green flowered plastic. Nelle sat with her pretty legs crossed, talking to Mary Foote. Grey was at her elbow. The little maid passed out canapés and shrimp. Light was still lingering in a clear sky barely pink at the edges. Pete skimmed leaves from the pool surface with a long-handled net. Lightning bugs winked and drifted, and the new little wife from Hattiesburg caught one or two in her palm and watched them crawl away, then take wing. "I used to do that," said Nelle. Then she shivered and Grey went for a shawl. It grew suddenly darker and one or two pale stars could be seen, then dozens. Pete, vanished inside, had started some records. Some people began to trail back in. And with another drink (the third, maybe?) it wasn't clear how much time had passed, when there came the harsh roar of a motor from the private road, growing stronger the nearer it got, a slashing of gravel in the drive out front, and a door slamming. And the first thing you knew there was Charlie Waybridge, filling the whole door frame before Pete or Hope could even go to open it. He put his arms out to everybody. "Well, whaddaya know!" he said.

His tie was loose two buttons down and his light seersucker dress coat was crumpled and open but at least he had it on. I went right to him. He'd been drinking, of course, I'd known it from the first sound of the car—but who wasn't drinking? "Hi ya, Baby!" he said, and grabbed me.

Then Pete and Hope were getting their greetings and were leading him up to meet the new people, till he got to the bar where he dropped off to help himself.

It was that minute that Perline, the little maid, came in with a plate in her hand. Charlie swaggered up to her and said, "Well, if it ain't Mayola's daughter." He caught her chin in his hand. "Ain't that so?" "Yes, sir," said Perline, "I am." "Used to know yo' mama," said Charlie. Perline looked confused for a minute, then she lowered her eyes and giggled like she knew she was supposed to. "Gosh sake, Charlie," I said, "quit horsing around and let's dance." It was hard to get him out of these moods. But I'd managed it more than once, dancing.

Charlie was a good strong leader and the way he danced, one hand firm to my waist, he would take my free hand in his and knuckle it tight against his chest. I could follow him better than I could anybody. Sometimes everybody would stop just to watch us, but the prize that night was going to Pete and Hope, they were shining around with some new steps that made the hoop skirts jounce. Charlie was half-drunk, too, and bad on the turns.

"Try to remember what's important about this evening," I said. "You know what Hope and Pete are trying for, don't you?"

"I know I'm always coming home to a lecture," said Charlie and swung me out, spinning. "What a woman for sounding like a wife." He got me back and I couldn't tell if he was mad or not, I guess it was half and half; but right then he almost knocked over one of Hope's floral arrangements, so I said, "Why don't you go upstairs and catch your forty winks, then you can come down fresh and start over?" The music stopped. He blinked, looked tired all of a sudden, and, for a miracle, like a dog that never once chose to hear you, he minded.

I breathed a sigh when I saw him going up the stairs. But now I know I never once mentioned Nelle to him or reminded him right out, him with his head full of oil leases, bourbon, and the road, that she was the real cause of the party. Nelle was somewhere else, off in the back sitting room on a couch, to be exact, swapping family news with Mary Foote, who was her cousin.

Dancing with Charlie like that had put me in a romantic mood, and I fell to remembering the time we had first got really serious, down on the coast where one summer we had all rented a fishing schooner. We had come into port at Mobile for more provisions and I had showered and dressed and was standing on deck in some leather sandals that tied around the ankle, a fresh white tee shirt and some clean navy shorts. I had washed my hair, which was short then, and clustered in dark damp curls at the forehead. I say this about myself because when Charlie was coming on board with a six-pack in either hand, he stopped dead still. It was like it was the first time he'd ever seen me. He actually said that very thing later on after we'd finished with the boat and stayed on an extra day or so with all the crowd, to eat shrimp and gumbo and dance every night. We'd had our flare-ups before but nothing had ever caught like that one. "I can't forget seeing you on the boat that day," he would say. "Don't be crazy, you'd seen me on that boat every day for a week." "Not like that," he'd rave, "like something fresh from the sea." "A catfish," I said. "Stop it, Eileen," he'd say, and dance me off the floor to the dark outside, and kiss me. "I can't get enough of you," he'd say, and take me in so close I'd get dizzy.

I kept thinking through all this in a warm frame of mind while making the rounds and talking to everybody, and maybe an hour, more or less, passed that way, when I heard a voice from the stairwell (Charlie) say: "God Almighty, if it isn't Nelle," and I turned around and saw all there was to see.

Charlie was fresh from his nap, the red faded from his face and his tie in place (he'd even buzzed off his five o'clock shadow with Pete's electric razor). He was about five steps up from the bottom of the stairs. And Nelle, just coming back into the living room to join everybody, had on a Chinese red silk shawl with a fringe. Her hair, so simple and shining, wasn't dark or blonde either, just the color of hair, and she had on the plain dove gray silk dress and the elegant sandals. She was framed in the door. Then I saw Charlie's face, how he was drinking her in, and I remembered the day on the boat.

"God damn, Nelle," said Charlie. He came down the steps and straight to her. "Where you been?"

"Oh, hello, Charlie," said Nelle in her friendly way. "Where have *you* been?"

"Honey, that's not even a question," said Charlie. "The point is, I'm *here.*"

Then he fixed them both a drink and led her over to a couch in the far corner of the room. There was a side porch at the Owens', spacious, with a tile floor—that's where we'd all been dancing. The living room was a little off-center to the party. I kept on with my partying, but I had eyes in the back of my head where Charlie was concerned. I knew they were there on the couch and that he was crowding her toward one end. I hoped he was talking to her about Grey. I danced with Grey.

"Why don't you go and break that up?" I said.

"Why don't you?" said Grey.

"Marriage is different," I said.

"She can break it up herself if she wants to," he said.

I'd made a blunder and knew it was too late. Charlie was holding both Nelle's hands, talking over something. I fixed myself a stiff drink. It had begun to rain, quietly with no advance warning. The couple from Hattiesburg had started doing some kind of talking blues number on the piano. Then we were singing. The couch was empty. Nelle and Charlie weren't there. . . .

It was Grey who came to see me the next afternoon. I was hung over but working anyway. Mr. McGinnis didn't recognize hangovers.

"I'm not asking her anywhere again," said Grey. "I'm through and she's through. I've had it. She kept saying in the car, 'Sure, I did like Charlie Waybridge, we all liked Charlie Waybridge. Maybe I was in love with Charlie Waybridge. But why start it up all over again? Why?' 'Why did you?' I said, 'that's more the question.' 'I never meant to, just there he was, making me feel that way.' 'You won't let me make you feel any way,' I said. 'My foot hurts,' she said, like a little girl. She looked a mess. Mud all over her dress and her hair gone to pieces. She had sprained her ankle. It had swelled up. That big."

"Oh, Lord," I said. "All Pete and Hope wanted was for you all— Look, can't you see Nelle was just drunk? Maybe somebody slugged her drink."

"She didn't have to drink it."

I was hearing Charlie: "All she did was get too much. Hadn't partied anywhere in months. Said she wanted some fresh air. First thing I knew she goes tearing out in the rain and whoops! in those high-heeled shoes—sprawling."

"Charlie and her," Grey went on. Okay, so he was hurt. Was that any reason to hurt me? But on he went. "Her and Charlie, that summer you went away up north, they were dating every night. Then her sister got sick, the one that died? She couldn't go on the coast trip with us."

"You think I don't know all that?" Then I said: "Oh, Grey!" and he left.

Yes, I sat thinking, unable to type anything: it was the summer her sister died and she'd had to stay home. I was facing up to Charlie Waybridge. I didn't want to, but there it was. If Nelle had been standing that day where I had stood, if Nelle had been wearing those sandals, that shirt, those shorts—Why pretend not to know Charlie Waybridge, through and through? What was he really doing on the Townshend property that night?

Pete, led by Hope, refused to believe anything but that the party had been a big success. "Like old times," said Pete. "What's wrong with new times?" said Hope. In our weakness and disarray, she was moving on in. (Damn Nelle Townshend.) Hope loved the new people; she was working everybody in together. "The thing for you to do about *that*—" she was now fond of saying on the phone, taking on problems of every sort.

When Hope heard that Nelle had sprained her ankle and hadn't been seen out in a day or so, she even got Pete one afternoon and went to call. She had telephoned but nobody answered. They walked up the long front walk between the elephant ears and up the front porch steps and rang the old turning bell half a dozen times. Hope had a plate of cake and Pete was carrying a bunch of flowers.

Finally Mrs. Townshend came shuffling to the door. Humpbacked, she had to look way up to see them, at a mole's angle. "Oh, it's you," she said.

"We just came to see Nelle," Hope chirped. "I understand she hurt her ankle at our party. We'd just like to commiserate."

"She's in bed," said Mrs. Townshend and made no further move, either to open the door or take the flowers. Then she said, "I just wish you all would leave Nelle alone. You're no good for her. You're no good I know of for anybody. She went through all those years with you. She doesn't want you anymore. I'm of the same opinion." Then she leaned over and from an old-fashioned umbrella stand she drew up and out what could only be called a shotgun. "I keep myself prepared," she said. She cautiously lowered the gun into the umbrella stand. Then she looked up once again at them, touching the rims of her little oval glasses. "When I say you all, I mean all of you. You're drinking and you're doing all sorts of things that waste time, and you call that having fun. It's not my business unless you come here and make me say so, but Nelle's too nice to say so. Nelle never would—" She paused a long time, considering in the mildest sort of way. "Nelle can't shoot," she concluded, like this fact had for the first time occurred to her. She closed the door, softly and firmly.

I heard all this from Hope a few days later. Charlie was off again and I was feeling lower than low. This time we hadn't even quarreled. It seemed more serious than that. A total reevaluation. All I could come to was a question: Why doesn't he reassure me? All I could answer was that he must be in love with Nelle. He tried to call her when I wasn't near. He sneaked off to do it, time and again.

Alone, I tried getting drunk to drown out my thoughts, but couldn't, and alone for a day too long, I called up Grey. Grey and I used to date, pretty heavy. "Hell," said Grey, "I'm fed up to here and so are you. Let's blow it." I was tight enough to say yes and we met out at the intersection. I left my car at the shopping center parking lot.

I remember the sway of his Buick Century, turning onto the interstate. We went up to Jackson.

The world is spinning now and I am spinning along with it. It doesn't stand still anymore to the stillness inside which murmurs to me, I know my love and I belong to my love when all is said and done, down through foreverness and into eternity. No, when I got back I was just part of it all, ordinary, a twenty-eight-year-old attractive married woman with family and friends and a nice house in Tyler, Mississippi. But with nothing absolute.

When I had a drink too many now, I would drive out to the woods and stop the car and walk around among places always known. One day, not even thinking about them, I saw Nelle drive by and this time there was no doubt who was with her—Robin Byers. They were talking. Well, Robin's wife mended the clothes when they were ripped or torn, and she sewed buttons on. Maybe they were going there. I went home.

At some point the phone rang. I had seen to it that it was "out of order" when I went up to Jackson with Grey, but now it was "repaired," so I answered it. It was Nelle.

"Eileen, I guess you heard Mama turned Pete and Hope out the other day. She was just in the mood for telling everybody off." Nelle laughed her clear, pure laugh. You can't have a laugh like that unless you've got a right to it, I thought.

"How's your ankle?" I asked.

"I'm still hobbling around. What I called for, Mama wanted me to tell you something. She said, 'I didn't mean quite everybody. Eileen can still come. You tell her that.' "

Singled out. If she only knew, I thought. I shook when I put down the phone.

But I did go. I climbed up to Nelle's bedroom with Mrs. Townshend toiling behind me, and sat in one of those old rocking chairs near a bay window with oak paneling and cane plant, green and purple, in a window box. I stayed quite a while. Nelle kept her ankle propped up and Mrs. Townshend sat in a tiny chair about the size of a twelve-year-old's, which was about the size she was. They told stories and laughed with that innocence that seemed like all clear things—a spring in the woods, a dogwood bloom, a carpet of pine needles along a sun-dappled road. Like Nelle's ankle, I felt myself getting well. It was a new kind of wellness, hard to describe. It didn't have much to do with Charlie and me.

"Niggers used to come to our church," Mrs. Townshend recalled. "They had benches in the back. I don't know why they quit. Maybe they all died out—the ones we had, I mean."

"Maybe they didn't like the back," said Nelle.

"It was better than nothing at all. The other churches didn't even have that. There was one girl going to have a baby. I was scared she would have it right in the church. Your father said, 'What's wrong with that? Dr. Erskine could deliver it, and we could baptize it on the spot.' "

I saw a picture on one of those little tables they had by the dozen, with the starched linen doily, and the bowed-out legs. It was of two gentlemen, one taller than the other, standing side by side in shirt sleeves and bow ties and each with elastic bands around their upper arms, the kind that used to hold the sleeves to a correct length of cuff. They were smiling in a fine natural way, out of friendship. One must have been Nelle's father, dead so long ago. I asked about the other. "Child," said Mrs. Townshend, "don't you know your own grandfather? He and Sid thought the world of one another." I had a better feeling when I left. Would it last? Could I get it past the elephant ears?

I didn't tell Charlie about going there. Charlie got it from some horse's mouth that Grey and I were up in Jackson that time, and he pushed me off the back steps. An accident, he said; he didn't see me when he came whamming out the door. For a minute I thought I, too, had sprained or broken something, but a skinned knee was all it was. He watched me clean the knee, watched the bandage go on. He wouldn't go out—not to Pete and Hope's, not to Rose and John's, not to anywhere—and the whisky went down in the bottle.

I dreamed one night of Robin Byers, that I ran into him uptown but didn't see a scar on his face. I followed him, asking, Where is it? What happened? Where's it gone? But he walked straight on, not seeming to hear. But it was no dream that his house caught fire, soon after the cleaning shop opened again. Both Robin and Nelle said it was only lightning struck the back wing and burned out a shed room before Robin could stop the blaze. Robin's daughter got jumped on at school by some other black children who yelled about her daddy being a Tom. They kept her at home for a while to do her school work there. What's next?

Next for me was going to an old lady's apartment for Mr. McGinnis, so she could sign her will, and on the long steps up to her door, there was Robin Byers, fresh from one of his deliveries.

"Robin," I said, at once, out of nowhere, surprising myself, "you got to leave here, Robin. You're tempting fate, every day."

And he, just as quick, replied: "I got to stay here. I got to help Miss Nelle."

Where had it come from, what we said? Mine wasn't a bit like me; I might have been my mother or grandmother talking. Certainly not the fun girl who danced on piers in whirling miniskirts and dove off a fishing boat to reach a beach, swimming, they said, between the fishhooks and the sharks. And Robin's? From a thousand years back, maybe, superior and firm, speaking out of sworn duty, his honored trust. He was standing above me on the steps. It was just at dark, and in the first street light I could see the white scar, running riverlike down the flesh, like the mark lightning leaves on a smooth tree. When we passed each other, it was like erasing what we'd said and that we'd ever met.

But one day I am walking in the house and picking up the telephone only to find Charlie talking on the extension. "Nelle . . ." I hear. "Listen, Nelle. If you really are foolin' around with that black bastard, he's answering to me." And blam! goes the phone from her end, loud as any gun of her mama's.

I think we are all hanging on a golden thread, but who has got the other end? Dreaming or awake, I'm praying it will hold us all suspended.

Yes, praying—for the first time in years.

The Wars of Heaven

•

RICHARD CURREY

Richard Currey was born in Parkersburg, West Virginia. Among several awards and prizes, he has twice received National Endowment for the Arts writing grants and the D. H. Lawrence Fellowship in Literature. His books include Fatal Light, *a novel, and* Crossing Over: A Vietnam Journal. *He has lived with his family in New Mexico since 1979.*

Listen. Hear me talking to you. Rockwell Lee Junior remembering the glow in your kitchen, Momma, the light that was a mix of gold and blue on a winter's night and the way our talk drifted around like big slow birds in the warm air and Oh what I wouldn't give for one more day in the sweetness of what I didn't know back when, the days before, when I was just a grinning boy in a dirty white shirt, an innocent yes indeed. Or the afternoons sitting at your kitchen table when you'd make me a mug of your coffee, Momma, and sweeten it with clover honey and color it with goat's milk. Always liked your coffee, you know that I did, even when I was a kid I'd ask you for a taste and you'd let me sip from your cup and Daddy grinning at me from across the table. I remember the little circle of heat that would come up from your cup, touch my lips, and what I wouldn't have given for a cup of your coffee, trapped as I was in that icehouse of a sky full of snow where any direction I looked and as far as I could see it was white, whiteness in the trees, humped up against the mountains, whiteness. At least the wind had died down, that was the morning of St. Valentine's Day, at least I could say that because that's what kills you,

that's what steals the air out of your lungs, steals the light straight out
of your eyes, if anything can do that it's the wind in winter across a
field of snow bearing down on you like a ghost train out of nowhere.
Early that morning the wind passed off to the north, I could nearly see
it go, so God was merciful and I thanked God for that. I dropped to
my knees taking care to keep my rifle butt-down and upright leaning
against my left shoulder, and I prayed. Thank you Jesus. No wind
today. No wind to freeze what life I got left, to steal the light out of
my eyes. Thank you Jesus. One more day of life. And Momma you
might ask how it was the condemned man still prayed to his God in
the wilderness, you'll say, What could I have to say to God and Jesus
out there on the run. Where could I be going that was any salvation at
all after what I done. Maybe this is all I really wanted, a chance at
rectitude, restitution by myself and alone and in a place of my own
choosing. A simple place where what dreams I might still have har-
bored could die a tranquil death, lonely as time itself and peaceful as
light. And you know the Sheriff's posse caught up to me here at Judson Church so there may be a justice in this, an understanding. You
know you always said that dreams were made of water and human
desire, that dreams went no mortal place at all, they were only man's
way to confuse himself and convince himself that a fire was lit at the
heart of things. You always said it was nothing but cinder and ashes
and now I don't know, the way I walked out there in that whole world
of snow with that posse surely on my trail, I don't know, I swear I
can't be sure. When I shot that girl you know I saw her fall down right
there on her Daddy's porch, fall down like a puppet whose strings got
cut and I swear I saw the life drawing out of her like light coming out
of a window at night. And I was not the man you knew. In that
instant I was not the man you ever knew. I was that skeleton engineer
on the phantom locomotive in that scare-story you told when I was a
kid, I was just one headlong scream into oblivion, I swear. At the
moment she fell down like an empty sack and I knew what I had done
I was lost as I am right now up here in the hills in the snow. Now that
it's all too late I think you were wrong, Momma, I think that there is a
light down somewhere in the center of things and that if a man knew
that for a solid fact he could go down to that place and warm his

hands on a cold night. Because how could I be so desperate and finished and on the run and see everything so beautiful and transfixing
and everlasting, everywhere I turned was like looking forever, like a
picture up on somebody's wall so I had to stop and stand and look
into the world for the first and last time, wondering why I never saw it
before.

When I got to Judson Church there was enough wood to light a fire
and I hung my coat and warmed myself over that stove and thanked
the Lord there was no moon that night, no moonlight to let any
Sheriff's posse see my smoke. No moonlight to show my footprints
walking across the snowfield and right up to the church steps. I'd been
on the move at night, hiding in tumble-down houses all day with my
rifle up and ready and afraid to sleep, and I had my time to think,
reflect on things, see where it had all gone bad and Momma, you know
I think it was losing Daddy that did it to us, both of us. It was losing
Daddy that took the life out of you, took your own life away from
you, that made you so hard and tired and unforgiving. That let your
own bitterness rail against you inside like a snow-wind of the very
heart and soul I swear, that made you turn away in your loss and
violent mind. Momma, I think you died on that old covered bridge
with Daddy, I swear I think you did. Daddy was the true anchor, he
was the root our lives were growing from when he died only we didn't
know it, we were innocents, the two of us. So you claim you know
Daddy's killer, that you'd know the face of the devil if you looked
straight into that face, and maybe so. But I don't know. All we know
is Daddy's body was found on that bridge with his watch and money
gone, that's all we really know, and it could have been anybody, it
could have been a neighbor or a stranger and we'll never know and
that's a fact.

So it's a terrible strange thing that I came to be the very one that
killed Daddy for a pittance in the cover of darkness. For we are all of
one bad wind, you know that Momma, all of us robbers and murder-
ers are one evil man split down into a hundred wild boys, all doing the
cruel bidding of some kind of master within. I had heard that before
and now I know it to be true but I never once thought about it, what
was happening to me, I never once saw it all coming as I should. I

could have turned back a hundred times but I didn't, I was like a man on a spooked horse, riding straight into the eyes of a fire and just hanging on for dear life.

You could say it was friends or circumstance or some of both but I can feel now it was simply Daddy going out the way he did, lost the way he was in some terrible whirlpool of time and I swear I was nothing but a useless boy hanging on a spike thrown this way and that, born under a bad sign, condemned to howl at the moon, to preach to the wind, and I drifted like a rotting boat cut loose on floodwaters after a hard rain, breathing from one tree to another until I was out in the main current and running. And that's the way it goes, out there in the deep water with some other power under you and driving you, keeping you whole until finally you hit the rapids and go over the falls.

That's how I come to be in on the robbery of Strother's Store over in the mining camp. There was the other boys wanted to do it, claimed old Strother kept a mint under the floor behind the cashbox and I said Well OK. When we got over there I felt no fear, I still cannot explain how I walked right up on the porch and butted my rifle right through the plate glass and opened the door and walked inside like it was my store and not Strother's, but let me tell you it inspired a measure of confidence in those boys that went inside behind me, yes indeed. And you know the strange thing is, I walked into that store holding my rifle up like I was looking to shoot something, walked in and straight back past them tables all laid up with can-goods and linens and bottled water, right back to the rear wall where Strother had all his bridles and reins hung up and I turned around to face front, leaned against the wall and just stood there. I didn't want a goddamned thing. I didn't care about money, or the things worth stealing in that store. I felt then as I did ever since. I felt mad with temper, and like I could just keep it under my skin if nobody pushed at me. And so goddamned afraid. Afraid of what I've never been truly sure, but I know if the Sheriff walked into the middle of that robbery or any other one and shot us all down I wouldn't have much cared, that's the kind of feeling I'm speaking of. And I felt that way until the day I hit Judson Church and looked back on what had gone before, and knew I had to wait in that little house of the Lord, wait there for my redemption in whatever form it was coming and at least I was in a sanctified place.

So I just stood there in Strother's Store while the boys whooped it up and made a mess of the place, and Bob Hanks come back to me, said Rocky what's the matter? And I said I'm just fine, Bob. You just go on and do what you came to do, that's all. And Bob looked at me strange a moment but went on back to work, and when the boys was still and quiet and standing in the doorway with their bags full up I walked over to where they stood and past them and out the door. I stepped down to the road and got in behind the wheel of your truck, Momma, started it up. The boys all filed down and got in, climbed onto the bed, and nobody said a word to me.

They had found old Strother's money pile and split it five ways. Three thousand dollars and change. Everything Strother had in the world and Bob Hanks come over to me with six one-hundred dollar bills saying This here's your share Rock. And I said Thank you kindly and Bob drew on the whisky bottle he'd been carrying round and grinned at me. Well sir, he said, you're quite welcome.

And you know Momma it was all my plans after that, the branch bank over in Federalsville, the general store out to Middle River, right down to the night I shot Betty Shadwell dead on her daddy's front porch and knew I had become the man who speaks to you now in the sure voice of death, dead in the ice, you might even say in the frozen waste of time. Out here in the snow it is surely the end of the world. I could hear the sound of my breath setting up against the air like a rasp: the end of the world I swear.

Outside the church it was going to sunset, the day's light drawing down to that twilight filled with fire-color that burns on the snow before it proceeds to die right into the night. I stirred the wood on the grate and was thankful for that bit of stove-heat, wrapped my coat around me and tried to lay down on a pew and saw it wasn't going to work. So I went on and lay down on the floor up against the back wall of the church with a Philadelphia hymnal under my head and the Winchester right there in easy reach. But sleep wasn't about to come. No ma'am. I just lay there, listening to the mice scrap and itch around the floorboards, thieves like me, looking for what isn't there, for what

will never be there and you know how your mind goes into a kind of
trance when you're too tired to sleep, how you think crazy things,
think the moon moves faster than it does? I lay there on the floor of
Judson Church and lived in that half-a-dream, and I saw your face
Momma, and I saw Daddy's, and I saw Rita Clair's face too, it was
Rita as I saw her the last time up on the hill over town, sitting on a
blanket with that man's workshirt on over nothing, her dress and
underwear laid to one side on the grass. We made love up there on that
hill, squatting down on that old blanket and moving together and the
bees moaning around us and crickets working, every now and again a
hot breeze come to rustle in our hair. I had my hands up under that
shirt, all over her like I wanted to be more than just inside her, I
wanted to melt into her. As if I could just disappear and become part
of that one moment, forever, lost in it, outside of this voice that speaks
to you now. I raised my face to the sky and the sky was blue as I had
never seen and there were clouds as white and soft and eternal-looking
as you can imagine and I swear it was as if me and Rita were being
raised together into that sky, lifted up, me holding Rita and her in my
lap, the both of us panting and wheezing and crying out. We went up
in the air floating right out over the brow of that hill, then we started
to come down like we were stones settling to the bottom of a slow
river, coming down through green light and silence, our ears filled up,
our eyes covered over and I thought then, that's right, we're just like
rocks thrown into a river. You don't know where you come from or
where you're gone, you just get picked up and thrown. But you can
have one little moment, yes sir, you can have Rita Clair's sweet fine
body on a hill in the middle of a hot summer so as to have a glimpse of
what might have been, like looking through a little crack into the
future or the past and not knowing which way you're looking, but
seeing it all filled up with light and the smell of honey. I laid there,
Momma, remembering everything I tell you now, Daddy going the
way he did, you turning away from me in your grief, having that little
taste of Rita Clair, that little glimpse of heaven and knowing I wasn't
fit to have no more than that, and the way I went to stealing and could
hate myself so bad and still be so calm, standing at the window of the
church and seeing the Sheriff and his deputies out there at the treeline

like I knew they would be, just shapes out there in those long coats and big hats and the straight black lines of their rifle barrels up against the snow.

There was a thin light seeping into the church, that watery first light you get on a winter dawn. I stood up and shook out of my coat and went to the window and there they were, standing out there looking at my trace across the snowfield, the way it ended right at the church steps.

I turned away from the window, sat down in a pew. They wouldn't just walk up to the door and knock. No sir. Not with a man like me inside. Sheriff'd try to get me to come out peaceable, lay down my gun, throw it out in the snow. But he'd be prepared to shoot me.

I got my rifle and went to the window on the other side of the church, unlocked it an slid it up. The stained-glass face of Jesus rose up in front of me and then I saw the snow stretching down to Rucker's Creek and I leaned out and propped my piece against the outside wall of the church, let myself out and down to the snow, waited. I heard nothing. I knew they wouldn't come across the pasture, not with the risk of me being inside the church. They'd be fanning out just inside the treeline, trying to surround me. I started for the trees thinking I could at least get into the woods myself. The snow was frozen over, a crust my boots dropped through an inch and I saw they'd track me anywhere I went but I had to go, there was nothing else to do. I was halfway to the treeline when I heard my name called out, hollow, booming around in the air. I turned and it was Stewart McCarty standing under the stained-glass window I'd left out of with his scattergun trained on me. *Mr. Lee,* he called out, *just stand where you are real still and put down your rifle.* I could see the smoke of his breath. I raised my Winchester and fired, hit Stewart somewhere above the waist and he grunted, slammed back against the church and slid a red streak down the wall, flopping around in the snow and I turned and ran for the trees.

I could hear the sound of the creek and a man I thought looked like Roy John stepped around in some birches up to my right, and then I knew it was him when he yelled to me *Rockwell Lee, give yourself up now. No use in running no more.*

I turned to the direction of his voice. New snow started to fall. His shape moved back and forth in the trees. *Roy,* I called out. *Roy, help me. What happened, it was an accident.*

Roy John came into full view, aiming his rifle at me. I thought I saw movement behind him. Snow filled the air.

Roy, I said. *Roy, you know me. You know my Momma.*

I know what you done, Rock. You're gonna have to come home with us.

The peculiar thing is that I had no intention of killing anyone at the Shadwell place, there or any other place, we just meant to get on out of there with the silver because Bob Hanks knew where the old man kept it in the house. If the old man hadn't come out of the house firing his pistol. I just meant to let go a warning shot, blow out a front window, I swear I didn't even see Betty there on the porch, what was she doing there anyway? You answer me that. I didn't even see her till she fell. Rockwell Lee Junior may have been a robber but he was no murderer. That was a pure accident. It was never meant to be. No sir. So when I lifted my rifle with the intent to throw it down and give myself up and tell my story, Roy John blew off my left shoulder.

The force of it shoved me back and I stumbled, and I had the strangest feeling of surprise but I stayed on my feet and kept hold of my gun. Blood and bone and muscle had sprayed out over the snow like a mist, I could look right down into the hole in my coat where my shoulder had been, an awful burning and the falling snow melting in the wound, steam wisping up out of the hole and my shoulder looking that way got me angry, mad with temper all over again and that terrible fear and I raised my Winchester over my head with my right arm yelling *Goddam you, Roy, look what you done.*

The second shot was a shotgun, catching me square in the chest, I went off the ground, legs kicking and the force of that shot knocking my right boot off. Damn if I was going to let them take me laying on the ground, I got up again and don't you know I was an awful mess, I looked like the mouth of hell, blood everywhere and my coat hanging on me in rags.

I swayed there in the falling snow. My breath was hard to come by, I could hear air sucking right in through the holes in my chest and the whole lot of them come out of the trees then, the Sheriff, Roy John, the rest of the deputies just coming up around me and looking at me and I could see it was Stewart McCarty who fired the shotgun round. He was back on his feet under that Jesus window and at first I thought I had been shot by a ghost but then I knew I had only wounded him. My eyesight began to go on me then, frayed around the edges in all that whiteness and air filled with snow like an old sheet hung out to dry and coming apart in a heavy wind. Roy John walked up to me and took off his long coat and put it around me. The Sheriff came up behind Roy to handcuff my wrists together and standing there half-dead for sure I heard the sound of bells, out in the distance of that snowy air, out in some reach of that wild snowy air there was the slow music of bells and I looked out to the hills and clouds trying to see where that music came from and why it was coming to me. Roy John looked at me and said *What is it, Rock?*

And I said *Roy, don't you hear 'em? Like church bells.* I raised the handcuffs, my hands clasped together in a fist pointed west and said *Out there.*

I turned back to Roy John and my knees went to plain water, I fell straight down in the snow on my knees, like a man about to pray, a man calling for mercy. And that is one thing I did not want to be, a man calling for mercy. I did not want to ask for anything, not food or water, no rest, not even for my own life, and I said *Roy, Help me up, now. Don't let me stay down here.* The Sheriff stood beside Roy, his shape as big as a tree, the two of them lifting me up, one on either side, and the Sheriff said *Let's go, Roy.* And they led me across that snowcovered meadow with the rest of the posse behind us, me with one boot gone and walking short-legged in a sock the same meadow I'd walked across the night before to get to Judson Church. The treeline moved up on us as if the trees were sailing in from a long way off and I could see the sleigh and the two roans snorting and blowing wet smoke in that air and I hope you're happy, Momma, because this is the first and last time you will ever hear this story, your only son shot at Rucker's Creek not five miles from his place of birth, his blood running over the ice like oil and into the water to cloud up colored like a rose and swirl away. I've always heard it said the wars of heaven are fought on righteous ground, Momma, and the godly man shall be the victor. So Roy John helped me up into that sleigh and threw a saddle blanket over me and I lay where I lay, an end to my so-called life of crime, nobody to know how lost I truly was, the man who built his own gallows in the snow, out behind the house of the lord. I am the man who sought restitution by himself and alone in a place of his own choosing. I am the man who surrendered with one boot gone on St. Valentine's Day, the year of our lord nineteen hundred and thirteen, with the smell of salt and woodsmoke and gunpowder in the air.

The last of this Lee family is gone now, Daddy crossed over, Rockwell Junior the robber and murderer shot down at Judson Church, and Momma you know you died with Daddy on that covered bridge and are as gone as me and him, yes you are, sad and gone, and we have suffered for what we didn't know back when and what we couldn't find, and for what we didn't even know we'd lost. And now we are gone, we are history. We are stories nobody tells, Momma, we have disappeared back down to the bottom of that river once and for all.

We are in the company of time. Ours is the testament of snow. We are alone together.

The Place to Be

•

════ SHIRLEY HAZZARD ════

Born in Australia, Shirley Hazzard has lived in New York City and in Italy for many years. She has published five works of fiction, and one volume of social history concerning the United Nations, where she worked for ten years. Her most recent novel, The Transit of Venus, received the National Book Critics' Circle Award in 1981. She is at present completing another novel.

In harbor on the first morning, Exley saw the pastel villas on the mountainside, here and there among vegetation: looted, unroofed, their marzipan interiors lined with rot; some of them rebuilding under bamboo scaffolding. Looking out from shipboard, he realized that from those slopes there would be a grand view over the straits to the mainland. Obviously, the place to be.

That same noon he stood by windows up at MacGregor Road, in the officers' quarters, while a skeptical soldier searched through papers for his name. While the soldier riffled colored pages, Peter Exley looked down the green mountain to the town scribbled along the shore: noting the cathedral, the post office, the governor's villa; and the bank, which was higher than the rest. It was all as he had supposed. Beyond the narrow harbor and the shipping there were small bleached mountains, at the verge of Asia.

He was aware of some consequential element he had not identified. And with indifference realized it was beauty.

There was no place for him at MacGregor Road, no record of his request. It would have been quiet up there, and relatively cool; just below the fog line—damp, of course, with the green smell Exley at first mistook for freshness and soon identified as decay. But there had been a mistake, and every room was taken.

Redirected to the barracks, he went down unsurprised on the cable car in the afternoon heat. The July air was a blanket, summer weight. The barracks looked like Scutari. Presenting himself, he was led along a creaking veranda and up a soiled stair. Everywhere, the breath of mold.

A corporal unlocked the door. There was a second, inner door, slatted and unlatched. Pledges of another presence were distributed about the room. At the center of things, marooned on wooden floor, a tin box was stencilled with name and number. The better bed, by the window, was heaped with dirty laundry and overhung by a dingy clump of mosquito net. There was the quiescent menace of a gramophone.

"Can't I get a room to myself, at least?"

"Put you down sir, soons we got one. Bit of a wait, I'd say." There was a fair-sized garrison in the colony—Buffs, Inniskillings, Gurkhas. In any case, no one would offer preference to Exley. He had no flair for attracting favors.

The corporal told him the mess hours. Exley asked, "Is there something like a library here?"

"Any books get left, they put em on a shelf near the stairs. Mostly duds, I'd say."

It was 1947, mid-July. His pocket diary said "Saint Swithin." Exley took off his tunic and sat on the inferior bed. His shirt stuck like a khaki skin. Overhead, there was the croak of a slow, ineffectual fan. Rails of light, red as electric elements, striped the shutters. Walls were distempered dun. There were marks where heads had greasily rested, where furniture and kit had been stored; where hands had sweated around knobs and switches. There were smudges of squashed insects, with adhering particles. Damp had got at the quicksilver of a long mirror on a mahogany stand. On the wall by the other bed, pinups were pinkly askew and printed signs carried insults, facetiously obscene.

The Place to Be

•

SHIRLEY HAZZARD

*Born in Australia, Shirley Hazzard has lived in New York City and in
Italy for many years. She has published five works of fiction, and one
volume of social history concerning the United Nations, where she
worked for ten years. Her most recent novel,* The Transit of Venus,
*received the National Book Critics' Circle Award in 1981. She is at
present completing another novel.*

In harbor on the first morning, Exley saw the pastel villas on the
mountainside, here and there among vegetation: looted, unroofed,
their marzipan interiors lined with rot; some of them rebuilding under
bamboo scaffolding. Looking out from shipboard, he realized that
from those slopes there would be a grand view over the straits to the
mainland. Obviously, the place to be.

That same noon he stood by windows up at MacGregor Road, in
the officers' quarters, while a skeptical soldier searched through papers
for his name. While the soldier riffled colored pages, Peter Exley
looked down the green mountain to the town scribbled along the
shore: noting the cathedral, the post office, the governor's villa; and
the bank, which was higher than the rest. It was all as he had supposed. Beyond the narrow harbor and the shipping there were small
bleached mountains, at the verge of Asia.

He was aware of some consequential element he had not identified.
And with indifference realized it was beauty.

There was no place for him at MacGregor Road, no record of his
request. It would have been quiet up there, and relatively cool; just

below the fog line—damp, of course, with the green smell Exley at first mistook for freshness and soon identified as decay. But there had been a mistake, and every room was taken.

Redirected to the barracks, he went down unsurprised on the cable car in the afternoon heat. The July air was a blanket, summer weight. The barracks looked like Scutari. Presenting himself, he was led along a creaking veranda and up a soiled stair. Everywhere, the breath of mold.

A corporal unlocked the door. There was a second, inner door, slatted and unlatched. Pledges of another presence were distributed about the room. At the center of things, marooned on wooden floor, a tin box was stencilled with name and number. The better bed, by the window, was heaped with dirty laundry and overhung by a dingy clump of mosquito net. There was the quiescent menace of a gramophone.

"Can't I get a room to myself, at least?"

"Put you down sir, soons we got one. Bit of a wait, I'd say." There was a fair-sized garrison in the colony—Buffs, Inniskillings, Gurkhas. In any case, no one would offer preference to Exley. He had no flair for attracting favors.

The corporal told him the mess hours. Exley asked, "Is there something like a library here?"

"Any books get left, they put em on a shelf near the stairs. Mostly duds, I'd say."

It was 1947, mid-July. His pocket diary said "Saint Swithin." Exley took off his tunic and sat on the inferior bed. His shirt stuck like a khaki skin. Overhead, there was the croak of a slow, ineffectual fan. Rails of light, red as electric elements, striped the shutters. Walls were distempered dun. There were marks where heads had greasily rested, where furniture and kit had been stored; where hands had sweated around knobs and switches. There were smudges of squashed insects, with adhering particles. Damp had got at the quicksilver of a long mirror on a mahogany stand. On the wall by the other bed, pinups were pinkly askew and printed signs carried insults, facetiously obscene.

Gloom without coolness. The mirror, unreflecting, was like the draped pelt of some desiccated leopard.

There was a century here of obscure imperial dejection: a room of listless fevers. Of cafard, ennui, and other French diseases. The encrusted underside of glory.

Exley, afterward, had no clear memory of seeing Roy Rysom for the first time—though sharply recalling that first sight of Rysom's dented tin box, its stencilled legend "WAR GRAVES COMMISSION" suggesting the decomposing contents. He remembered that he was reading when Rysom came in and set the jazz belting, dragged off his boots, flopped on his bed, and began twitching to the music. Rysom's foot in its dank sock stuck out from the military blanket, toes curling and uncurling erotically to the music; his fingers convulsively beat on his chest, like hands of the dying. Peter Exley had watched men clutch themselves and die, and be covered up by regulation blankets. Men shot to bits in the desert, blown in half by land mines, festered with infected wounds: the whole scarlet mess covered by the military blanket.

> *Oh, ya feets too big.*
> *Don't want ya cos yo feets too big.*
> *Mad at ya cos yo feets too big.*
> *Hate ya cos yo feets too big.*

Rysom's records were mostly jazz. Life with Rysom was suffused with noise: the messboy calling him to the telephone—"Mistah Rai-sam, Captain Rai-sam;" Rysom yelling for cold beer, as trams rattled in the road below and the dockyard siren hooted or the gun boomed noon. Rysom said it was funny they should both be Australians, he and Exley, and on loan to the British Army. He said, "You War Crimes lot," and hooted like the siren. Rysom could introduce disbelief into anything, unmasking was his vocation. With suspicion he turned over Exley's Chinese and Japanese textbooks, his volumes on international law: "A beaut racket." Spreading a double page of Japanese characters, he uttered a stream of mad, paralaliac sounds, his comic rendering of Japanese.

Rysom was forever doing imitations: of a language, an accent, a personality; a man.

Rysom had dreams from which he woke shouting: dreams, like
Exley's own, of men dismembered and sheets of flame. Each, in the
night, now fought alone the war that neither could survive.

On his cot at the barracks Exley now realized how much of his
soldiering had been spent flat on his back, waiting for war. War had
provided a semblance of purpose, reinforced by danger. Danger had
been switched off like a stage light, leaving the drab scenery. And
there they were at the barracks, he and Rysom, two years into peace
and bored to death by it. Each must scratch around, now, for some
kind of compromise and call it destiny.

On his first mornings in the colony, Exley set out early. The short
walk to his office led past the cricket ground, the club, the blotched
statue of queen and empress restored to its pedestal: a decorous few
hundred yards where Europeans were walking to their work in the
trading companies and government offices—the sun-dried men, sometimes accompanied by pale seemly wife or daughter in starched flowers or well-pressed pleats. At that hour, too, the tourists were coming
ashore from the President Lines, headed for tablecloths, carved ivory,
and cloudy jade. A sense of early purpose seemed to be leading to
something more than the chronic anticlimax of nightfall.

The harbor was an old photograph, a resumption: gray ships of war,
shabby freighters, and the stout passenger ships with banded funnels.
And the swarming sampans and lighters, the junks with dun sails
boned like fans and the dun-colored bony man working the yuloh at
the stern; the greater junks, like galleons; and the coastal steamers off
the praya, arriving from Amoy or Swatow, or from green Saigon.

The office was in the bank building, the best building, the white
block formed like a cenotaph that had been pointed out to Exley at the
time of his arrival: the highest building, and the only one air-condi-
tioned. The bank had thrown over the historic slow rotations of the
ceiling fan in favor of a new climate, man-made. In this building of
thirteen stories, Exley had a cubicle on a low floor, in a set of rooms
occupied by fellow officers. A group of translators in an inner room
were local staff. There was an admiralty clerk who did the legal draft-
ing, and a naval messenger had a chair near the door.

Three servicewomen worked in a room next to Exley's own: none of them pretty, none really young. One of them, Miss Brenda Mills, showed signs of ill nature. Of the other two, Exley could not be sure which was Monica and which Norah, and left it too long to ask. All three lived at the Helena May Hostel above the town. Each had been taken out in turn by the British officers on the floor, who had nothing favorable to report. One other woman in the office was Eurasian, of Portuguese descent: this was the typist, Miss Rita Xavier. There were also two Chinese amahs, who brought tea thickened with condensed milk, cleaned the rooms, and in their tiny antechamber laughed with gold teeth at the pidgin jokes of the admiralty clerk, who puffed his pipe at them in passing.

Here, through the mornings and long afternoons, Peter Exley explored a heap of files and despaired of justice. His office had access to a terrace paved in big red tiles, undulated by the rains. The terrace, rarely used, looked toward the harbor. Seagulls wheeled there, and a cormorant twice alighted. On fair afternoons Exley would go out and lean on the wide ledge. He would look at the war memorial on its patch of lawn, and at the parked cars and parked palm trees, and the sea beyond. The heat soon drove him indoors. Even so, he got a name for mooning.

That summer, in the steaming evenings, Exley would leave the barracks and walk east or west until the long streets became entirely, incontrovertibly Chinese. He would stroll past the hundred thousand stalls and tiny shops of food, of clothes, of soap and pots and bamboo baskets; past the minuscule dens hung with lanterns and braying out harsh music, where the soft smell of opium exuded into fumes of the street. From what would once have enthralled him he would bring away only a flare of alien color and raucous sound, a stench of crowds and cooking; and that scent, sickly as boredom.

Having walked this way an hour or two, he would then return by some divergent route, perhaps along the docks—ignoring appeals from venders and beggars, and the offers from women whose negligible bodies seemed weighted with gold teeth and platform shoes. It was difficult to invest those meagre frames with sensuality, or to covet the lean shanks displayed by the flowered dress slit to the thigh. In these districts Roy Rysom claimed to cut his swath almost nightly. Yet at the end of his own excursions Exley would often discover Rysom having dinner tamely enough—tame hardly describing Rysom's way with chopsticks—at the King Fu in the central district, where a scattering of officers was always to be found. Sometimes Exley sat down with Rysom's group, giving himself over once more to the uproar of loud companions, the clamor of Chinese diners and of waiters yelling to the kitchen. From the gallery above there was the incessant clack and crash of the mah-jongg pieces, the spitting and shouting of the players.

His fellow soldiers repeated the stale anecdotes of lonely men. If anyone told a joke against himself, Rysom laughed too loud—his need for advantage vigilant as fear. If they walked back together to the barracks, Rysom, turning solemn, would caution Exley against his expeditions in the Chinese town: "Filth."

Filth was in fact on Peter Exley's mind in those first weeks: the accretion filming the Orient, the shimmer of sweat or excrement. A railing or handle one's fingers would not willingly grasp; walls and objects grimed with existence; the limp, soiled money, little notes curled and withered, like shavings from some discolored central lode. Ammoniac reek, or worse, in paved alleys and under stuccoed arcades. Shaved heads of children, blotched with sores; gray polls of infants lolling from the swag that bound them to the mother's back. And the great clots and blobs of spittle shot with blood, unavoidable underfoot: what Rysom called "poached eggs." In such uncleanness, nothing could appear innocent, not even diseased chow dogs roaming the Chinese streets, or scrawny chickens pecking at street dirt.

What had not troubled Exley as a soldier in Egypt or South Italy now brought revulsion. He longed for a measure of cleanliness with which peace had somehow been associated. Returning to the barracks with Rysom, he said, "I realize now that I came out here to be well fed and housed, and to have people wait on me. I see now that was in my mind."

Rysom kicked open the door of their room. "Well, this is it, mate—the life of luxury."

The other thing was heat. In North Africa, the sun had been neutral, an impartial horror of war. Now, with cessation of hostilities, heat came out in its true colors as the enemy. The privileged of the colony clung to the mountainside. The rest took refuge in any merciful shadow or flutter of the humid air. The town never cooled: streets and street stalls broiled all night in the glare of naked electricity or paraffin lamps. A dry skin was the ultimate luxury, even for the privileged, even on a soft white body. Lust, if there was energy for it, must be consummated in a lather of sweat. And it was the same thing, no doubt, with love.

Exley's typist, the Portuguese Miss Xavier, was thin and possibly thirty. Skin like an apricot, with an apricot's minute brown flecks; straight black hair, not abundant, curved on shoulders. At her throat, in the hollow disclosed by a Western dress, a small gold crucifix quivered like a heart. Convent school days lingered about remote Miss Xavier. Someone—Brenda or Monica—told Exley that her four sisters were nuns.

"Eurasians," Brenda told him, "maintain a caste system of their own. It's no good mixing up in that."

It would have been pleasant to refute dogmatic Brenda. But in truth Miss Xavier of good family held aloof from Mr. da Silva, chief of the translators. Da Silva in turn condescended to his colleagues. All dealt brusquely with the Chinese.

Peter Exley wrote in his notebook: "There is a community of mixed races here claiming Portuguese descent through the Jesuit settlements of the East. They interpret the British to the Chinese, and vice versa. I don't refer only to language, though that is their essential service. I mean that they form a bridge by which business is done and power exercised. Disdained by both factions, ill-paid, indispensable, and far too obliging." If he wrote this to his mother, she would write back, "So interesting, pet," and put his letter with others in a cardboard box. She would tell some crony: "Peter always feels for the underdog."

In August, Exley was assigned to the interrogation of a Japanese officer charged with atrocities to prisoners of war. He had already no-

ticed the man in the exercise cages of cells behind the barracks, on a
private road that led through trees to the general's house. The prisoner
was listless, slight, still young; short limbs, cropped dark head. Sometimes the inexpressive eyes met Peter Exley's. It was difficult to say
then who was the accused.

Among those who gave evidence was the skipper of a Dutch mer-
chantman on the Surabaya-Kobe run. Exley's letter reached this man
on his way north, at Singapore or Penang; and ten days later, landing
in the colony, he came to make his deposition. He was something over
fifty, Hendriks by name: dark eyes unmoist in dry face, soft knob of
nose. His body itself, short and tough, announced taciturnity. He gave
his evidence in brief, competent assertions, and in correct, peremptory
English.

He had been taken prisoner at Tanjung-Priok, the port of Batavia,
early in 1942.

In Exley's little office, Hendriks told his appalling story with detachment. When the documents had been prepared and signed, the
Dutchman said, "We are in port some days. You shall lunch on
board."

On a Sunday of inhuman heat, Exley found himself on the mainland
docks, following the shadow of the godowns until forced out on an
asphalt wasteland where coolies hauled cargo for hoisting. The Dutch
ship, squat and shabby white, had a short white superstructure
cramped amidships. With driblets of rust on her hull and at the outlet
of the anchor cable, she recalled the smirched bathtub of some old
hotel. Exley was shown to a dim saloon, well enough kept up in its
dark old way, with panelling and polished brasses and heavy chairs
that had defied typhoons. On a long table, a snow-white cloth was set
with the dishes of the *rijsttafel*.

Hendriks came in at once, his seamed flesh emerging, at collar and
cuffs, from a uniform white as the table.

Bols was brought in a crock of ice, along with the circular baked
patties that, according to Roy Rysom, contained dog. As the indoor
contrast passed off, the heat in the saloon became terrific.

At table they were served, in silence, by a Malay and two Chinese.
The elaborate ordeal of drink, heavy food, and blazing sauces slowly

consumed the afternoon. It seemed easier to loll there than to cut the thing short, for Hendriks was clearly unprepared for an abrupt departure. Exley disliked his blunt manner with the servants, the orders rapped without a glance; and his unquestioning assumption of a right to bore. Drink settled in at eyes and temples, pulsating in purple rings. There were extended silences into which the ice collapsed with sharp sounds in crock and glasses, and both men softly mopped at eyes and jowls as if quietly weeping.

Exley realized that Hendriks was getting ready to talk.

Hot towels were brought, scented with sandalwood. Hendriks offered cigars from Havana, and maraschino in a pudgy bottle: "You shall have a glass." His hair, mouse-brown perhaps on a cool day, was dark with sweat and from some shiny unguent.

He said, "This Jap," pronouncing it "chap"—"This Jap of ours looks normal enough, would you say? Yes. He was a cadet, privileged. So he goes to war, he ties prisoners to trees for bayonet practice, he eats human flesh. Touch a nerve, the primitive is there." Hendriks chose a cigar and, with a small blade, clipped the tip. "You've been at war yourself, you've seen that."

Exley said, "I make a distinction between combat and perversion. Between soldiering and sadism. You may think that naïf."

"No, of course, I too wish to do so. There is cruelty beyond even that of battle. You look the man in the eye, then coolly kill him. Is it murder or is it war? Is war in any case murder? That is what your commission pretends to decide."

"You think it only a pretense, then."

"Excuse me, I use the word 'prétendre,' to claim." The Dutchman sucked on his cigar, crossed his foot on his knee. "Yes. I was in a freighter, off the coast of France, when Holland was overrun. Mid-May, that was, of 1940. Our captain was a small man, smaller than I, bowlegged. Ugly. We were bound for Rotterdam, when we had the news on our radio." Long wheeze of cigar. "The next morning, a U-boat surfaced across our bows.

"The captain of the U-boat—they are young in the submarines—the young captain stood out on deck with the megaphone. Two sailors at his side with the machine gun. We would be taken prisoner. This was the decent German, young man but old school. Unless we resisted we would not be sunk. No. He would force us to an occupied port—perhaps to Rotterdam itself—turn us over, and take our ship and cargo as a prize."

Hendriks pressed the towel to mouth, to eyes, and sighed.

"Well, we had our lives to save, we had families. Our skipper had four children. He stood on the bridge talking terms, reasonable, while the U-boat drifted closer. When she was right under our bows he suddenly gave the order: full speed ahead. And we plowed through that U-boat, we ripped her in two, the submarine and the young man and all the rest of them. They went down like skittles—you know how that is. We kept going, we didn't look back for survivors, we didn't stop until we reached Plymouth with the gash in our bow. At Plymouth we drank up, we laughed, we were proud." From his chair Hendriks turned his soft-nosed profile toward Exley. "I suppose that's all right?"

"Not all right, how could it be? But it was war, you defended yourselves."

"So we said, exactly. And our Jap—would he not also produce his justification? You say he took pleasure in the cruelty. And we, too, we rejoiced in it, I assure you. Never so happy, perhaps, before or again. That mild, pious, ugly man of ours turned murderer in a second, and was overjoyed with the result. Of course we were happy our skins were saved, and happy with our victory. But we were happy those men were dead and that we had killed them."

Hendriks knocked away a block of ash. "In any case, I took ship again, got to Portland, went on to Batavia, and ended up in prison all the same. Prisoner of war—that was a Western concept Japan wished to follow. In their emulation of the West, they allowed some of us to survive. Had they known my parentage, they might have dispatched me at the start." Peering into Peter Exley's eyes. "I'm part Javanese. You realized it?"

Exley stared.

"Yes. Grandmother East Indian. You didn't guess it? The tiny feet, the hands, the nose." Dispassionately indicating these, gesturing to the foot cocked on his knee as if it were disembodied. "In Holland they

know it, or in Java. With us it was not as with the British. We Dutch
—you notice I say that—we Dutch bred with the *indigènes,* we sometimes married them. And there are many such as I." Relapsed in his
chair, presenting the undulant profile. "One day it will all mean nothing."

"I don't know that it means anything now."

"Ah—caste remains a useful weapon. To defy it, one still must
suffer."

The revelation had made it impossible to get up and go. Some interlude was required in tribute, there could be no hastening away. Hendriks, having ceased pronouncing, fell into a silence in its own way
oracular. Exley hung on half an hour, the ship melting round him.
The two men took leave of one another at last, with assurances of a
reunion when Hendriks next came to port. It was clear to both that
this would not occur.

In September there were cooler days; and, at the barracks, an issue of
winter-weight blankets. At a Chinese tailor in Queen's Road, Peter
Exley was measured for a suit in dark-blue worsted. The tailor's shop,
upstairs, was called Old Bond's Treat. The tailor himself, dreaming
with open eyes, continually deferred the fittings.

Rysom said, "The bugger takes opium."

At the bank, refrigerated vapors mingled visibly with pipe tobacco.
Miss Rita Xavier now draped a linen jacket on her shoulders as she
typed and filed, and wore nylon stockings on her slender legs. Her
virginal aspect was on the turn for spinsterhood.

In the adjoining room, hefty Norah thumped her thighs and
shouted, "God, I'm getting porkers." And shaggy dark Brenda
scowled with unplucked brows—as she had scowled one evening at a
shipboard dance while returning Peter Exley's tipsy kiss. Rita Xavier's
face, by contrast, was very nearly impassive. If Westerners had con-
tributed expression to the human face, Exley wondered, were they to
be praised or blamed? Was responsiveness in itself something to be
proud of?

In his notebook Exley wrote: "Miss Xavier dislikes speaking Chinese. I hear her at it, directing the office cleaners—a pastiche of Man-

darin, Cantonese, and even Hakka, learned in childhood from her amahs. She has good French, taught by nuns. Some Portuguese, presumably. English excellent, cultivated—a better enunciation than my own. A fine vocabulary, curiously unrelated to any literary knowledge whatever: she chooses good words as they do in Latin countries, from having no alternative. Tells me she had an English governess, a young woman married to a noncommissioned officer stationed in the colony between the wars."

Exley closed his notebook on the governess. Some educated girl of good family, condemned by injudicious love to isolation in the colonial lower ranks. The colony was a backwater then, overshadowed by Shanghai. Shanghai was the place to be. The loneliness of such a life, the unfairness. The wilting pink-and-white, the ailments, the wretched economies. The damp getting to the quicksilver. The unforgiving good family: "She has made her bed and must lie in it." And the bed itself losing its magic. Some Camilla or Cassandra, fallen between two stools, between two wars.

The question of women, the absence of women, of pink-and-white women. Even the glowering Brendas were in demand, let alone the pretty Camillas, the English roses. In this respect the racial lines were quietly and implacably drawn. Hendriks the oracle, in his rusted bathtub, was perfectly right: to flout the agreement, you could not be casual; for you would be made to suffer.

"How terrible," said Monica or Norah, "when there are children of mixed race."

When Monica, Brenda, or Norah said this, Peter Exley was walking with all three of them, on a late afternoon, to the Helena May Hostel. They had gone up through the park and passed above the barracks. It was cool as they climbed. Simply to cease sweating was an inducement to thought, and Exley had forgotten his companions.

Monica gave him his cue: "Tragic, don't you think?"

They suspected Peter Exley of harboring large ideas which he would not have the gumption to assert.

Exley said, "Well, it happens."

Giggles, as if at something audacious. There are women, he thought, who can paralyze a man's best instincts.

He said, "As I see it, the mixed races seem indispensable here."

Brenda said, "Like the Virgin Rita." The three women laughed, pausing to do so with vehemence.

"That nun."

"A nun, like her sisters."

"Sister Rita."

"Santa Rita."

"Pretty prickly for a saint."

"Santa Claws."

He could not walk ahead or fall behind. An overhang of trees shadowed his face. There was the smell of green decay he had once mistaken for health.

At the hostel, in the lofty lounge, balancing his cup on the arm of a wicker settee, Exley watched these disputatious, thick-bodied women stumping off to fetch cake and a bowl of sugar with tongs; plumping down on the chintz roses of plumped down cushions, and fondling with near abandon the shamefaced, slavering Labrador belonging to the maiden directress. The airy room, the light of Asia, and strange red lilies in a vase could do nothing for them.

Brenda sat facing him, hair shoved back from ears, jowl distorted by a bad mosquito bite; flushed from nuzzling the salivating dog. While imploring Exley's advances, plainly summed him up as a poor thing. The low estimate had nothing to do with her yearning to be chosen and thus brought into existence. Judging him a poor thing, she would yet have married him and given him a devoted form of hell. Exley knew it. They had mutely agreed on the elements, if not the outcome.

As ever, his thoughts drawn by pathos; his imagination captured, when it might have been fired.

Mornings were crystalline, the mountain majestic. News from Europe was dark and pinched: they feared another winter like the last, no fuel, little food. A friend at Swindon wrote to thank Exley for a food package: "The corned beef saved us, actually."

Exley told Miss Xavier, "England is living out of tins."

Late in October, there was da Silva's wedding. Arriving one morning, Exley found an envelope on his desk. He was invited, in raised silver letters, to attend the wedding of Mercedes Prata and Jeronymo da Silva at the Catholic church near Happy Valley on a Saturday afternoon. A similar envelope was propped on Miss Xavier's table. The head of the office, Colonel Glazebrook, had also been asked. Just these three.

Exley left his acceptance on da Silva's desk at the same moment as Glazebrook brought his own regrets—appearing in the doorway cap in hand, for he was off to the airfield to meet a brigadier: "My best to your good lady."

The day before the wedding, Exley said to Rita Xavier: "If you're going to da Silva's wedding—"

"I don't think so."

He feared she intended to snub da Silva. "I was going to say we might go together." When she did not reply, he added earnestly, "Miss Xavier—forgive me—I hope you'll go."

"Captain Exley," said Rita Xavier, "I have no need to condescend to Jeronymo da Silva."

"You mean that I do. That I do condescend."

"You intend to be kind. But just—so far." Small, delicate chopping gesture; hands reclasped.

She was on to him, of course. He had never sought da Silva's company; strongly suspected da Silva to be boring. But he would go to the wedding and count himself a decent chap for giving up an hour of his far from precious Saturday. And was eager to enlist others in this undemanding humanity.

He would have said, "You're right," but the realization might appear too swift.

She said, "Since you mind, then, I'll come." Ironic or resigned.

Monica told him: "As Nanny used to say, there'll be tears before bedtime."

On Saturday, Exley took Rita Xavier to Happy Valley in a downpour. Rain rocked the cab, and drenched them as they ran for the church. They were shown to a forward pew, where Rita sank at once to her knees and Exley took short breaths of church air heavy with incense and tuberoses, and with emanations from the mold that streaked the apse. In the half-dark, Oriental women under hats of

Western tulle turned to see them. Da Silva, pin-striped and atremble, stood by the altar. A pin-striped brother was best man.

Lights went up to the music of an organ, and the congregation stood. A priest appealed to God in the tone, at once mechanical and unctuous, of a cabaret crooner. The Latin seemed bizarre, but Latin has many nationalities.

The bride was rising from her knees.

In front of Exley, a heavy woman was showing fear of thunder.

The bride's veil was being raised. Her hand, inert, was linked with da Silva's. In the curio shops of Queen's Road there were armies of just such ivory Madonnas: an impassivity not quite Christian.

The priest resumed his colonial Latin, in which the congregation joined. Peter Exley, from Australia, was the only European.

After the ceremony the bride and groom stood in the portico. The bride's right hand, in tight white glove, repeatedly touched her throat. There were dark depressions below her eyes. Above her head, the veil was bunched like mosquito net. Her father was crying. Exley hardly knew how, in the circumstances, to congratulate da Silva; but did so heartily, and was introduced all round.

How often one could be both moved and bored at the same time.

When the rain let up, the guests stood in a muddy enclosure outside the church, dodging drops from the trees. Photographs were taken, during which the women laughed with nervous constraint, dabbing away raindrops and tears. There was a general shy deference to Peter Exley, as if he in some way presided; and modified homage to Rita Xavier. It was clear that Rita had gained, at least in the short run, from appearing with Exley, and that for the moment they made some kind of couple.

Da Silva thanked him too much for coming. They would all have a better time when he was gone.

Crunching on sodden gravel toward a taxi, Exley invited Rita Xavier for a drink.

They sat in the upstairs gallery of a small café off Wellington Street. Below them, in the pit, there was a smoky crowd. Youth and uniforms recalled the time of war, but there was none of war's suspense. In wartime one was always expecting a finality that peace, achieved, could not provide: in a place like this there would have been the hopeful songs—"When the Lights Go On Again" or "There's a great day dawning." When dawn came, it seemed all Europe had died in the night.

Rita Xavier put back her hair, and it fell behind her shoulders. The crown of her head was beaded with rain. Her silk dress was patterned with small roses, and the gold cross hung at her throat.

She said, "This is pleasant."

He hoped she wasn't going to be appreciative. He'd had enough of humility for the time being.

Exley had a glass of whiskey. Coffee came in a white crock. In the pit below, the officers sat in groups of three or four, without women. There was a wet-weather crowd of Chinese couples, but no families.

"What happened to you in the war?" It had never occurred to him before to ask her this off-duty question.

"We moved to my uncle's place at Macao. People left here, if they could, after the Japanese came. We thought there would be air raids, another bombardment."

She would have been in her early twenties then. A family of pious girls, hiding from soldiers.

"Many Chinese left, too, for the countryside." Her cup nursed in both hands, an unfamiliar gesture in this climate. "Of course, this island was never empty. But when there's fear, there's a kind of emptiness—no liveliness . . ." She looked in her cup, seeking her right to a complex notion.

"I know," said Exley. "Silence falls."

"So—we were at Macao. Portugal being neutral, Macao had many refugees." She was younger, talking of her youth, her hair about her shoulders; her good silk dress and silky skin. On cheeks and brow, the tiny moles or sunspots were not displeasing. "We were crowded into my uncle's house. We missed our home. There was loneliness, but no privacy. A small thing to complain of in a war."

The five girls—and the male presence in which they ate, washed, dressed, undressed. "You have four sisters, if I'm right?"

"Only two." Surprised.

"And both are nuns?"

"One is a nun. The other is married and has children."

Below the balcony where they sat, the pianist was taking his seat. Looking over the railing, Rita said, "He's Russian." She ate a little dod of cake, Chinese translation of the scone. "His parents live in Shanghai. When the Communists take over, what will they do? They fled once, where can they go now, having no passport?" She said, "Stateless people cannot even become refugees."

The pianist was playing Chopin. Rita said, "He himself has a French wife." After a hesitation, went on, "She's old, an invalid. Some say mad."

"So he married a nationality."

Slight, sad smile; suggestion of a shrug. "Some people marry a fortune, some marry social standing. And some a passport."

Such people must pick up any nationality going. They could not expect to enjoy national pride, or other dangerous convictions of birthright.

Now, from the piano, it was Cole Porter. Exley ate a Chinese scone. The piano was quietude itself, after the blare of Rysom's gramophone. He said this to Rita, adding a few words about his life at the barracks: the incautious relief of telling about oneself, not indulged for a long time.

There had been loneliness, but no privacy.

She asked, "But can't you get away from that?"

"Yes, I must push harder for a different room." She was right, of course, but disappointing. Women's sympathy should be complete, untainted by the reproach of common sense.

The pianist had come round again to his first number.

She asked, "What's that song?"

"It's an étude by Chopin."

"I thought there was a song."

"You're right, someone put words to it. 'Deep in the Night,' something like that."

" 'So Deep Is the Night.' " In a low, tuneful voice she sang some phrases: " 'No moon tonight, no friendly star to guide me with its light . . .' " The occasion had gone to her head, tinging her cheek-bones a tipsy pink. " 'Be still my heart . . .' "

Her very hands looked unpracticed in the actions of love.

The pianist was on to Rachmaninoff: "The Floods of Spring."

"I should leave soon." She perhaps felt she had shown excitement, and lapsed into apathy or reticence. He saw that the afternoon's mild pleasure had occurred to her as a source of possible trouble.

The return to guardedness offended him—this countering of a possibility so slight. The afternoon, leading nowhere, had yet possessed its particle of valid life; and she herself had said, "With fear, there is no liveliness." Well, Rita, he thought, are you alive or dead?

Soon, however, fairness rolled over him again, like fog, and he applied the question to himself. Evasion, after all, took many forms: in her, repressiveness; and, in himself, the general amnesty for human-kind.

He said, "I suppose da Silva's reception is in full spate." The wedding was by now a memory, dankly streaked with green.

"Oh yes. There are two or three places where those things are held. The families expect it. It would be impossible to do anything different, of one's own."

He supposed her sister had toed the line.

It occurred to him how few choices she had—intermarriage in the small community; or the convent. Or the marginal position in the arid, ill-paid office. And he thought of all the girls, fastidious and intelligent, who had shed their bloom and developed their defenses, like Rita.

As they went out he was greeted here and there from the crowd. In a dim mirror saw himself—stooping, tall, with faded khaki strokes of uniform and hair; and Rita beside him, subdued in the noisy scene.

Rita lived with her parents on the mainland. She and Exley strolled down Ice House Street, heading for the ferry. The footpath was too narrow for them both, and Peter Exley walked in the puddled road. Rita said, "Thank you for urging me to come."

Her indifference to da Silva's wedding might now be seen in a new light. Exley said, "It's taken me all this time to like the place."

"And now you do?"

"Well enough." He felt he should enlarge this revelation, but let it stand.

The next wedding invitation was from the Glazebrooks, who were giving, in raised gold letters, cocktails at the club on the occasion of the royal marriage. Colonel Glazebrook's good lady, ethereally fair and interestingly young, was said to have been an actress or model. Exley had sometimes seen the Glazebrooks in the street, arm in arm. A previous good lady had been bettered.

Before the party, Exley had to go to the parade ground, where guns were fired for the far-off princess—whose photograph in that morning's paper had shown her buxom, bridal, smiling: bedecked for lineal procreation.

It was November, but summer flared that day for the last time. On beaten sand the men marched in the heat, saffron kilts swirling, blue bonnets undulant. Complex formations intersected, to a barbaric skirl of pipes. "Flowers of the Forest" was played, and "Hearts of Oak." The climactic anthem brought collective rigidity, followed by slow dispersal.

There was one incident only. During the parade, a huge soldier fainted, left in the sun on the ground until taken up with other debris when all was over. The misadventure enlivened the hot watching—the show of precision having created, in onlookers, a desire for some conspicuous error. The image of this collapsed soldier—pleats rucked up on raised belly, pale knees awry—lingered with Peter Exley as he walked down to the club. A discarded man, like the bole of an uprooted tree. By disowning and dishonoring the failure, authority had transformed it to an assertion.

The Glazebrooks' party was held in an upstairs room at the annex. There were flowers, long windows, and a floor of polished teak. Mrs. G., in fragile dress, stood near the door. As Exley arrived she drew him aside: "Do something about that potted palm and I'm your slave." Exley slid a ficus in its brass cachepot over glossy boards, and looked back for her approval. She blew him a kiss, lifting a lacy sleeve. She was called Hermione: fair curls, a red laughing mouth, and the loose, pale dress with lavender ribbons.

When people were spontaneous, Peter Exley was ready to love them.

Monica and Brenda stationed themselves each side of Exley, a brace of female warders. Planning escape, he got a boy to bring Gimlets. He knew the women would refer to his afternoon with Rita; and, when they did so, said, "Don't be daft."

The Colonel came up. "Who are you daft over now, girls?"

"Peter's potty about Miss Xavier."

Glazebrook said, "Miss Xavier. Ah. Miss Xavier is serious. There would be no trifling with Miss Xavier."

The women howled, as if this were witty. As their sputtering subsided, Glazebrook went on, "And now I must tear myself from you charmers." As he and Exley drew away, he made a low, sighing sound. "Poor clots. Can't stand em, frankly."

The room filled up with older officers and their wives, and with the young unwed. There were also the merchants and bankers, the bishop, the harbormaster. The Colonial Secretary might look in, on his way to something grander. All the blotched statues, restored to their pedestals. The French consul, known to be the Sûreté man, arrived with pretty daughter. The actors doubled their parts—villain in one scene, bystander in another. The same few players represented a crowd, the same sparse voices called for Caesar.

Exley took his leave of blond Hermione: "That's a pretty dress."

"Thank God you like it. My husband says it looks like underwear."

"Then you must have lovely underwear."

"Famous for it." Laughing into his eyes.

Exley, at her side, basked in the little flirtation. As he admired her dress, however, it struck him that she might be pregnant; and the idea, with its utter exclusion, drained his good spirits. He had already turned from her when Glazebrook himself came to ask his wife if she would like something fetched for her, food or drink. At her refusal, the husband murmured, in the amused undertone of love, "You're supposed to have cravings. Don't you crave anything?"

And her laughing soft reply: "Only your indulgence."

When he left the party, Exley walked along in the night, thinking of Hermione—imagining some Hermione, animated, charming, and quite without pathos, who might be his own. And why, he wondered, should she be merely without pathos? Since she was in any case a figment, let her be downright lucky. He laughed unhappily, sounding drunker than he was. It was long since he had given affection or received it. He seemed to have dribbled away a lot of feeling in a kind of running sensibility, like a bad cold.

He sometimes had dreams of tenderness in love, as others might dream of its eroticism.

He passed through the green marble arcade that led to the best hotels. There was a dance floor up red-carpeted stairs. And here he found a table, ordered a Tom Collins, and sat watching the dancers and tapping his foot abstractedly. It seemed an age since the military scene at the parade ground. He could scarcely recall now the huge soldier collapsed among his marching comrades.

In the emotional befuddlement of a third drink, he suddenly spotted Rysom among the dancers. Rysom in civilian clothes—orange jacket, clean white shirt, and a tie forked with emerald lightning—was trundling a heavy woman round the floor, while the band played "La Vie en Rose" and the lights turned pink. It was Rysom all right, even if his expression—earnest to the point of urgency—was unfamiliar. Nothing in Rysom's account of himself had suggested he might at last be found in this established and expensive place, intently circulating in the dance.

The emergence of Roy Rysom at the center of the very vortex that he himself derided was disquieting. In taking Rysom more literally, or more sincerely, than Rysom took himself, Peter Exley might have been left behind yet again in the general stampede to safety. Exley had imagined he knew at least who Rysom was. Now it appeared that Rysom had stolen a march on him by unabashedly having things both ways. He and Rysom had agreed on one another's debility. Now Rysom had broken faith.

When the cold weather came, after Christmas, it surprised less by severity than by its effect of clearing the air. Looking across the strait, you now saw, as if from a great height, the interior life of the mainland: grouped habitations, laborious paddies, serpentine paths, and the smoke of small necessary fires. There was the detailed foreground; far off, the forms and colors of other, unsuspected hills; and to the north, like a signal, the mountain called Tai Mo Shan.

Such a place must hold revelations, if one only had the nerve to elicit them.

The island itself was less fictitious now, newly populated by quilted crowds, newly smelling at dusk of charcoal and wood smoke. You were no longer out from Europe or out from anywhere, but drawn inward to a continent. You approached, so Peter Exley thought, the immense reality, or your own acceptance of it. One January night, passing under the arcades—where, beside shops selling chocolate truffles and crystallized fruits, small families had set braziers on the flagstones—Exley realized there was nowhere he would prefer to be. In those moments he was not dissatisfied, and that fact itself was happiness; for he was aware that his desires, if examined, might be considered exorbitant.

The intense cold lasted little more than a month. With the Chinese New Year, which fell that year on Shrove Tuesday, the days became less revelatory. Visibility departed like hallucination, in light that, however beautiful, was charged with returning heat. And you drew away again, from cold China, cold Russia; from that interlude of climatic seriousness in which normality had seemed a spiritual condition.

Exley said to Rita Xavier: "Perhaps cold places really are more self-respecting, as one is taught to believe."

"One is taught to believe that," she said, "only in cold places."

"Not in my own case. We looked to the cold north for instruction. North was the place to be." The indelible equatorial ring on the huge tub of the world. He said, "There's something in it, after all. Heat, if immoderate, debilitates. If enjoyable, it encourages silliness." Her look was politely neutral. Since he was talking to himself anyway, he supplied her side of the dialogue: "Hard to strike a balance."

He wished to declare his identity, for, by maintaining her defenses, Rita appeared to class him with the Brenda girls and all the rest. What would become of Rita Xavier without defenses he did not pretend to foresee. The coffee outing, repeated once or twice, had come to nothing. Attempts to deliver something of his soul miscarried, but Exley returned to them—because he could not help believing in the sensibility of wounded persons. Or because he could not leave well enough alone.

One Saturday in spring, Peter Exley was walking toward Queen's Road. In the course of afternoon errands he had been to the post office and was now headed for the tailor. At the corner he ran into Rita, about to cross. She was going to the King's Theatre. After weeks of Margaret Lockwood, there was a new film—hours long, Chinese.

They stood in the shade under a scaffolding. Everything was in repair now, hung with straw flaps, framed by bamboo rods. Gray stucco was blotched with white. The air was granulated dust, with plaster smells of some great prosperity astir.

"Would you mind if I joined you?"

She said, "It doesn't begin till four."

They stood aside from the crowd, and from all that noisy life they might have liked to join—if they could do so just occasionally and set their terms.

Rita said, "I was going to have something to eat. I've had no lunch." There was a restaurant in the theatre, one flight up.

"I'm on my way to the tailor." He pointed out the sign: "Old Bond's Treat." She did not smile, but agreed to meet him in the restaurant ten minutes later.

Beside a shop that sold materials, shabby stairs led to the tailor's door. This door, usually open, was today closed and locked. Exley rapped on the frosted glass. A Chinese in American clothes, coming from the floor above, smiled in passing and made a gesture to his head.

Exley asked, "What's wrong?"

The youth, surprised, replied in Cantonese: "Liu isn't working today."

"Is he there?"

The tailor lived in the shop with his wife and child. Exley had never seen the woman, although the little girl sometimes ran out from behind a plywood partition, and could often be heard prattling or crying there. He had been told the wife was kept in seclusion. Rysom had said, "He's got the old trouble-and-strife in purdah.'

The man on the stairs said, "Yes. But not working." Another smile, another gesture of seersucker sleeve.

"I only have to collect a package."

The man passed on down the stairs. Exley thought how puzzling they were, even such small encounters with the unfamiliar. Recalling his arrangement with Rita Xavier, he was about to leave, when there was the sound of a bolt slowly drawn, and a shadow blurred the glass. When he tried the door again, it opened.

The tailor's wife was standing just inside. She wore the black clothes of an amah, jacket and pantaloons. On the crown of her head the braids were coiled and lacquered in a formal structure contrasting with her primitive commotion of expression. Exley had never seen a more afflicted face. He crossed the threshold. The windows were covered by rattan blinds, and the room smelt vilely of opium and uncleanness. Liu, lying sideways on a bench where customers usually sat, gave Exley an anesthetized smile.

Exley said to the woman, "Is he ill?" He could not understand her grief: it was as if she wept without sound or tears. He said, "Tell me."

She motioned him to the partition. Behind it, in household clutter, a child was lying on an arrangement of clothes and rags. He knew this must be Liu's daughter, but could not recognize the sunken face—or the tiny, diminished body, perfectly still, head turned at an angle, showing a small gold hoop through the ear. Mouth slackly open, eyes closed. Exley thought, The child is dead.

Seeing his thought, the woman spoke for the first time. At the same moment, Exley saw the girl draw breath. He said, "What about a doctor, what about the hospital?" and, squatting down, lifted the child a little. The limbs resettled like wayward sticks. There was an aroused stench of untended illness. He asked, "How many days?"

The woman now began to weep aloud, kneeling by the child but not touching it, rocking her own head in her hands. Exley saw that she herself was merely adolescent—a daughter, possibly, of the sampan people, traded off at puberty: so small in her black garments, and yet with a child of her own. The human frame was often, to him, incommensurate with all it must evince and bear.

He said, "I'll get help."

He went out, ran down the stairs. From the shop there was a loud wrangle of negotiation, and the thump of bolts of cloth. Exley crossed to the King's Theatre. The bright, coherent world resumed—all color, animation, and indifference. In the busy restaurant upstairs Rita Xavier was eating, with chopsticks, small gobbets from a bowl.

He came up to her: "Rita."

She said at once, "What's wrong?" And he saw that his tunic was marked with the child's sickness.

"Would you help me?" He sat on the edge of a chair and explained: a curious moment, in which he knew all that the next few minutes would contain. And, as he was speaking, noted her relaxation of alarm and recovery of detachment. He thought, She feels I should not mix up in it. He said, "I can't let the child die"—to compel her, or justify himself; and in either case, as he felt, unworthily.

"It may die, whatever you do."

He asked, "Will the public-health people come?"

"One must take the child to them, to the hospital." Then she said, "Even for you, they would not come"—defining, with that imperial You, the distance between them.

It would have to be the troublesome act of humanity, or nothing. He started to ask, "Will you help me persuade the mother?" But said instead, "Will you excuse me, then?" And got up.

She also stood, resigned and nearly ironic as when they had discussed da Silva's wedding; making clear she considered Peter Exley self-deluding—he who did the one excited thing, rather than the thousand daily others. On this occasion he met her knowingness unconvinced. And began then and there to forget her.

He took her bill and paid the cashier. Going out, they were trapped in the exodus from the previous showing of the film. Just below them on the crowded stairs was Brenda Mills.

Exley said, "Brenda." Throwing Rita over.

Brenda made a champing motion with her jaws. "Don't speak to me."

He stared.

She said, "They stole my handbag. When I got up for the anthem." Flushed to a color like claret, quivering near tears. "One of these swine," she said. "During 'God Save the King.' The vileness. Don't speak to me."

Exley left them together. Pushed his way from the King's Theatre, and crossed the street without waiting for a change of light. While Brenda was saying, "Nothing of value, it's not that," and Rita was silently praying not for pardon but excuse, Exley was already on the dirty stairs that led to Liu's door. He returned to the foul-smelling room, to its certainties, with relief. In addition, there was the sense of familiarity: hardship is never quite alien.

He sat again on the floor and supported the child on his knees. The head lolled as before, showing the irrelevant earring. The bed, improvised from remnants of material, was all plaids and florals, and striped shirtings. He saw that the child's mother, even in her despair, was disturbed—like the rest—by his improbable behavior. Mistrustful of a sudden change for the better. He understood this perfectly. He was also aware his intervention might go wrong, and was pretty sure of being blamed somewhere along the line. All of this seemed a small price to pay for health.

It was his own health he had in mind, his long convalescence over.

While Brenda was complaining to the management and Rita stood irresolute at the curb, and Roy Rysom somewhere was exposing civilization for a fraud, Peter Exley was only acknowledging the simple truth. This is generally called a revelation.

He told the woman what he meant to do. She cried out to him in a dialect he could hardly understand, and he let her speak while he considered what came next. He thought about the taxi ride, and wondered if Liu's wife had ever ridden in a car. These moments passed, and the child lay against him, still animate, valuable, and part of prodigious being.

He thought with relief of the hospital. He had forgotten there would be people to help him.

"All right, then," he said in English. "Time to go."

Yarrow

•

—— **JOYCE CAROL OATES** ——

*Joyce Carol Oates lives in Princeton, New Jersey, where she teaches at
the university and helps edit* The Ontario Review. *Her most recent
novel is* You Must Remember This *(E. P. Dutton). "Yarrow" will be
included in her next collection of short stories,* Blue Skies. *She has
previously appeared in the* O. Henry Prize Stories *collections.*

He was afraid to borrow the money from a bank.

It was a Saturday morning in early April, still winter, soft wet snow
falling, clumps the size of blossoms.

A messy season, flu season, dirt-raddled snow drifted against the
edges of things, mud thawing on the roads. A cavernous-clouded sky
and blinding sunshine and it was the longest drive he'd made in his
truck in memory, three miles to his cousin Tyrone Clayton's house.

Tyrone saw it in his face. Asked him inside, asked him did he want
an ale?—Irene and the children were in town shopping.

The radio was turned up loud: Fats Domino singing "Blueberry
Hill."

Mud on Jody's boots, so he said he wouldn't come all the way into
the house, he'd talk from the doorway. Didn't want to track up Irene's
clean floor.

He could only stay a minute, he said. He had a favor to ask.

"Sure," Tyrone said. Laying his cigarette carefully in an ashtray.

"I need to borrow some money."

"How much?"

"Five hundred dollars."

Jody spoke in a low quick voice just loud enough for Tyrone to hear. Then exhaled as if he'd been holding his breath in for a long time.

Tyrone said, keeping his voice level and easy, "Guess I can manage that."

"I'll pay you back as soon as I can," Jody said. "By June at the latest."

"No hurry," Tyrone said.

Then they were silent. Breathing hard. Excited, deeply embarrassed. Tyrone knew that Jody needed more than five hundred dollars —much more than five hundred dollars—but the way things were right now he couldn't afford to lend him more. He just couldn't afford it and even five hundred dollars was going to be hard. He knew that Jody knew all this but Jody had had to come to him anyway, knowing it, asking the favor, knowing that Tyrone would say yes but knowing that Tyrone could barely afford it either. Because Jody was desperate and if Tyrone hadn't quite wanted to understand that until this minute he had to understand it now.

His cousin's young, aggrieved, handsome face inside that sallow face blurred and pocked by fatigue. Three days' growth of whiskers on his chin and he wouldn't meet Tyrone's eyes—he was that ashamed.

Tyrone said he could get to the bank Monday noon, would that be soon enough?

Jody said as if he hadn't been listening that he wanted to pay the going rate of interest on the loan. "Ask them at the bank, will you?— and we'll work it out."

"Hell no," Tyrone said, laughing, surprised. "I don't want any interest."

"Just find out," Jody said, an edge to his voice, "and we'll work it out."

Tyrone asked how was Brenda these days, he'd heard from Irene she was getting better? But his voice came out weak and faltering.

Jody said she *was* getting better, she rested a lot during the day, the stitches from the surgery had come out but she still had a lot of pain and the doctor warned them about rushing things, so she had to take it slow.

He did the grocery shopping, for instance. All the shopping. Not that he minded—he didn't—he was damned glad Brenda was alive—but it took time and he only had Saturdays really.

Then this afternoon if the snow didn't get worse he was hoping to put in a shift at the quarry, three or four hours. Shoveling mainly, some clean-up—

He was speaking faster, with more feeling. A raw baffled voice new to him and his eyes puffy and red-rimmed as if he'd been rubbing at them.

All this while Jody's truck was idling in the driveway, spewing out clouds of exhaust. He'd left the key in the ignition, which Tyrone thought was a strange thing to do, almost rude.

Snowflakes were falling thicker now, blown in delicate skeins by the wind. Twisting and turning and looping like narrowing your eyes to shift your vision out of focus so that it's your own nerve-endings you see out there.

Wet air, colder than the temperature suggested. Flu season and everybody was passing it around to everybody else.

Something more needed to be said before Jody left but Tyrone couldn't think what it was.

He stood in the doorway watching Jody maneuver the truck out onto the road. It was a heavy-duty dump truck, Jody's own truck, a '49 Ford he'd have to be replacing soon. Tyrone was thinking they should have shaken hands or something but it wasn't a gesture that came naturally or easily to them. He couldn't remember when he had last shaken hands with somebody close to him as Jody and this morning wasn't the time to start.

He watched Jody drive away. He hadn't gotten around to shaving yet that morning himself and he stood vague and dazed, rubbing his stubbled jaw, thinking how much it had cost Jody McIllvanney to ask for that five hundred dollars, and how much it would cost him.

For the past year or more Jody's wife Brenda had been sick. Twenty-eight years old, thin, nervous, red-haired, pretty, she'd had four children now ranging in age from Dawn, who was thirteen years old and said to be troublesome, to the baby boy, who was only eighteen months. In between were two more boys, ten years and six years. Brenda had never quite recovered from the last pregnancy, came down with a bladder infection, had to have an operation just after Christmas —at a city hospital forty miles away, which meant people in Yarrow had to drive eighty miles round-trip to see her. Which meant, too, more medical bills the McIllvanneys couldn't afford.

The day before she was scheduled to enter the hospital, Brenda spoke with Irene Clayton on the phone and said she was frightened she was going to die.

"Don't talk that way," Irene said sharply.

Brenda was crying as if her heart were broken and Irene was afraid she too would start to cry.

"I just don't think Jody could manage without me," Brenda was saying. "Him and the children—and all the bills we owe—I just don't think he could keep going."

"You know better than to talk that way," Irene said. "That's a terrible thing to say." She listened to Brenda crying and felt helpless and frightened herself. She said, "You hadn't better let Jody hear you going on like that."

The McIllvanneys lived in Brenda's parents' old farmhouse, which wasn't by choice but all they could afford. Some years ago Jody had started building his own house at the edge of town but he ran out of money shortly after the basement was finished—Jody was a trucker, self-employed; his work tended to be local, seasonal, not very reliable —and for more than a year the family lived in the basement, below-ground. (The roof was tar-papered over and there were windows but still the big single room was damp, chilly, depressing—the children were always coming down with colds. Dawn called it a damn dumb place to live, no wonder the kids on the school bus laughed at them all. Living like rats in a hole!) After Brenda's mother died they moved into the old farmhouse, which was free and clear, no mortgage, except it had been built in the 1880's and was termite-ridden and needed repairs constantly. Rotting shingles—leaky roof—earthen cellar that flooded when it rained: you name it. Bad as the Titanic, Jody said. He wished the damn thing *would* sink.

When Brenda got pregnant for the fourth time Jody began working part-time at the limestone quarry in Yarrow Falls: hard, filthy, back-breaking work he hated but it paid better than anything else he could find and he didn't have to join a union. Jody handled a shovel, he climbed ladders, he operated drills and tractors and wire-saws; when it rained he stood in the pit water to his knees. Coughing up phlegm, his feet aching as if they were on fire. Just temporary work he hoped wouldn't kill him.

Worse yet, he told Tyrone, he might develop a taste for the quarry. Like most of the quarriers. The limestone, the open fresh air, the weird machines that were so noisy and dangerous—it was work not just anybody could do. You had to have a strong back and the guts for it and anything like that, it tended to get under your skin if you weren't careful. It brought some pride with it after all.

The Clayton children Janice and Bobby were fond of their Uncle Jody—as they were taught to call him: Janice knew he was really a cousin of theirs, just as he was a cousin of their father's—except when he was in one of his bad moods. Then he wouldn't really look at them, he'd just mutter hello without smiling. He had a worse temper than their father and he was a bigger man than their father—muscled arms and shoulders that looked as if they were pumped up and that the flesh would hurt, ropy veins and skin stretched tight. But he could be funny —loud-laughing as a kid—with a broad side-slanting grin and a way of teasing that left you breathless and excited as if you'd been tickled with quick hard fingers. Their own father was lean and hard and soft-spoken; an inch or two shorter than his cousin. He worked at the Allis-Chalmers plant in town and never had anything interesting to say about it—just that it was *work,* and it *paid*—while Jody had all sorts of tales, some believable and some not, about driving his truck. Never a dull minute with Jody around! Irene always said. Tyrone said that was true but—"You know how he exaggerates."

One summer when Janice was a small child her Uncle Jody came over to the house with a half-dozen guinea chicks in a cardboard box, a present for them, and Janice had loved the chicks tiny enough to stand in the palm of her hand—they didn't weigh anything! No feathers like the adults, just fuzzy blond down, stubby wings and legs disproportionately long for their bodies. They were fearless, unlike the adults that were so suspicious and nerved-up all the time.

"They're pretty birds," Jody said. "I like seeing them around the place—you get kind of used to them."

The Claytons tried to raise the guinea fowl according to Jody's instructions but they died off one by one and in the end even Janice lost her enthusiasm for them. She'd given them special names—Freckles, Peewee, Queenie, Bathsheba—but they disappointed her because all they wanted to do was eat.

They only liked her, she said, because she fed them.

After Jody borrowed the five hundred dollars from Tyrone he didn't drop by the house for a long time. And Tyrone didn't seek him out, feeling embarrassed and uncomfortable: he didn't want Jody to think he was waiting to be paid back or even that he was thinking about the money.

(Was he thinking about it? Only occasionally, when it hit him like a blow to the gut.)

Irene didn't hear from Brenda very often either, which was strange, she said, and sad, and she hoped the money wouldn't come between them because Brenda was so sweet and such a good friend and needed somebody to talk to, what with Jody and Jody's moods—and that Dawn was a handful too, judging from what Janice said. (Dawn was a year older than Janice but in her class at school.) Irene said, "Why don't we invite them over here for supper or something?—we haven't done that in a long time." But Tyrone thought the McIllvanneys might misunderstand. "He'll think I'm worried about that money," Tyrone said.

It wasn't until midsummer that Jody made what he called the first payment on the loan, one hundred and seventy-five dollars he gave Tyrone in an envelope, and Tyrone was relieved, and embarrassed, and tried to tell him why not keep it for a while since probably he needed it —didn't he need it?—and there wasn't any hurry anyway. But Jody insisted. Jody said it was the least he could do.

Then: word got back to Tyrone that Jody had borrowed money from a mutual friend of theirs at about the time he'd borrowed the five hundred dollars from Tyrone *and he had paid all of it back.* Three hundred and fifty dollars and he'd paid all of it back in a lump sum and Tyrone was damned mad to hear about it and Irene tried to tell him it didn't mean anything, only that Jody knew Tyrone better, was closer to Tyrone, like a brother; also if he'd only borrowed three hundred and fifty dollars from the other man it was easier to pay it all back and close out the debt. Sure, said Tyrone. That makes me the chump.

But he didn't mean it and when a few days later, or a week later, Irene brought the subject up again, wondering when Jody was going to pay the rest of the money, he cut her off short saying it was his money, not hers, and it was between him and Jody and hadn't anything to do with her, did she understand that?

Janice didn't want to tell her mother but: when they went back to school in the fall Dawn McIllvanney began to behave mean to her. And Dawn could be really mean when she wanted to be.

She was a chunky, thickset girl, swarthy skin like her father's, sly eyes, a habit of grinning so it went through you like a sliver of glass—not a bit of friendliness in it. Called Janice *"Jan*-y" in a sliding whine and shoved her on the school bus or when they were waiting in the cafeteria line, "Oh excuse me, *Jan*-y!" she'd say, making anyone who was listening laugh. Dawn was the center of a circle of four or five girls who were rough and pushy and loud, belligerent as boys; she got poor grades in school not because she was stupid—though she might have been a little slow—but because she made a show of not trying, not handing in homework, wising off in class and angering her teachers. Janice thought it was unfair that Dawn McIllvanney had such a pretty red-haired mother while she had a mother who was like anybody's mother—plain and pleasant and boring. She'd always thought, before the trouble started, that Brenda McIllvanney would rather have had *her* for a daughter than Dawn.

Janice soon understood that Dawn hated her and she'd better keep her distance from her but it happened that in gym class she couldn't and that was where Dawn got her revenge: threw a basketball right into Janice's face one time, broke Janice's pink plastic glasses, claimed afterward it was an accident—*"Jan-y"* got in her way. Another time, when the girls were doing gymnastics, Dawn stuck her big, sneakered foot out in front of Janice as Janice—who was wiry and quick, one of the best gymnasts in the class—did a series of cartwheels the full length of the mat, and naturally Janice fell, fell sideways, fell hard, seeing as she fell her cousin's face pinched with hatred, the rat-glittering little eyes. Pain shot like a knife, like many knives, through Janice's body and for a long time she couldn't move—just lay there sobbing, hearing Dawn McIllvanney's mock-incredulous voice as the gym instructor reprimanded her, *Hey I didn't do anything, what the hell are you saying, look it was her, she's the one, it was her own damn fault, the little crybaby—*

Janice never told her mother about the incident. She tried not to think that Dawn, who was her cousin after all, had wanted to hurt her really—break her neck or her backbone, cripple her for life. She tried not to think that.

One warm autumn day Irene Clayton met Brenda McIllvanney in the A&P in town—Brenda whom she hadn't seen in months—Brenda who was thin, almost gaunt, but wearing a flowery print dress—red lipsticked lips and hard red nails and a steely look that went through Irene like a razor. And Irene just stood there staring as if the earth had opened at her feet.

In her parked car in the lot Irene leaned her forehead against the steering wheel and began to cry. She made baffled sobbing sounds that astonished and deeply embarrassed the children—Janice and Bobby had never seen their mother cry in such a public place, and for so little reason they could understand. She usually wept in a rage at them!

Bobby threw himself against the back seat, pressing his hands over his ears. Janice, in the passenger's seat, looked out the window and said, "Momma, you're making a fool of yourself," in the coldest voice possible.

Tyrone wasn't accustomed to thinking about such things, poking into his own motives, or other people's. But he'd known, he said. As soon as he'd handed Jody the money, that was it.

Irene said she didn't believe it.

She knew Brenda, and she knew Jody, and she didn't believe it.

Jody had thanked him but he hadn't wanted to look at him, Tyrone said. Took the money 'cause he couldn't not take it but that was that.

"I don't believe it *really,*" Irene said, wiping at her eyes.

Tyrone said nothing, lighting up a cigarette, shaking out the match. His movements were jerky and angry these days, these many days. Often it looked as if he was quarreling with someone under his breath. Irene said, "I don't believe it *really.*"

Jody sold his truck, gave up trucking for good, worked full-time now at the limestone quarry, still in debt, and that old house of theirs looked worse than ever—chickens and guinea fowl picking in the grassless front yard amid tossed-out trash, Brenda's peony beds overgrown with weeds as if no woman lived in the house at all—but still—somehow—Jody managed to buy a '53 Chevrolet up in Yarrow Falls; and he and Brenda were going out places together again, roadhouses and taverns miles away where no one knew them. Sometimes they were alone and sometimes they were with another couple. Their old friends rarely saw them now.

Tyrone was always hearing from relatives that the McIllvanneys couldn't seem to climb out of their bad luck though Jody was working ten, twelve hours a day at the quarry, etcetera; poor Brenda had some kind of thyroid condition now and had to take medicine so expensive you couldn't believe it, etcetera; and Tyrone listened ironically to all this and said, "O.K. but what about me?—*what about me?*" And there never seemed to be any answer to that.

If Tyrone ran into Jody in town it was sheerly by accident. And damned clumsy and embarrassing: Jody pretended he didn't see Tyrone, turned nonchalantly away, whistling, hands in his pockets, turned a corner and walked fast and disappeared.

Asshole. As if Tyrone didn't see *him.*

Tyrone complained freely of his cousin to anyone who would listen, old friends, mutual acquaintances, strangers. He was baffled and bitter and hurt and furious, wondering aloud when he'd get his money back. And would he get it *with interest* as Jody had promised.

When he'd been drinking a bit Tyrone said that nobody had ever thought Jody McIllvanney would turn out the way he had—a man whose word wasn't worth shit—not much better than a common crook—a man who couldn't even support his wife and children. "Anybody that bad off, he might as well hang himself," Tyrone would say. "Stick a shotgun barrel into his mouth and pull the trigger."

He had to stop thinking about Jody all the time, Irene said. She was getting scared he'd make himself sick.

She'd lain awake too many nights herself thinking about the McIllvanneys—Brenda in particular—and she wasn't going to think about them any longer. "It isn't healthy," she said, pleaded. "Ty?—it eats away at your heart."

But Tyrone ignored her, he was calculating (sitting at the kitchen table, a sheet of paper before him, pencil in hand, bottle of Molson's Ale at his elbow) how much Jody was probably earning a week up at the Falls now that he'd been promoted from shoveler to drill-runner. It made him sick to think that—subtracting union dues, Social Security and the rest—Jody was probably making a few more dollars a week than he made at Allis-Chalmers. And if Jody could get an extra shift time-and-a-half on Saturdays he'd be making a damn sight more.

When Tyrone stood he felt dizzy and panicky, as if the floor was tilting beneath his feet.

Most people in Yarrow were on Tyrone's side but he sensed there were some on Jody's side and lately he'd begun to hear that Jody was saying things about *him*—bad-mouthing him so you'd almost think it was Tyrone Clayton who owed Jody McIllvanney money and not the other way around. Hadn't Jody helped him put asbestos siding on his house when he and Irene had first moved in—? (Yes but he, Tyrone, had helped Jody with that would-be house of his, helping to put in the concrete, lay the beams for the basement ceiling, tar-paper the goddamned roof in the middle of the summer.) Tyrone went out drinking to the places he'd always gone and there were the men he'd been seeing for years, men he'd gone to school with, but Jody wasn't there, there was a queer sort of authority in Jody's absence, as if, the more *he* said, the more his listeners were inclined to believe *Jody.* "I know things are still bad for Jody and Brenda," he'd say, speaking passion-

ately, conscious of the significance of his words—which might be repeated after all to Jody—"and I don't even want the fucking money
back but I do want respect. I do want respect from that son of a
bitch."

(Though in fact he did want the money back: every penny of it.)

(And he tended to think Jody still owed him five hundred dollars,
the original sum, plus interest, no matter he'd insisted at the time of
the loan that he didn't want "interest" from any blood relation.)

There were nights he came home drunk, other nights he was so
agitated he couldn't sit still to eat his supper because he'd heard something at work that day reported to him and Irene tried to comfort him,
Irene said he was frightening the children, Irene said in a pleading
voice, Why not try to forget?—forgive?—like in the Bible?—wasn't
that real wisdom?—and just not lend anybody any money ever again
in his life. "What the hell was I supposed to do?" Tyrone would say,
turning on her furiously. "Tell my own cousin that I grew up with that
I wouldn't help him out? Tell him to get out of that doorway there?"
Irene backed off saying, "Ty, I don't know what you were supposed to
do but it turned out a mistake, didn't it?" And Tyrone said, his face
contorted with rage and his voice shaking, "It wasn't a mistake at the
time, you stupid bitch. *It wasn't a mistake at the time.*"

One night that fall the telephone rang at nine p.m. and Irene answered and it was Jody McIllvanney, whose voice she hadn't heard in
a long time, drunk and belligerent, demanding to speak to Tyrone—
who luckily wasn't home. So Jody told Irene to tell him he'd been
hearing certain things that Tyrone was saying behind his back and he
didn't like what he'd heard and if Tyrone had something to say to him
why not come over to the house and tell it to his face and if Tyrone
was afraid to do that he'd better keep his mouth shut or *he'd* come
over *there* and beat the shit out of Tyrone.

Jody was shouting, saying he'd pay back the goddamn money when
he could, that was the best he could do, he hadn't asked to be born,
that was the best he could do, goddamn it—And Irene, speechless,
terrified, slammed down the receiver.

Afterward she said she'd never heard anyone anywhere sounding so

crazy. Like he'd have killed her if he'd been able to get hold of
her. . . .

A chilly breezy November day but there was Jody McIllvanney in
coveralls and a T-shirt, no jacket, bareheaded, striding along the sidewalk, not looking where he was going: and Janice Clayton stared at
him, shocked at how he'd changed—my God he was big now! almost
what you'd call *fat!*—weighing maybe two hundred sixty pounds, bar-
rel-chested, big jiggly stomach pressing against the fabric of his coveralls, his face bloated too and his skin lumpy. It was said that stone
quarriers ate and drank like hogs, got enormous, and there was Jody
the shape of a human hog, even his hair long and shaggy, greasy, like a
high-school kid or a Hell's Angel. Janice stood frozen on the sidewalk,
her schoolbooks pressed against her chest, hoping, praying, her Uncle
Jody wouldn't glance up and see her or if he did he wouldn't recognize
her though her heart kicked and she thought *I don't hate him like I'm
supposed to.*

But he looked up. He saw her. Saw how she was shrinking out
toward the curb to avoid him and so he let her go, just mumbled a
greeting she couldn't hear, and the moment was past, she was safe, she
pushed her glasses up her nose and half-ran up the street to escape.
She remembered how he used to call out "How's it going?" to her and
Bobby instead of saying hello—winking to show that it was a joke
(what did any adult man care about how things were going for children) but serious in a way too. And she'd never known how to answer,
nor had Bobby. "O.K.," they'd say, embarrassed, blushing, flattered.
"All right I guess."

(Janice had no anticipation, not the mildest of premonitions, that
that would be the last time she'd see her Uncle Jody but long afterward the sight of him would remain vivid in her memory, powerful,
reproachful, and the November day too of gusty winds and the smell
of snow in the air, a texture like grit. Waiting for the bus she was
dreamy and melancholy watching how the town's south-side mills
gave off smoke that rose into the air like mist. Powdery, almost irides-

cent, those subtle shifting colors of the backs of pigeons—iridescent gray, blue, purple shading into black.

The guinea fowl had long since died off but Janice had snapshots of her favorites, their names carefully recorded.)

* * *

Shortly after the New Year Tyrone was driving to town when he saw a man hitchhiking by the side of the road, and sure enough it was Jody McIllvanney—Jody in his sheepskin jacket, a wool cap pulled low over his forehead, thumb uplifted. His face looked closed-in as a fist; he might have recognized Tyrone but gave no sign just as Tyrone, speeding past, gave no sign of recognizing him. It had all happened so swiftly Tyrone hadn't time to react. He wondered if Jody's new car had broken down and he laughed aloud harshly, thinking, Good. Serve him right. Serve them all right.

He watched his cousin's figure in the rearview mirror, diminishing with distance.

Then: for some reason he'd never be able to explain he decided to turn his car around, drive back to Jody; maybe he'd slow down and shout something out the window, or maybe—just maybe—he'd give the son of a bitch a ride if it looked like that might be a good idea. But as he approached Jody it was clear that Jody intended to stand his ground, didn't want any favors from him, you could see from his arrogant stance that he'd rather freeze his ass off than beg a ride from Tyrone: he'd lowered his arm and stood there in the road, legs apart, waiting. A big beefy glowering man you could tell wanted a fight even without knowing who he was.

Tyrone's heart swelled with fury and righteousness.

Tyrone hit the horn with the palm of his hand to scare the son of a bitch off the road.

He was laughing, shouting, *thief! liar! lying betraying bastard!*

What did he do then but call Jody's bluff, aim the car straight at him, fifty miles an hour and he'd lost control even before he hit a patch of cobbled ridged ice and began to skid—hardly had time before the impact to turn the wheel, pump desperately at the brakes—and he saw his cousin's look of absolute disbelief, not even fear or surprise, as the left fender slammed into him, the chassis plowed into his body and threw it aside and out of Tyrone's sight.

The steering wheel caught Tyrone in the chest. But he was all right. He was coughing, choking, but he was all right, gripping the wheel tight and pumping the brakes as the car leveled out of its wild swerve and came to a bumpy rest in a ditch. Scrub trees and tall grasses clawing at the windshield and Jesus his nose was bleeding and he couldn't see anything in the rearview mirror but he knew Jody was dead: that sickening thud, that enormous impact like a man-sized boulder flung against the car, that's what it meant.

"Jesus . . ."

Tyrone sat panting in his car, the motor racing, clouds of exhaust lifting behind; he was terrified, his bladder contracted, heart pumping like crazy and it couldn't have happened, could it?—that quickly?—hairline cracks on his windshield and his nose clogged with blood?—except he'd felt the body snapping beneath the car, it wasn't something you were likely to mistake as anything but death.

He didn't have to drive back another time. Didn't have to see the bright blood on the snow.

He pressed his forehead against the steering wheel. A terrible hammering in his chest he'd have to wait out.

"Damn you fuck you *Jody* . . ."

He'd done it on purpose, hadn't he!

Tyrone busied himself maneuvering his car out of the ditch, rocking the chassis, concentrating on the effort which involved his entire physical being; he was panting, grunting, whispering *C'mon baby c'mon for Christ's sweet sake,* then he was free and clear and back on the road and no one knew.

He'd begun to shiver convulsively. Though he was sweating too inside his clothes. And his bladder pinched in terror as he hadn't felt it in a long, long time.

But he was all right, wasn't he? And the car was operating.

That was the main thing.

He drove on, slowly at first, then panic hit him in a fresh wave and he began to drive faster, thinking he was going in the wrong direction but had had to get somewhere—where?—had to get help.

Police, ambulance. He'd go home and telephone.

There's a man dead on the road. Hitchhiker and he'd stepped in front of the car and it was over in an instant.

Blood dripping from his nose onto his fucking jacket and those hairline cracks in the windshield, like cracks in his own skull. He was crying, couldn't stop.

He'd tell Irene to make the call. Wouldn't tell her who it was he'd hit. Then he'd drive back to Jody, *Hey you know I didn't mean it why the hell didn't you get out of the way I was just kidding around then the ice, why the hell didn't you get out of the way goddamn you you did it on purpose didn't you—*

But maybe it would be better if he stopped at the first house, a neighbor's house.

Police, or the ambulance? Or both? There was an emergency number he'd never memorized the way you were supposed to. . . .

His mind was shifting out of focus, going blank in patches empty and white-glaring as the snowy fields.

Those fields you could lose yourself in at this time of year. Staring and dreaming, stubbled with grass and grain and tracked over with animal prints but you couldn't see that at a distance—everything clean and clear, dazzling blinding white. At a distance.

It was a secret no one knew: Jody McIllvanney was dead.

Bleeding his life out in a ditch. In the snow.

He hadn't survived the impact of the car, Tyrone knew that. No chance of it, plowing into a human being like that full in the chest and the gut, he'd felt the bones being crushed, the backbone snapped—*felt* it.

He'd feel it all his life!

He'd seen bodies crumpled, Jesus he'd seen more than his fair share. Kids his own age, Americans, Japs, in uniform, near-naked, bleeding, broken bones, eyes rolled up into their skulls. But mostly he'd been lucky enough to come upon them after death had come and gone and only the body was left.

No witnesses.

No one on the road this time of day.

He had to get help but help was a long way off.

His foot pressing down hard on the accelerator then letting up when the tires began to spin, it was dangerous driving in the winter along these roads, dangerous driving any time the roads were likely to be slippery, now approaching a single-lane bridge crashing over the bridge the floorboards bouncing and kicking and the car trembling, Oh sweet Jesus help me.

Explaining to someone, a patrolman on the highway, how it wasn't his fault. The hitchhiker standing flat-footed in the road not dodging out of the way even when the car began to skid.

He'd lost control of the car. But then he'd regained it.

No witnesses.

How could he be held to blame?

If Jody had paid in installments for instance twenty-five dollars, even ten dollars every month or so. Paring back on the debt just to show his good faith. His gratitude.

He couldn't be held responsible. He'd kill himself if they came to arrest him.

Except: no witnesses.

Except: his car was damaged.

The fender crushed, the bumper, part of the hood—that's how they would know. Blood splashed on the grill.

That's how they would find him.

That's how they would arrest him.

He and Jody used to go deer hunting farther north; you sling the carcass over the fender unless it's too big—then you tie it to the roof of the car. Twine tied tight as you can tie it.

He'd known without having to look.

Asshole. Bleeding his life out back in a ditch.

But who would know? If he kept going.

If he drove on past his house—just kept driving as if it weren't any house he knew, any connection to him—drive and drive up into the northern part of the state until something happened to stop him. Until his gas gave out.

Dolphin Dreaming

•

——————— PETER LaSALLE ———————

Peter LaSalle grew up in Rhode Island and graduated from Harvard. He currently divides his time between Austin, Texas, where he teaches at the University of Texas, and Narragansett, Rhode Island. His books include a novel, Strange Sunlight, *and a story collection,* The Graves of Famous Writers.

I

The day he was supposed to go to the studios of the television station in Providence, Burns woke up from another Dolphin dream. Whoever said that you don't dream in color, Burns thought as he looked over to the travel alarm clock, had never played professional football.

Burns dreamed often in those colors of the uniforms. So bright. In this case, they were wearing home uniforms, aqua jerseys with white, orange-trimmed numerals. They were playing the Chargers in their blue jerseys and enameled helmets trimmed with gold lightning bolts. That probably made them their home uniforms too, because such things could happen in dreams. But they were definitely playing in the Orange Bowl. It was night, the strong stadium lights almost aching in their intensity, and what was strange was that there were no fans in the cavern of white-painted stands. In fact, the game was just grinding on and on, at this point on a third-and-short-yardage for the Chargers. The Orange Bowl's astro carpet was greener than any spring grass. The Floridian sky stretched enormous, hugely black and splattered with the tropical stars that always seemed so close to Burns.

Setting up on defense in the left linebacker spot, Burns again tried

to shout to them all. "Hey, there's something wrong here. Hey, look
around, there are no fans, maybe we got the wrong night and . . ."

The quarterback's signals drowned him out, a staccato of double
digits, and then there was that initial crack of plastic on plastic as the
linemen's helmets smacked. Some grunting, and the rush of running
past Burns himself, who quickly read the medium-out, a favorite pat-
tern of the rookie Charger tight end, and backpedaled a few steps to
cut and keep up with him. Except Burns wasn't trying to cover. He
only wanted to catch him, to loop his arms around the kicking, blue-
and-gold calf stockings even if the man didn't snag a pass.

In the dream, he had to make sure that somebody else was there,
even though it *looked* as if they were. *He got scared to think that
maybe the players too would disappear: he had no idea what he would
do if it turned out that he actually was alone in his uniform there in the
concrete bowl in the swallowing Miami night.*

II

Of course football at this point was over for Burns. It had been for
more than five years. Burns had never thought he would play professional football. To be honest, nobody else had ever thought he would.

He hadn't taken football seriously in high school in upstate New
York, and though he started on the squad, he prided himself on being
able to say the coach never considered him one of his "boys." The
coach was a gung-ho Korean War veteran, a crew-cut bull who was so
taken up with his job that on warm days in the off-season he would
stroll around the upstate city with his wife—downtown shopping or to
the new Grand Union—in his high-school-issued, green coach's ber-
muda shorts, polo shirt, and baseball cap. Burns considered him a
fool, and he suspected that the coach detected his sentiments. Meanwhile, Burns possibly fancied himself an intellectual. He wasn't a
grind, but he made the honor roll with more A's than B's, and that
was taking all the honors-section classes. He was quite sure that he
was the first in his high school to discover Bob Dylan in the early
sixties. A kid named Burroughs challenged that distinction. One afternoon, Burroughs brought over to Burns' house the first Dylan Columbia album, simply titled "Bob Dylan." It was the one that showed

Dylan—not long after having changed the name from Zimmerman—off to one side of a sky-blue background. He wore a cheap sheepskin coat, had a leather cap pushed back on his curly tuft on top, and looked decidedly cherubic to the point that the cover photographer could have touched up the cheeks to make them that rosy.

"This is the first album. Check the serial number. That should prove that it's an early run too," Burroughs said snootily.

"Kiddies' play," Burns had told him. He wouldn't have laid it so heavily on Burroughs. But Burroughs had been obnoxious about it. "Ever hear of Blind Boy Grunt, Burroughs?"

"All right, you can be the one who discovered Blind Boy, whatever you said. I'll take credit for Dylan."

"Burroughs, I think you're going to be surprised." And poor Burroughs was when he heard the nasal twang, admittedly with the then-uncharacteristic electric back-up, but obviously Dylan nevertheless.

"Ah, don't feel bad, Burroughs. I mean these things are rare. He wasn't sixteen when he cut them. I came across them when I first got into blues a few years ago."

Burns' parents were working people, and Burns would have had no trouble getting a scholarship to at least a local state college. However, an uncle in Seattle who had had something to do with inventing the freeze-dry process had left money in a trust for college educations for Burns and his two sisters. Burns applied to Harvard, Yale, and Williams, and was accepted by Harvard and Williams. He felt no disappointment about having been turned down by the New Haven school, and there was some satisfaction in knowing that he hadn't played up to the Brooks-suited Yalie—hornrimmed glasses and all—who he met one afternoon for an interview over in Syracuse. (Alumni handled such screening for the university.) The man was a stockbroker, certainly proud of his calling. He seemed sure that a high school kid like Burns would be awed when he came to his firm's office. Phones rang and figures flashed across black electronic screens, showing closing quotations for the New York Exchange. "The brokerage business is quite fascinating. Why don't we start with my giving you a tour of our plant."

"Ah, if it's all right, maybe we could skip that. I mean it looks like it might snow, and I wouldn't mind being back on the freeway before it does." The self-satisfied Yalie was cold after that. Burns hadn't meant to rattle him, but he was there for an *interview*, and he didn't want to tramp around a boring office in Syracuse for an hour. The Yalie was about twenty-five. He turned pompous with Burns, and with a fine-point Bic pen, he performed some scratchy figuring on canary note paper. He came up with what he said would be Burns' scholastic average if he had gone to his school—"an old prep operation," as he emphasized. Burns had heard of the place, or at least he had read the name in the begging "Schools" advertisements he happened to flip through once while reading the *New York Times* magazine section.

"A C average, a low C, I'd say," the broker pronounced.

"I think I see some flakes now." Burns wanted to be out of there.

Burns chose Williams because it offered a fuller program in studio art than Harvard did. Burns had become obsessed with modern sculpture in high school, and an art teacher there, Ed Zabracki, introduced him to arc welding for metal freeforms. He didn't major in art at the handsome little college in the green Berkshires, but he did manage to take a studio course each semester. He studied English Literature. The major had loose enough requirements to allow him to fit in all the necessary biology and organic chemistry courses required to establish a pre-med preparation. And he played football.

Football at Williams in a way was more tolerable for him than it had been at his high school. It wasn't taken too seriously, and Burns didn't mind going out to the practices. And practice was held only three afternoons a week. If he ever did associate any pleasure with the game, he associated it with football at Williams. A November late afternoon, and the sky would start to pinken over the mountains' saw-toothed silhouette. The air had that ammonia-clear something of coming winter, and the practice field was frozen just enough so that you felt the steel-tipped nylon cleats through your shoes' soles because the cleats couldn't sink into the ground. They would be congregated in ragged white scrimmage garb, tossing the ball around just to keep warm, while Smith, the assistant coach, said that if the coach himself didn't show in ten minutes, he too was going to call it quits for the day.

They lost most of their games.

Burns knew that Williams players weren't the usual jocks he would find at places that offered big athletic scholarships, even at Harvard. He liked the guys on the team, and they liked him. His best friend, however, was a short design major, Calavetti. Calavetti had already decided that MIT was the best graduate school of architecture, and as a freshman he announced that MIT would be where he would eventually study. Burns and Calavetti could spend hours goofing around in the library's lounge, dodging their assigned study and passing back and forth art history books like a couple of pre-teenagers poring over hot-rod magazines.

"How about Zurbaran," Burns said. "Wow, will you look at the way he uses black. He must be the best painter of black. All right, without looking at this, tell me what your favorite Zurbaran is."

"First of all, I think that there should be no doubt," Calavetti said, "that everybody's favorite Zurbaran is the 'Vision of St. Peter Dreaming,' the one with the golden city of heaven floating in the clouds above. Secondly, you're sure you can make a sound argument for Zurbaran as the best painter of black over Velasquez?"

"Positive. Listen." It would go on and on like that.

Burns dated many "interesting" girls from Skidmore and Mount Holyoke, or as many as living in Williamstown and having to borrow a car for a weekend would allow. He was handsome with prematurely thinning blond hair he brushed straight back. He wore round, steel-rimmed spectacles. He was also big. In high school, it seemed he was just tall and skinny. Now, in college, he filled out, and at six-five he was almost a textbook-perfect figure of a linebacker—shoulders as wide as a tackle's and a waist and legs trim enough to belong to a sprinter. He was voted to the first squad of the Little Three All-Star team in his junior and senior years. He honestly thought that might have made him good enough not to get cut from, though never see any action for, one of those Midwestern or West Coast university teams that played in televised games before massive stadium crowds, as opposed to Williams' Saturday contests, sometimes in the morning, before a handful of classmates and dates.

If you had asked Burns what he considered his major accomplishment in college, he would have said it was organizing with Calavetti a chapter of the Students for a Democratic Society at Williams. In 1968, his sophomore year, he and Calavetti thought the college needed a little shaking up. They held the SDS meetings in a fraternity house assembly room, a spot with the usual varnished knotty-pine walls and a green linoleum floor that would never be fully free from beer stickiness. Some on campus liked to joke that the meetings never entailed anything more than discussions of the progress of the members' beard growth, but Burns knew that the Williams SDS was responsible for a curriculum reassessment by the administration. Also, they could be counted on to mobilize at least thirty bodies to march in any Boston anti-war demonstration.

Burns graduated and was free from the draft because of a minor shoulder injury. He planned to take a year off from study, maybe for VISTA volunteer work and a bit more sculpting, before taking the boards for medical school. A buddy from the Williams team, the place-kicker, talked him into driving with him up to Montreal that June for the Montreal Alouettes training camp, an open affair during which most anybody with the slightest college football credentials could try out. The place-kicker was thinking of writing a freelance piece on Canadian football to start his own journalistic career. If Burns had suspicions that he never did like football much, they were more than confirmed during that scorching week or so on the burnt-yellow field of the McGill Stadium where they practiced, and in the motel where everybody trying out lived with about all the grace of mongrels in a city pound. The Canadian League started regular play in the summer, and it attracted hungry graduates of American schools who hadn't been picked up in the NFL draft. Burns felt bad for them when he saw how desperate they were. A fullback from Iowa State seemed to believe that he would increase his own chances of making the team by methodically picking fights with, and so eliminating, each of the other candidates for the position. He must have boxed, probably Golden Gloves, somewhere along the line. But, in the end, sheer numbers were against him and five fights in as many days were too much for him. Burns was up early one morning to check the bus schedule for the trip back to Boston. He saw the fullback checking out in the motel lobby, a duffle bag over his shoulder. He looked as if he had had a hard time of it in the bout the night before. A ring most likely caused the deep gash above his eye, stitches X'ing over the maroon caked blood. His cheeks had puffed to twin blue sacks from the constant battering. Later, making sure he had everything (and trying not to listen to the burly black guard from Texas Tech who wept next door exactly at one every afternoon), Burns told his buddy that he couldn't take the depressing scene any longer. "At least you think you'll get an article to peddle. I say I've seen enough for experience's sake."

Two things resulted from the trip to Canada. One: Burns realized that though he wouldn't have made the cut even if he did stick it out on a lark in Montreal, the professional prospects—admittedly only prospects for the Canadian League—weren't much better than he was. And two: a week later, he got a person-to-person call from the linebacker coach of the Miami Dolphins. Apparently, the team, a losing expansion club, took any stray tip from another camp, being so desperate themselves to shake up their personnel and win some games. The coach said that a friend of his passing through Montreal had told him that Burns was quite agile for his size. The coach also admitted he had never heard of Williams College. Burns talked to the VISTA coordinator in Philadelphia by telephone, and he said they could keep a spot open for Burns in that city's North Side program till September. "It won't be that long, I don't think," Burns explained. "I'll guarantee I'll be there by August first."

By August first, after a month of camp, Burns had signed a one-year contract with the Dolphins at the 1970 league minimum of sixteen-thousand dollars. By October first, three games into the season, he was a starting outside linebacker. By November first, it was obvious the Dolphins were a changed team.

That first year was worth it, as far as Burns was concerned, if only for the experience of seeing what the whole business of professional sports was like. He played decently, if not outstandingly, while the famed "No-Name Defense" itself was making its mark. The second year, he didn't find it much fun at all, despite the Dolphins becoming the proverbial "Cinderella Team." They were Super Bowl contenders, receiving more publicity than any expansion club in the history of

sports, excepting maybe the Mets the year they mysteriously metamorphosed from a group of men who didn't know what to do with a
ground ball that came their way for fielding to World Series Champi-
ons. The sports commentators loved Burns.

It was exactly the kind of thing that would launch Howard Cosell
into one of his nasalized raptures of forced vocabulary. "And there's a
young man in on that last play, Dandy. Number 53, Connell Burns. A
graduate of that tiny, but su-per-ior insti-tu-tion of higher education
nestled in the Berkshires and founded in 1793—Williams College for
Men. An in-tel-ligent, soft-spoken fellow who was determined to serve
his country as a VISTA volunteer before em-barking on a career of
medi-cal study to become a surgeon. Then the Miami organization
called Connell Burns and invited him South for their peru-sal. Connell
Burns never had thought of a future in football, and now he is an inte-
gral part of this Dolphins success story."

"Ah, Howard, how do you know that college was founded in
1793?"

"Dandy, it surely was founded in 1793, and I can tell you that in
1793 there not only was not your own es-teemed alma mater SMU,
but there was not your es-teemed city of Dallas, or, for tha-at matter,
your es-teemed state of Texas itself."

"Whatever you say, Howard."

The print media went Dolphin-wild too. There were entire articles
giving detailed accounts how the orange and aqua team colors were
chosen, after much deliberation, as being the hues most representative
of the region—the orange for the citrus fruit of that name and the
aqua for the warm coastal waters. There were articles on the local fans
in the sunny Orange Bowl. By the end of the year, Don Shula was on
the cover of *Time* magazine. Naturally, Csonka and Kiick monopo-
lized the bulk of the publicity about the individual players. But Burns
got maybe more than his share—as an oddity. A big spread in *Sports
Illustrated,* titled "Super Minds and Super Jocks," featured the stories
of three young athletes: Burns; the forward for the Atlanta Flames
who graduated from Brown, where he studied Slavic Languages, and
who said in the article that he read Dostoevsky in the locker room and
memorized a word from *Webster's* every day; and the rather outspoken

center for the Detroit Pistons who in the off-season was working on a Rhodes Scholarship and preaching internationally the virtues of health food in general and radishes in particular.

Burns didn't pay much attention to the publicity. He still disliked football. He didn't like the city of Miami either, from the yellow heat of the hot months to the torpor of being surrounded by all the tanned, aging vacationers. He didn't have much in common with most of the players. On the whole, they were self-satisfied and egocentric. They were overgrown, bragging boys who had thrived on people telling them how athletically gifted they were from age eight onward. Burns roomed with the Cyprian place-kicker who had played European soccer and certainly wasn't the standard NFL product. Other than that kicker, the blacks from rural Southern colleges like Grambling and Bethune-Cookman were the only teammates who interested Burns. They were less affected, decidedly more honest than the rest. That year Miami did make it to the championship game. They lost to Dallas, but no forecaster doubted they would be back in the Super Bowl the next season.

Right after that second season, Burns became seriously involved with a stewardess for Braniff. Penny was a beautiful girl from San Diego who had played bit parts in three "Fury" television shows as a child actress. Wispily tall, she had honey hair and a slight cast to one eye. That was the kind of rarity, Burns thought, that could constitute an exquisiteness that an old master would have recognized in choosing a model to pose for an ageless portrait. She usually managed to get four-day lay-overs, and she spent them at Burns' condominium in Coconut Grove. Still exhausted from the season, Burns found it comfortable to relax with one girl and to have her around in her tennis shorts and a T-shirt from her endless collection of them, each stencilled with a name of a different rock band. Maybe that comfort—the barbecues, the evenings of low stereo jazz, the ocean fishing together—deluded Burns into the seriousness. Because, eventually he had to admit that Penny wasn't much different from the other athletes' groupies he had dated before, simply out of convenience. They broke up in the spring, and she seemed surprised that Burns as much as questioned if she were doing the right thing by quitting her stewardess job and taking off to Malibu to live with a twenty-year-old stunt man who promised to make the contacts she needed to get her back in the television business. "Do you realize what an *opportunity* this is for me?"

That was when Burns decided to quit pro football. He admitted that there was the danger that if he kept playing, he might find himself, ten years hence, content with the absurdity of sportswriters fawning over him while he himself waited for the next mindless stewardess to tag after him.

He didn't do it right away. But he confided to Calavetti, his best friend from Williams, that he would play one season more. He saw Calavetti late that spring in Chicago where he was representing the Dolphins in an NFL Players Association meeting. (That "super-brain" publicity convinced the team that he was the one they wanted to make sure the owners understood the players' point of view concerning their pensions and other matters under discussion.) Calavetti had graduated from the MIT Design School. He was an architect with a top Chicago firm and he was married to a girl who was finishing at the University of Chicago Law School. One evening, Burns and Calavetti managed to go off on their own. Burns was at the padded wheel of the rented silver Audi. The car had a sun roof, and the drive started off as an excursion to view the famous Chicago skyscrapers, by night and a little stoned on grass Burns supplied. The towers rose above them, all that glass (blue-mirroring or dark-tinted) of the giants lining Lake Shore Drive, North Michigan and Wabash. The smooth Audi gargled along. The taillights from the sparse traffic streaked redly, as Burns and Calavetti inhaled a few more spicy puffs in the fine May night. "Wow. How about that Mies Van Der Rohe," Burns rhapsodized. "I mean can you believe the way he just slaps those steel beams into the sky." They gawked through the sun roof. And it was like the old sessions with Calavetti at Williams, and, in a way, quite unlike them too. Calavetti kept asking about football. He kept talking about Csonka and Kiick. Mercury Morris and Nick Buoniconti. That bothered Burns.

Burns approached that final season as a job. If the Dolphins won the AFL title, as they were picked to do, and then took the Super

Bowl, Burns would make over sixty-thousand dollars. The Super Bowl money alone was twenty thousand. He needed that money for medical school and he had to make sure the team did well. He had an exceptional year. He led the conference's linebackers in interceptions. His tackling took on a new aggressiveness, and in the Patriots game at Foxboro, he had ten unassisted pull-downs for short yardage. By this time, all of them on the "No-Name Defense" were quite known. Burns was a star. The Dolphins disposed of the Redskins more easily than the 14 to 7 score would indicate in the Los Angeles Coliseum for the Super Bowl. In between that game and the Pro Bowl, Burns flew to Boston for an interview at the Harvard Medical School. He announced to the stunned Miami management in March, when his acceptance to Harvard came, that he was leaving football. The announcement attracted a flurry of laudatory publicity, but, deep in the hockey and basketball seasons, the sports writers were too busy with other matters to ramble on about what a noble move Connell Burns was making.

III

Burns didn't last a year at Harvard.

His performance was an embarrassment to the admissions officers. They had originally agreed that though Burns' scores on the medical boards weren't at all high, they had to compensate for his having been away from school for a few years. And so, he was admitted. Now they realized they had overcompensated. An alumnus whose son had been denied admission that year was threatening to the dean that he would demand an investigation of the school's admission policies in general; he charged those admissions were becoming "a bloody celebrities sweepstakes." Burns couldn't keep up. He failed every anatomy and chemistry course, passing only a "gut" seminar in hypnotism. He studied so intensely that he lost thirty pounds, and it did no good. In April, the dean called him in and flatly announced, "It just wouldn't be right for us to take your money any longer, Connell."

He was quite drunk quite often till August, when word arrived from a small pre-intern medical school in St. Joseph, Missouri, that they could fit him into the fall class. There he passed two courses and they didn't do him the service of advising him he was wasting his money. His letter of dismissal didn't come till the end of June—after all fees had been paid. A surgeon on the teaching staff tried to console Burns by saying that he thought Burns should look into their R.N. program, to become a registered nurse, or even the L.P.N. program, to become a licensed practical nurse. "As a nurse you can show that admirable dedication to help people that you obviously have, even if you don't have, the, ah, ah, the gray matter to be a doctor." It was all Burns could do to keep from slugging him. He was quite drunk quite often for the next year and a half.

In Chicago, shortly before Christmas one year, Burns caused a terrible scene at a Christmas party at Calavetti's home. Calavetti had recently bought a Frank Lloyd Wright prairie-school original in Oak Park. By now Burns had moved from Missouri back to Boston. He had been receiving treatment for his drinking problem at the Newton General Hospital. To cheer himself up one night, he called Calavetti who told him about the house and how busy he was getting ready for an upcoming house-warming party. "If you're having a party, then I'm damn well coming, Cal. You just watch." He flew from Logan the next day.

He arrived in Oak Park by Yellow Cab in a snowstorm. He knew he shouldn't have drunk so much tequila in the bar of the Essex Hotel in the city. But what the hell, he was going to see his old best friend. He slipped the black driver a bill, telling him to keep the change. Burns' vision was blurred from the alcohol, and he was sure only that the bill was green—it could have been a twenty, fifty, or hundred. Inside, the people were mostly architects from Calavetti's firm and their wives. The men in blazers and red or green tartan-plaid slacks, and the wives in simple cocktail sheaths. Those women reminded Burns of the girls he used to know at Skidmore and Mount Holyoke. It could have been their broad, educated accents. The Wright house, a designated Oak Park landmark, was more form than function. The ceilings were abnormally low to make for that low-slung profile outside. Burns' head seemed to barely miss brushing them, and he probably looked like a giant in there. The streamlined woodwork was auburn-stained. The fireplace, trimmed with olive ceramic tile, was a work of art in itself.

There was a moveable leaded-glass divider of those classic Wright rectangles. It too was an original.

Burns never wandered far from the bar. He told the red-jacketed waiter behind the linen-blanketed table to keep the bottle of Cutty Sark to one side for him. He didn't listen to the men trying to talk to him about football, trying to tell him how well they remembered a particular play he made in a particular quarter in a game in Baltimore or Minnesota. He remembered going into a rant about Frank Lloyd Wright. He remembered shouting how he, Burns, was smarter than any of the architects present, and he knew more about Wright—understood more of the man's sense of the prairie's vastness, his poetic design—than any of them would ever have a chance of understanding. He called them phonies. He shouted for Calavetti to back him up. He shouted for Calavetti to tell them how they two were the great minds of their class at Williams. He flailed his arms, and the heavy Scotch glass flew free. It shattered two purple-tinted panes in the leaded-glass divider.

Now it was Calavetti's wife's turn to shout. She demanded that Calavetti throw "that stinking, drunk animal" out of her house. Maybe she was tipsy too. "And people wonder why America is the way it is today. We wonder when oafs like this are our children's heroes!"

IV

That day he woke in Providence after having had another Dolphin dream, Burns dressed neatly in a tan, tapered-waist suit, a blue shirt, and a dark-blue tie. He walked from the downtown motel to the studios of the local television station. (This was almost a couple of years after the Chicago incident. Since then, Burns had gone on the talk circuit sponsored by the NFL Players Association, lecturing Elks, Boy Scouts, and high schoolers in the Greater Boston area. He wasn't drinking heavily anymore. He had filled in to do some radio color commentary for a few Patriots home games, and this job reading sports in Providence could be the break he needed in television.)

Providence in August was hot, and the downtown looked like what it was—the heart of a tired, forgotten city. An attempt at a pedestrian shoppers' mall didn't help much. A street had been closed off from traffic. Some of the stores in the old Victorian buildings were vacant. The pavement had been covered with red brick laid like herringbone, and the evergreens in huge redwood tubs here and there were gray from a lack of watering. He thought satisfiedly that a blue shirt was best for television, as he walked alongside his reflection in the display-window glass of a deserted place. It must have once been a posh department store, judging from the frills carved in the brownstone, and all the brass trimming the doors that were padlocked shut. A scruffy teenager was banging a transistor radio against the bench on which he sat, maybe trying to get it to work. Burns remembered that dream he woke from, the way he wanted to make that tackle to make sure that the San Diego receiver actually *was* there.

At the studios, he read high-school baseball scores off a teletype sheet for half an hour in front of a video camera. The station manager said his articulation was excellent. After that, Burns went upstairs a floor, to the offices of the executives—one sending him to the office of the next, who sent him on to the office of the next, etc. He talked windily about his Dolphins days and what an honor it was to have been part of "The Dynasty." (Retired, Burns would always be remembered that way, as the star linebacker who challenged so many records in the first year that the Miami team took the Super Bowl. Burns too didn't have much sense anymore of those articles that for a while were concerned with his being the "thinking man's" athlete.)

On his way down the tangerine carpeting to the next office, he overheard two older men talking. They looked like former newspaper reporters, both bald and both in drip-dry shirts with cheap wide ties. They probably wrote copy at the station.

"Did you see that Connell Burns this morning? The size of him. The build. Like one of those Greek Gods."

"Athletic ability of that calibre is a gift."

"The way he used to hit them. An explosion. The man didn't know his own strength." Then they saw Burns.

"Hey, Mr. Burns. I'm Bill Ajootian of the news department." They came out into the hall together. Ajootian, the shorter, shoved his hand out first. His friend followed.

"They sure do make you blab a lot in this business," Burns said. "Before I go to see this next big-wig, I think I need me a little aqua simplex to wet the old whistle." They were fans, and Burns, bending that big frame over the gray-metal water fountain, saw his face reflected in the chrome dish of the thing. He was sure of what he was going to do. It would be easy.

He put his meaty hand on the pivoting knob and twisted in a short, stinging jerk. The plastic piece snapped cleanly. Burns held it up, as if he were surprised, "Ah, this is all I need." He shook his head and grinned. "I guess I can count this job out."

"Will you look at that," Ajootian said, smiling and satisfied himself, almost mesmerized.

"I guess it just sort of reminded me of one of old Bob Hayes' little ankles," Burns said. They all roared.

Leaving them there, Burns had no doubt that he would get the job. This crowd was lucky to have a celebrity like him, a former Dolphin Super Bowler, in a place like Providence, he told himself. And they knew it. "Carol," he thought. Yes, that was the name of the receptionist downstairs, the cute little girl no more than twenty with the hot-comb-curled, auburn hair. He would bet she had unbuttoned the crisp seersucker shirtdress so low like that when she saw him coming. It was an obvious come-on, and, almost to the next executive's office, Burns told himself she was a sure thing for dinner and probably a tumble back at the motel afterwards.

He stopped before knocking on the black door. This was the big boy, the one who would talk to him about salary. Burns pushed his hand through his thin hair, and he told himself now that this guy wouldn't get off easy. He would *pay*. That last year he played should have been enough to prove to anybody that he was one of the best—who knows, maybe *the* best—who had ever mastered the linebacking position. He was amazed himself when he thought of those ten unassisted tackles in the Patriots game.

He grabbed the doorknob of the black door, and tried again not to think of that dream.

Rot

•

JOY WILLIAMS

Joy Williams is the author of two novels, State of Grace *and* The Changeling, *and a collection of stories,* Taking Care. *A new novel will be published by Vintage Contemporaries in June. She lives in Florida.*

Lucy was watching the street when an old Ford Thunderbird turned into their driveway. She had never seen the car before and her husband, Dwight, was driving it. One of Dwight's old girlfriends leapt from the passenger seat and ran toward the house. Her name was Caroline, she had curly hair and big white teeth, more than seemed normal, and Lucy liked her the least of all of Dwight's old girlfriends. Nevertheless, when she came inside, Lucy said, "Would you like a glass of water or something?"

"I was the horn," Caroline said. "That car doesn't have one so I was it. I'd yell out the window, 'Watch out!' "

"Were you the brakes too or just the horn?" Lucy asked.

"It has brakes," Caroline said, showing her startling teeth. She went into the living room and said, "Hello, rug." She always spoke to the rug lying there. The rug was from Mexico with birds of different colors flying across it. All of the birds had long, white eyes. Dwight and Caroline had brought the rug back from the Yucatan when they had gone snorkeling there years before. Some of the coves were so popular that the fish could scarcely be seen for all the suntan oil floating in the water. At Garrafon in Isla Mujeres, Dwight told Lucy, he had raised his head and seen a hundred people bobbing facedown over the rocks of the reef and a clean white tampon bobbing there among them. Caroline had said at the time, "It's disgusting, but it's obviously some joke."

Caroline muttered little things to the rug, showing off, Lucy thought, although she wasn't speaking Spanish to it, she didn't know Spanish. Lucy looked out the window at Dwight sitting in the Thunderbird. It was old with new paint, black, with a white top and portholes and skirts. He looked a little big for it. He got out abruptly and ran to the house as though through rain, but there was no rain. It was a grey, still day in spring, just before Easter, with an odious weight to the air. Recently, when they had been coming inside, synthetic stuff from Easter baskets had been traveling in with them, the fake nesting matter, the pastel and crinkly stuff of Easter baskets. Lucy couldn't imagine where they kept picking it up from, but no festive detritus came in this time.

Dwight gave her a hard, wandering kiss on the mouth. Lately, it was as though he were trying out kisses, trying to adjust them.

"You'll tell me all about this, I guess," Lucy said.

"Lucy," Dwight said solemnly.

Caroline joined them and said, "I've got to be off. I don't know the time, but I bet I can guess it to within a minute. I can do that," she assured Lucy. Caroline closed her eyes. Her teeth seemed still to be looking out at them, however. "Five ten," she said after a while. Lucy looked at the clock on the wall which showed ten minutes past five. She shrugged.

"That car is some cute," Caroline said, giving Dwight a little squeeze. "Isn't it some cute?" she said to Lucy. "Your Dwight's been tracking this car for days."

"I bought it from the next of kin," Dwight said.

Lucy looked at him impassively. She was not a girl who was quick to alarm.

"I was down at the Aquarium last week looking at the fish," Dwight began.

"Oh, that Aquarium," Lucy said. The Aquarium was where a baby seal had been put to sleep because he was born too ugly to be viewed by children. "I like fish," Dwight had told Lucy when she asked why he spent so much of his free time at the Aquarium. "Men like fish."

"And when I came out into the parking lot, next to our car was this little Thunderbird and there was a dead man sitting behind the wheel."

"Isn't that something!" Caroline exclaimed.

"I was the first to find him," Dwight said. "I'm no expert but that man was gone."

"What did this dead man look like?" Lucy asked Dwight.

He thought for a moment, then said, "He looked like someone in the movies. He had a large head."

"He didn't resemble you, did he?" she asked.

"Oh no, darling, not in the slightest."

"In any case," Lucy said a little impatiently.

"In any case," Dwight said, "this car just jumped at me, you know the way some things do. I knew I just had to have this car, it was just so pretty. It's the same age as you are, darling. That was the year the good things came out."

Lucy made a face for she wearied of references to her youth. She was almost twenty-five years younger than Dwight. Actually, theirs was rather a peculiar story.

"This car is almost cherry," Dwight said, gesturing out at it, "and now it's ours."

"That car is not almost cherry," Lucy said. "A man died in it. I would say that this car was about as un-cherry as you can get." She went on vehemently in this way for a while.

Caroline gazed at her, her lips parted, her teeth making no judgment. Then she said, "I've got to get back to my lonely home." She did not live far away; only a few of Dwight's old girlfriends had ever left town. "Now you two have fun in that car, it's a sweet little car." She kissed Dwight and he patted her back in an avuncular fashion as he walked her to the door. The air outside had a faint, thin smell of fruit and rubber. A siren screamed through it.

When Dwight returned, Lucy said, "I don't want a car a man died in for my birthday."

"It's not your birthday coming up, is it?"

Lucy admitted it was not, although Dwight often planned for her birthday months in advance. She blushed.

"It's funny how some people live longer than others, isn't it," she finally said.

Lucy and Dwight had been married for five years. When Dwight had first seen her, he was twenty-five years old and she was a four-month baby.

"I'm gonna marry you," Dwight said to the baby. People heard him. He was tall and had black hair, and was wearing a leather jacket that a girlfriend had sewed a violet silk liner into. It was a New Year's Eve party at this girlfriend's house and the girl was standing beside him. "Oh, right," she said. She didn't see anything particularly intriguing about this baby. They could make better babies than this, she thought. Lucy lay in a white wicker basket on a sofa. Her hair was sparse and her expression solemn. "You're gonna be my wife," Dwight said. He was very good with babies and good with children too. When Lucy was five, her favorite things were pop-up books in which one found what was missing by pushing or pulling or turning a tab, and for her birthday Dwight bought her fifteen of these, surely as many as had ever been produced. When she was ten he bought her a playhouse and filled it with balloons. Dwight was good with adolescents as well. When she was fourteen, he rented her a horse for a year. As for women, he had a special touch with them, as all his girlfriends would attest. Dwight wasn't faithful to Lucy as she was growing up, but he was attentive and devoted. Dwight kept up the pace nicely. And all the time Lucy was stoically growing up, learning how to dress herself and read, letting her hair grow, then cutting it all off, joining clubs and playing records, doing her algebra, going on dates, Dwight was out in the world. He always sent her little stones from the places he visited and she ordered them by size or color and put them in and out of boxes and jars until there came to be so many she grew confused as to where each had come from. This depressed her at first, then alarmed, then annoyed her. At about the time Lucy didn't care if she saw another little stone in her life, they got married. They did some traveling of their own, then bought a house and settled in. The house was a large, comfortable one, large enough, was the inference, to accommodate growth of various sorts. Things were all right. Dwight was like a big strange book where Lucy just needed to turn the pages and there everything was already.

They went out and looked at the Thunderbird in the waning light.

"It's a beauty, isn't it," Dwight said. "Wide whites, complete engine dress." He opened the hood, exposing the gleaming motor. Dwight was happy, his inky eyes shone. When he slammed the hood shut there was a soft rattling as of pebbles being thrown.

"What's that?" Lucy asked.

"What's what, my sweet?"

"That," Lucy said, "on the ground." She picked up a piece of rust, as big as her small hand and very light. Dwight peered at it. As she was trying to hand it to him, it dropped and crumbled.

"It looked so solid, I didn't check underneath," Dwight said. "I'll have some body men come over tomorrow and look at it. I'm sure it's no problem, just superficial stuff."

She ran her fingers behind the rocker panel of the door and came up with a handful of flakes.

"I don't know why you'd want to make it worse," Dwight said.

The next morning, two men were scooting around on their backs beneath the T-Bird, poking here and there with screwdrivers and squinting at the undercarriage. Lucy, who enjoyed a leisurely breakfast, was still in the kitchen, finishing it. As she ate her cereal, she studied the milk carton, a panel of which made a request for organs. Lucy was aware of a new determination in the world to keep things going. She rinsed her bowl and went outside just as the two men had slipped from beneath the car and were standing up, staring at Dwight. Gouts and clots of rust littered the drive.

"This for your daughter here?" one of them said.

"No," Dwight said irritably.

"I wouldn't give this to my daughter."

"It's not for anyone like that!" Dwight said.

"Bottom's just about to go," the other one said. "Riding along, these plates give, floor falls out, your butt's on the road. You need new pans at least. Pans are no problem." He chewed on his thumbnail. "It's rusted out too where the leaf springs meet the frame. Needs some work, no doubt about that. Somebody's done a lot of work but it needs a lot more work for sure. Donny, get me the Hemmings out of the truck."

The other man ambled off and returned with a thick brown catalogue.

"Maybe you should trade up," the first man said. "Get a car with a solid frame."

Dwight shook his head. "You can't repair it?"

"Why sure we can repair it!" Donny said. "You can get everything for these cars, all the parts, you got yourself a classic here!" He thumbed through the catalogue until he came to a page which offered the services of something called *The T-Bird Sanctuary*. The Sanctuary seemed to be a wrecking yard. A grainy photograph showed a jumble of cannibalized cars scattered among trees. It was the kind of picture that looked as though it had been taken furtively with a concealed camera.

"I'd trade up," the other man said. "Lookit over here, this page here, *Fifty-seven F-Bird supercharged, torch red, total body-off restoration, nothing left undone, ready to show . . .*"

"Be still, my heart," Donny said.

"You know if you are going to stick with this car you got," the other man said, "and I'm not advising you to, you should paint it the original color. This black ain't original." He opened the door and pointed at a smudge near the hinges. "See here, Powderblue."

"Starmist blue," Donny said, looking at him furiously.

The men glared at each other and when it appeared that they were about to come to blows, Lucy returned to the house. She stood inside, thinking, looking out at the street. When she had been a little girl on her way to school, she had once found an envelope on the street with her name on it, but there hadn't been anything in the envelope.

"We're getting another opinion," Dwight said when he came in. "We're taking it over to Boris, the best in the business."

They drove to the edge of town, to where another town began, to a big brown building there. Lucy enjoyed the car. It handled very well, she thought. They hurtled along, even though bigger cars passed them.

Boris was small, bald and stern. The German shepherd that stood beside him seemed remarkably large. His paws were delicately rounded but each was the size of a football. There was room, easily, for another German shepherd inside him, Lucy thought. Boris drove the Thunderbird onto a lift and elevated it. He walked slowly beneath it, his hands on his hips. Not a hair grew from his head. He lowered the car down and said, "Hopeless." When neither Lucy nor Dwight spoke, he shouted, "Worthless. Useless." The German shepherd sighed as though he had heard this prognosis many times.

"What about where the leaf springs meet the frame?" Lucy said. The phrase enchanted her.

Boris moved his hands around and then clutched and twisted them together in a pleading fashion.

"How can I make you nice people understand that it is hopeless? What can I say so that you will hear me, so that you will believe me? Do you like ripping up one-hundred-dollar bills? Is this what you want to do with the rest of your life? What kind of masochists are you? It would be wicked of me to give you hope. This car is unrestorable. It is full of rust and rot. Rust is a living thing, it breathes, it eats and it is swallowing up your car. These quarters and rockers have already been replaced, once, twice, who knows how many times. You will replace them again. It is nothing to replace quarters and rockers! How can I save you from your innocence and foolishness and delusions. You take out a bad part, say, you solder in new metal, you line-weld it tight, you replace the whole rear end, say, and what have you accomplished, you have accomplished only a small part of what is necessary, you have accomplished hardly, anything! I can see you feel dread and nausea at what I'm saying but it is nothing compared to the dread and nausea you will feel if you continue in this unfortunate project. Stop wasting your thoughts! Rot like this cannot be stayed. This brings us to the question, What is man? with its three subdivisions, What can he know? What ought he do? What may he hope? Questions which concern us all, even you, little lady."

"What!" Dwight said.

"My suggestion is to drive this car," Boris said in a calmer tone, "enjoy it, but for the spring and summer only, then dump it, part it out. Otherwise, you'll be putting in new welds, more and more new welds, but always the collapse will be just ahead of you. Years will pass and then will come the day when there is nothing to weld the weld to, there is no frame, nothing. Once rot, then nothing." He bowed, then retired to his office, which was sheeted with one-way glass.

Driving home, Dwight said, "You never used to hear about rust and rot all the time. It's new, this rust and rot business. You don't know what's around you any more."

Lucy knew Dwight was depressed and tried to look concerned, though in truth she didn't care much about the T-Bird. She was distracted by a tune that was going through her head. It was a song she remembered hearing when she was a little baby, about a tiny ant being at his doorway. She finally told Dwight about it and hummed the tune.

"Do you remember that little song?" she asked.

"Almost," Dwight said.

"What was that about anyway," Lucy asked. "The tiny ant didn't do anything, he was just waiting at his doorway."

"It was just nonsense stuff you'd sing to a little baby," Dwight said. He looked at her vaguely and said, "My sweet . . ."

Lucy called up her friend Daisy and told her about the black Thunderbird. She did not mention rot. Daisy was ten years older than Lucy and was one of the last of Dwight's girlfriends. Daisy had recently had one of her legs amputated. There had been a climbing accident and then she had just let things go on for too long. She was a tall, boyish-looking woman who before the amputation had always worn jeans. Now she slung herself about in skirts, for she found it disturbed people less when she wore a skirt, but when she went to the beach she wore a bathing suit, and she didn't care if she disturbed people or not because she loved the beach, the water, so still and so heavy, hiding so much.

"I didn't read in the paper about a dead man just sitting in his car like that," Daisy said. "Don't they usually report such things? It's unusual, isn't it?"

Lucy had fostered Daisy's friendship because she knew she was still in love with Dwight. If someone, God, for example, had asked Daisy if she'd rather have her leg back or Dwight, she would have said, "Dwight." Lucy felt excited about this and at the same time mystified and pitying. Knowing it always cheered Lucy up when she felt out of sorts.

"Did I tell you about the man in the supermarket with only one leg?" Daisy asked. "I had never seen him before. He was with his wife and baby and instead of being in the mother's arms the baby was in a stroller so the three of them took up a great deal of room in the aisle, and when I turned down the aisle I became entangled with this little family. I felt that I had known this man all my life, of course. People were smiling at us. Even the wife was smiling. It was dreadful."

"You should find someone," Lucy said without much interest.

Daisy's leg was in ashes in a drawer in a church garden, waiting for the rest of her.

"Oh no, no," Daisy said modestly. "So!" she said, "You're going to have another car!"

It was almost suppertime and there was the smell of meat on the air. Two small, brown birds hopped across the patchy grass and Lucy watched them with interest for birds seldom frequented their neighborhood. Whenever there were more than three birds in a given place, it was considered an infestation and a variety of measures were taken which reduced their numbers to an acceptable level. Lucy remembered that when she was little, the birds that flew overhead sometimes cast shadows on the ground. There were flocks of them at times and she remembered hearing the creaking of their wings, but she supposed that was just the sort of thing a child might remember, having seen or heard it only once.

She set the dining-room table for three as this was the night each spring when Rosette would come for dinner, bringing shad and shad roe, Dwight's favorite meal. Rosette had been the most elegant of Dwight's girlfriends, and the one with the smallest waist. She was now married to a man named Bob. When Rosette had been Dwight's girlfriend, she had been called Muffin. For the last five springs, ever since Lucy and Dwight had been married, she would have the shad flown down from the North and she would bring it to their house and cook

it. Yet even though shad was his favorite fish and he only got it once a
year, Dwight would be coming home a little late this night because he
was getting another opinion on the T-Bird. Lucy no longer accompanied him on these discouraging expeditions.

Rosette appeared in a scant, white cocktail dress and red high-
heeled shoes. She had brought her own china, silver, candles and wine.
She reset the table, dimmed the lights and made Lucy and herself
large martinis. They sat, waiting for Dwight, speaking in a desultory
way about things. Rosette and Bob were providing a foster home for
two delinquents whose names were Jerry and Jackie.

"What awful children," Rosette said. "They're so homely too. They
were cuter when they were younger, now their noses are really long
and their jaws are odd-looking too. I gave them bunny baskets this
year and Jackie wrote me a note saying that what she really needed
was a prescription for birth-control pills."

When Dwight arrived, Rosette was saying, "Guilt's not a bad thing
to have. There are worse things to have than guilt." She looked admir-
ingly at Dwight and said, "You're a handsome eyeful." She made him
a martini which he drank quickly, then she made them all another
one. Drinking hers, Lucy stood and watched the T-Bird in the driveway. It was a dainty car, and the paint was so black it looked wet.
Rosette prepared the fish with great solemnity, bending over Lucy's
somewhat dirty broiler. They all ate in a measured way. Lucy tried to
eat the roe one small egg at a time but found that this was impossible.

"I saw Jerry this afternoon walking down the street carrying a
Weedwacker," Dwight said. "Does he do yard work now? Yard work's
a good occupation for a boy."

"Delinquents aren't always culprits," Rosette said. "That's what
many people don't understand, but no, Jerry is not doing yard work,
he probably stole that thing off someone's lawn. Bob tries to talk to
him but Jerry doesn't heed a word he says. Bob's not very convinc-
ing."

"How is Bob?" Lucy asked.

"Husband Bob is a call I never should have answered," Rosette
said.

Lucy crossed her arms over her stomach and squeezed herself with delight because Rosette said the same thing each year when she was asked about Bob.

"Life with Husband Bob is a long twilight of drinking and listless anecdote," Rosette said.

Lucy laughed, delighted, because Rosette always said this, too.

The next day, Dwight told Lucy of his intentions to bring the T-Bird into the house. "She won't last long on the street," he said. "She's a honey but she's tired. Elements are hard on a car and it's the elements that have done this sweet little car in. We'll put her in the living room which is under-furnished anyway and it will be like living with a work of art right in our living room. We'll keep her shined up and sit inside her and talk. It's very peaceful inside that little car, you know."

The T-Bird looked alert and coquettish as they spoke around it.

"That car was meant to know the open road," Lucy said. "I think we should drive it till it drops." Dwight looked at her sorrowfully and she widened her eyes, not believing she had said such a thing. "Well," she said, "I don't think a car should be in a house, but maybe we could bring it in for a little while and then if we don't like it we could take it out again."

He put his arms around her and embraced her and she could hear his heart pounding away in his chest with gratitude and excitement.

Lucy called Daisy on the telephone. The banging and sawing had already begun. "Men go odd in different ways than women," Daisy said. "That's always been the case. For example, I read that men are exploring ways of turning the earth around toxic waste dumps into glass by the insertion of high-temperature electric probes. A woman would never think of something like that."

Dwight worked feverishly for days. He removed the picture window, took down the wall, shored up the floor, built a ramp, drained the car of all its fluids so it wouldn't leak on the rug, pushed it into the house, replaced the studs, put back the window, erected fresh Sheetrock and repainted the entire room. Lucy was amazed that it was so easy to tear a wall down and put it back up again. In the room, the car looked like a big doll's car. But it didn't look bad inside the house at all and Lucy didn't mind it being there, although she didn't like it when Dwight raised the hood. She didn't care for the hood being raised one bit and always lowered it when she saw it was up. She thought about the Thunderbird most often at night when she was in bed lying beside Dwight and then she would marvel at its silent, un-seen presence in the room beside them, taking up space, so strange and shining and full of rot.

They would sit frequently in the car, in their house, not going any-where, looking through the windshield out at the window and through the window to the street. They didn't invite anyone over for this. Soon, Dwight took to sitting in the car by himself. Dwight was tired. It was taking him a while to bounce back from the carpentry. Lucy saw him there one day behind the wheel, one arm bent and dangling over the glossy door, his eyes shut, his mouth slightly open, his hair as black as she had ever seen it. She couldn't remember the first time she had noticed him, really noticed him, the way he must have first no-ticed her when she'd been a baby.

"I wish you'd stop that, Dwight," she said, "sitting there pale like that."

He opened his eyes. "You should try this by yourself," he said. "Just try it and tell me what you think."

She sat for some time in the car alone, then went into the kitchen where Dwight stood, drinking water. It was a grey day, with a grey careless light falling everywhere.

"I had the tiniest feeling in there that the point being made was that something has robbed this world of its promise," Lucy said. She did not have a sentimental nature.

Dwight was holding a glass of water in one of his large hands, frowning a little at it. Water poured into the sink and down the drain, part of the same water he was drinking. On the counter was a televi-sion set with a picture but no sound. Men were wheeling two stretchers out of a house and across a lawn and on each stretcher was a long still thing covered in a green cloth. The house was a cement-block house with two metal chairs on the porch with little cushions on them, and under the roof's overhang a basket of flowers swung.

"Is this the only channel we ever get?" Lucy said. She turned the water faucet off.

"It's the news, Lucy."

"I've seen this news a hundred times before."

"This is the Sun Belt, Lucy."

The way he kept saying her name began to irritate her. "Well, Dwight," she said. "Dwight, Dwight, Dwight."

Dwight looked at her mildly and went back to the living room. Lucy trailed after him. They both looked at the car and Lucy said to it, "I'd like an emerald ring. I'd like a baby boy."

"You don't ask it for things, Lucy," Dwight said.

"I'd like a Porsche Carrera," Lucy said to it.

"Are you crazy or what?" Dwight demanded.

"I would like a little baby," she mused.

"You were a little baby once," Dwight said.

"Well, I know that!"

"So isn't that enough?"

She looked at him uneasily, then said, "Do you know what I used to like that you did? You'd say, 'That's my wife's favorite color . . .' or 'That's just what my wife says . . .'" Dwight gazed at her from his big, inky eyes. "And of course your wife was me!" she exclaimed. "I always thought that was kind of sexy."

"We're not talking sex any more, Lucy," he said. She blushed.

Dwight got into the Thunderbird and rested his hands on the wheel. She saw his fingers pressing against the horn rim which made no sound.

"I don't think this car should be in the house," Lucy said, still fiercely blushing.

"It's a place where I can think, Lucy."

"But it's in the middle of the living room! It takes up practically the whole living room!"

"A man's got to think, Lucy. A man's got to prepare for things."

"Where did you think before we got married," she said crossly.

"All over, Lucy. I thought of you everywhere. You were part of everything."

Lucy did not want to be part of everything. She did not want to be part of another woman's kissing, for example. She did not want to be part of Daisy's leg which she was certain, in their time, had played its part and been something Dwight had paid attention to. She did not want to be part of a great many things that she could mention.

"I don't want to be part of everything," she said.

"Life is different from when I was young and you were a little baby," Dwight said.

"I never did want to be part of everything," she said excitedly.

Dwight worked his shoulders back into the seat and stared out the window.

"Maybe the man who had this car before died of a broken heart, did you ever think of that?" Lucy said. When he said nothing, she said, "I don't want to start waiting on you again, Dwight." Her face had cooled off now.

"You wait the way you want to wait," Dwight said. "You've got to know what you want while you're waiting." He patted the seat beside him and smiled at her. It wasn't just a question of moving this used-up thing out again, she knew that. Time wasn't moving sideways the way it had always seemed to her to move but was climbing upward, then falling back, then lurching in a circle like some poisoned, damaged thing. Eventually, she sat down next to him. She looked through the window of the car into the other window, then past it.

"It's raining," Lucy said.

There was a light rain falling, a warm spring rain. As she watched, it fell more quickly. It was silverish, but as it fell faster it appeared less and less like rain and she could almost hear it rattling as it struck the street.

The Gangster's Ghost

•

===== SALVATORE La PUMA =====

*Salvatore La Puma was born in Brooklyn, and now lives in Santa Barbara, California. In 1987 the University of Georgia Press published his first book of stories—*The Boys of Bensonhurst.

Lying on the couch in the parlor with his shoes off thinking of his dead father, Ernesto got up when his mother called him from the kitchen, and felt his way in the dark. The lights had gone out when Costanza plugged her electric iron in the three-way socket the radio and electric heater were already in. Now his mother was handing him the plaster Virgin Mary's candles burning in red glasses.

"Ernesto, go down the basement. On top of the fuse box. Find the new fuse," said Costanza.

To his friends in 1939, Ernesto Foppa, fifteen, with his furry arms, chest, and back, uncovered in summer, and with his meaty body, was known as "Bear," and he was thought to be a little slow, too, especially by his teachers. He was a poor student who disliked reading and arithmetic. His hands, though, had an intelligence of their own, as untaught he rebuilt gummy carburetors, a dying toaster, radios with too much static, and for twenty-five dollars from Louie Perrino, disconnected the alarm at Morrie's Watches without getting an electric shock.

In the basement in his socks, Ernesto set the two candles on the old dresser, the flickering points silent metronomes dancing with the shadows. Before he replaced the fuse, something in the dresser's mirror startled him. He polished the mirror with his sweater sleeve. The faint shape seemed to take on a chin, a nose, and eyes, becoming a face as gray as the ashes he shoveled from the coal burner. The face kept developing. The red votive lamps were dabbing in rosy cheeks. Then in shock he recognized his dead father no longer dead. First Ernesto himself was as still as death. Then he bolted and tripped over a box of Christmas ornaments, hurting his toes and alarming his mother at the top of the stairs.

"Ernesto? You hurt? Answer me."

With little light to guide her, rushing down as if she were a feather instead of lumpy cushions, Costanza found Ernesto on the damp cement floor, his face against his knees.

"In the mirror," he said. "It's Pa."

"You hurt your head?" said Costanza, searching his scalp for blood and bumps.

"I saw him. He's there."

In the mirror the widow didn't see her husband's ghost, only her own face made old by sorrow and poverty. Having identified Romero in the morgue, she knew that with his vanity as Rudolph Valentino's near double he wouldn't show himself now that his face was shot full of holes.

Women had been attracted to Romero, and he had often broken his marital vows, but he always came home to Costanza, for he loved only her. Besides, honor had to be accorded to his wife or his associates would have held him in contempt. The Sicilian wife was thought to preserve the family's sanctity, and could be tossed out only if *she* were the unfaithful one. She, however, should tolerate her wayward lion who had seed enough for a pride of females. But Costanza never accepted Romero's prowling.

She was regretting now that she couldn't see his ghost in the mirror. She had saved up a list of grievances from nights alone in her bed. At the top of her list was Romero's foolish lack of fear, resulting in his early death for a cause paying a few paltry dollars a week.

Even though she was armed to send him shuffling back to his grave, before he left Costanza would kiss his ghostly face, just as she had when it was torn and bloodied. She ached so much for his gaiety and

for his attention in bed, even to praising the excesses of her body. And
she still adored the dead man.

Coming back to Ernesto and soothing her son's face with the palms
of her hands, Costanza detected again Romero's high brow, his rakish
black eyes, and she wondered why the vision had come to Ernesto and
not to herself.

"I can even touch the floor in back," said Bianca Bassano, sixteen,
the landlord's daughter, as the day's light was fading. Most boys ignored her because of her big nose, but Ernesto liked her for her doubt
that he really was slow.

"You can't," he said.

"I'm double-jointed. Watch this," said Bianca, turning on her hands
by the handball courts in the yard of New Utrecht High School. Upside down, her sterling silver miraculous medal on the silver chain
around her neck fell into her mouth, and her skirt fell, showing her
pink cotton underpants.

Until now, Bianca hadn't stirred up feelings in Ernesto. But they
were suddenly there, in his limbs, on his face, in his mouth. She
seemed made of bunches of the wine grapes which her father grew in
the backyard of the house on 79th Street in Bensonhurst. "That's
pretty good," said Ernesto. "I could show you a ghost."

"Bear, there's no such thing," said Bianca, disapproving of his su-
perstition, tossing her chestnut curls which she put up in rags at night,
although she knew curls wouldn't shrink her nose. She wanted to be
noticed by the boys, as were her cousins Tina and Julia. Not that
Bianca liked any boy more than Ernesto. Ernesto was the big teddy
bear who had rescued her the winter before from fresh boys throwing
snowballs.

"You can see it yourself. Come down the basement," he said. "By
the outside doors, so my mother, she won't see me bringing you
down."

"Why she care?" said Bianca, twinkling, sensing his growing interest. "What would you do?"

"Nothing. Talk. Play cards." Ernesto was acting the dunce teachers
and others thought he was. The ploy enabled him to escape uncom-

fortable questions, but proved to himself at least that he could fool people confident of their own superior intellect.

"If I see your ghost, Bear, will you watch me stand on my head? I can do it in the basement."

"I'll watch you," said Ernesto.

From eight kitchens in apartments on both sides of the alley, cooking smells made an antipasto for Ernesto's young appetite as they were sneaking by, bending low under the windows. He wondered if he should have gone in for his dinner instead. Reaching the backyard, Bianca pressed flat against the building while Ernesto wrestled with the double doors that covered the basement steps.

The candles having been returned to the Virgin, Ernesto first tried conjuring up the ghost by striking matches, while Bianca peered in the mirror earnestly, wishing it there. The matches were soon used up without the ghost appearing. So Ernesto turned on the electric light, and then he ahhhhed.

"See. It's him. My father," he said, chills on his spine, but not running, for it would be shameful to be afraid in front of a girl.

"That isn't anything," said Bianca, after some detective work.

"Watch," he said, pulling his sweater from his back and polishing the glass. "See him now? Hello, Pa."

"The mirror in back is just worn out," she said. "Sort of looks like somebody. But it's just the mirror."

"That you, Pa? I see you in there. Can you talk? Something you want? You want to come back? Is that why you're there? You want your body back, Pa? It's all shot up, you know. Out in Calvary, in Queens where the World's Fair is. If you want, maybe I could dig it up."

Bianca was becoming annoyed that Ernesto wasn't paying her any attention now that she had disproved his ghost. So she went to stand on her head, bracing herself against the wall, her stocking feet pointing to the ceiling. "You don't know anything," she said, upside down when Ernesto came to sit on the floor. "I know all about sex. My mother has a book. I read it. She doesn't know."

"Does your head hurt that way?" he said. "I know about sex too. We could go on the couch."

Bianca came down and, putting out the light, went to the couch. Its stuffing was coming out, and it smelled of cobwebs and coal dust. She presented herself to be circled in his arms and kissed. Then he picked up her skirt. When she didn't protest, he started tugging on her underpants. They were practically glued on her waist and thighs with unyielding elastic. He was wishing for more light from the dimming small windows. It seemed to him that half the fun of taking her pants down was to look. But if her parents or his mother were coming downstairs, the darkness would allow them seconds to be modest again.

"Now you," said Bianca, underpants around her knees.

"What?" he said.

"Bear, take off your pants."

"What for?"

"You're dumb. I knew it. I knew you're dumb."

"I don't want to give you no baby."

"You taking them off? Or not?"

"I'm taking them *down.* Not off."

"And your shorts. Now come over and lie on top."

Ernesto's heart was pounding like mad and his breath was coming short. And he was sticking out when he got on top. She put her hand there, leading him to the right place.

"You have to put it in," she said.

"Where is it?" he said.

"Right there," she said.

"I can't see it in the dark," he said.

"You don't have to see it," she said.

"I can't even find it," he said.

Ernesto was slipping off the couch, still holding Bianca, pulling her to the floor too. There he tried again and was making what he thought was some progress. Then Bianca started making peculiar sounds. She was sort of singing a hymn, and Ernesto didn't know whether to go forward more or to pull back and put his shorts on again. The decision was made for him.

"Holy cow!" he said.

Bianca said, "Oh my God. Oh my God. Jesus, Joseph, and Mary, have mercy on me. It's so wonderful. I think I'm going to die. More, more, Bear. God forgive me. I'm going to hell. Bear, pray for me."

"I can't," he said. "I have to get up."

"We're damned," said Bianca, stretching out her crucified arms. "Like Father Valenti says, we're sinners. We made a mortal sin. God forgive us. Let's say the rosary. Then I'll do my back flip."

"I never say the rosary," he said.

"You should," she said. "It always makes me feel better."

"Eating makes me feel better," he said.

A few weeks later, on her wedding anniversary, Costanza found it impossible to get the memory of her husband out of her bed. Her desire was so strong she cried and punched Romero's pillow, and would've killed him if he weren't already dead.

In the kitchen she consoled herself with a small glass of marsala, and then another. No other man could take Romero's place. She would wear the black dress and the black stockings the rest of her life, as if she were in Sicily, not in Bensonhurst. Besides, no other man would want a woman with too much of everything, even a widow. A widow was thought to be more available to sleep with, if not to marry, by the single men in the neighborhood. She would save herself for Romero, for when she would be with him again.

After another marsala, she found herself in the interior of the night with only the corner train passing every half hour. The stillness was in contrast to the storm in her soul. Remembering Ernesto's ghost and having enough wine to believe that maybe her husband really was in the mirror, she began to retrace her son's steps, going in the hall to the inside stairs and down to the basement carrying the burning candles in their red glasses.

After a minute, at this late hour, desperately wanting him, Costanza gradually accepted the tarnished oval as Romero in the mirror, not there vividly, but smoky as a vision. "You been a traitor to me. Always I was here. Always I took you between my legs. Sometimes you smelled bad. Your beard was rough, but I took it to my breast. But now you don't come home no more. I hate you. And I love you. So what am I to do?"

In his robe, Ernesto sat on the top step, awakened by Costanza's wanderings, following her voice, unsure now if he should enter the privacy of his parents' meeting at the mirror. He was waiting to lend a hand if she called for him, as she often did, simply to have him near, to share a moment together, to soften her sorrow.

"You miss your Costanza? You have other women there? Please don't, Romero. Wait for me. I won't be long. When Ernesto becomes the man. Then there'll be nothing for me."

Costanza kissed the glass and blessed herself, making the sign of the cross as if she had witnessed her personal miracle. At peace, at least for this night, and finally ready to sleep, she took up the red glasses and, turning, saw Ernesto there. His arms opened to her. He embraced her as a son would his wounded mother.

"I think he wants to come back," he said.

"The dead rot in the ground," said his mother.

"Pa was strong. Maybe he won't rot."

"He was stupid," said Costanza. "He liked the new suit. The car. And he had the gun. You carry the gun, you stupid too."

"A guy could make some easy money," said Ernesto.

Louie Perrino also lived on 79th Street and belonged to the same gang Romero had been in. Louie was in business for himself on the side, pulling small jobs to supplement his low gang wages. His regular duties were to hurt guys trying to hurt girls in the houses in Harlem, and to hurt other guys who forgot to pay back loans from the gang. Louie never had trouble sleeping after he hurt someone, since the guy always deserved it, and Louie did only enough damage to be persuasive; he didn't hate the guy he was beating up either, as if his victim were just the punching bag at Mel's Gym.

So far Louie hadn't killed anybody, but he packed the snub-nosed .32 in a belt holster under his jacket. He doubted he would ever pull the trigger, since word would get back to his mother. Louie knew she would never leave him in peace. To be on the safe side, he always kept his gun unloaded.

"Ain't nothing to it," said Louie. "We just pull up to the curb. You look straight ahead. I go ask the dame, nice like. Nobody's around, the show being half over. And she gives me the loot. Then you step on the gas."

"My mother would figure it out if I have a bunch of change," said Ernesto.

"Okay. I take it," said Louie. "You get tens."

"I don't know," said Ernesto.

"Your mother on relief ain't doing good. You have to help out. The son has to," said Louie.

"We have enough to eat," said Ernesto.

"She's in that same ratty dress. She needs a new one. Buy it for her," said Louie.

"I can't buy a lady's dress," said Ernesto.

"Look. You're the only guy I trust," said Louie. "Do this favor. I could put in a good word. When you get older, want to take your father's place? I could say, you're a guy has brass balls. I could say I saw them. Because you did this job."

On Saturday morning Bianca knocked on the Foppa door. Costanza, opening it, puckered disapprovingly, suspicious of this bosomy girl. With a woman's intuition, Costanza immediately sensed that Bianca had an interest in her son. But he was too young for girls. For now, he had a widowed mother to think about. That was enough. He didn't need a girl who swung her eggplants front and back going to the store. Besides, he could have a pretty girl without a nose he could hang his coat on. Ernesto, exiting from the toilet, went in the hall with Bianca, leaving his mother behind the closed door.

"I ain't seen you," he said.

"I've been around," she said.

"You want to come down? See the ghost?" he said.

"I got scared the last time," she said.

"You didn't," he said.

"Not by the ghost. But I missed. You know what that means? God. I thought the world was coming to an end. But it didn't. Maybe I won't be so lucky next time."

"We could just hold hands. Talk," said Ernesto.

"If we could read stories," said Bianca.

"I can't, so good," he said.

"Bear, you have to try. Can't you try?"

"What's the use?" he said. "I'm going in the rackets anyway."

"See what happened to your father?" said Bianca. "Maybe you really *are* dumb."

Ernesto went down the basement and threw open the outside doors. Three days a week he filled the ashcans and hauled them up into the alley. He did it for a dollar a week from Bianca's father. Mr. Bassano liked Ernesto, and since Romero's death nine months before, he had secretly adopted the boy as the son he wished he had. Ernesto liked Mr. Bassano too, but when he said, "You smoke. You cough. You get sick, Bear. Don't be like your father. Go learn yourself a trade," Ernesto played dumb.

His chore finished, Ernesto went to see if his father's ghost was there now in daylight too. Leaning on his elbow before the mirror for many minutes, he was remembering his father in a sleeveless undershirt presenting him with two baseball mitts on his twelfth birthday, one for each of them. Then they went out to the middle of the street early that morning and pitched to each other, Ernesto in pajamas, a few cars honking to get by. Now he sometimes played catch with the guys in the school yard, but he never lent any of the guys his father's mitt.

At first that morning Ernesto didn't see his father's face. He explained it to himself that ghosts were probably out during the day looking for work. The longer he studied the glass, however, the more his father's eyes were taking shape right before his own. He wasn't afraid now, even though he was alone with the ghost, and wondered if it had something to say to him, an important message from the grave. Then he thought he heard his father's voice. It was coming out of the glass softly, the way his father had spoken when waking him for school—regretting the disturbance of his dreams, but doing what a father must.

"I miss you, my son. I used to think of the days when you'd be grown up, as a good guy, not making my mistakes. I'm sorry I won't see that. And I'm sorry I can't help you out. You have to do it by yourself."

"I don't know what to do, Pa."

"Be good to your mother, but not tied to her apron. And don't be crooked. Otherwise, you'll get holes in your head."

"You had a bad break, Pa."

"Tonight, Ernesto, I ask you. Don't go drive Louie's car. Stay home. Listen to Eddie Cantor on the radio, with your mother. Louie's got a warm heart, but he leads you the wrong way."

"He's giving me fifty bucks."

"But what if you break your mother's heart? Don't go, Ernesto. Your father's telling you."

"I hear you," said Ernesto.

"Another thing," said the ghost in the mirror. "That Bianca. You could get her in trouble. You shouldn't do that. She's a little mixed up. But nice. She could be a good friend. So give me your promise."

Ernesto was silent for what seemed a long while. He was still caught by the eyes in the mirror. Finally, to break the spell, he said, "I promise, Pa." As he went up for breakfast with his mother, he wasn't so sure he meant it.

Whenever he went out at night his mother had to know where he was going and with whom. So that Saturday night he said he was going to the Hollywood to see *Jesse James* with Tyrone Power. With his developing cunning, he even asked if she would like to come along, knowing that in mourning she was denying herself even the movies.

For an hour, while he played pinball in the corner candy store under the elevated with other guys hanging around wondering what to do, Ernesto's mechanical genius had an audience. By gently tilting the machine, he was scoring to cheers, and winning more free games than he had time to play.

At eight o'clock he said he was taking in the show. Instead he took the ten-minute walk to Lorenzo's gas station, supposedly closed for the night. Alone in the office was Louie Perrino in his pin-striped suit, blue shirt, and white tie. As a sort of greeting, Louie took his fedora from the peg on the wall and tried the broad-brimmed hat on Ernesto's head.

"Pretty soon you get one fits," said Louie. "Your head must be pretty big. Or you need a haircut pretty bad."

Ernesto's hair was black, thick, straight, and unruly, while Louie's was fine, gray-blond, and thinning, with skin horns up from his forehead. Old enough to be Ernesto's father, but younger than dead Romero, Louie was slim and neat. He was unmarried because his widowed mother needed him and because in his line of work, if things didn't go right, he wouldn't be coming home some night like Romero; it wasn't fair leaving a wife and kids.

"My pa said I shouldn't do this."

"Your pa? Romero? He didn't have no tongue left to say boo. How could he be talking to you?"

"I saw his ghost. He don't want me doing this, Louie."

"It's up to you, Bear. I ain't twisting your arm. Your father says don't, so don't. But I thought you was a pal."

"I just said he don't want me to," said Ernesto. "I could use the dough for a suit."

"You afraid?" said Louie.

"Nope," said Ernesto.

"Listen, Kid. I ain't letting nothing happen to you. I know your old lady don't have no one else. Since you're here and all, just do this one. I won't even ask no more."

After the second feature started, at nine-thirty, Ernesto pulled up in the black '37 sedan. He was surprised at not being scared. But his belly felt like heaving up his mother's veal parmigiana. He wondered if his father was making him sick. Maybe it was lucky his father was dead. He had once put his fist through the bathroom door when Ernesto was in there smoking, and Ernesto hadn't had a cigarette again until after the funeral.

Strolling over to the box office, Louie showed his gun and said, "Please. Give me everything. You won't get shot."

Behind the glass the old bottle redhead turned and opened the back door, handing out two sacks of coins and a few slim packets of bills. As Louie was running back to the car, the redhead sang like Aida.

Then a cop with his tunic unbuttoned was coming out of the theater. Louie didn't get a chance to slam the car door before Ernesto had the pedal to the floor. Looking back, Ernesto saw the pistol, but all he heard was the thundering train overhead. Then Louie slumped down. Ernesto kept driving. After a few blocks, Louie half straightened up.

"Maybe . . . we should've listened . . . to your old man," Louie gasped.

Lorenzo's was closed and no one was around, and to make matters worse, Louie had passed out, but he wasn't bleeding much. Ernesto didn't know what to do next. He could leave Louie in the car at the gas station and hope that Lorenzo would find him in the morning. But tomorrow was Sunday and the gas station would be closed. Or he could drive to Louie's mother's house, but she was very old and might have a heart attack seeing her son passed out from a bullet that had gone in one side of his shoulder and out the other. Going to the hospital was out. He had learned that from his father. Doctors and nurses called the cops before helping. So that left only one place to go, even though he would get in hot water up to his ears.

Costanza could be awkward, a blimp floating in a couple of directions at once, but she was now mustering unexpected strength, looping Louie's arm over her shoulders and bearing most of his weight into the Foppa apartment. Ernesto held up Louie's other side. They laid him out on the parlor's oak floor to save the couch from bloodstains. Costanza took off Louie's jacket, tie, and shirt and held him in his undershirt in her lap. She cleaned his wounds with alcohol and iodine. Ernesto was also on the floor, away from his mother, as if to avoid her seething anger temporarily held in check until the immediate problem was solved. Costanza had wrapped Louie's shoulder in gauze and tape, but he was still out cold. And he was cold in her arms, so she sent Ernesto for blankets, overcoats, sweaters, and Romero's trousers, and buried Louie in them. After twenty minutes, sweat beading on his forehead, he opened his eyes unsurely, and Costanza called, "Louie. Louie. Gangster," and then he was awake and touching her face.

"I must be dead. You an angel," said Louie.

"Watch your mouth," said Costanza. "I'm a married woman."

"You don't have no husband," he said. "Maybe I'll stay *here*. You take care of me."

"What for? To see you get killed? Go home to your mother. Let her bury you. I don't bury no more husbands."

"Sorry to put you through this," said Louie, putting on his ripped jacket with her help. "I'll come back in a week, Signora Foppa, to show my appreciation. I hope you let me in."

"No gangster comes in my door. This time my son brought you. He thought you was dying."

"I like a woman with a little meat on her bones," said Louie.

Costanza was sewing her new dress. It was one size smaller—a print, navy blue with yellow flowers. Louie was coming to Sunday dinner again. He was the driver for Califano's hearse now.

With Costanza's approval, Ernesto and Bianca were on the couch in the parlor. Bianca was reading aloud a story in the *Daily News* one word at a time. And Ernesto, stumbling, read aloud the same story. It wasn't as hard as he thought it would be. They read four or five stories and captions under pictures. Then Ernesto practiced the multiplication tables, and Bianca tested him. If he recited a table without a mistake, she allowed him to catch her breast in her blouse for one second before she shooed his hand away.

"My father says you can have the job in his garage," said Bianca. "But at night you have to study mechanics."

"I know how to be a mechanic," he said.

"You only know easy things. He says you can't rebuild a clutch or do a ring job," she said.

"If I see it once, I could," said Ernesto.

"I've decided to be a teacher," said Bianca.

"If I was a mechanic, would you marry me?"

"I would."

"Even if you went to college? And could read things I couldn't?"

"Someday, Ernesto, you could own my father's garage, maybe own ten. And I'd keep the books. And we'd have lots of kids, with big noses."

"I like your big nose, Bianca."

Bumblebees

•

======== BOBBIE ANN MASON ========

Bobbie Ann Mason is the author of In Country, *a novel published by Harper & Row, 1985, and* Shiloh and Other Stories, *Harper & Row, 1982.* Shiloh and Other Stories *which won the Ernest Hemingway Foundation Award for best first fiction. Bobbie Ann Mason has received a Guggenheim Fellowship and other grants. She is a native of Mayfield, Kentucky.*

From the porch, Barbara watches her daughter, Allison, photographing Ruth Jones out in the orchard. Allison is home from college for the summer. Barbara cannot hear what they are saying. Ruth is swinging her hands enthusiastically, pointing first to the apricot tree and then to the peach tree, twenty feet away. No doubt Ruth is explaining to Allison her notion that the apricot and the peach cross-pollinate. Barbara doesn't know where Ruth got such an idea. The apricot tree, filled with green fruit, has heart-shaped leaves that twirl in clusters on delicate red stems. Earlier in the year, the tree in bloom resembled pink lace.

Allison focusses the camera on Ruth. Ruth's hand is curled in her apron. Her other hand brushes her face shyly, straightening her glasses. Then she lifts her head and smiles. She looks very young out there among the dwarf trees.

Barbara wonders if Ruth is still disappointed that one of the peach trees, the Belle of Georgia, which Barbara chose, is a freestone. "Clingstones are the best peaches," Ruth said when they planted the trees. It is odd that Ruth had such a definite opinion about old-fashioned clingstones. Barbara agrees that clingstones are better; it was just an accident that she picked Belle of Georgia.

They were impatient about the trees. Goebel Petty, the old man Barbara and Ruth bought the small farm from two years before, let them come and plant the trees before the sale was final. It was already late spring. Barbara chose two varieties of peach trees, the apricot, two McIntoshes, and a damson plum, and Ruth selected a Sweet Melody nectarine, two Redheart plums, and a Priscilla apple. Ruth said she liked the names.

The day when they planted the trees was breezy, with a hint of rain —a raw spring day. Mr. Petty watched them from the porch as they prepared the holes with peat moss. When they finished setting the balled-and-burlapped roots into the hard clay, he called out, "Y'all picked a bad place—right in the middle of that field. I had fescue planted there." Later, he said to them, "The wind will come rip-roaring down that hill and blow them trees over."

Barbara could have cried. It had been so long since she had planted things. She had forgotten that Georgia Belles were freestones. She didn't notice the fescue. And she didn't know about the wind then. After they moved in, she heard it rumble over the top of the hill, sounding like a freight train. There were few real hills in this part of western Kentucky, but the house was halfway up a small one, at the end of a private road. The wind whipped across the hickory ridge. Barbara later discovered that particular kind of wind in a Wordsworth poem: "subterraneous music, like the noise of bagpipers on distant Highland hills."

Now, as Ruth and Allison reach the porch, Ruth is laughing and Allison is saying, "But they never teach you that in school. They keep it a secret and expect you to find it out for yourself." Allison tosses her hair and Barbara sees that several strands stick to the Vaseline she always has on her lips to keep them from chapping. Allison brushes the hair away.

"Ruth, do you remember what you said that day we planted those trees?" asks Barbara.

"No. What?" Ruth has a lazy, broad smile, like someone who will never lose her good humor—like Amelia Earhart, in one of those photographs of her smiling beside her airplane.

Barbara says, "You said you wondered if we'd last out here together long enough to see those trees bear."

"I reckon we're going to make it, then," Ruth says, her smile fading.

"Y'all are crazy," says Allison, picking a blade of grass from her bare knee. "You could go out and meet some men, but here you are hanging around a remote old farm."

Barbara and Ruth both laugh at the absurdity of the idea. Barbara is still bitter about her divorce, and Ruth is still recovering from the shock of the car accident three years before, when her husband and daughter were killed. Barbara and Ruth, both teachers at the new consolidated county high school, have been rebuilding their lives. Barbara took the initiative, saying Ruth needed the challenge of fixing up an old farmhouse. Together, they were able to afford the place.

"We're not ready for men yet," Ruth says to Allison.

"Maybe in the fall," Barbara says idly.

"Maybe a guy will come waltzing up this road someday and you can fight over him," Allison says.

"I could go for that Tom Selleck on 'Magnum, P.I.,' " Ruth says.

"Maybe he'll come up our road," Barbara says, laughing. She feels good about the summer. Even Allison seems cheerful now. Allison had a fight with her boyfriend at the end of the school year, and she has been moody. Barbara has been worried that having Allison around will be too painful for Ruth, whose daughter, Kimberly, had been Allison's age. Barbara knows that Ruth can't sleep until Allison arrives home safely at night. Allison works evenings at McDonald's, coming home after midnight. The light under Ruth's door vanishes then.

"I never heard of two women buying a farm together," Mr. Petty said when they bought the farm. They ignored him. Their venture was reckless—exactly what they wanted at that time. Barbara was in love with the fields and the hillside of wild apples, and she couldn't wait to have a garden. All her married life she had lived in town, in a space too small for a garden. Once she got the farm, she envisioned perennials, a berry patch, a tall row of nodding, top-heavy sunflowers. She didn't mind the dilapidated condition of the old house. Ruth was so excited about remodelling it that when they first went indoors she didn't really mind the cracked linoleum floors littered with newspapers and Mr. Petty's dirty clothes. She was attracted by the larkin desk and the upright piano. The barn was filled with Depression-style furniture, which Ruth later refinished, painstakingly brushing the spindles of the chairs to remove the accumulated grime. The house was filthy, and the floor of an upstairs room was covered with dead bumblebees. Later, in the unfinished attic they found broken appliances and some unidentifiable automobile parts. Dirt-dauber nests, like little castles, clung to the rafters.

On the day they planted the fruit trees, they explored the house a second time, reëvaluating the work necessary to make the place livable. The old man said apologetically, "Reckon I better get things cleaned up before you move in." As they watched, he opened a closet in the upstairs room with the bumblebees and yanked out a dozen hangers holding forties-style dresses—his mother's dresses. He flung them out the open window. When Barbara and Ruth took possession of the property two weeks later, they discovered that he had apparently burned the dresses in a trash barrel, but almost everything else was just as it had been—even the dead bumblebees littering the floor. Their crisp, dried husks were like a carpet of autumn leaves.

Ruth would not move in until carpenters had installed new plasterboard upstairs to keep bees from entering through the cracks in the walls. In the fall, Barbara and Ruth had storm windows put up, and Barbara caulked the cracks. One day the following spring, Ruth suddenly shrieked and dropped a skillet of grease. Barbara ran to the kitchen. On the windowpane was a black-and-yellow creature with spraddled legs, something like a spider. It was a huge bumblebee, waking up from the winter and sluggishly creeping up the pane. It was trapped between the window and the storm pane. When it started buzzing, Barbara decided to open the window. With a broom, she guided the bee out the door, while Ruth hid upstairs. After that, bees popped up in various windows, and Barbara rescued them. Ruth wouldn't go outdoors bareheaded. She had heard that a sting on the temple could be fatal. Later, when the carpenters came to hang Masonite siding on the exterior of the house the bees stung them. "Those fellows turned the air blue with their cussing!" Ruth told friends. In the evenings, Barbara and Ruth could hear the wall buzzing, but the sounds gradually died away. One day after the carpenters left, Barbara heard a trapped bird fluttering behind the north wall of the living room, but she did not mention it to Ruth. This summer, Barbara has noticed that the bees have found a nook under the eaves next to the attic. Sometimes they zoom through the garden, like truck drivers on an interstate, on their way to some more exotic blossoms than her functional marigolds, planted to repel insects from the tomatoes.

Barbara's daughter has changed so much at college that having her here this summer is strange—with her cigarettes, her thick novels, her box of dog biscuits that she uses to train the dog. The dog, a skinny stray who appeared at the farm in the spring, prowls through the fields with her. Allison calls him Red, although he is white with brown spots. He scratches his fleas constantly and has licked a place raw on his foreleg. Allison has bandaged the spot with a sanitary napkin and some wide adhesive tape. Allison used to be impatient, but now she will often go out at midday with the dog and sit in the sun and stare for hours at a patch of weeds. Barbara once asked Allison what she was staring at. "I'm just trying to get centered," Allison said with a shrug.

"Don't you think Ruth looks good?" Barbara asks Allison as they are hoeing the garden one morning. Allison has already chopped down two lima-bean plants by mistake. "I like to see her spending more time out-of-doors."

"She still seems jittery to me."

"But her color looks good, and her eyes sparkle now."

"I saw her poking in my things."

"Really? I'm surprised." Barbara straightens up and arches her back. She is stiff from stooping. "What on earth did she think she was doing?"

"It made me feel crummy," Allison says.

"But at least she's coming out of her shell. I wish you'd try to be nice to her. Just think how I'd feel if you'd been killed in a wreck."

"If you caught me snooping, you'd knock me in the head."

"Oh, Allison—"

Allison lights a cigarette in the shade of the sumac, at the edge of the runoff stream that feeds into the creek below. She touches a thistle blossom.

"Come and feel how soft this flower is, Mom," she says. "It's not what you'd expect."

Barbara steps into the shade and caresses the thistle flower with her rough hands. It is a purple powder puff, the texture of duck down. Honeybees are crawling on some of the flowers on the stalk.

Allison picks a stalk of dried grass with a crisp beige glob stuck on it. "Here's another one of those funny egg cases," she says. "It's all hatched out. I think it's from a praying mantis. I saw it in my biology book." She laughs. "It looks like a hot dog on a stick."

Every day Allison brings in some treasure: the cracked shell of a freckled sparrow egg, a butterfly wing with yellow dust on it, a cocoon on a twig. She keeps her findings in a cigar box that has odd items glued on the lid: screws, thimbles, washers, pencils, bobbins. The box is spray-painted gold. Allison found it in the attic. Barbara has the feeling that her daughter, deprived of so much of the natural world during her childhood in town, is going through a delayed phase of discovery now, at the same time she is learning about cigarettes and sex.

Now Allison crushes her cigarette into the ground and resumes her hoeing, scooping young growth from the dry dirt. Barbara yanks pigweed from the carrot row. It hasn't rained in two weeks, and the garden is drying up. The lettuce has shot up in gangly stalks, and the radishes went to seed long ago.

Barbara lays down her hoe and begins fastening up one long arm of a tomato plant that has fallen from its stake. "Let me show you how to pinch suckers off a tomato vine," she says to Allison.

"How do you know these things, Mom? Did you take biology?"

"No. I was raised in the country—don't you remember? Here, watch. Just pinch this little pair of leaves that's peeping up from where it forks. If you pinch that out, then there will be more tomatoes. Don't ask me why."

"Why?" says Allison.

In her garden diary, Barbara writes, "Thistles in bloom. Allison finds praying mantis egg carton." It is midmorning, and the three of them are having Cokes on the porch. Ruth is working on quilt pieces, sewing diamonds together to make stars. Her hands are prematurely wrinkled. "I have old-people hands and feet," she once told Barbara merrily. Ruth's face doesn't match. Even at forty, she has a young woman's face.

A moment ago, Allison said something to Ruth about her daughter and husband, and Ruth, after pausing to knot a thread and break it with her teeth, says now, "The reason I don't have their pictures scattered around the house is I overdid it at first. I couldn't read a book without using an old school picture of Kimberly for a bookmark. I had her pictures everywhere. I didn't have many pictures of him, but I had lots of her. Then one day I realized that I knew the faces in the pictures better than I knew my memories of their faces. It was like the pictures had replaced them. And pictures lie. So I put away the pictures, hoping my memories would come back to me."

"Has it worked?"

"A little bit, yes. Sometimes I'll wake up in the morning and her face will come to me for a second, and it's so vivid and true. A moment like that is better than seeing the pictures all the time. I'm thinking the memory will get clearer and clearer if I just let it come." Ruth threads her needle in one purposeful jab and draws the ends of the thread together, twisting them into a knot. "I was at my sister's in Nashville that night and we stayed out late and they couldn't get in touch with us. I can't forgive myself for that."

"You couldn't help it, Ruth," Barbara says impatiently. Ruth has told the story so many times Barbara knows it by heart. Allison has heard it, too.

As Ruth tells about the accident, Allison keeps her book open, her hand on the dog. She is reading "Zen and the Art of Motorcycle Maintenance." It isn't just about motorcycles, she has told them.

Her needle working swiftly, Ruth says, "It was still daylight, and they had pulled up to the stop sign and then started to cross the intersection when a pickup truck carrying a load of turnips rammed into them. He didn't stop and he just ran into them. There were turnips everywhere. Richard was taking Kimberly to baton practice—she was a third-place twirler at the state championships the year before." Ruth smooths out the star she has completed and creases open the seams carefully with her thumbnail. "He died instantly, but she just lingered on for a week, in a coma. I talked to that child till I was blue in the face. I read stories to her. They kept saying she never heard a word, but I had to do it anyway. She might have heard. They said there wasn't any hope." Ruth's voice rises. "When Princess Grace died and they turned off her machines? They never should have done that, because there might have been a miracle. You can't dismiss the possibility of miracles. And medical science doesn't know everything. For months I had dreams about those turnips, and I never even saw them! I wasn't there. But those turnips are clearer in my mind than my own child's face."

The mail carrier chugs up the hill in his jeep. Allison stays on the porch, shaded by the volunteer peach tree that sprang up at the corner of the porch—probably grown from a seed somebody spit out once—until the jeep is gone. Then she dashes down to the mailbox.

"Didn't you hear from your boyfriend, hon?" Ruth asks when Allison returns.

"No." She has a circular and a sporting-goods catalogue, with guns and dogs on the front. She drops the mail on the table and plops down in the porch swing.

"Why don't you write him a letter?" Ruth asks.

"I wrote him once and he didn't answer. He told me he'd write me."

"Maybe he's busy working," Ruth says kindly. "If he's working construction, then he's out in the hot sun all day and he probably doesn't feel like writing a letter. Time flies in the summer." Ruth fans herself with the circular. "He's not the only fish in the sea, though, Allison. Plenty of boys out there can see what a pretty girl you are. The sweetest girl!" She pats Allison's knee.

Barbara sees the three of them, on the porch on that hillside, as though they are in a painting: Allison in shorts, her shins scratched by stubble in the field, smoking defiantly with a vacant gaze on her face and one hand on the head of the dog (the dog, panting and grinning, its spots the color of ruined meat); Ruth in the center of the arrangement, her hair falling from its bobby pins, saying something absurdly cheerful about something she thinks is beautiful, such as a family picture in a magazine; and Barbara a little off to the side, her rough hands showing dirt under the fingernails, and her coarse hair creeping out from under the feed cap she wears. (Her hair won't hold curl, because she perspires so much out in the sun.) Barbara sees herself in her garden, standing against her hoe handle like a scarecrow at the mercy of the breezes that barrel over the ridge.

In the afternoon, Barbara and Ruth are working a side dressing of compost into the soil around the fruit trees. The ground is so hard that Barbara has to chop at the dirt. The apricot is the only tree in the orchard with fruit, and some of the apricots are beginning to blush with yellow. But the apple leaves are turning brown. Caterpillars have shrouded themselves in the outermost leaves and metamorphosed already into moths.

Ruth says, "Imagine a truckload of apricots. It almost seems funny that it would be turnips. You might think of apples or watermelons. You see trucks of watermelons all the time, and sometimes you hear about them rolling all over the highway when there's a wreck. But turnips!" She picks up her shovel and plunges it into the ground. "God was being original," she says.

"The nectarine tree looks puny," Barbara says abruptly. "I had my doubts about growing nectarines."

"That man that ran into them in his turnip truck? They said he didn't look. He just plowed right into them. The police swore he hadn't been drinking, but I believe he was on dope. I bet you anything—"

Suddenly screams waft up from the house. It is Allison shrieking. Barbara rushes down the path and sees her daughter in front of the house shaking her head wildly. Then Allison starts running, circling the house, pulling at her hair, following her own voice around the house. Her hair was in ponytail holders, but when she reappears it is falling down and she is snatching the bands out of her hair. As she disappears around a corner again, Barbara yells, "Mash it, Allison! Mash that bee against your head!"

Allison slams to a stop in front of the porch as Barbara catches her. In a second Barbara smacks the bumblebee against the back of her daughter's head.

"He was mad at me," sobs Allison. "He was chasing me."

"It's that perfume you've got on," says Barbara, searching through Allison's hair.

"It's just bath oil. Oh, my head's stung all over!"

"Be still."

Barbara grabs one of Allison's cigarettes from the package in her shirt pocket. She pushes Allison up onto the porch, where she sits down, trembling, in the wicker rocker. Barbara tears the paper of the cigarette and makes a paste out of tobacco shreds and spit in the palm of her hand. She rubs the paste carefully into the red spots on Allison's scalp.

"That will take the sting out," she says. "Now just relax."

"Oh, it hurts," says Allison, cradling her head in her hands.

"It won't last," Barbara says soothingly, pulling her daughter close, stroking her hair. "There, now."

"What's wrong with Allison?" asks Ruth, appearing from behind the lilac bush as though she has been hiding there, observing the scene. Barbara keeps holding Allison, kissing Allison's hair, watching the pain on Ruth's face.

After that, Ruth refuses to wear her glasses outdoors, because the tiny gold "R" decorating the outer corner of the left lens makes her think a bee is trying to get at her eye. But now the bees are hiding from the rain. For two days, it has been raining steadily, without storming. It rarely rains like this, and Barbara's garden is drowning. In the drizzle, she straightens the Kentucky Wonder vines, training them up their poles. The peppers and peas are turning yellow, and the leaves of the lima beans are bug-eaten. The weeds are shooting up, impossible to hoe out in the mud. The sunflowers bend and break.

With the three of them cooped up, trying to stay out of each other's way, Barbara feels that the strings holding them together are both taut and fragile, like the tiny tendrils on English-pea vines, which grasp at the first thing handy. She's restless, and for the first time in a long while she longs for the company of a man, a stranger with sexy eyes and good-smelling after-shave. The rain brings out nasty smells in the old house. Despite their work on the place, years of filth are ingrained in it. Dust still settles on everything. Ruth discovers a white mold that has crept over the encyclopedia. "An outer-space invasion," Allison says gleefully. "It's going to eat us all up." Ruth bakes cookies for her, and on Friday evening, when Allison has to work, Ruth videotapes "Miami Vice" for her. Allison's tan is fading slightly in the gloomy weather, and her freckles remind Barbara of the breast of a thrush.

The creek is rising, and the dog whines under the front porch. Allison brings him onto the enclosed back porch. His bandage is muddy and shredded. She has the mail with her, including a letter from her father, who lives in Mobile. "Daddy wants me to come down this fall and live," she tells Barbara.

"Are you going?"

"No. I've made a decision," Allison says in the tone of an announcement.

"What, honey?" Ruth asks. She is mixing applesauce cake, from a recipe of her grandmother's, she promised to make for Allison.

"I'm going to quit school for a year and get a job and an apartment in Lexington."

"Lexington?" Barbara and Ruth say simultaneously. Lexington is more than two hundred miles away.

Allison explains that her friend Cindy and she are going to share an apartment. "It'll be good for us to get out in the real world," she says. "School's a drag right now."

"You'll be sorry if you don't finish school, honey," Ruth says.

"It doesn't fit my needs right now." Allison picks up her music and heads for the piano. "Look, think of this as junior year abroad, O.K.? Except I won't be speaking French."

Barbara jerks on her rain slicker and galoshes. In the light drizzle, she starts digging a trench along the upper side of the garden, to divert the water away from it. The peppers are dying. The cabbages are packed with fat slugs. She works quickly, fighting the rivulets of water that seep through the garden. The task seems useless, but belligerently she goes on, doing what she can.

Ruth comes slogging up the muddy path in her galoshes, blinking at the rain. She's not wearing her glasses. "Are you going to let her go to Lexington?" Ruth asks.

"She's grown," Barbara says.

"How can you let her go?"

"What can I do about it?"

Ruth wipes the raindrops from her face. "Don't you think she's making a mistake?"

"Of course, God damn it! But that's what children are—people with a special mission in life to hurt their parents."

"You don't have to tell me about hurt, Barbara. Do you think *you* know anything about that?"

Furiously, Barbara slaps the mud with her hoe. Next year she will relocate the garden above the house, where the drainage will be better.

The next day, the rain lets up, but it is still humid and dark, and a breeze is stirring over the ridge, as though a storm is on its way. Allison is off from work, and she has been playing the piano, picking out nonsense compositions of her own. Barbara is reading. Suddenly, through the picture window, Barbara sees Ruth in the orchard, pumping spray onto a peach tree. Barbara rushes outside, crying, "Ruth, are you crazy!"

The cloud of spray envelops Ruth. Barbara yells, "No, Ruth! Not on a windy evening! Don't spray against the wind!"

"The borers were going to eat up the peach tree!" Ruth cries, letting the sprayer dangle from her hand. She grabs a blob of peach-tree gum from the bark and shows it to Barbara. "Look!"

"The wind's blowing the spray all over *you,* not the tree," Barbara says sharply.

"Did I do wrong?"

"Let's go inside. The storm's coming."

"I wanted to help," Ruth says, in tears. "I wanted to save the tree."

Later, when Barbara and Allison are preparing supper and Ruth is in the shower washing off the insecticide, Allison says, "Mom, when did you realize you weren't in love with Daddy anymore?"

"The exact moment?"

"Yeah. Was there one?"

"I guess so. It might have been when I asked him to go have a picnic with us over at the lake one day. It was the summer you were a lifeguard there, and I thought we could go over there and be together —go on one of those outdoor trails—and he made some excuse. I realized I'd been married to the wrong man all those years."

"I think I know what you mean. I don't think I'm in love with Gerald anymore." Studiously, Allison chops peppers with the paring knife.

Barbara smiles. "You don't have to be in a hurry. That was my trouble. I was in a hurry. I married too young." Hastily, she adds, "But that's O.K. I got you in the bargain."

Allison nods thoughtfully. "What if you wanted to get married again? What would you do about Ruth?"

"I don't know."

"You'd have to get a divorce from *her* this time," Allison says teasingly.

"It would be hard to sell this place and divide it up." Barbara is not sure she could give it up.

"What's going on with Ruth, anyway?" Allison is asking. "She's so weird."

"She used to be worse," Barbara says reassuringly. "You remember how she was at first—she couldn't even finish the school year."

"I didn't want to tell you this, but I think Ruth's been pilfering," Allison says. "I can't find my purple barrette and that scarf Grandma gave me. I bet Ruth took them." Allison looks straight out the window at the water washing down the runoff stream, and a slight curl of satisfaction is on her lips. Barbara stares at the dish of bread-and-butter pickles she is holding and for a moment cannot identify them. Images rush through her mind—chocolate chips, leftover squash, persimmons.

That night, Allison has gone out to a movie, and Barbara cannot sleep. The rain is still falling lightly, with brief spurts of heavy rain. It is past midnight when Allison's car drives up. The dog barks and Ruth's light switches off, as if this were all some musical sequence. Earlier in the evening, Barbara glimpsed Ruth in her room, shuffling and spreading her pictures on the bed like cards in a game of solitaire. She keeps them in a box, with other mementos of Kimberly and Richard. Barbara wanted to go to her with some consolation, but she resisted, as she resisted mothering Allison too closely. She had the feeling that she was tending too many gardens; everything around her was growing in some sick or stunted way and it made her feel cramped. As she hears Allison tiptoeing down the hall, Barbara closes her eyes and sees contorted black motorcycles, shiny in the rain.

Early the next morning, Allison calls them outdoors. "Look how the creek's up," she cries in a shrill voice.

The creek has flooded its banks, and the bridge is underwater, its iron railing still visible.

"Oh, wow," Allison says. "Look at all that water. I wish I was a duck."

"It's a flood," Barbara says matter-of-factly. Her garden is already ruined and she has decided not to care what happens next.

At breakfast, a thunderous crack and a roar send them out to the porch. As they watch, the bridge over the creek tears loose and tumbles over, the railing black against the brown, muddy stream. The violence of it is shocking, like something one sees in the movies.

"Oh, my God," Ruth says quietly, her fingers working at her shirt.

"We're stranded!" says Allison. "Oh, wow."

"Oh, Lord, what will we do?" Ruth cries.

"We'll just have to wait till the water goes down," Barbara says, but they don't hear her.

"I won't have to work," Allison says. "I'll tell McDonald's I can't get there, unless they want to send a rescue helicopter for me. Or they could send the McDonald's blimp. That would be neat."

"Isn't this sort of thrilling?" Barbara says. "I've got goose bumps." She turns, but Ruth has gone indoors, and then Allison wanders off with the dog.

Barbara heads out through the field. From the edge of the woods, she looks out over the valley at the mist rising. In the two years Barbara and Ruth have lived here, it has become so familiar that Barbara can close her eyes and see clearly any place on the farm—the paths, the stand of willows by the runoff stream that courses down the hill to feed the creek. But sometimes it suddenly all seems strange, like something she has never seen before. Today she has one of those sensations, as she watches Allison down by the house playing with the dog, teaching him to fetch a stick. It is the kind of thing Allison has always done. She is always toying with something, prodding and experimenting. Yet in this light, with this particular dog, with his frayed bandage, and that particular stick and the wet grass that needs mowing—it is something Barbara has never seen before in her life.

She continues up the hill, past the woods. On the path, the mushrooms are a fantastic array, like a display of hats in a store—shiny red Chinese parasols, heavy globular things like brains, prim flat white toadstools. The mushrooms are so unexpected, it is as though they had grown up in a magical but clumsy compensation for the ruined garden. Barbara sidesteps a patch of dangerous-looking round black mushrooms. And ahead on the path lies a carpet of bright-orange fungi, curled like blossoms. She reaches in the pocket of her smock for her garden diary.

On Tuesday the sun emerges. The yard is littered with rocks washed out of the stream, and the long grass is flattened. The bumblebees, solar-activated, buzz through the orchard.

From the orchard, Barbara and Ruth gaze down the hill. The runoff stream still rushes downhill, brown and muddy, and Barbara's trench above the garden has widened.

"The apricots are falling off," Ruth says, picking up a sodden, bug-pocked fruit.

"It's O.K.," Barbara says, toeing the humps of a mole tunnel.

"I thought I'd fix up a room for Allison so she won't have to sleep in the living room," Ruth says. "I could clean out the attic and fix up a nice little window seat."

"You don't need to do that, Ruth. Don't you have something of your own to do?"

"I thought it would be nice."

"Allison won't be around that long. Where is she, anyway? I thought she was going to try to wade the creek and meet her ride to work."

"She was exploring the attic," Ruth says, looking suddenly alarmed. "Maybe she's getting into something she shouldn't."

"What do you mean, Ruth? Are you afraid she'll get in your box?"

Ruth doesn't answer. She is striding toward the house, calling for Allison.

Allison appears on the porch with a dusty cloth bundle she says she has found under a loose floorboard in the attic.

"Burn it!" Ruth cries. "No telling what germs are in it."

"I want to look inside it," Allison says. "It might be a hidden treasure."

"You've been reading too many stories, Allison," says Barbara.

"Take it out in the driveway where you can burn it, child," Ruth says anxiously. "It looks filthy."

Allison fumbles with the knot, and Ruth stands back, as though watching someone light a firecracker.

"It's just a bunch of rags," says Barbara skeptically. "What we used to call a granny bag."

"I bet there's a dead baby in here," says Allison.

"Allison!" Ruth cries, covering her face with her hands. "Stop it!"

"No, let her do it, Ruth," says Barbara. "And you watch."

The rags come apart. They are just stockings wound tightly around each other—old stockings with runs. They are disintegrating.

"My old granny used to wear her stockings till they hung in shreds," Barbara says breezily, staring at Ruth. Ruth stares back with frightened eyes. "Then she'd roll them up in a bundle of rags, just like this. That's all it is."

"Oh, crap," says Allison, disappointed. "There's nothing in here."

She drops the stockings on the damp gravel and reaches in her pocket for a cigarette. She strikes a match, holds it to her cigarette and inhales, then touches the match to the rags. In the damp air, the flame burns slowly, and then the rags suddenly catch. The smell of burning dust is very precise. It is like the essence of the old house. It is concentrated filth, and Allison is burning it up for them.

Cecil Grounded

•

RICHARD PLANT

*Richard Plant was born in Oklahoma City in 1959. A graduate of
Oklahoma State University and Washington University in St. Louis,
he currently teaches writing at Southwestern Oklahoma State University. "Cecil Grounded" is his first published story.*

Nothing to it, Cecil said to himself while the stick jolted crazily in his
hand and the engine made its final throaty coughs. He cleared the
Goebels's barn by eight feet, then dropped, didn't see now how he'd
ever make it over the jagged farmhouse shingles and into the meadow
beyond; so he fought the stick hard left and tried to hold her to the
tractor path running into Goebels's corn. It's all right, he yelled inside
his head, the engine dead now and only the wind roaring in his ears,
pounding insistently through the flaps of his aviator's cap but refusing
to tell him a damn thing. So he thought nothing when the wheels set
down on the earth with a knock that sent his jaw nigh through his
nose, and only *Lord,* this single word of prayer, as the plane crashed
through the corn: stalks snapping around him, dust and severed leaves
drifting onto the shuddering wings and into his face. Then the only
sounds were the hiss from the engine, voiceless sighs and crackles
(death rattle of the broken plants), and the thunder of blood in his
own head.

Goebels and his wife were already out of the house, running, when
Cecil stepped through the corn. He raised his hands over his head and
grinned at them. Grinned because there was nothing else to do; because he was alive; because he'd just pictured the hysteria he must

have caused buzzing the farmhouse: rattling the dishes in Mrs. Goebels's breakfront, scaring the farmhouse dogs into corners; and grinning because, after all, there'd been nothing to it.

Goebels was the first to reach him. Cecil thought the farmer had been cussing or mumbling something along the way, but he was only smacking his lips over a lunch left at table. "You hurt?"

"No sir. Not one bit."

"Your lip's bleeding."

Cecil tasted blood and grinned. "Must of bit it some."

"Criminy Moses. What happened up there?"

He shrugged. "Can't say exactly. Could be a busted fuel line."

"This happen before? You ever land on a whim like this before?"

"No sir, this is the first time Maybelline's gotten that idea."

Now Mrs. Goebels was beside her husband, and Cecil could grin and say, "Sorry about the corn, Ma'am. Looks like I owe you a few ears."

"Corn?" Her voice floated up like the toot of a penny whistle. "Don't talk about corn, when all the time running I kept thinking what was I going to tell your parents. Ringing them up to say you'd died in my cornfield."

Cecil said he was sorry for the scare, sorry too that he'd left a ten-acre swath undusted when the problem started. The Goebels walked him to the house, but he wouldn't go inside on account of the dirt and the chemicals coating his clothes and his hair. So they fed him a lunch on the porch. Mrs. Goebels came out to hand him a slice of ice for his lip one minute, a steaming cup of coffee the next. The fuss both embarrassed and tickled him. Overall, it seemed a good thing after the wind's roar in his ears and the stick bucking in his hands like something alive.

From the Goebels's porch he could see Maybelline's tail. Broken corn stalks dangled sorrowfully on either side of the plane's five-yard furrow, some leaves and whitish silks dripped from the stabilizers—making it look like the furry tail of some animal asleep in its burrow.

Finally he and Goebels went to look her over. Now Cecil felt in control again, not angry, ready to forgive Maybelline her pique or

illness, ready to start over from scratch. He lifted the cowling and
poked around.

"Is she broke?" Goebels asked.

Coming down he must have cracked a couple of struts in the undercarriage; the plane was listing heavily to the left. As for the engine, he
could conclude only, "Too hot to see much."

"We'll have to pull her out. Rain's coming in, too."

"Wet don't matter," Cecil said.

Goebels told him that his tractor already had disks mounted behind
so he wanted to turn over the twenty acres as he'd planned before
pulling them off and hitching the tractor to Maybelline. He said he'd
park her next to the barn, but if it rained before he got to her, she'd
probably be drier in the corn anyway.

"Lor-raine!" Goebels shouted, leaning inside the kitchen door with
Cecil standing behind him watching the purple streaks in the eastern
sky and stamping both boots to knock off the foul-smelling dust.
"What we going to do about Cecil Perkins? Take him on as scarecrow?"

"I guess he's stuck all right," she answered, unseen.

Goebels slammed the screen shut. "Lorraine'll drive you home." He
folded his arms over the denim pockets on his chest and stared into his
battered corn. "That must of took some flying, bringing her down that
way. Shake you up some?"

"No sir," Cecil said. "I had no doubts she'd make it down, just
didn't know how slow or fast."

Goebels gave a wheezy laugh. "I hope it ain't broke bad. You do a
real good job with that machine. Everybody says so. Course your
brother's regarded the famous one in your family, but nobody's got a
bad word to say for you neither, Cecil, and that's the truth."

"I guess I know it," he said for something to say.

Once again in motion, with an engine roaring smoothly and a wind
that, if he'd cared to lower the glass, could only be whistling, Cecil
leaned back luxuriously alive in the front seat of the Goebels's big
Packard and let the farmer's still-pretty wife ask him questions about
Emmett Wayne—which was fine, which was best, which was like shar-

ing something better than you between you, the way some folks could wear your ear about Jesus Christ or President Roosevelt, or the pilots in Little Rock could light up about Ford Tri-Motors.

"What's he studying there?"

"Politics. 'Course he takes classes in lots of subjects, math and chemistry and classics and such, but the main one's politics."

"He could be Governor."

"Might could," Cecil agreed out of real feeling and not just politeness. And he went on to describe his younger brother's wins in high school debate, the speech he wrote for commencement; described how Principal West had found himself short-handed one year and hired Wayne to teach a class of eighth graders before Wayne had even graduated high school himself.

But there were some things he didn't tell, details that emerged then settled back into his mind, unspoken, like the dust he saw in the car's side mirror, swirling and settling silently behind them. Cecil sometimes sent Wayne money, and Wayne sent back letters, different from the ones his parents received. These were meant only for him, Cecil, and carried Wayne's own voice on the slanted backs of his spidery ciphers: "I fell asleep to some *Fall and Decline,* woke to what I thought was the stomp of Roman legions, but was only Josh Hoppe drunk upstairs teaching his roommate the tango. If college is the gateway to high culture, it sure seems funny that Yale men are reduced to dancing with other men, more like lonely cowboys or lumberjacks." Or, on another occasion: "Fred McDeal (Ohio man) drove me down to New York last weekend. Wish you could have seen the airfield we passed. More planes than Arkansas has cars! Big passenger birds, too. I have seen the future and it's you, boy." But these were months old.

"Wayne was my alarm clock in summer," Cecil was saying instead. He told Lorraine Goebels about rising before dawn to dig fish bait, how it was Wayne's job to wake him, and so the first thing he'd see at four a.m. would be the kerosene lantern on the floor, hot from burning all night, and Wayne in the opposite bed leaning toward him and hissing his name, a book lying face down on Wayne's lap like a cat he'd stroked to sleep and didn't want to wake.

"Neither of our boys seems much taken with books," Lorraine Goebels said, sighing a mother's sigh.

Before this remark, Cecil had been thinking how much younger than her husband Mrs. Goebels looked, idly sketching out a story of child bride, bored and lonesome. In the fantasy he'd scripted, after a minute's silence Lorraine would begin to sing "Flat Foot Floogie with a Floy Floy," tilting her head forward just enough to smooth out the faint creases under her chin and casting wayward glances at the miraculously spared young flyer beside her. With a thin show of weariness she might propose that they pull over at the Negro jukejoint a mile this side of the Perkins house on the county road for a quick sad song from Lester Lincoln's guitarbox and a cool glass of shine. But of course these things didn't transpire, so when she stopped in front of the desolate barnlike structure Cecil was a little reluctant to call his home, he only thanked her and asked her to tell Goebels to look for him that evening.

"Give your family our best," she said. "And when you write your brother make sure he knows we wish him well."

"Thanks," he said. "I guess I'll see you."

The Packard rolled on toward town while Cecil stood in front of his house, trying to decide what to do first. About the plane, he'd best call Willet Yoates. Yoates was a farmer and self-employed mechanic who had originally bought the Martin biplane from Alvin Barlowe, the bank president, when the bank had started to slip under. Yoates already owned the fastest automobile and the strongest tractor in two counties and couldn't resist owning an aeroplane as well. But Yoates had it only for four years. Then his wife, Clarissa, discovered that the bottom half of their wheat wasn't getting plowed since Willet never had enough gas in the tractor to plow it, and he never had enough gas because he used it for Saturday joyrides in Maybelline. So for $1,750, paid out over three years, Willet Yoates sold his aeroplane to Cecil, who still lived at home then and worked in his father's brick kiln, making extra money from his fishbait business (which he could now recall in detail, perhaps because Maybelline had put his present vocation in jeopardy: getting up at four to dig the nightcrawlers that he sold to fishermen at sunrise, seated on a clover hummock by the side of the dirt turn-off to Carson Lake, his commodity squirming beside him in tin buckets).

Yoates had taught him to fly and take care of Maybelline, which came easy to someone as hand-minded as Cecil. He had given Cecil his leather cap at no charge; he would have thrown in his gloves, but they were too small for Cecil's big hands.

In Little Rock Cecil was certified by a man whose pilot's license had been signed by Orville Wright himself.

"Where you going to keep that thing?" his father had asked. And just the sight of it hulking out back was nearly all it took to make his mother cry with worry. So he'd bought this land on the edge of town and built a hangar for it, and this took so much of his time that he put up a board shack for himself and just started living out here. In spite of all these investments, he'd somehow managed to keep from spending his last cent, and after his father and his brother DeForrest both put in some money he'd wrangled a start in the crop-dusting business, probably because folks had always trusted him to do a good sturdy job, just as they trusted the sun to set in the west and the frogs to sing when it did.

Wayne's letters he kept in a cardboard box on the shelf beside the coffee can he filled with spare coins. And because Lorraine Goebels's well-wishes were more concrete and resonant than his fuzzy projections for fixing Maybelline or otherwise working out the day's remainder, he took these down. The last letter, now a week old, had been the most troubling of the series, tainting Cecil's eager encomiums with a ragged temptation to worry.

"Dear Cecil," it had begun. "I am well and hope you and the folks are the same. Give them my love." But then, instead of the worldly anecdotes and ironic asides he was used to gleaning, nurturing, and then scattering through town like wildflower seeds or insecticide dust, Cecil had read another, serious sort of message:

> I'm writing to you because you have always been so strong in my eyes and secretly so much wiser than your snot-nosed brother who went away to Yale and now is cracking up. How do I describe this? I go to class as always, get on with my professors, but more and more

I have less and less to say. There is a nervousness in my head that's been building like a boiler fire. Professors Wharton and Summers deduce that I'm ill prepared, that I don't read the texts, that I lack the necessary interest. Now I confide in you what I couldn't explain to them. You, Cecil, know I need no great excuse to exercise my eyes by lamplight. The pages are still turning, but my brain is losing its grip. I no longer have ideas. I can't even remember where ideas come from. And when I am presented with two ready-made ideas and asked to make a choice, I cannot. I don't remember how to judge.

On occasion I've flat looked ridiculous in class, mumbling apologies or proffering ludicrous guesses when called upon. But my fears are even worse: every day I sit at the end of a row of scholars and drive my spine down into the hard wood of my seat while I wait in terror for the sound of my name. If a professor calls me out I shall certainly scream, or gurgle unintelligible baby sounds while the rest of the class looks on, horrified.

When other students speak I am amazed. Where do they find the words and how do they know the proper sequence? I feel like applauding. I feel like all these other men find words magically etched across the glowing curve of their skull, while my eyes look in and see only darkness, an empty black cavern where the wind whistles through empty crannies and corners and bounces back from nothing at all.

Cecil, I can't imagine how this looks to you. I read it once and see that I have exaggerated my problem unforgivably. I read it a second time and find this account only a pale reflection of my terror. I don't mean to frighten you. I think I'm telling you this so that now I can afford myself the comforting picture of you holding my letter in your big hands, giving your head a pragmatic shake of disgust and telling me to remember who I am and what I am. Tell me this latest crisis is just a twinge of being sensitive to the point of womanly weakness. And even though you're there in Arkansas, I want to feel you shake me and slug me with your brick-baking, cloud-hopping hands, knocking the fluff out of my skull and putting me to rights.

Already I feel some relief. I trust you not to speak of this to Mom or Dad. My next letter, I hope, will be none of this sop but some real news.

                                                            Love, Wayne

After he had read this letter through the first time, a week ago, Cecil had opened the door of his handmade house and watched the sun slip off the edge of the blood-tinted cotton field across the road. Tomorrow should be good weather for dusting, he had figured. Little or no wind—the dust would be allowed to nestle into Sharp's corn like snow; then if his almanac was right, there would be rain later in the week to tamp it down.

Cecil had gone back in the house and read the letter a second time. Finally he put it down, stroked his long, stubbly jaw, and grinned. Hadn't he always known his brother Emmett Wayne to be the family genius, and didn't this high-pitched letter just confirm it all again? Cecil had never been to college himself, but vaguely knew that great men at college were supposed to experience crises of the heart and soul, lose God and then find him in another shape, and finally emerge viewing the world in a light and a language above the murky understanding of the common man—the common man being himself, Cecil. What else, he had tried to persuade himself, did Wayne expect of him but a slap and a grin?

Cecil found some hosing, clamps, and copper tubing easily enough in the nest of materials that had accumulated against the north wall of his aeroplane hangar. So before dark he'd wrestled a new fuel line into Maybelline's innards and gotten her to burn, without dying, a full gallon of petrol. But the rejuvenated engine rocked violently and uncharacteristically to one side, and Cecil had no idea why. Also, in dragging the plane from the corn to the lee of his barn, Goebels had done further damage to the broken landing gear, a mangled mess of splintered wood and twisted brackets that could only be replaced, not repaired.

Over the telephone in the Goebels's kitchen, where bare-armed Lorraine was kneading dough for her Saturday dumplings, Cecil, a stranger in this house, heard the disembodied voice of Clarissa Yoates; so that for an instant he could fancy himself capable of transcending the normal laws of space and time and maybe even sex, flitting from the tinkling voice of one woman to the sight (and smell?) of another.

"Willet's gone to Shreveport, Cecil. His brother there passed on last night."

"I'm real sorry," he said, suddenly small and mortal again.

She explained that the funeral was to be in two days, but Willet was likely to stay longer. "What was it you wanted?"

"It's no real matter," he said. "I thought maybe Willet would like to dirty his hands on Maybelline once more, but it'll wait. Is there something I can do for you folks?"

She said no, but would call him if there was. Cecil did not explain that his own house did not have a phone. He hung up, smiled his thanks to Mrs. Goebels, and before spreading the Yoates tragedy before her, shrugged at his own relatively comic share of misfortune and declared, "I'm grounded."

"You must think I'm tracking you." This was Cecil's greeting when he stepped through the barber's door and saw Goebels there with his youngest.

"Hi-you, Cecil. Lance here's getting too shaggy for Mama's taste. You know Mr. Perkins, son?"

"You fly the aeroplane."

"Yessir. Gus, you going to give ole Lance a shave today?" All three of the waiting chairs were filled, so Cecil sprawled in the black, wrought-iron shoeshine seat. Not yet noon and already the Saturday bucks had started to slink in for their haircuts and shaves, for a sprinkle of witch hazel on the back of the neck and behind the ears. Cecil was amused, although he was himself a courting sort of buck, though come to it late.

"I hear you taught that aeroplane some tricks, Cecil," Gus teased.

"She's a puppy dog. I say 'git' and she goes. I say 'roll over' and she do."

"What'd you say in Val Goebels's cornfield?"

"Play dead."

As the men chortled he pictured Maybelline listing against the side of Goebels's barn, shrouded in a canvas tarpaulin, and Willet Yoates bowed at graveside somewhere in Louisiana.

One buck, a teenager named Mitch'L Leeds, picked up the banter.

"Perkins, you pay Gus extra to scrape all them poor squashed flies, gnats, and nits off your face?"

Cecil had a reputation as a man who loved a good ribbing, to give or receive. "Mitch'L," he said, "you so soft, you go up in an aeroplane for five minutes with those little buggies slapping your face, I bet you come down looking like a bruised banana. I bet they knock you senseless."

"You was born senseless," Mitch'L replied.

"That's likely true."

"They held back his brains so Emmet Wayne could have a double dose," Gus said.

"I think that's so, and one smart feller per family suits me fine."

"How's Wayne doing?"

"Stupendous. Him at that college is like Jesus teaching the elders."

"He's a genius," Mitch'L Leeds said flatly, as though he were giving the time of day. "I went through school with him."

Shorn and bored, Lance turned to his father in the chair beside his. "What's *genius?*"

"Smarts, boy."

"Brains."

"Kentucky quarterhorse running in his traces."

"Might could be President."

"It means," Cecil said, looking serious, "when my little brother rides through this here town on his presidential train with the banners waving and the bands a-playing, the squirrels in the trees and the pigs in their sty better nod politely to him or else."

"Else what?"

"Else I'll pick them right up and make them nod," he shouted, bounding from the shoeshine dais, the iron chair vibrating as though struck by a violent wind—"Like this"—plucking the boy from the barber chair into the cradle of his arms, swinging the open-mouthed towhead back and forth, the barber's towel twisted and flapping.

"You!" shrieked the boy. "Hey you!"

Outside, Cecil could feel stray hairs creeping down his overalls, his shirt collar, teasing his skin like little shivers of ice. If he had any brains, he'd invent a new kind of barber's bib to protect customers from this lingering itch. As he paused, bending to brush the loose hairs from his head and face, Cecil heard a snuffle and moan. He took a peek down the alley behind the barber shop's west wall and saw a familiar dark huddle on the ground, shivering in the shadow of the bricks.

"Hey you, Lester."

The huddle raised its head but continued to shake. "What that?"

Cecil leaned into the alley. With one arm he pulled Lester Lincoln to his feet. "All right?"

The thin black man's head wobbled from side to side. He refused to raise his focus from the ground, as though that seat had become a warm, fondly remembered place. "Ain't me," he rasped, the words punched from inside.

Cecil pulled him gently into the sunlight and, satisfied that this dark skeleton could stand, released his arm and pressed some money into his palm. "Look here, Lester. Shaking so bad you could jar the bricks from this wall, be like Joshua's trumpet at Jericho. Now take this four-bits and buy yourself a drink."

Lester stared at the coins and finally tilted an eye up at Cecil. It almost made Cecil shiver himself, this glassy yellow puddle threaded with red, cocked up at him from a body that trembled like a thing possessed. "You a Christian man."

"May be," Cecil said. "But I suspect the dog what bit you done also snapped at me."

Cecil took the boardwalk in long, driving strides, testing the stretch and balance of his own muscles now, proving himself king of his own big body: sharp and strong, chewing the planks beneath his heels, spitting them out behind him.

The Eubanks Grocery reminded Cecil of a well-stocked cave, cool and clean and fragrant. When he heard the shiny cedar floorboards creak and shift beneath his weight, he thought instead of ships at sea and tilting decks. He bought a pound of sugar-cured bacon, apples, bread, canned beans, and wine. He teased the butcher for his cleaver's dullness, juggled apples for the register girl, and—full of himself once more—took up Eubanks's challenge to move the pickle barrel four feet to the south. There was a mousehole behind it they needed to stuff. The men waited until the store's other two customers left, then Eubanks closed the door and put Cecil's purchases next to the register.

"Don't hurt yourself."

"No chance," he said. "I waltz with barrels bigger than this in my sleep." The pickle barrel had water up to a foot from the top. He first tried to lift it by reaching around the highest metal hoop, which felt wonderfully cool but was too slick to grasp. So he squatted once more and this time hugged the staves beneath, pushing in until his wrists, his forearms, and his shoulders all tingled from the pressure. Nothing to it, he said behind clenched teeth. Then, straightening his legs, he hoisted it off the floor and tottered the necessary three steps while the floorboards sang in complaint. Some of the pickle water sloshed out when he set the barrel down, making a dark place on the shiny wood. They cheered him—Fred the butcher, Eubanks, and the girl who ran the register—and Eubanks reopened the street door.

"Don't ring up those apples, Grace. This lunkhead earned those at least."

Cecil rubbed his wrists and winked at the girl.

"You're Wayne Perkins's brother."

"I guess I must be."

"Hear from him much?"

"Now and then. Want me to say hi?"

"From Grace," she said, smiling. "I played clarinet in high school band."

"I don't recollect Wayne playing in band."

"Well, no, but that's probably the only way he'd remember me. I never stood out much but for the clarinet."

Cecil smiled back at this girl with the single talent and promised to mention her in the next letter.

Clouds were moving in. Cecil stood on the boardwalk with his bag of groceries, his clipped hair prickling the back of his neck, and watched the clouds. He sniffed for rain. It had missed them last night but wouldn't be long in coming now. Cecil was excited by the prospect of rain, the challenge of dodging showers long enough to pick up Patrice and make his parents' house without getting soaked.

Somehow informed of his trouble at Goebels's, Cecil's mother would likely start up on the dangers of flying, citing once more—this time for Patrice's benefit—the deaths of Wiley Post and Will Rogers, Amelia Earhart slipping into the ocean like a slender, fallen feather. She thought they should ban Jimmie Allen from the radio, prohibit his weekly adventures and tin aeroplane toys from stirring kids up about flying. As though an aeroplane were something wicked. Tonight Cecil would drop his heavy elbows on the table and argue. It's nothing but a machine, Ma. Why do you talk this way? Look, an aeroplane is just metal and wood, wire and petrol. You don't have to talk to it or pray to it or be real smart about it, you just have to know what little lever does what job. An aeroplane is no more mysterious than your own hands and feet, no more mysterious. (And all this time Maybelline would be crouching under a tarpaulin in a strange farmyard, the raindrops coursing across her canvas cover like tears across a face.) To avoid an argument, they'd talk instead about DeForrest, who was in the service, or Wayne, who would soon be home from Yale. He would lose at Hearts after dinner in the room where his stuffed pheasant and Wayne's debating trophy and a picture of DeForrest in uniform crowded the mantel. He and Patrice would excuse themselves to go to the picture show, but instead they would huddle together in his buggy, away from the rip in the roof, and head for Cecil's house on the outskirts of town. There they would shuck their wet clothes by candlelight and go to bed with the drops hitting the roof tiles and spattering against the windows and, likely as not, leaking through to pop on the floorboards like sparks from a fire. Racing the rain tonight would be like racing against gravity before lifting off in Maybelline.

Patrice was busy behind the post office counter weighing packages for an old-timer with a cane, so Cecil stood with his hands behind his back reading the familiar Wanted posters. Dillinger had been gone for years. Now there was round-headed Franklin Dobbs, sought for kidnapping. Armed and dangerous. What crime would he, Cecil, be most likely to join this roster of the infamous for? The F.B.I. did not waste their time and bullets on mere fornicators, show-offs, men who flew too close to the ground.

He turned and opened the door for the old man.

"You got a letter," Patrice said and disappeared behind the wall of silver-trimmed mailboxes. Cecil leaned on the counter; tried to pick out the smell of her.

"Here," she said, returning. "I was going to bring it tonight."

"Isn't that a crime, taking other folks' mail?"

Patrice leaned over her side of the counter. With her face beside his, she whispered, "You could lead me into a life of crime, Cecil DeLoss Perkins. Deep into it."

Cecil felt the top of his ear getting hot, there where Gus had clipped the hair close to his head. "It's fixing to rain. I should be by early."

She said, "Yes. You better."

He could hear someone step up behind him, so he straightened and asked for three stamps.

"Here. Nine cents."

"You say *nonsense?*" He spoke loudly, in feigned confusion. She wrinkled her forehead and pursed her lips in a crooked pucker. He found the coins in his bib pocket and pressed the last penny into Patrice's hand slowly, all four fingers curled into her open palm, caressing her fingertips as he lifted, turned, and left.

Cecil read Wayne's new letter seated in his buggy.

New Haven
April 29, 1938

Dear Cecil,

Things are getting worse. I may have to get help. The last two days I went to class but got nothing from the lectures. I know the teachers are speaking, I can see their lips move. But I can't make sense of the sounds that come out. I'm supposed to study for final exams. I'm looking over these notes that read now like something written by another person.

I think different people peak at different times. Mozart peaked early and Beethoven later in life. I've peaked and am now sinking fast. Maybe high school was my peak. At the regional debate tournament I delivered my rebuttal without even looking at my notes or pausing to think of a next sentence. They just came to me, gifts. I was like a spigot running full blast. And while I was speaking I did not lose a beat but felt like I moved outside myself and watched myself and it was wonderful. This sounds vain or stupid, I know, but it was a moment when I felt in love with myself and grateful I could filter ideas out of thin air. And now all I feel is a dread, a sinking into silence and ignorance. The spigot is shut off. I hope to limp through finals and come home. I want to come home very much. But I must pull myself together first. Mother and Dad can't see me like this. It's a frightened dead stone that I've become. Pray.

Love, Wayne

The air's moisture made Cecil's cotton shirt feel clammy before the first drops even fell. He tried to concentrate on the grayness of the horizon, on the rhythm of the hoofbeats, on the intervals between lightning flashes in the clouds—not on his brother's letter nor on the reply that before returning to town for Patrice he'd carefully scrawled and stamped:

Dear Wayne,
    Ignorance is no sin in my book. I hope you feel better about yourself. You have worked too hard and need a rest. Come home now. Grace who plays clarinet says hello. Here is fifteen dollars.

Love, Cecil

But since these diversions did not work, he tried to concentrate on Patrice, who leaned into his side but was quiet.

Although *loneliness* was a word Cecil had little truck with, sometime after Wayne had gone to school and he had moved out to his home-hangar, loneliness had begun to eat big holes in him, holes that flying and liquor and ribbing couldn't fill. He needed a woman was all. So when Patrice Jackson showed him that first sign of tenderness he had jumped for her like a startled buck jumps for the safety of trees. And she was sweet to him, lord she was sweet. She knew what he liked without even saying: such as pulling off her long stockings, like peeling a clean, sweet piece of fruit. When he had little to say she let him sit silent with no bother nor worried little bird-glances. And he never told her so, but he liked the way in bed her hands would push against his chest, not pushing him away but lying open against him and following him like flowers follow the power of the wind.

On Tuesday, Willet Yoates was still in Louisiana and it was still raining. Cecil should have been dusting five hundred acres ten miles east of the river. The cotton field across the way was saturated, water spilling from its furrows onto the road like parallel creeks emptying into a single river. He could look between the porch planks, through cracks under his feet, and see floating twigs, the dull reflection of water.

It was a quiet rain. Loudest was the drumming it made on the big chemical mixing tank behind the house. Cecil heard the bicycle's squeak before he looked down the road and saw the boy and the bicycle. The Western Union boy's yellow slicker was the only thing of color, the boy and the bicycle the only things moving under the dark blanket of rain. When the boy came alongside Cecil's house, he looked up. Now he knows I've been standing here watching him, Cecil thought. The boy looked more angry than miserable as he stomped to Cecil's porch, rain running off his hat brim and mud oozing from under his boots.

"Telegram," he said, opening a hard leather case on his belt and handing Cecil the paper. He said the words like a challenge, like something nobody should have to ride two miles in the rain to pronounce to a big man in his bare feet with nothing better to do than stand on his rickety porch and watch boys getting soaked, but he had done all that anyway, so there.

"Come in," Cecil said. The boy took off his hat and hit it against the porch rail. He had red hair, matted high on his forehead. The boy followed Cecil far enough for Cecil to shut the door behind him, then shivered once, like a wet dog. "I have some coffee," Cecil said, but went instead to his money can and picked out a dime for the boy.

"Yessir. Why don't you read it," the boy said. "You might want to send an answer."

Cecil stop checked into hospital for mental stop will not be home next
week as planned stop school wants to inform parents but I am telling
you instead stop make something up for me stop don't worry stop Wayne

When he looked up, Cecil was surprised to see the Western Union boy
still there, looking at him. "There's no answer," he said. The boy
opened the door himself and went back out into the rain.

Cecil took a wet rag and cleaned the floor where the boy had stood
in his muddy boots, then worked on the rest of the house, pushing the
rag in long, furious strokes. When he finally straightened up to shove
his bed aside, there was a cramp hammering at his back. He took
down the whiskey bottle and kept it open beside him. He carried his
three rugs outside and shook them out, flapping them one at a time up
and down like a giant bat wing; little swirls of dust became airborne in
the gray rain.

Inside the house he washed his drinking glasses. He emptied the
whiskey bottle into a clean glass, and after he'd drunk that down
washed the glass a second time.

Soon after, he heard the porchboards creak, the door swing open,
and there was Patrice. She tracked red mud in his doorway, but her
hat and her shoulders looked dry. The rain had let up.

"I wish you'd get a damn telephone out here."

"Hello," he said.

"You got a telegram from Connecticut. Is everything all right?"

Cecil felt like shouting at her, demanding to know how it was that
every weakness in his life became public knowledge, how news traveled so fast through thin air and became bad news only from the grime
of ears and tongues it touched on its way. Then he remembered that
Patrice worked in the post office, and that the Western Union desk was
also in the post office. He said, "Is that why you're here?"

"I was a little worried, yes." She had taken off her hat and coat and
hung them by the door. Now she was unlacing her shoes.

"Wayne," Cecil said, as he felt the story making itself up and cutting sharply through the whiskeyweight on his tongue, "was asked to
help a teacher with some research project. It's an honor and it pays.
So he's not coming home next week like we thought."

"Is that all?" Patrice pushed her hair back with her fingers and smiled at him.

"Yeah," he said. "Excuse me a minute." He made a sweep with his hand, something to indicate *Would you sit down? Help yourself? Whatever the hell you want.* Then he went out the back door. The stones that led to the outhouse were cold under his bare feet. They were also slick with mud, and Cecil was a little unsteady from the whiskey. He nearly fell.

The rain smelled like something alive.

Cecil closed the door. He sat to the right of the shithole, rounded and black beside him like a grin, and pressed his shoulder against the outhouse wall. Now I must make this something I can touch, something I can carry, he argued. After all, he was made to carry loads. His back was strong, his hands were strong, he was made of muscle and bone and will. Cecil pulled on his lower lip with his teeth, trying to taste the whiskey again. He could board a train for the East tonight, run down a moving boxcar outside of Shantytown if need be, and get there by Thursday. He could find Emmett Wayne and haul him right out of that hospital, lift him up with these hands, heft him over his shoulder. He could plow through whitecoats as if playing high school football. He could carry Wayne home like a conqueror.

What a strong and wonderful picture of himself, clearer now than the black earth between his feet. Isn't this what Wayne would expect of him, and so what he had to do? This vision hovered just overhead, tugging him after. And the warm whiskey was expanding and pushing him out of himself, up toward the vision. Then between these two forces, not trying too hard, he felt his spirit pushing out at his taut shoulders, pushing out at his neck, jumping with a frenzy he never expected of his own lazy, half-lidded soul. Now he could feel it ooze free, rising two or three wobbly feet in the outhouse dark. Cecil DeLoss looked down. What he saw was his own big agonized self all bent and heaving with a wet glisten on the hair of his forearms. He heard himself moan, and his soul slipped back in like a kiss.

Honey

•

========= **ANN BEATTIE** =========

*Ann Beattie was born in Washington, D.C., and now lives in Char-
lottesville, Virginia. A monograph,* Alex Katz by Ann Beattie, *was
published by Abrams in 1987. She is at work on a novel.*

Elizabeth's next-door neighbors were having a barbecue. Though Elizabeth and Henry had lived in the house since his retirement three
years before, they had only once eaten dinner next door, and the
neighbors had only once visited them. After Henry's car accident, the
Newcombs had called several times, but when Henry returned, they
again only silently nodded or waved across the wide expanse of lawn
when they caught sight of each other through the scrub pines that
separated their property. Mrs. Newcomb was said to be an alcoholic.
The boys, though, were beautiful and cheerful. When they were not
joking with each other, their expressions became dreamy. The way
they wore their hair, and their direct gazes, reminded Elizabeth of
Clark Gable. She often saw the boys in Bethel. They were inseparable.

Though Elizabeth was re-potting geraniums, her mind was partly
on the boys next door, partly on her daughter, Louisa, who lived in
Atlanta and who had had a baby the week before, and partly on Z,
who had phoned that morning to say that he would stop by for a visit
on the weekend. Her thoughts seemed to jump between those people
in time with the slap of the softball into the catcher's mitt next door.
As they tended the barbecue grill, the brothers were tossing a ball
back and forth. The air smelled of charred meat.

The day before, backing out of a parking place next to the market,

Elizabeth had hit a trashcan and dented the side of Henry's car. Louisa had not wanted her to come to Atlanta to help out. Z's fiancée drank a bit much.

Elizabeth forced herself to smile, so that she would cheer up. Wind chimes tinkled and a squirrel ran across a branch, and then Elizabeth's smile became genuine. It had been a month since Z's last visit, and she knew that he would be enthusiastic about how verdant everything had become.

Verdant? If a dinosaur had a vocabulary, it might come up with the word verdant. She was almost forty-five. Z was twenty-three. After Z's last visit, Henry had accused her of wanting to be that age. She had gotten a speeding ticket, driving Z's convertible.

Henry suspected the extent of her feelings for Z, of course. The attachment was strong—although the two of them talked around it, privately. She often thought of going to see the remake of "Reckless" with Z at a matinee in New Haven. They had shared a tub of popcorn and licked butter off each other's fingers. Another time, they brown-bagged a half-pint of Courvoisier and slugged it down while, on the screen, Paul Newman drove more crazily than Elizabeth would ever dare to drive.

A few days ago, returning from the train station, Elizabeth had come to an intersection in Weston, and as she came to a stop, Paul Newman pulled up. He went first. Rights of the famous, and of who has the newer car. Although convertibles, in this part of the world, were always an exception and went first.

Next door, the boys had stopped playing ball. One probed the meat, and the other changed the station on the radio. Elizabeth had to strain to hear, but it was what she had initially thought: Janis Joplin, singing "Cry, Baby."

The best songs might be the ones that no one could dance to.

On Saturday, sitting in a lawn chair, Elizabeth started to assign her friends and family roles. Henry would be emperor. . . . The lawn sprinkler revolved with the quick regularity of a madman pivoting, spraying shots from a machine gun.

Henry would be Neptune, king of the sea.

A squirrel ran, stopped, dug for something. It seemed not to be real, but the creation of some animator. The wind chimes tinkled. The squirrel ran up the tree, as if a bell had summoned it.

Ellen, Z's fiancée, was inside, on the telephone, getting advice about how to handle Monday's follow-up interview. She was leaning against the corner of the bookcase, drinking bourbon and water. Z detoured from the kitchen to the dining room to nuzzle her neck. He had come in to help Elizabeth, when she left the yard to get trays. One tray was oval, painted to look like a cantaloupe. The other was in the shape of a bull. She had bought them years ago in Mexico. Devilled eggs were spread out on the bull. The canteloupe held a bottle of gin and a bottle of tonic. A lime was in Z's breast pocket. A knife was nestled among the eggs.

Elizabeth held the back door open, and Z walked out. Henry's friend and lawyer, Max, was there, and a friend of Max's named Len. Dixie had stopped by for a drink, en route to her new house in Kent. Dixie was in the process of ending an affair with her architect. He had gotten religion during the building of the house. He had put skylights everywhere, so that God's radiance could shine in.

Z and Max were discussing jade. The man who used to deliver seltzer to Max was now smuggling jade into the country. Max was saying that people were fools to swallow prophylactics filled with drugs: look at the number of deaths. If jade spilled into somebody, it would just be like jellybeans that would never be digested.

Ellen came out of the house. She had had several drinks and, chin up, trying to look sober, she looked like a stunned soldier. She called out to Elizabeth that Louisa was on the phone. "The minute I put it back in the cradle, it rang," Ellen said.

Elizabeth thought: the cradle of the phone; the cradle she had ordered for Louisa's child . . . She was smiling when she picked up the phone, so it came as a surprise that Louisa was angry with her.

"I offered to come," Elizabeth said. "You said you had enough people underfoot."

"You *offered,*" Louisa said. "You never said you *wanted* to come. I could hear it in your voice."

"I wanted to come," Elizabeth said. "I was quite hurt you didn't want me. Ask your father."

"Ask my father," Louisa said. She snorted. "So who's there today?" she said. "Neighbors? Friends from far and wide?"

In recent years, Elizabeth had begun to realize that Louisa was envious of her knowing so many people. Louisa was shy, and when she was a child, Elizabeth had thought that surrounding her with people might bring her out. When she taught, she did seem to find many interesting people.

"Oh, go ahead and go back to your party," Louisa said.

"Please tell me to come to Atlanta if you want me," Elizabeth said.

"Yes, *do* conclude this foolishness," Louisa said.

Sometimes Louisa was so good at mocking what she thought were her mother's attitudes that Elizabeth actually cringed. As they hung up, Elizabeth said a silent prayer: Please let her have had this baby for the right reason. Please let it not be because she thinks that if someone needs her, he loves her.

Z was in the doorway when she opened her eyes. She looked at him, as startled as if the lights had just come up in the movies.

"Headache?" he said.

She shook her head no.

"Your eyes were closed," he said. "You were standing so still."

"I was talking on the phone," she said.

He nodded and left the room. He opened the refrigerator to get more ice. She heard the cubes cracking as he ran water, then twisted the tray.

Outside, Dixie was volunteering to go into town and get movies. Henry told her to get one serious one and one funny one. Most people did that when they went to Videoville, to allow for the possibility that they might want to be silly, after all. Elizabeth realized that it was harsh of her to judge Henry—it was overreacting to think of his insisting that Dixie get what he called "a comedy and a tragedy" as ambivalence.

"It was right there," Henry was suddenly saying to Max. "Riiiight there, and I tapped it with the cane. Looked at Jim, back in the cart, and he looked away, to let me know he hadn't noticed. Hell, I *had* done good to land it there, with one leg that wouldn't even swivel. Who's going to criticize somebody who's half crippled? It'd be like taking exception to finding a blind man in the ladies' room."

On Wednesday Len stopped by, having guessed that the bracelet in his car must have been Dixie's, lost when she borrowed his car to go to Videoville. Henry was upstairs, taking his afternoon nap, when Len arrived. Elizabeth invited him in for an iced tea. He countered with an offer of lunch. He was house-sitting for his brother, whose house was about fifteen miles away. She didn't know she would be driving thirty miles when she got in the car. Why take her there, instead of into Bethel, or to Westport, for lunch? she wondered. He probably thought that she was more fun than she was, because they had gotten involved in a drunken game the other night, playing matador in the backyard with the tablecloth and the bull tray.

She had put on Dixie's bracelet for safekeeping: copper strands, intertwined, speckled with shiny blue stone. The stones flashed in the sunlight. Always, when she was in someone else's yard, she missed the music of the wind chimes and wondered why more people did not hang them in trees.

She and Len strolled through the backyard. She waited while Len went inside and got glasses of wine to sip as they surveyed the garden. The flowers were rather chaotic, with sunflowers growing out of the phlox. Scarlet Sage bordered the beds. Len said that he had been surprised that she did not have a garden. She said that gardening was Henry's delight, and of course, so soon after the accident, he wasn't able to do it. He looked at her carefully as she spoke. It was clear to her that she was giving him the opportunity to ask something personal, by mentioning her husband. Instead, he asked about the time she had taught in New Haven. He had been accepted there years ago, he told her, but he had gone instead to Duke. As they strolled, she learned that Max and Len had been college roommates. As he spoke, Elizabeth's attention wandered. Was it possible that she was seeing what she thought?

A duck was floating in a washtub of water, with a large fence

around it. Phlox was growing just outside the wire. Bees and butterflies flew around the flowers. There was a duck, floating.

Len smiled at her surprise. He said that the pen had been built for a
puppy, but his brother had realized that he could not give the puppy
enough time, so he had given it away to an admirer. The duck was
there in retirement.

"Follow me," Len said, lifting the duck out of the tub and carrying
it into the house. The duck kicked, but made no noise. Perhaps it was
not kicking, but trying to swim through the air.

Inside, Len went to the basement door, opened it, and started down
the steps. "This way," he hollered back.

She followed him. A fluorescent light blinked on. On one corner of a
desk piled high with newspapers, there was a rather large cage with
MR. MUSIC DUCK stencilled across the top. The cage was divided
into two parts. Len put the duck in on the right and closed the door.
The duck shook itself. Then Len reached in his pocket and took out a
quarter and dropped it into the metal box attached to the front of the
cage. A board rose, and the duck turned and hurried to a small piano
with a light on top of it. With its beak, the duck pulled the string,
turned on the light, and then began to thump its beak up and down
the keyboard. After five or six notes, the duck hurried to a feed dish
and ate its reward.

"They were closing some amusement park," Len said. "My brother
bought the duck. The guy who lives two houses over bought the dancing chicken." He reached in the cage, removed the duck, and smiled.
He continued to smile as he walked past her, duck clasped under his
arm, and started to walk upstairs. At the top, he crossed the kitchen,
pushed open the back door, and carried the duck out to the pen. She
watched through a window. The duck went back to the water silently.
Len looked at it a few seconds, then turned back toward the house.

In the kitchen, Len poured more wine and lifted plates out of the
refrigerator. There was cheese and a ham butt. He took out a bunch of
radishes—bright red, some of them cracked open so that white worms
appeared to be twisted around the bulbs. He washed them and cut off
the tops and tips with scissors.

They ate standing at the counter. They talked about the sweaty bicycle riders who had been pouring over the hilly highways near Elizabeth's house all summer. She looked out the window and saw the duck swim and turn, swim and turn. She poured a third glass of wine. That finished the bottle, which she left, empty, in the refrigerator. Len reminisced about his days at Duke. He asked then, rather abruptly, if he should drive her home.

In the car, he put on the radio, and she remembered the crashing keys under the duck's bill as it played the piano. Drinking wine had made her think of the brandy in the bag, and of sitting in the matinee with Z.

She wondered what she would say to Henry about how she had spent the afternoon. That she had eaten lunch and watched a duck play the piano? She felt foolish, somehow—as if the day had been her idea, and a silly idea at that. To cover for the way she felt, and in case Len could read her mind, she invited him to Sunday brunch. He must be lonesome, she realized; presiding over someone else's house and someone else's duck was probably not his idea of a perfect day, either. But who was he, and why had he not said? Or: why did she think that everything had to have a sub-text?

She shook his hand when he dropped her off. His eyes were bright, and she realized that the ride back had been much faster than the ride to the house. His eyes riveted on the stones in the bracelet. Henry, too, noticed the bracelet the minute she came in, and told her that he was glad she had gone out and bought herself something pretty. He seemed so genuinely pleased that she did not tell him that it was Dixie's bracelet. It hurt her to disappoint him. It would have saddened him if she had admitted that the bracelet was not hers, just as he had been very worried when she told him, some time ago, that the college where she taught in New Haven was no longer using part-time faculty, and that she would not be teaching there after the end of the semester. She had been able to say that, in spite of his sad face, but of course other thoughts remained private.

Z had young hands. That was what had stopped her. Or maybe she thought that because she wanted to think that there had been one thing that stopped her. He had large, fine hands and long, narrow feet. Sometimes it seemed that she had always known him in summer.

She searched her mind for the title of the poem by Robert Browning about the poor servant girl who had only one day off a year.

Here it was Sunday, and she was entertaining again. Z (without Ellen, who was having a snit); Len; Max; Margie and Joe Ferella, who owned the hardware store; Louisa and the baby.

What a week it had been. Phone calls back and forth between Connecticut and Atlanta, between herself and Louisa, between Louisa and Henry, between Louisa's husband and both of them—and finally, through a flood of tears, after Louisa accused Elizabeth of every example of callousness she could think of, she had said that not only did she want to be with Elizabeth and Henry, but that she wanted to be with them *there*. She wanted them to see the baby.

The baby, in a cotton shirt and diapers, slept on Louisa's chest.

Louisa's hand hovered behind the baby's head, as if it might suddenly snap back. Elizabeth was reminded of the duck, held in the crook of Len's arm—how lightly it rode there, going downstairs to play the piano.

Ellen came after all, in a pink sundress that showed off her tan, wearing high-heeled sandals. She went to the baby and lightly touched its shoulder. She said that the baby was miraculous and fawned over him, no doubt embarrassed that she had made a scene with Z earlier. She did not seem to want to look at Z. He was obviously surprised that she had come.

They were drinking Soave, with a little Cointreau mixed in. A big glass pitcher of golden liquid sat on the center of the table. The food was vegetables that had been sautéed in an olive oil as green as Max's treasured jade; a plate with three kinds of sausages; a wooden tray with bunches of radishes (she had placed scissors on the board, to see if Len would say anything, just as a reminder of the day); strawberries; sourdough bread; cornbread and honey.

Everyone was exclaiming. Several hands reached for the pitcher at once. Beads of sweat streamed down the glasses. Z complimented Elizabeth on the meal, as he poured more of the wine mixture into her glass. It was so easy to please people: to take advantage of a summer day and to bring out attractive food, with trays rimmed with sprigs of mint, studded with daisies. Even Louisa cheered up. She lifted a sausage with her fingers and smiled. She relinquished the baby to Ellen, and soon Ellen's lips were resting on the baby's tiny pink ear. Pretty, pretty, Elizabeth thought—even though she did not like Ellen much. Pretty the way her lips touched the baby's hair. Pretty the way her diamond sparkled.

She looked around the table, and thought silently: Think only about the ways in which they are wonderful. Henry's cheeks, from the long morning in the sun, were pink enough to make his eyes appear more intensely brown. Next to him, Z raised the lid off the honey pot and she looked at those fingers she loved—the ones that, as he gestured to make a point, seemed to probe the air to see if something tangible could be brought forward. Margie and Joe were as attuned to each other as members of a chorus line (he looked at the cornbread, and her hand pulled the tray forward). Max was so complacent, so at ease, that any prankster would have known where to throw the firecracker for best results. Len, sitting next to Louisa, edged his shoulder a little closer and—as Louisa had done earlier—cupped his hand protectively behind the baby's head. And Louisa, though there were dark circles under her eyes, was still the child—half charming, half exasperating— who picked out her favorite vegetables and left the others.

Next door the brothers, again lighting the barbecue, again tossing the softball, shouted insults to each other and then cracked up at their inventiveness. One threw the ball and it rolled away; the other threw it back underhand, so that it arched high.

What happened, then, out on the lawn, was this: Henry swatted at a bee with a roll of paper towels, and suddenly three or four more buzzed low over the table. Hardly had any of them begun to realize what was happening when bees began to appear everywhere, dropping down on the table like a sudden rain, swarming, so that in a few seconds anyone who had not seen the honey pot on the table to begin with would have seen only a cone of bees the size of a pineapple. And then—however wonderful they had been—Max became in an instant the coward, chair tipped back, colliding almost head-on with Margie Ferella; Henry reached for his cane and was stung on the wrist; as a bee flew past Ellen's nose, she screamed, shooting up from the chair, knocking over her glass of wine. Joe Ferella put his hands over his head and urged the others to do the same. Louisa snatched the baby back from Ellen, hate in her eyes because Ellen had only been concerned with her own safety, and it had seemed certain that she would simply drop the baby and run.

When Elizabeth remembered the afternoon, late that night, in bed, it was as if she had not been a part of it. She had the sense that the day, like a very compelling movie, was something half dreamed. That there was something inevitable and romantic about the way she and Z had risen in unison and reached toward each other reflexively.

Later, Henry had told her that her hand and Z's, clasped across the table, had reminded him of the end of a tennis match, when the winner and the loser gripped hands perfunctorily. And then he had stopped himself. What an odd thing to think of, he had said: clearly there had been no competition at all.

Don't Worry About the Kids

(for Jerry Perlman)

•

========= JAY NEUGEBOREN =========

Jay Neugeboren is the author of nine books, most recently The Stolen
Jew, *which won the* Present Tense *award of the American Jewish
Committee for Best Novel of 1981, and* Before My Life Began, *which
won the Edward Lewis Wallant Memorial Prize for Best Novel of
1985. He is Writer-in-Residence at the University of Massachusetts in
Amherst, and lives in Northampton, Massachusetts.*

Michael imagined that he could see the fragrances coming at him in
waves, that each wave was a different color. He sat in a small Italian
restaurant in the Cobble Hill section of Brooklyn, Langiello, the
court-appointed investigator, across from him. Langiello was talking
about his own marriage and divorce, about how he had begun living
with his second wife before he had even filed for a separation. It was
crazy, he said, what love could do to you when it took hold.

Michael tried to smile, felt his upper lip quiver, stared at his plate.
The gnocchi seemed to be carved from balsa wood, floured with potato dust. He thought of radio waves, outside the restaurant, shimmer-
ing in the air, passing through the metal roofs of automobiles, the
brick walls of apartment houses, the windows of office buildings and
storefronts. He inhaled, tried to separate the fragrances, to name
them. He saw low smoky-green S-curves for basil, high rolling mountains of barn-red for tomatoes, graceful ripples of ivory for garlic.

"So you can relax, Mike, let me tell you right off that I think the present custody setup is lousy and that I'm going to recommend some changes." Langiello smiled easily. "Okay?"

Michael nodded. He liked Langiello, like the man's manner: the streetwise directness, the rough-edged tenderness. Langiello reminded him of the Italian guys he'd gone to grade school and high school with.

"I read the complaint you filed, and I read all the diary stuff you gave me. You've been through some rough times."

"I suppose."

"We never had kids, me and my first wife, but I feel for guys like you, when their wives use the kids against them. I mean, it's one thing if some broad tries to kick shit out of you herself. It's another if she gets your kids to start kicking too. How can you fight that?"

"I don't know."

"Still hard for you to talk, isn't it?"

Langiello reached across, put his hand on top of Michael's. Michael swallowed hard. He felt like a child. Why? At the present time Michael had his children with him only one out of every four weeks, and he'd known that in filing for primary custody he would be blamed by them for stirring things up. It would be the same old story—their mother's story: that he didn't really love them, that he only wanted to prove he could get his way. He had been prepared for this. What had surprised him, though, was how tiring it had become to hold back, to *not* answer his children's accusations. *When did you stop loving your children?* The question was there, in his head, and the only thing more absurd than the question, he knew, was that, in Langiello's presence he felt what he sometimes felt when he was with his children: the need to answer it.

"Listen. I was nervous too, before I met you the first time—all I remembered from when we were in high school, you being such a hot shot. I mean, two guys like us, two old schoolyard ballplayers from Brooklyn, we'll get along fine."

The waiter appeared, glanced at Michael's plate, asked if everything was all right. He spoke to Langiello in Italian. He wore a midnight blue tuxedo, fingered the dark lapel. Langiello and the waiter laughed together, and Michael imagined Langiello as a boy of seven or eight coming across the ocean on a ship, huddled inside a blanket.

The waiter was gone. Langiello was buttering a piece of bread. Michael touched his napkin, thought of white drapes around an open wound, a scalpel in his palm. He saw the skin spread and bleed. He saw subcutaneous tissue, the layer of pale yellow fat below that. He saw muscles, like brown steak, thin tissues of white tendon being peeled away. He smelled onions, parsley, sweet red peppers. He imagined Coleman, his anesthesiologist, staring into a green monitor, at hills and valleys of fragrances that flowed above and below sea level. Oregano. Grated cheese. Lemon. Michael wanted to reach out and touch the smells, to flatten them to the horizon. He wanted the moment he was living in to become a thin white line, to disappear.

"Tell me what to do," Michael said.

"First thing?"

"First thing."

"Eat."

Langiello grinned, skewered a strip of scungili on his fork, talked about how his father had brought him to the restaurant when he was a boy. Michael felt frightened, in need of reassurance. He tried to visualize himself earlier in the day, taking the subway from Brooklyn to Manhattan, entering the hospital, greeting receptionists, nurses, doctors, residents. He saw himself in the operating suite, putting the x-rays on the viewbox, hanging his clothes in the locker, walking into the operating room. Bach's Suite Number One, his favorite, was already playing. His nurse helped him scrub up, tie his gown, put on his slippers. She held a pair of gloves for him, stretched the wrists wide. Langiello talked about the diary he had kept while he was going through his own divorce, about how crazy things had been.

Michael closed his eyes, could feel the thin skin of latex coat his hands like a film of talcum. The hip was exposed, draped inside a white rectangle less than a foot square. He prepped the area, watched his fingers, smooth and white like a dead man's, work inside the wound. His fingers retracted muscles, moved to deeper muscle, cut, cauterized. His resident suctioned blood. He told the resident to be careful of the sciatic nerve, to move it aside gently. If you harmed it, the woman would have a dropped foot forever after. Bach became Mahler—the Andante Moderato from the Second Symphony. They were using his tapes today, not Coleman's. His fingers worked on. Mahler became Bach again: Preludes and Fugues on harpsichord. Landowska.

He held an electric saw as if it were a pistol, cut through the bone, removed it. With a mallet, he banged a reamer into the middle of the bone, inside the hip, put down his trial prosthesis. He removed the remaining cartilage, drilled holes, cleaned them with a water pik, washed out the femur, the socket. He mixed cement, white and creamy like Elmer's glue.

He chewed his gnocchi now, imagined a piece lodging in his throat, Langiello leaning across, grabbing his jaw, prying his mouth open, reaching in with a hooked finger. He saw himself suturing heavy tendons with violet thread. He smelled potatoes, butter, sausage.

Langiello asked about his brother, about how it felt to have a brother who was crazy. Michael wanted to protest, to explain that Jerry was not crazy—that he was retarded, perhaps, damaged, disabled—but he told Langiello that he had stopped by the day-care center before coming to the restaurant. Jerry was heavily sedated: two thousand units of Thorazine a day, Benadryl for the side effects. Michael was concerned about Jerry's eyesight: the corneas were becoming filmy, glazed. He must remember to call later, to suggest an exam, a change in medication. He imagined the top of Jerry's head, sliced open, lifted up as if on hinges, and he saw himself standing on a stepladder, pouring a mixture of glue and corn meal into Jerry's head.

"You said that he's been like that most of his life, that he was never really normal."

"That's right."

"I don't mean to pry. It's just that I like to find out these things—so I can get the big picture, you know what I mean?"

Michael had long ago stopped believing in the diagnostic terms the doctors used: autism, schizophrenia, manic-depression. Who would ever know what had actually happened thirty-nine years ago—genetically, neurologically, in utero?

Michael saw himself closing the wound, binding the skin with a staple gun, laying on the dressing. Langiello asked Michael to describe his marriage and Michael gave Langiello a few sentences, then talked about how hard things were on the children, about how he wished he could get them into counseling. Langiello nodded sympathetically, said that he might be able to make a recommendation, that he didn't think their objectives were far apart.

"Then you *agree* with me?" Michael asked. "You really do think I should have the children with me more?"

"Sure. Only you have to remember that I don't have final say. I do my investigation, I file my report, I make recommendations if I want." Langiello winked. "But don't worry. We have leverage. My uncle just happens to be the judge, or did I tell you that already?"

Michael felt his heart surge, pump. He tried to show nothing.

"You got some time?" Langiello asked.

"Time?"

"Afterwards. You got any appointments, or are you free?"

"I have time. I left the afternoon open. I don't have to be back in the city until four-thirty."

"Good. So how about after lunch, we walk around the neighborhood? I'll show you where I was born—where my old man had his store."

If Jerry were reasonably calm, Michael thought, he would bring him here the next time. Jerry loved Italian food. If they succeeded in getting through the meal without incident, he decided, he would bring the children the time after that. Michael looked down, knew that the spirals on the gnocchi were there so that they would resemble seashells. He ate. He told Langiello that he would love to walk around the neighborhood with him, and while he talked he thought of the ocean, of Brighton Beach, of sand castles. He saw himself on the beach with Jerry, smoothing down a spiral runway that ran from the top of the castle to the bottom. He set a pink ball at the top, watched it circle downwards. Jerry clapped. They dug out tunnels that let in the ocean. They built moats. They mixed water and sand and let the mixture drip onto the castle's turrets.

Michael thought he tasted sand in his mouth. Jerry's back was red. Their father screamed at him, slammed a newspaper against his head, kicked in the castle. Jerry wailed. Their father yelled at Michael for letting his brother burn up while he kept himself protected. He grabbed at Michael's polo shirt but Michael was too quick for him. He ran off. All he ever thought about was himself, his father shouted. His father was kissing Jerry's back in a way that made Michael feel embarrassed. Michael looked down, watched the ocean foam around his ankles.

His father was dead, Jerry was crazy. Michael was forty-four years old, a successful orthopedic surgeon, the divorced father of two boys and a girl. Well. He had worked for seventeen years to create the kind of family he himself had never had, and now that family was gone, had *been* gone for over two years. Why, then, was he still so surprised?

They walked along Court Street, turned left, passed the Baltic Street Day Care Center. A line of patients, Jerry not among them, moved toward a Dodge mini-van. Most of the patients were in their thirties and forties. They wore housecoats and ragged furs, plaid shirts over heavy wool sweaters, brightly colored silk scarves, frayed slippers, men's ties for belts. Such sad flamboyance, Michael thought. The patients shuffled along in pairs, eyes downcast, skin colorless, holding hands like schoolchildren, looking as if they were emerging from a bad flight, airsick.

Next to the van a young Hispanic couple embraced. The man wore a long olive-drab Army coat. He was about thirty years old. While his eyes and shoulders showed fatigue, his mouth and jaw were set in anger. The woman was attractive, young, her glossy black hair pulled back neatly, her eyelids shaded in pale lavender. Michael watched her lips move at the man's ear. *I love you,* she said. *Oh I love you.*

The woman stepped into the van. The man started to walk away, turned.

"Don't worry about the kids," he called back. "You hear me? Don't you worry about the kids."

Then he pivoted, raced across the street at a diagonal. Cars screeched, honked. He was gone.

"That's heavy, isn't it?" Langiello said, touching Michael's arm.

Michael saw that Langiello's eyes were moist. Had he misjudged

him? By the end of their lunch, as now, Michael had become quiet
again, uneasy. He wanted desperately to make a good impression. He
wanted Langiello to know just how much he loved his children, and
yet, without his children physically there, he was afraid that anything
he said would sound hollow.

Langiello talked about the neighborhood, about what it had been
like growing up there. Michael answered questions. Yes, he liked to
cook, to clean, to shop, to do the dishes, to do the laundry, to help the
children with their homework. Yes, he had worked out a schedule
with his partners that allowed him to be at home most days after
school. He was on call only one out of every four weekends. He *liked*
being a father, being at home with his children. And yes, as he had
written in his diary, he did fear for his ex-wife's sanity, for her influ-
ence on the children. For months, before and after the divorce, she
had threatened to commit suicide by hanging herself from the boys'
climbing rope. She had thrown scissors and bricks and kitchen knives
at him. She had threatened to harm the children.

She continued to tell the children that she had never wanted a
divorce, that she had done everything to save the marriage. She told
them that Michael had left her for another woman, that he had been
playing around all through the marriage. She told them that he had
beaten her. She told them that he was planning to abandon them, to
leave New York and take a job at the Mayo Clinic in Minnesota.
Langiello nodded sympathetically, said that he'd seen a lot of guys in
Michael's spot, that he admired Michael.

"Sometimes—" Michael said, encouraged by Langiello's words
"—sometimes I feel like the Jackie Robinson of divorce." Michael
paused. Langiello smiled, and when he did Michael felt his own heart
ease. "What I mean is, sometimes I feel that I have to take all the crap
my kids can throw at me, yet have the courage *not* to fight back."

"Sure," Langiello said. "I know what you mean. Don't I remember
Jackie, what it was like for him that first year, everybody calling him
nigger, going at him with their spikes?"

Langiello touched Michael's arm, pointed to a set of windows on
the second floor of a three-story building, to the apartment in which
he had lived for the first twenty-six years of his life. Bruno's Pastry

Shop, on the ground floor, had always been there, Langiello said. They entered the shop. Langiello told Mrs. Bruno that Michael was a friend, a famous surgeon. Mrs. Bruno inclined her head, as if in the presence of a priest. Michael closed his eyes, inhaled the fragrances: butter, almond, chocolate, yeast. He saw Jerry, in the bathtub, himself on his knees, beside the tub, rinsing shampoo from Jerry's hair. He was carrying Jerry to the bedroom in an enormous pea-green bath towel. He was sprinkling talcum on Jerry, rubbing baby oil into his scalp, inclining his head to Jerry's head, closing his eyes, inhaling the strange, sweet fragrance.

Michael and Langiello walked along Court Street, passing fish markets, antique stores, restaurants, funeral parlors. Langiello said that his father had been a shoemaker, that when he was a boy he had believed the neighborhood was called Cobble Hill because of men like his father—all the Italian cobblers who worked there. Langiello pointed to the narrow store, now a locksmith shop, that had once been his father's. Langiello said that his great regret in life was that he had never been able to let his father, who died when he was fourteen years old, know how much he had loved him.

"My father died when I was sixteen," Michael said.

Briefly, Langiello put his arm around Michael's shoulder, and when he did Michael found that he wanted to tell Langiello *everything*. They passed a yellow brick building set back from the road like a small museum: The Anthony Anastasios Memorial Wing of the Longshoreman's Medical Association. In the distance, no more than half a mile away, Michael could see the Gowanus Parkway, the gray turrets and smokestacks of ships beyond it. Michael talked about his father, who had been a bookkeeper for a small manufacturing company, Wonderwear Hosiery. His mother had worked as a practical nurse, taking care of invalids at home. Whenever she was on a case—this was before Jerry was hospitalized at the age of twelve—he would be in charge of Jerry and of the house: of cooking, cleaning, shopping, laundry. It was one reason, he sometimes thought, taking care of his own children came so naturally for him.

They sat on a bench together in Carroll Gardens, watching old men in black jackets playing *bocce,* schoolchildren playing tag. The sky seemed lower, as if being pushed down by an enormous slab of gray steel. Michael thought of aircraft carriers, their decks stripped and removed by giant cranes, then welded together until they stretched across the heavens. Had Michael resented having to care for Jerry? Some. Still, the days he had spent alone in their apartment with his brother were among the happiest of his childhood—the only times when the rooms were quiet, when he could be close to Jerry, could tend to him without being scolded, times that Jerry felt free to return Michael's affection.

Langiello asked if Michael had talked with his ex-wife since their last interview. She had called two nights before, Michael said, at three in the morning, exploding at him with obscenities, threats, accusations; and she had called again just a few hours ago, before he left for the hospital, to wish him good luck in his interview with Langiello. She had sounded rational, normal. She had told him that she was still willing to get back together.

"And I'll bet she's been giving the kids the same line," Langiello offered. "Sure. I know all about it. The kids need a punching bag and you're it. They'll know the difference, though, Mike. Kids are resilient. I mean, they'll take her side now—she's the victim, right?—but you'll get your reward some day."

"Maybe."

"You will, Mike. I've seen enough of these cases to know. The open agenda is reconciliation—the hidden agenda is revenge. Hot and cold, cold and hot. The problem is that they had this great family once upon a time, see, and now they don't—and she gives them a story that helps them make sense of what can never really make sense. It's what I was trying to tell you before, about going to court: it's not who's right or wrong that counts, but who comes up with the best story. What you need is a good *story*, Mike."

"Jackie's story?"

"Not a bad idea." Langiello laughed. "What a guy he was. I got close to him once, at this clinic for our team at Ebbets Field. I was in a group assigned to him, him showing us how to take a lead, get a jump on the pitcher. Jesus! I forgot about that for ages."

"Where did you go—New Utrecht?"

"Yeah. I played second base, only I wasn't much. Good-field no-hit. You play baseball at Erasmus?"

"No."

"I remember how great you were in basketball—first team all-city, right?"

"Yes."

"For a little guy you were something else, Mike. We had these two big Italian guys that clogged up the middle—surf and turf, we called them—and in practice our coach got this kid from the JV to try to imitate you, the way you'd dribble through any defense we could throw up."

"You were on the team?"

"Sure."

"Why didn't you say so before?"

"Maybe I was hoping you'd remember me." Langiello punched Michael on the arm, playfully. "Ah, I wasn't much. Seventh man, my senior year. They'd send me in for surf or turf if they got into foul trouble."

Michael tried to picture Langiello as an eighteen-year-old, in uniform. He tried to recall the game but instead he saw Jerry running in circles around the schoolyard, screaming with joy, a basketball held tightly against his stomach.

Langiello laughed. "You faked me out of my jock once, going in for a drive, I didn't know what happened, you were so quick." Langiello leaned forward, hands clasped. "You were all-Ivy at Dartmouth too—I remember following you in the papers, but you never went to the pros. In those days I guess you could make more being a hotshot doctor than an athlete. You read about the contracts these guys get now, out of college? It really pisses me off, you want the truth, twenty-year-old kids making all that dough." Langiello paused, cocked his head to one side. "Let me ask you something, Mike. How much do you think I earn, the job I got?"

"I don't know. You have a law degree, don't you?"

"I have a law degree. Brooklyn Law School, Class of '68. But take a guess at how much I make. C'mon—"

"I'd rather not."

"Eighteen thousand."

"That's *all?*"

"That's all. Sure. But I got no complaints. I mean, I like my work, right? Child-abuse cases mostly—I get to be *guardian ad litum* for a lot of kids, get to make a difference in their lives." He stood. "And I get to meet some fascinating people too, right?"

Langiello suggested that he walk Michael to the subway, that Michael had more important things to do than to pass the time of day with a guy like him. Michael clenched his fists, angry with himself because he hadn't seen that each time Langiello had asked him a question he had doubtless been hoping Michael would ask one back, would show interest. They stopped at the Gowanus Canal, leaned on the bridge railing, looked down into water that seemed thick with black clouds. He answered a few of Langiello's questions, then asked him about his work with child-abuse cases.

"Ah—crazy things go on behind doors once people close them," he said. "And the craziest thing of all is how most of the time, the women and the kids, banged up to hell, all they want is for us to get the fathers to live with them again. They'll almost always drop the charges if only the bastard will come back home."

"I'm not surprised," Michael said.

"You know what the hardest thing in the world is, Mike? It's getting a kid *not* to love a parent." They came to the Bergen Street subway station. Langiello said he would be seeing Mike's ex-wife later in the afternoon. Langiello smiled. "But don't worry, okay? You'll get more time with the kids. I promise—"

"Thanks," Michael said. He moved toward Langiello, wanting to touch the man. "I wish I—"

"No need to say anything," Langiello said. "I mean, it's been good to reminisce about the old days, the way things were when we were growing up. Times change, Mike. Times change and who's ever ready?"

They shook hands. Michael watched Langiello walk off, then started down the steps. He felt exhausted suddenly—drained—and he couldn't understand why. All he wanted to do was to lie down, to sleep, to dream of lush green lawns and pale blue skies. Three teenagers, two in black leather jackets, stood below, where the staircase turned.

At the landing he made a right turn, then saw bright lights flare inside his head, welding sparks spraying crazily. A hand was jammed over his mouth so that his teeth cut into his lips, drew blood. He was being dragged backwards by both arms. He resisted, saw a knife blade flash. He relaxed, let himself be led to an alcove. He stood on a soft mass of wet newspapers. Above him were rusting girders, sagging wires, a clogged grating coated with swirls of brown slime.

"Don't fight back. We ain't your enemies, okay? We don't want to hurt you unless we have to."

Michael nodded. They were taller than he was. The man in front of him was well built, wore a black T-shirt, the sleeves cut off. His brown eyes were dull.

"You a friend of Langiello's?"

"Not exactly."

"What's it worth to you if we take care of him?"

"I don't understand."

"Don't give me crap. We know what Langiello does, the hold he got on you. You want us to do a job on him, it'll cost you five thousand bucks, cash, unmarked bills. Five thousand ain't much for a rich guy like you, the clothes you got on."

"Hey Lobo—ask him if he owns oil wells."

"Shut up, jerk." Lobo pulled on Michael's tie. His eyes were without cleverness. Michael thought of sludge at the bottom of the Gowanus Canal. Why did he call himself Lobo, Spanish for wolf, when he was not Spanish? "What do you do for a living?"

"I'm a doctor."

"Oh yeah? What kind?"

"A surgeon. An orthopedic surgeon."

"Langiello makes bundles off guys like you."

"You're wasting your time," Michael said coldly. "I have nothing against Mr. Langiello."

"But he got plenty against you, I bet. He always does. Who'd you beat up, your wife or your kids? You rape your seven-year-old daugh-

ter, mister, or are you one of them new kinds of pervert who gets off
on old people?"

"I haven't touched anybody. You've made a mistake."

"Don't crap with us." Lobo sliced buttons from Michael's jacket,
one at a time. "What's he got on you? C'mon. How much you gotta
pay him so he don't have his uncle send you up the river?"

Michael moved forward.

"If you'll excuse me, I—"

He saw the gun pointed at his chest.

"We're on your side, mister," Lobo said. "Believe me, okay? We just
want to talk with you for your own good, understand? You want the
truth, there's lots of guys on your side. Lots of guys would chip in for
a contract on Langiello. His uncle's the judge, see—"

"I know that."

"Only there's no profit in us killing the judge. You kill one judge,
there's another judge in his seat the next day. But Judge DiGregorio,
he only got one investigator who's his nephew. You get rid of the
nephew, you're home free. You think it over, who you can trust, us or
Langiello. Like they say, our rates are competitive."

"My story is different," Michael said. "I'm not involved in child
abuse. I was divorced. I have three children. My ex-wife and I are in
court because of a custody dispute. I don't think Mr. Langiello means
me any harm. Really. I—"

"Let him go," Lobo said.

The two men released Michael's arm. He heard a switchblade click
shut, but not before it had slashed his jacket, upwards, on the right
side, from the waist to the armpit.

II

Langiello smiled and shook Michael's hand, asked if Michael had had
breakfast yet. He tapped a manila envelope, said that his report was
finished, ready for the judge. He was sorry he'd made Michael come
out so early, but he had to be in court by ten o'clock for a child-abuse
hearing. Michael took off his raincoat, ordered coffee, talked about
how cold it was outside—a freakish hailstorm turned to slashing rain,
crazy for the first week of spring—and of how, coming along the street

from the subway station, he had seen daffodils and crocuses sheathed inside ice, looking as if they were made of stained glass.

Michael was surprised at how good he felt, how relieved he was to know that the report was complete, that the ordeal, for him and the children, would soon be over. And he was pleased too, he knew, simply to be in Langiello's presence again, to feel that he had an ally, somebody who understood that, despite all his worldly successes, he was still just an old Brooklyn schoolyard ballplayer heading for his middle years.

Michael sipped coffee, talked about his children, his brother. He said that when the trial was over he intended to have his children meet Jerry, to spend time with him. He wondered: could he mention having met Lobo and his two henchmen the week before? He didn't want even to *appear* to be testing Langiello, to be doubting him.

"Listen," Langiello said. "I always like to do this with clients—not all investigators do—but before I file my report I like to sit down with them and tell them what's going to be in it. I like to be up front."

"Of course."

"Your case has been a real tough one for me, Mike, and I guess the main thing I want to say to you—and I hope this is a help, given how much pain you've been in—"

"Pain?"

"The stuff you told me last time about how it hurts you to take crap from your kids all the time, to be their nigger—how your kids are always taking their mother's side."

"I don't understand."

"Your kids love you, Mike," Langiello said. "Absolutely." He paused, leaned forward, his eyes suddenly bright. "But they don't *like* you. Do you understand what I'm saying?"

Michael tried to laugh. "I know they love me," he said. "I never doubt that. As for liking me—well, they're in a real bind, as I explained. If they even let themselves *think* they like me—that I'm not the monster who made everything go bad—it makes them feel they're rejecting their mother. The more they punish me emotionally, the more brownie points they earn with her. That's why I—"

"Mike," Langiello said sharply, his hand flat on the table as if he had slapped it. "You're not *listening* to what I'm saying. That's one of the things the kids said too—that you never really listen to them, that you always have to be right, that you think you're perfect."

"That's ridiculous." In his mind, Michael was on the court at Madison Square Garden, looking toward the bench, seeing the coach tell him to slow down, to take his time in setting up the next play. "Look," he offered, forcing a laugh, hoping to appeal to their common past. "I missed a foul shot in a game against Jefferson that almost cost us the championship my senior year, didn't I?"

Langiello stared at Michael without expression. Michael thought of Lobo's dull brown eyes. He thought of daffodils thawing, wilting. He thought of reaching inside his chest, of sawing ribs, retracting muscles, of stroking his own heart gently, of calming it.

"I mean, there are dozens of times I admit to them that I was wrong about something, that I made a mistake," Michael continued.

"They love you, Mike, but they don't like you. Can you *hear* what I'm saying? I'm telling you the truth. I'm trying to help you."

"I don't understand," Michael said. "Last week you said that you were going to give me more time with them, that—"

"I hadn't met your kids yet. I hadn't met your wife either." Langiello paused, as if daring Michael to reply. "They're good kids, Mike, and she's a terrific mother. And what I think is that they've shown a lot of courage in putting their lives back together since the divorce."

"Courage?"

"The kids want to live with their mother, Mike. Can you hear me?"

"But they *have* to say that. If they don't they're scared she'll stop loving them—don't you see *that?*"

"No, Mike. I really don't. I don't think you give your kids enough credit. They said that too—that you never believe them."

"Oh come on," Michael said. "I've never said such things to them. What's going on is your garden-variety emotional blackmail and you know it. I mean, ask yourself this question: Would the kids ever be able to tell her that they want to live with *me?*" Michael stopped, realized that his voice was rising. "When they're afraid to reject me or criticize me, then I'll worry. Then—"

"You're not listening to me, Mike." Langiello sat back. Michael saw himself passing off, circling under the basket, getting his wind back. He wondered if Langiello had an arrangement with Lobo, had *sent* Lobo. He wanted to be ready for Langiello's moves, to be alert to all possibilities.

"I don't understand," Michael said again. He looked down. Play defense, he told himself. Stall. He decided to try letting Langiello think he was bewildered, wounded. Perhaps if he didn't threaten him, if he gave him his ounce of flesh . . .

"Let me put it this way," Langiello said. "I met your kids and I met your wife. She's a wonderful woman, Mike—soft-spoken and somewhat shy, I'll admit, but warm and loving and gentle and—"

"Sure. When she doesn't have a knife in her hand."

"You're interrupting me again." Langiello smiled. "You can't resist, can you?"

Michael said nothing. He tried to let his mind go blank. He tried to let it fill up with air, but as it did he saw gray swirls of smoke, he smelled coffee and bacon, he saw fragrances drifting through his head as if through canals, as if they were dyes that had been injected into his spinal column and were journeying toward his brain.

"I listened to everyone," Langiello went on, "and what I kept asking myself was this: What was it that could have caused a woman like this to act the way she did? I mean, I admit her behavior's been bizarre—but what I wanted to know was what made her *get* that way?"

Michael let his shoulders sag. There was no way he was going to win, he realized, and what surprised him was neither Langiello nor his own foolishness in having trusted Langiello, but something else: that he was *still* willing to trust Langiello, if in a totally unexpected way. He almost smiled, but he didn't want to give himself away, he didn't want Langiello to know that what he was tempted to do suddenly was to throw aside all his old rules—his crazy devotion to *fairness.* For the first time in his life he was tempted, he realized, to make a deal, to offer a bribe, and the discovery delighted him.

He tried to play the scene out in his head, before it happened. What if Langiello were to double-cross him after being paid off? What if

Langiello took the money and submitted his report without changing it? Michael could, he saw, lose both ways: he could lose the children *and* lose in his own eyes—for having betrayed a set of values that . . . that what? Michael looked up.

"And what did you decide?" he asked. "What was your answer?"

"You're a tyrant, Mike," Langiello said. "It's as simple as that. You were always the big shot—the powerhouse. She showed me notes you left for her when she was putting you through medical school, when she didn't do things exactly the way you wanted—"

"But that was *before* our problems—almost twenty years ago."

"There's no doubt in my mind that she struck out at you through the kids and did a lot of crazy things—I mean, who doesn't when a marriage breaks up?—but it's also clear to me, and this is the essence of my report, that you drove her to it."

"Sure," Michael said, and he smiled for the first time. "The devil made me do it, right?"

"They talked about that too—her and the kids—the way you get sarcastic whenever you can't face up to taking the blame. I *learned* from them, Mike. It wasn't difficult to figure out why they were willing to talk about the marriage and you weren't."

"But the marriage is over," Michael said. "It's been over for two years. I didn't think it was *important* to talk about it. I thought that what was important was putting all the old battles to rest so we could get on with our lives." Michael stopped, aware that the words were coming out automatically, that he himself hardly believed in them. "All right. If you want to talk about the marriage, let's talk. What do you want to know?"

"Too late." Langiello tapped the envelope. "I've already put more time into your case than I usually do."

Michael hesitated, shook his head sideways, spoke: "You're not giving me a fair shake."

"Could be." Langiello gestured, palms up. "You and your lawyer are always free to ask for another investigator."

"No." Michael saw himself wandering around an empty court, looking up at the game clock, at championship banners, at ducts and wiring and fans of bright lights. Was the game over already? He supposed he could do it—that he could compromise his values in order to save his kids, to win for all of them—that he could humble himself if he had to, even if he *and* Langiello knew he was only putting on an act. "I just want to put all this behind me, but I suppose that as long as she can stay involved with me, one way or the other, she's gratified."

"But the two of you *are* still involved, Mike. You're still mother and father to these kids. She showed me letters—the way you tried to persuade her to come back into the marriage when you found out she was having affairs. But what else could she do? The men she loved didn't run her down the way you did, Mike. They were kind and gentle. They—"

"They were married and they had kids, damn it!" Michael felt his heart blaze. He stood. "I really don't have to listen to this. I don't have to sit here and—"

Langiello was smiling. Michael stopped in midsentence. Had he, by accident, given the man what he was looking for?

"You're angry, Mike. You're a very angry guy, aren't you?"

Michael sat. He looked into Langiello's eyes and he imagined himself making small incisions in the corneas. When the corneas were deprived of oxygen they drew blood vessels from surrounding territory. Michael imagined Langiello's eyes laced with spider webs of pale red threads. He imagined himself lifting the corneas—peeling them off—freezing them so that they would be ready for the lathe. He shivered. Refractive surgery—flattening the corneas to correct nearsightedness—was the one new surgical procedure that, in his imagination, could give him chills. He saw diamond blades cut into his own eyes, into the eyes of his children, into Jerry's eyes.

"I'm upset," Michael said. He tried to be ready for what was coming. He tried to prepare himself for asking Langiello how much money he wanted, and how and when he wanted it. "I mean, you're telling me I may lose my children."

"That's right."

Michael smelled sausage, onions. He felt nauseated. "I love my children," Michael said. "I mean, how can I *not* be upset?"

"But when you don't get your way you also get a little crazy."

"No."

"Your kids say different. They say you're like your brother sometimes."

"But my kids don't even remember my brother."

"I wondered about that too—why you didn't want me to meet your brother last time, us going right past his place. Your wife says that after visiting him you throw fits sometimes, you hurl things around the house."

"It's not so."

"The kids say it is. Your wife says that you used to wake her in the middle of the night to go on crazy tirades."

"It's not so." Michael looked down, head in hands, hoping Langiello would think he was fighting back tears.

"Are you ashamed of him?"

"Of who?"

"Of your brother."

"No." Michael looked up. "Did she say that *too?*"

"You should see your face, Mike. You should go look in a mirror. I have to say I agree with her, that there's something off-center there when you get angry. And you did have a breakdown once."

"It's not so."

"But you told me you had once put yourself under psychiatric care."

"I was in analysis for six years. When Jerry was—"

Michael considered saying more—considered talking about the analysis: why he entered it, how difficult and rewarding the work had been. He smiled. "Can I ask you a question—a few questions?"

"Shoot," Langiello said.

"I take it you're going to recommend that my ex-wife get primary custody of the children and I assume nothing I say now will change your mind. But tell me, Mr. Langiello—is a good parent one who *lies* to her children about the other parent? Is a good parent one who threatens to put her children in a foster home when they don't do what she wants? Does a wonderful parent deny counseling for her children? Does she threaten to kill them and maim them? Does she encourage her children to lie for her, to spy on their father, to steal things for her, to join in her war against him?"

"Who knows?" Langiello said. "Wouldn't you tell lies to protect your kid?" Michael said nothing. "I mean, who knows what a good parent is, Mike? Who really knows?"

At the corner, Michael went into a telephone booth, called the hospital. He spoke to a nurse who said that because of the weather the vans had not gone to Brooklyn. Would Michael be coming out to Staten Island? Michael said that he had office hours midafternoon, but he promised he would visit Jerry later in the week. The nurse said that Jerry had been telling everybody in the ward that he was going to a fancy restaurant with his brother; he had spent most of the morning preparing—washing, shaving, deciding which clothes to wear. She had never seen him dressed so handsomely.

"I'll be there," Michael said. "Tell him it may take me a while—I'll go by ferry—but I'll be there."

Michael called his office and arranged for one of his partners to cover for him, then took the subway to Manhattan, exited at South Ferry, paid his quarter. When he arrived on the Staten Island side he would take a taxi to the hospital.

The rain had stopped. Michael stayed at the back of the ferry, on deck. Despite what had happened with Langiello, he was looking forward to seeing Jerry. A group of schoolchildren were on tour, and a middle-aged ferry-boat captain was telling them that cows had once walked across the Bay, near where the Brooklyn Battery Tunnel was, from Brooklyn to Manhattan; if the cows did not get back before the tide came in, they would often drown. Michael watched Manhattan grow smaller. Gulls followed the boat, the captain said, not for garbage, as most people thought, but because the warm water churned up by the boat's propellers brought fish to the surface.

When the schoolchildren went inside, Michael stayed on deck, looking not toward Brooklyn, but toward the Statue of Liberty, Ellis Island, New Jersey. The water seemed pockmarked, a murky brown spotted with filmy stars of blue and black and green. The ship rolled gently through row after row of whitecaps. Michael thought of dirty dishwater. He thought of Jerry on a stepladder, remembered teaching Jerry how to wash dishes, how to use the sponge and soap and steel wool. He saw raw spinach rising to the surface of cloudy water. Was he inventing the picture, or had Jerry once tried to wash spinach leaves as if they were dishes? He recalled his father coming home and praising Jerry, ranting at him.

Michael walked to the port side. Brooklyn was gone, bathed in gray fog, and Michael sensed some light—the sun, behind the mist, slowly transforming the air to the color of unwashed ivory. Despite the fact that the air was now warm and moist, almost feathery in its tangible balm, Michael found that he was trembling, his teeth clicking. He should go inside, buy a cup of tea, rest. He should forget Langiello. He should tell himself again and again that the hard thing would be to believe in his heart what he understood in his mind: that there was, literally, nothing he could do about what had happened and nothing he could have done. All he really wanted was to get to the other side of the Bay, to see Jerry, to spend time with him.

Were Jerry to ask him about the children and were he to begin to tell Jerry the story of what had happened, he knew that Jerry would walk away, turn in circles. He wished that it wasn't so important to him that others understand what, in fact, had truly happened. He wished he could be certain that he cared more for his children than he did about losing them, about losing his fight *for* them.

Michael rubbed the iron railing, reminded himself to stop on the other side, to buy something to bring for Jerry—a magazine, a pipe, a box of chocolates. He smiled. Jerry would doubtless turn at once and hand the gift to another patient. Michael would tease Jerry about always giving things away and Jerry would laugh, would say something about their childhood that only he and Michael would understand. What do you think this is anyway, he would ask. Your birthday?

The craziest thing of all, he sometimes thought, was that the two of them actually liked being together, enjoyed spending time with one another even though they both knew that their conversations made no ordinary sense.

Jerry loved to ask Michael questions about surgery, to walk around his ward reciting the procedures to everyone he met. Jerry had an uncanny memory that made Michael believe he was not brain-damaged so much as brain-scrambled—all the pieces there, but in the wrong places. Michael considered: he could pretend that he needed Jerry to help him in surgery, that there was this guy he knew they had to operate on, so that the man would never walk again.

Michael could imagine taking Jerry to the Italian restaurant, Jerry's eyes bright with pleasure as he explained the procedure, repeated Michael's words back to him: first you make an incision in the knee and put the fiber-optic light in. Then you look into the TV camera and you fill the knee with saline fluid. Then you make a cut of about five millimeters. Then you make an incision on the other side and you watch in the camera while you work with your scalpel and clamps and trocar and Army-Navy retractors. If there's too much bleeding you buzz the veins.

Michael smiled. Jerry loved the idea of buzzing veins and arteries—cauterizing them with lasers—loved to use the word *buzz* as often as possible. The anterior or posterior cruciate ligaments would be the ones they'd cut, Michael explained, so that forever after the knees would—without warning, but regularly—give way. Or perhaps they could, Jerry offered, go into the neck and slice the carotid artery, or one of the vertebral arteries, so that, as if the guy had had a stroke, his brain would never again be able to tell his body what to do.

The ferry slowed, turned, began backing into its spot in the harbor, foam boiling up above green scum. Michael went inside, moved quickly, pushing his way through the crowd so that he would be first off.

The Halfway Diner

•

========= **JOHN SAYLES** =========

John Sayles was born in Schenectady, New York, in 1950. He is the author of the novels Pride of the Bimbos, Union Dues, *and the short story collection* The Anarchists' Convention. *He is the writer/director of the feature films* Return of the Secaucus Seven, Lianna, Baby, It's You, The Brother from Another Planet, Matewan, *and* Eight Men Out.

Some of the other girls can read on the way but I get sick. I need somebody to talk to, it don't matter who so much, just someone to shoot the breeze with, pass time. *Si no puedes platicar, no puedes vivir,* says my mother and though I don't agree that the silence would kill me, twelve hours is a long stretch. So when Goldilocks climbs on all big-eyed and pale and almost sits herself in Renee's seat by the window I take pity and put her wise.

"You can't sit in that seat," I say.

Her face falls like she's a kid on the playground about to get whupped. "Pardon?" she says. *Pardon.*

"That's Renee's seat," I tell her. "She's got a thing about it. Something about the light."

"Oh. Sorry." She looks at the other empty seats like they're all booby-trapped. Lucky for her I got a soft heart and a mouth that needs exercise.

"You can sit here if you want."

She just about pees with relief and sits by me. She's not packing any magazines or books which is good cause like I said, I get sick. If the person next to me reads I get nosy and then I get sick plus a stiff neck.

"My name's Pam," she says.

"It would be. I'm Lourdes." We shake hands. I remember the first time I made the ride, four years ago, I was sure somebody was gonna cut me with a razor or something. I figured they'd all of them be women who'd done time themselves, a bunch of big tough mamas with tattoos on their arms who'd snarl out stuff like "Whatsit to you, sister?" Well, we're not exactly the Girl Scout Jamboree, but mostly people are pretty nice to each other, unless something happens like with Lee and Delphine.

"New meat?" I ask her.

"Pardon?"

"Is your guy new meat up there?" I ask. "Is this his first time inside?"

She nods and hangs her head like it's the disgrace of the century. Like we're not all on this bus for the same reason.

"You hear from him yet?"

"I got a letter. He says he doesn't know how he can stand it."

Now this is good. It's when they start to get comfortable up there you got to worry. We had this girl on the bus, her guy made parole first time up, only the minute he gets home he starts to mope. Can't sleep nights, can't concentrate, mutters to himself all the time, won't take an interest in anything on the outside. She lives with this a while, then one night they have a fight and really get down and he confesses how he had this kid in his cell, this little *mariquita,* and they got to doing it, you know, like some of the guys up there will do, only this guy fell in *love.* These things happen. And now he's *jealous,* see, cause his kid is still inside with all these *men,* right, and damn if a week later he doesn't go break his parole about a dozen different ways so he gets sent back up. She had to give up on him. To her it's a big tragedy, which is understandable, but I suppose from another point of view it's kind of romantic, like *Love Story,* only instead of Ali McGraw you got a sweetboy doing a nickel for armed robbery.

"What's your guy in for?" I ask.

Pam looks at her feet. "Auto theft."

"Not *that*. I mean how much *time*."

"The lawyer says he'll have to do at least a year and a half."

"You don't go around asking what a guy's rap is in here," I tell her. "That's like *per*sonal, you know? But the length of sentence—hey, everybody counts the days."

"Oh."

"A year and a half is small change," I tell her. "He'll do that with his eyes closed."

The other girls start coming in then. Renee comes to her seat and sets up her equipment. She sells makeup, Renee, and her main hobby is wearing it. She's got this stand that hooks onto the back of the seat in front of her, with all these drawers and compartments and mirrors and stuff and an empty shopping bag for all the tissues she goes through during the trip. I made the mistake of sitting next to her once and she bent my ear about lip gloss for three hours straight, all the way to the Halfway Diner. You wouldn't think there'd be that much to say about it. Then after lunch she went into her sales pitch and I surrendered and bought some eye goop just so I wouldn't have to hear her say "our darker-complected customers" one more time. I mean it's all relative, right, and I'd rather be my shade than all pasty-faced like Renee, look like she's never been touched by the sun. She's seen forty in the rearview mirror though she does her best to hide it, and the big secret that everybody knows is that it's not her husband she goes to visit but her *son*, doing adult time. She just calls him "my Bobby."

Mrs. Tucker settles in front with her knitting, looking a little tired. Her guy is like the Birdman of Alcatraz or something, he's been in since back when they wore stripes like in the Jimmy Cagney movies, and she's been coming up faithfully every weekend for thirty, forty years, something incredible like that. He killed a cop way back when is what Yayo says the word on the yard is. She always sits by Gus, the driver, and they have these long lazy Mr. and Mrs. conversations while she knits and he drives. Not that there's anything going on between them off the bus, but you figure over the years she's spent more time with Gus than with her husband. He spaces out sometimes,

Gus, the road is so straight and long, and she'll bring him back with a poke from one of her needles.

The ones we call the sisters go and sit in the back, talking nonstop. Actually they're married to brothers who are up for the same deal but they look alike and are stuck together like glue so we call them the sisters. They speak one of those Indio dialects from up in the mountains down south, so I can't pick out much of what they say. What my mother would call *mojadas*. Like she come over on the *Mayflower*.

Dolores comes in, who is a sad case.

"I'm gonna tell him this trip," she says. "I'm really gonna do it."

"Attagirl."

"No, I really am. It'll break his heart but I got to."

"It's the only thing to do, Dolores."

She has this boyfriend inside, Dolores, only last year she met some nice square Joe and got married. She didn't tell him about her guy inside and so far hasn't told her guy inside about the Joe. She figures he waits all week breathless for her visit, which maybe is true and maybe is flattering herself, and if she gives him the heave-ho he'll fall apart and kidnap the warden or something. Personally I think she likes to collect guilt, like some people collect stamps or coins or dead butterflies or whatever.

"I just feel so *guilty,*" she says and moves on down across from the sisters.

We got pretty much all kinds on the bus, black girls, white girls, Chicanas like me who were born here and new fish from just across the border, a couple of Indian women from some tribe down the coast, even one Chinese girl, whose old man is supposed to be a very big cheese in gambling. She wears clothes I would kill for, this girl, only of course they wouldn't look good on me. Most of your best clothes are designed for the flat-chested type, which is why the fashion pages are full of Orientals and anorexics like Renee.

This Pam is another one, the kind that looks good in a man's T-shirt, looks good in almost anything she throws on. I decide to be nice to her anyway.

"You gonna eat all that?"

She's got this big plastic sack of food under her feet, wrapped sandwiches and fruit and what looks like a pie.

"Me? Oh—no, I figure, you know—the food inside—"

"They don't let you bring food in."

Her face drops again. "No?"

"Only cigarettes. One carton a month."

"He doesn't smoke."

"That's not the point. Cigarettes are like money inside. Your guy wants anything, wants anything done, he'll have to pay in smokes."

"What would he want to have done?"

I figure I should spare her most of the possibilities, so I just shrug. "Whatever. We get to the Halfway you get some change, load up on Camels from the machine. He'll thank you for it."

She looks down at the sack of goodies. She sure isn't going to eat it herself, not if she worked at it for a month. I can picture her dinner plate alone at home, full of the kind of stuff my Chuy feeds his gerbil. A celery cruncher.

"You want some of this?" she says, staring into the sack.

"No thanks, honey," I tell her. "I'm saving myself for the Halfway Diner."

Later on I was struck by how it had already happened, the dice had already been thrown, only they didn't know it. So they took the whole trip up sitting together and talking and palling around unaware that they weren't friends anymore.

Lee and Delphine are as close as the sisters only nobody would ever mistake them for relatives, Lee being blonde and Delphine being one of our darker-complected customers. Lee is natural blonde, unlike certain cosmetics sales-women I could mention, with light blue eyes and a build that borders on the chunky although she would die to hear me say it. Del is thin and sort of elegant and black like you don't see too much outside of those documentaries on TV where people stick wooden spears in lions. *Negro como el fondo de la noche* my mother would say and on Del it looks great. The only feature they share is a similar nose, Del because she was born that way and Lee because of a field-hockey accident.

Maybe it was because they're both nurses or maybe just because they have complementary personalities, but somehow they found each other on the bus and since before I started riding they've been tight as ticks. You get the feeling they look forward to the long drive to catch up on each other's lives. They don't socialize off the bus, almost nobody does, but how many friends spend twelve hours a week together? Some of the black girls are friendly with some of the white girls, and us Chicanas can either spread around or sit together and talk hometalk, but black and white as tight as Lee and Del is pretty rare. Inside, well, inside you stay with your own, that's the beginning and the end of it. But inside is a world I don't even like to think about.

They plunk down across from us, Del lugging all these magazines— *Cosmo, People, Vogue, Essence*—that they sort of read and sort of make fun of, and Lee right away starts in on the food. Lee is obsessed with food the way a lot of borderline-chunky girls are, she can talk forever about what she didn't eat that day. She sits and gets a load of the sack at Pam's feet.

"That isn't food, is it?" she asks.

"Yeah," Pam apologizes. "I didn't know."

"Let's see it."

Obediently Pam starts shuffling through her sack, holding things up for a little show-and-tell. "I got this, and this," she says, "and this, I thought, maybe, they wouldn't have—I didn't know."

It's all stuff you buy at the bus station—sandwiches that taste like the cellophane they're wrapped in filled with that already-been-chewed kind of egg and chicken and tuna salad, stale pies stuffed with mealy applesauce, spotted fruit out of a machine. From all reports the food is better in the joint.

"How old are you, honey?" I ask.

"Nineteen."

"You ever cook at home?" Lee asks.

Pam shrugs. "Not much. Mostly I eat—you know, like salads. Maybe some fish sticks."

Del laughs. "I tried that fish-sticks routine once when Richard was home," she says. "He ask me, 'What is this?' That's their code for 'I don't like the look of it.' It could be something *basic*, right, like a fried egg starin up at em, they still say, 'What's this?' So I say, 'It's fish, baby.' He says, 'If it's fish, which end is the *head* and which is the *tail?*' When I tell him it taste the same either way he says he doesn't eat nothin with square edges like that, on account of inside they always be cookin everything in these big cake pans and serve it up in squares—square egg, square potato, square macaroni. That and things served out in ice-cream scoops. Unless it really *is* ice cream Richard don't want no *scoops* on his plate."

"Lonnie's got this thing about chicken bones," Lee says, "bones of any kind, but especially chicken bones. Can't stand to look at em while he's eating."

"Kind of rules out the Colonel, doesn't it?"

"Naw," she says. "He *loves* fried chicken. We come back with one of them buckets, you know, with the biscuits and all, and I got to go perform surgery in the kitchen before we can eat. He keeps callin in— 'It ready yet, hon? It ready yet? I'm starvin here.' I'll tell you, they'd of had those little McNugget things back before he went up our marriage woulda been in a lot better shape."

They're off to the races then, Lee and Del, yakking away, and they sort of close up into a society of two. Blondie is sitting there with her tuna-mash sandwiches in her lap, waiting for orders, so I stow everything in the sack and kick it deep under the seat.

"We get to the Halfway," I tell her, "we can dump it."

Sometimes I wonder about Gus. The highway is so straight, cutting up through the Valley with the ground so flat and mostly dried up, like all its effort goes into those little square patches of artichokes or whatever you come past and after that it just got no more green in it. What can he be thinking about, all these miles, all these trips, up and down, year after year? He don't need to think to do his *yups* and *uh-huhs* at Mrs. Tucker, for that you can go on automatic pilot like I do with my Blanca when she goes into one of her stories about the tangled who-likes-who in her class. It's a real soap opera, *Dallas* for fifth-graders, but not what you need to concentrate on over breakfast. I wonder if Gus counts the days like we do, if there's a retirement date in his head, a release from the bus. Except to Mrs. Tucker he doesn't say but three things. When we first leave he says, "Headin out, ladies, take your seats." When we walk into the Halfway he always says, "Make it simple, ladies, we got a clock to watch." And when we're about to start the last leg, after dinner, he says, "Sweet dreams, ladies, we're bringin it home." Those same three things, every single trip. Like Mrs. Tucker with her blue sweater, always blue. Sometimes when I can't sleep and things are hard and awful and I can't see how they'll ever get better I'll lie awake and invent all these morbid thoughts, sort of torture myself with ideas, and I always start thinking that it's really the same exact sweater, that she goes home and pulls it apart stitch by stitch and starts from scratch again next trip. Not cause she wants to but cause she has to, it's her part of the punishment for what her husband done.

Other times I figure she just likes the color blue.

For the first hour or so Renee does her face. Even with good road and a fairly new bus this takes a steady hand, but she is an artist. Then she discovers Pam behind her, a new victim for her line of cosmetics, and starts into her pitch, opening with something tactful like, "You always let your hair go like that?" I'm dying for Pam to say, "Yeah, whatsit to you, sister?" but she is who she is and pretty soon Renee's got her believing it's at least a misdemeanor to leave the house without eye-liner on. I've heard all this too many times so I put my head back and close my eyes and aim my radar past it over to Lee and Del.

They talk about their patients like they were family. They talk about their family like they were patients. Both are RNs, they work at different hospitals but both on the ward. Lee has got kids and she talks about them, Del doesn't but wants some and she talks about that. They talk about how Del can eat twice as much as Lee but Del stays thin and Lee gets chunky. They talk about their guys, too, but usually not till we get pretty close to the facility.

"My Jimmy," Lee says, "is now convinced he's the man of the house. This is a five-year-old squirt, he acts like he's the Papa Bear."

"He remembers his father?"

"He likes to think he does, but he doesn't. His favorite saying these days is 'Why should I?' "

"Uh-oh."

"At least he doesn't go around saying he's an orphan like his sister. I introduce her, 'This is my daughter, Julie,' right, she says, 'Hi, I'm a orphan.' Cute."

"I used to do that," says Delphine. "Evertime my daddy spanked me that's what I'd spread round the neighborhood."

"So Julie says she's an orphan and Jimmy says his father works for the state."

Del laughs. "That's true enough."

"And he picks up all this stuff in the neighborhood. God I want to get out of there. Lonnie makes parole this rotation I'm gonna get him home and get his head straight and get us moved outa there."

"Like to the country or something?"

"Just anywheres it isn't so mean and he's not near his asshole so-called buddies."

"Yeah—"

"And I want—oh, I don't know, it sounds kinda stupid, really—"

"What?" Del says.

"I want a *dish*washer."

Del laughs again. Lee is embarrassed.

"You know what I mean—"

"Yeah, I know—"

"I want something in my life I just get it started and then it takes care of itself."

"I hear you *talk*in—"

"The other night Jimmy—now I know some of this is from those damn He-Man cartoons and all, but some of it is not having a father, I swear—he's in their room doing his prayers. He does this thing, the nuns told him praying is just talking to God, that's the new breed of nuns, right, so you'll go by their room and you'll hear Jimmy still up, having like these one-sided telephone conversations. 'Uh-huh, yeah, sure, I will, no problem, I'll try, uh-huh, uh-huh,' and he thinks he's talking with *God*, see, like a kid does with an imaginary friend. Or maybe he really *is* talking to God, how would I know? Anyhow, the other night I peek in and he's doing one of these numbers only now he's got that tough-guy look I hate so much pasted on his face like all the other little punks in the neighborhood and he's quiet for a long

time, listening, and then he kind of sneers and says—'Why should
I?' "

We all sort of pretend the food is better at the Halfway than it really is.
Not that it's bad—it's okay, but nothing to write home about. Elvira,
who runs the place, won't use a microwave, which makes me happy.
I'm convinced there's vibes in those things that get into the food and
ten years from now there'll be a national scandal. Whenever I have
something from a microwave I get bad dreams, I swear it, so if something comes out a little lukewarm from her kitchen I don't complain.

The thing is, Elvira really seems to look forward to seeing us, looks
forward to all the noise and hustle a busload of hungry women carry
into the place, no matter what it is that brung them together. I imagine pulling into someplace different, with the name of the facility
rolled up into the little destination window at the front of the bus, us
flocking in and the waitresses panicking, the cooks ready to mutiny,
the other customers sure we're pickpockets, prostitutes, baby-snatch-
ers—no way José. So maybe the food here tastes better cause it comes
through Elvira, all the square edges rounded off.

She's a big woman, Elvira, and if the country about here had a face
it would look like hers. Kind of dry and cracked and worn, but
friendly. She says she called the Halfway the Halfway because every-
place on earth is halfway between somewhere and somewhere else. I
don't think being halfway between the city and the facility was what
she had in mind, though.

When we bust in and spill out around the room there's only one
other customer, a skinny old lizard in a Tecate cap and a T-shirt,
never once looking up from his grilled-cheese sandwich.

"Make it simple, ladies," Gus says. "We got a clock to watch."

At the Halfway it's pretty hard to make it anything but simple.
When they gave out the kits at Diner Central, Elvira went for bare
essentials. She's got the fly-strip hanging by the door with a dozen
little boogers stuck to it, got the cornflakes pyramided on a shelf, the
specials hand-printed on paper plates stuck on the wall behind the
counter, the morning's Danishes crusting over under their plastic
hood, the lemon and chocolate cream pies with huge bouffants of

meringue behind sliding glass, a cigarette machine, a phone booth, and a machine that tells your exact weight for a quarter which Lee feeds both coming in and going out.

"Have your orders ready, girls!" Elvira calls as we settle at the counter and in the booths, pretty much filling the place. "I want to hear numbers."

Elvira starts at one end of the counter and her girl Cheryl does the booths. Cheryl always seems like she's about to come apart, sighing a lot, scratching things out, breaking her pencil points. A nervous kid. What there is to be nervous about way out there in the middle of nowhere I couldn't tell you, but she manages. I'm sitting at the counter with Mrs. Tucker on one side, Pam on the other, then Lee and Del. Lee and Del get talking about their honeymoons while Pam goes off to pump the cigarette machine.

"So anyhow," says Lee, "he figures we'll go down to Mexico, that old bit about how your money travels further down there? I don't know how *far* it goes, but after that honeymoon I know how *fast*. He was just trying to be sweet, really, he figured he was gonna show me this wonderful time, cause he's been there and I haven't and he knows what to order and I don't and he knows where to go and all that, only he *doesn't,* you know, he just *thinks* he does. Which is the whole thing with Lonnie—he dreams things up and pretty soon he believes they're *true,* right, so he's more surprised than anybody when the shit hits the fan."

"Sounds familiar," says Del.

"So he's heard of this place—jeez, it's so long ago—Santa Maria de la Playa, something like that—" Lee looks to me for help. "You must know it, Lourdes. It's on the coast—"

"Lots of coast down there."

"There's like these mountains, and the ocean—"

"Sorry," I tell her. "I've never been to Mexico."

Delphine can't feature this. "You're shittin me," she says. *"You?"*

"You ever been to Africa?"

Del cracks up, which is one of the things I like about her. She's not oversensitive about that stuff. Usually.

"Anyway," says Lee, "he says to me, 'Baby, we're talkin Paradise here, we're talkin Honeymoon *Heaven*. I got this deal—' "

"They *al*ways got a deal," says Del.

Elvira comes by then with her pad, working fast but friendly all the time. "Hey, girls," she says, "how's it going? Mrs. Tucker?"

"Just the water," Mrs. Tucker says. "I'm not really hungry."

She doesn't look too good, Mrs. Tucker, kind of drawn around the eyes. Elvira shakes her head.

"Not good to skip lunch, Mrs. Tucker. You got a long ride ahead."

"Just the water, thank you."

Lee and Del get the same thing every week. "Let's see, we got a Number Three and a Number Five, mayo on the side," Elvira says. "Ice tea or lemonade?"

They both go for the lemonade and then Pam comes back dropping packs of Camels all over.

"How bout you, hon?"

"Um could I see a menu?" More cigarettes tumble from her arms. I see that Pam is one of those people who is accident-prone for life, and that her marrying a car thief is no coincidence. A catastrophe waiting to happen, this girl. Elvira jerks a thumb to the wall. Pam sees the paper plates. "Oh um—what are you having?"

"Number Three," says Lee.

"Number Five," says Delphine.

"Oh. I'll have a Number Four, please. And a club soda?"

"You know what a Number Four *is*, hon?"

"No, but I'll eat it."

Elvira thinks this is a scream but writes it down without laughing. "Four and a club," she says and moves on.

"So he's got this deal," says Del, getting back to the story.

"Right. He's got this deal where he brings these tapes down to San Miguel de los Nachos, whatever it was, and this guy who runs a brand-new resort down there is gonna give us the royal-carpet treatment in exchange—"

"Like cassette tapes?"

"Fresh from the K mart. Why they can't go to their own stores and buy these things I don't know—what's the story down there, Lourdes?"

"It's a mystery to me," I say.

"Anyhow, we got thousands of the things we're bringing through without paying duty, a junior version of the scam he finally went up for, only I don't know because they're under the back seat and he keeps laying this Honeymoon Heaven jazz on me."

"With Richard his deals always have to do with clothes," says Del. "Man come in and say, 'Sugar, what size dress you wear?' and my stomach just hits the *floor.*"

"And he brings the wrong size, right?"

"Ever damn time." Del shakes her head. "We took our honeymoon in Jamaica, back when we was livin high. Girl, you never saw nobody with more fluff in her head than me back then."

"You were young."

"Young ain't no excuse for *stupid.* I had one of those posters in my head—soft sand, violins playing, rum and Coke on ice and I was the girl in the white bikini. I thought it was gonna be like that *always.*" Del gets kind of distant then, thinking back. She smiles. "Richard gets outa there, gets his health back, we gonna *party,* girl. That's one thing the man knows how to do is party."

"Yeah, Lonnie too. They both get clear we should all get together sometime, do the town."

As soon as it's out Lee knows different. There's a silence then, both of them just smiling, uncomfortable. Guys inside, black and white, aren't likely to even know who each other is, much less get together outside and make friendly. It does that to you, inside. Yayo is the same, always on about *los gachos gavachos* this and *los pinches negros* that, it's a sickness you pick up there. Or maybe you already got it when you go in and the joint makes it worse. Lee finally breaks the silence.

"I bet you look great in a white bikini," she says.

Del laughs. "That's the *last* time I been to any *beach,* girl."

Cheryl shows with the food and Mrs. Tucker excuses herself to go to the ladies'. Lee has the diet plate, a scoop of cottage cheese with a cherry on top, Del has a BLT with mayo on the side, and Pam has the

Number Four, which at the Halfway is a Monte Cristo—ham and cheese battered in egg, deep fried, and then rolled in confectioner's sugar. She turns it around and around on her plate, studying it like it fell from Mars.

"I think maybe I'll ask him this visit," says Del. "About the kids."

"You'd be a good mother," says Lee.

"You think so?"

"Sure."

"Richard with a baby in his lap . . ." Del grimaces at the thought. "Sometimes I think it's just what he needs—responsibility, family roots, that whole bit, settle him down. Then I think how maybe he'll just feel more *pres*sure, you know? And when he starts feelin pressure is when he starts messin up." Del lets the thought sit for a minute and then gives herself a little slap on the cheek as if to clear it away. "Just got to get him healthy first. Plenty of time for the rest." She turns to Pam. "So how's that Number Four?"

"It's different," says Pam. She's still working on her first bite, scared to swallow.

"You can't finish it," says Lee, "I might take a bite."

Del digs her in the ribs. "Girl, don't you even *look* at that Number Four. Thing is just *evil* with carbohydrates. I don't wanta be hearing you bellyache about how you got no willpower all the way home."

"I got willpower," Lee says. "I'm a goddamn tower of strength. It's just my *app*etite is stronger—"

"Naw—"

"My appetite is like Godzi*l*la, Del, you seen it at work, layin waste to everything in its path—"

"Hah-*haaah!*"

"But I'm gonna whup it—"

"That's what I like to hear."

"Kick its butt—"

"Tell it, baby—"

"I'm losin twenty pounds—"

"Go for it!"

"An I'm quittin smoking too—"

"You can do it, Lee—"

"And when that man makes parole he's gonna buy me a dish-washer!"

"Get *down!*"

They're both of them giggling then, but Lee is mostly serious. "You know," she says, "as much as I want him out, sometimes it feels weird that it might really happen. You get used to being on your own, get your own way of doing things—"

"I hear you talkin—"

"The trouble is, it ain't so bad that I'm gonna leave him but it ain't so good I'm dying to stay."

There's hardly a one of us on the bus hasn't said the exact same thing at one time or another. Del looks around the room.

"So here we all are," she says, "at the Halfway Diner."

Back on the road Pam gets quiet so I count dead rabbits for a while, and then occupy the time imagining disasters that could be happening with the kids at Graciela's. You'd be surprised at how entertaining this can be. By the time we pass the fruit stand Chuy has left the burners going on the gas stove and Luz, my baby, is being chewed by a rabid Doberman. It's only twenty minutes to the facility after the fruit stand and you can hear the bus get quieter, everybody but Dolores. She's still muttering her good-bye speech like a rosary. The visits do remind me of confession—you go into a little booth, you face each other through a window, you feel weird afterward. I think about the things I don't want to forget to tell Yayo. Then I see myself in Renee's mirror and hit on her for some blush.

The first we know of it is when the guard at security calls Lee and Del's names and they're taken off in opposite directions. That sets everybody buzzing. Pam is real nervous, this being her first visit, and I think she is a little afraid of who her guy is going to be all of a sudden. I tell her not to ask too much of it, one visit. I can't remember me and Yayo just sitting and talking a whole hour that many times *before* he went up. Add to that the glass and the little speaker boxes and people around with rifles, and you have definitely entered Weird City. We always talk home-talk cause all the guards are Anglos and it's fun for Yayo to badmouth them under their noses.

"Big blowout last night in the mess," he says to me. *"Anglos contra los negros.* One guy got cut pretty bad."

I get a sick feeling in the pit of my stomach. The night Yayo got busted I had the same feeling but couldn't think of anything to keep him in the house. "Black or white?" I ask.

"A black dude got stabbed," he says. "This guy Richard. He was a musician outside."

"And the guy who cut him?" I say, although I already know without asking.

"This guy Lonnie, was real close to parole. Got him up in solitary now. *Totalmente jodido."*

It was just something that kind of blew up and got out of control. Somebody needs to feel like he's big dick by ranking somebody else in front of the others and when you got black and white inside that's a fight, maybe a riot, and this time when the dust clears there's Lee's guy with his shank stuck in Del's guy. You don't ask it to make a lot of sense. I tell Yayo how the kids are doing and how they miss him a lot but I feel this weight pulling down on me, knowing about Lee and Del, I feel like nothing's any use and we're wasting our time squawking at each other over these microphones. We're out of rhythm, it's a long hour.

"I think about you all the time," he says as the guard steps in and I step out.

"Me too," I say.

It isn't true. Whole days go by when I hardly give him a thought, and when I do it's more an idea of him than really him in the flesh. Sometimes I feel guilty about this, but what the hell. Things weren't always so great when we were together. So maybe it's like the food at the Halfway, better to look forward to than to have.

Then I see how small he looks going back inside between the guards and I love him so much that I start to shake.

The bus is one big whisper when I get back on. The ones who have heard about Lee and Del are filling in the ones who haven't. Lee gets in first, pale and stiff, and sits by me. If I touched her with my finger she'd explode. Pam steps in then, looking shaky, and I can tell she's disappointed to see I'm already by someone. When Del gets on everybody clams up. She walks in with her head up, trying not to cry. If it had been somebody else cut her guy, somebody not connected with any of us on the bus, we'd all be around bucking her up and Lee would be first in line. As it is a couple of the black girls say something but she just zombies past them and sits in the very back next to Pam.

It's always quieter on the way home. We got things that were said to chew over, mistakes to regret, the prospect of another week alone to face. But after Del comes in it's like a morgue. Mrs. Tucker doesn't even knit, just stares out at the Valley going by kind of blank-eyed and sleepy. Only Pam, still in the dark about what went down inside, starts to talk. It's so quiet I can hear her all the way from the rear.

"I never thought about how they'd have those guns," she says, just opening up out of the blue to Del. "I never saw one up close, only in the movies or TV. They're *real*, you know? They look so heavy and like if they shot it would just take you *apart*—"

"White girl," says Del, interrupting, "I don't want to be hearin bout none of your problems."

After that all you hear is the gears shifting now and then. I feel sick, worse than when I try to read. Lee hardly blinks beside me, the muscles in her jaw working as she grinds something out in her head. It's hard to breathe.

I look around and see that the white girls are almost all up front but for Pam who doesn't know and the black girls are all in the back, with us Chicanas on the borderline between as usual. Everybody is just stewing in her own thoughts. Even the sisters have nothing to say to each other. A busload of losers slogging down the highway. If there's life in hell this is what the field trips are like. It starts to get dark. In front of me, while there is still a tiny bit of daylight, Renee stares at her naked face in her mirror and sighs.

Elvira and Cheryl look tired when we get to the Halfway. Ketchup bottles are turned on their heads on the counter but nothing is sliding down. Gus picks up on the mood and doesn't tell us how we got a clock to watch when he comes in.

Pam sits by me with Dolores and Mrs. Tucker on the other side. Dolores sits shaking her head. "Next time," she keeps saying. "I'll tell him next time." Lee shuts herself in the phone booth and Del sits at the far end of the counter.

Pam whispers to me, "What's up?"

"Big fight in the mess last night," I tell her. "Lee's guy cut Delphine's."

"My God. Is he okay?"

"He's alive if that's what you mean. I've heard Del say how he's got this blood problem, some old drug thing, so this ain't gonna help any."

Pam looks at the booth. "Lee must feel awful."

"Her guy just wrecked his parole but good," I say. "She's gettin it with both barrels."

Elvira comes by taking orders. "Rough trip, from the look of you all. Get your appetite back, Mrs. Tucker?"

"Yes, I have," she says. Her voice sounds like it's coming from the next room. "I'm very, very hungry."

"I didn't tell him," Dolores confesses to no one in particular. "I didn't have the heart."

We order and Elvira goes back in the kitchen. We know there is a cook named Phil but we have never seen him.

I ask Pam how her guy is making out. She makes a face, thinking. I can see her in high school, Pam, blonde and popular, and her guy, a good-looking charmer up to monkey business. An Anglo version of Yayo, full of promises that turn into excuses.

"He's okay, I guess. He says he's going to do his own time, whatever that means."

I got to laugh. "They all say that, honey, but not many manage. It means like mind your own business, stay out of complications."

"Oh."

Delphine is looking bullets over at Lee in the phone booth, who must be calling either her kids or her lawyer.

"Maybe that's how you got to be to survive in there," I say. "Hell, maybe out here, too. Personally I think it bites." Mrs. Tucker puts her head down into her arms and closes her eyes. It's been a long day. "The thing is," I say to Pam, "we're all of us doing time."

Lee comes out of the booth and goes to the opposite end of the counter from Del. It makes me think of me and Graciela. We used to be real jealous, her and me, sniff each other like dogs whenever we met, on account of her being Yayo's first wife. Not that I stole him or anything, they were bust long before I made the scene, but still you got to wonder what's he see in this bitch that I don't have? A natural human reaction. Anyhow, she's in the neighborhood and she's got a daughter by him who's ahead of my Chuy at the same school and I see her around but it's very icy. Then Yayo gets sent up and one day I'm stuck for a baby-sitter on visiting day. I don't know what possesses me, but desperation being the mother of a whole lot of stuff I ask Graciela. She says why not. When I get back it's late and I'm wasted and we get talking and I don't know why but we really hit it off. She's got a different perspective on Yayo of course, talks about him like he's her little boy gone astray which maybe in some ways he is, and we never get into sex stuff about him. But he isn't the only thing we got in common. Yayo, of course, thinks that's all we do, sit and gang up on him verbally, and he's not too crazy about the idea. We started shopping together and sometimes her girl comes over to play or we'll dump the kids with my mother and go out and it's fun, sort of like high school where you hung around not necessarily looking for boys. We go to the mall, whatever. There's times I would've gone right under without her, I mean I'd be *gonzo* today. I look at Lee and Del, sitting tight and mean inside themselves, and I think that's me and Graciela in reverse. And I wonder what happens to us when Yayo gets out.

"Mrs. Tucker, can you hear me? Mrs. Tucker?"

It's Gus who notices that Mrs. Tucker doesn't look right. He's shaking her and calling her name, and her eyes are still open but all fuzzy, the life gone out of them. The sisters are chattering something about cold water and Cheryl drops a plate of something and Pam keeps yelling, "Where's the poster? Find the poster!" Later she tells me she meant the anti-choking poster they're supposed to have up in restaurants, which Elvira kind of hides behind the weight-telling machine cause she says it puts people off their feed. Mrs. Tucker isn't choking, of course, but Pam doesn't know this at the time and is sure we got to look at this poster before we do anything wrong. Me, even with all the disasters I've imagined for the kids and all the rescues I've dreamed about performing, I've never dealt with this particular glassy-eyed-older-lady type of thing so I'm no help. Gus is holding Mrs. Tucker's face in his hands, her body gone limp, when Lee and Del step in.

"Move back!" says Lee. "Give her room to breathe."

"You got a pulse?" says Del.

"Not much. It's fluttering around."

"Get an ambulance here," says Del to Elvira and Elvira sends Cheryl running to the back.

"Any tags on her?"

They look around Mrs. Tucker's neck but don't find anything.

"Anybody ever hear her talk about a medical problem?" asks Del to the rest of us, while she holds Mrs. Tucker's lids up and looks deep into her eyes.

We rack our brains but come up empty, except for Gus. Gus looks a worse color than Mrs. Tucker does, sweat running down his face from the excitement. "She said the doctor told her to watch her intake," he says. "Whatever that means."

"She didn't eat lunch," says Elvira. "You should never skip lunch."

Lee and Del look at each other. "She got sugar, maybe?"

"Or something like it."

"Some orange juice," says Lee to Elvira and she runs off. Mrs. Tucker is kind of gray now, and her head keeps flopping if they don't hold it up.

"Usually she talks my ear off," says Gus. "Today she was like depressed or something."

Elvira comes back out. "I brung the fresh-squoze from the fridge," she says. "More vitamins."

Del takes it and feeds a little to Mrs. Tucker, tipping her head back to get it in. We're all of us circled around watching, opening our mouths in sympathy like when you're trying to get the baby to spoon-feed. Some dribbles out and some stays down.

"Just a little," says Lee. "It could be the opposite."

Mrs. Tucker takes another sip and smiles dreamily. "I like juice," she says.

"Here, take a little more."

"That's good," she says in this tiny, little-girl voice. "Juice is good."

By the time the ambulance comes we have her lying down in one of the booths covered by the lap blanket the sisters bring, her head pillowed on a couple of bags full of hamburger rolls. Her eyes have come clear and eventually she rejoins the living, looking up at all of us staring down around her and giving a little smile.

"Everybody's here," she says in that strange, far-off voice. "Everybody's here at the Halfway Diner."

The ambulance guys take some advice from Lee and Del and then drive her away. Just keep her overnight for observation is all. "See?" Elvira keeps saying. "You don't never want to skip your lunch." Then she bags up dinners for those who want them cause we have to get back on the road.

Nobody says anything, but when we get aboard nobody will take a seat. Everybody just stands around in the aisle talking about Mrs. Tucker and waiting for Lee and Del to come in and make their move. Waiting and hoping, I guess.

Lee comes in and sits in the middle. Pam moves like she's gonna sit next to her but I grab her arm. Delphine comes in, looks around kind of casual, and then like it's just a coincidence she sits by Lee. The rest of us settle in real quick then, pretending it's business as usual but listening real hard.

We're right behind them, me and Pam. They're not talking, not looking at each other, just sitting there side by side. Being nurses together might've cracked the ice but it didn't break it all the way through. We're parked right beneath the Halfway Diner sign and the neon makes this sound, this high-pitched buzzing that's like something about to explode.

"Sweet dreams, ladies," says Gus when he climbs into his seat. "We're bringin it home."

It's dark as pitch and it's quiet, but nobody is having sweet dreams. We're all listening. I don't really know how to explain this, and like I

said, we're not exactly the League of Women Voters on that bus but
there's a spirit, a way we root for each other and somehow we feel that
the way it comes out between Lee and Delphine will be a judgment on
us all. Nothing spoken, just a feeling between us.

Fifty miles go past and my stomach is starting to worry. Then,
when Del finally speaks, her voice is so quiet I can hardly hear one
seat away.

"So," she says. "San Luis Abysmal."

"Huh?" says Lee.

"Mexico," says Delphine, still real quiet. "You were telling me
about your honeymoon down in San Luis Abysmal."

"Yeah," says Lee. "San Something-or-other—"

"And he says he speaks the language—"

You can feel this sigh like go through the whole bus. Most can't
hear the words but just that they're talking. You can pick up the tone.

"Right," says Lee. "Only he learned his Spanish at Taco Bell. He's
got this *deal*, right—"

"Finalmente," one of the sisters whispers behind me.

"¡Qué bueno!" the other whispers. *"Todavía son amigas."*

". . . so we get to the so-called resort and he cuts open the back
seat and all these cas*settes* fall out, which I know nothing about—"

"Course not—"

"Only on account of the heat they've like *liq*uified, right—"

"Naw—"

"And this guy who runs the resort is roped off but so are we cause
this so-called brand-new resort is so brand-new it's not *built* yet—"

"Don't *say* it, girl—"

"It's just a con*struc*tion site—"

"Hah-*haaah!*"

The bus kicks into a higher gear and out of nowhere Gus is
whistling up front. He's never done this before, not once, probably
because he had Mrs. Tucker talking with him, but he's real good, like
somebody on a record. What he's whistling is like the theme song to
some big romantic movie, I forget which, real high and pretty and I
close my eyes and get that nice feeling like just before you fall to sleep
and you know everything is under control and your body just relaxes.

I feel good knowing there's hours before we got to get off, feel like as long as we stay on the bus, rocking gently through the night, we're okay, we're safe. The others are talking soft around me now, Gus is whistling high and pretty, and there's Del and Lee, voices in the dark.

"There's a beach," says Lee, "only they haven't brought in the *sand* yet and everywhere you go these little fleas are hoppin around and my ankles get bit and swole up like a balloon—"

"I been there, girl," says Del. "I hear you talkin—"

"Honeymoon Heaven, he says to me—"

Del laughs, softly. "Honeymoon *Heaven.*"

The Mountain

•

SHEILA KOHLER

*Sheila Kohler was born in Johannesburg and spent some years in
Europe before coming to New York City to study writing at Columbia
University. "The Mountain" is her first published story.*

The man I met in Gerzett—I think I met him in Gerzett; I can't be
quite sure—said something about a fly. It was what he said about the
fly that made me remember.

At any rate, I did not notice the man coming toward me because I
was reading or sipping a cup of tea or doing both, or perhaps I was
simply gazing at the lake. I was looking across the smooth green grass
that dipped down toward the lake like a sigh and saw, I think, the
silver-blue of the water reflected for a moment in the breast of a bird
as it swept down low across my vision.

Naturally, I did not notice the man.

He was not really the sort one notices, even coming toward one,
even in those shoes: thick crepe-soled shoes that give beneath the foot
with a slight lurch and squeak mournfully as one moves. Besides, I
was used to handling this sort of thing, or what I thought was this sort
of thing. I went on doing whatever it was I had been doing before.

Even when the fellow was quite close to me, blocking the afternoon
light, his shadow before him, I did not look up. It usually works best
—ignoring them—I mean, if that is what they are after, which this
fellow, in fact, was not. When he began to speak, I did not even hear
what he was saying to me, until he had said it twice, and even then it

was only the name that I heard. It was the name which struck me; it was not the sort of name one would forget entirely.

All of that month of May I had lingered on somewhat reluctantly in Gerzett. Despite what the doctors had told me about the therapeutic quality of the Swiss air, I found that the place was far too high for me; the air was too thin; I was constantly breathless.

I definitely did not like that lake. Just the thought of that still, trapped water was somehow dreadfully depressing. But it was the mountains, those towering snow-tipped peaks, with their steep craggy treeless surfaces, which filled me with an almost physical malaise, an impression of being shut in, or perhaps it was shut out.

Actually, I've never been able to remain for very long in the mountains. There is something about their stark beauty brooding eternally above one that daunts me and gives me somehow a sense of the impoverishment of life, a sense of doom which can literally bring on an attack of nausea or giddiness in my particular constitution.

Between you and me, I've never really liked Switzerland. The people are courteous, of course, but frightfully dull, and the whole place has always looked somehow "preserved" to me, rather like pickles in a jar. And too many cows, I always say, there are just far too many cows, and as for those wretched cow bells, which wake one in the morning and ring constantly through the day, they are enough to send one dashing off into that lake.

The hotel, which had been recommended to me as secluded and well appointed, turned out, of course, to be somewhat dilapidated. It was quiet, naturally, surrounded as it was by acres of lawns and wooded areas and that depressing lake. There were the usual sort of mixed borders and spreading oaks and sad cypresses. But the whole place was not a little in need of repair. It had seen better days.

Actually, it rather amazed me that the place had any clients at all. It was one of those hotels so refined in its elegance that the elegance was really only visible in the price of the room. The bathrooms, though fortunately very clean, had undoubtedly not been touched since 1930, and the walls of the corridors and dining room had been painted some sort of ghastly pale lime-green that seemed to glow with an almost ghostly light.

At that time of year, there was hardly anyone there except a handful of solid English dowagers whom I heard at meal-times rather than saw, bent over their plates, beside the potted palms, scraping their way noisily through the indigestible food in the vast half-empty dining room.

But, I must say, I had managed to secure a not entirely uncomfortable room after a long and vituperative argument with the hotel manager. I insisted on that particular accommodation because it was away from the main body of the hotel, almost entirely self-contained and consequently very quiet—I suffer from insomnia and absolutely anything wakes me—and because of the honeysuckle which grew up the wall and almost into my window.

The gardener had had to come and cut back the creeper from the window while I was staying in that room. He had come and hacked at the plants with a blunt instrument, a short semicircular blade or sickle, and I had had to ask him not to cut the creepers back too much but to let them grow along the windowsill so that I could see them from my bed when I woke in the mornings.

The room was large and sunny, with a wide soft double bed and a reading lamp which you could actually read by, a rarity in hotels, I always find; a steel table and chair on a not unbearably narrow private area where I was able to enjoy the weather, which was, I will admit, passably fair for that time of year: the light clear and bright from dawn to sunset and the wind still.

And the doctors, after all, had gone on at considerable length to recommend the place to me, praising the dry, clean air and the sunny climate, what they had the audacity to call the plain healthy food, and pointing out that the secluded nature and general restfulness of the place were ideal for someone suffering from my eternal complaint; so I stayed on for a while, partly out of lethargy—the spring has always made me, not restless, but apathetic—but also waiting to see if the doctors' advice might eventually prove to be salutary.

Every evening, from five to seven, I sat on the main terrace of the hotel overlooking the lake under the wooden window boxes of mul-

ticolored geraniums. I had arranged my time carefully; it is my custom to arrange my time carefully and to follow my schedule exactly: I
broke each day up into a number of identical segments which, by their
abiding uniformity, never gave me the impression that the day was
passing either too fast or too slowly: every morning I took as lengthy a
walk as I could manage in the woods, lunched generally in some
restaurant in the town, and came back to the hotel for a long siesta in
my room with the shutters closed; after a bath, I spent the rest of the
afternoon on the terrace looking over the lake, with a cup of tea or a
drink, my inhalator in my lap in its zippered bag, a book or the
newspaper or sometimes nothing at all, just the changing light in the
leaves to amuse me.

Of course, at night, at times, there were men—not the type who
could cause one any trouble.

As for this one, the one who came over to me on the terrace of the
hotel, he said, I believe, after some preliminary excuses for the disturbance he was causing, "Were you not related to Claire Richdale?" or
perhaps, "You were a friend of Claire Richdale's, it seems to me?" or
something of that sort.

I do not pretend to reproduce the man's particular vernacular. I'm
afraid I did not pay sufficient attention to his words to render them
with any sort of authenticity but can only attempt to give the general
gist of what he said. He spoke, I believe, without any sort of elegance,
but at the same time as a man of not a little education would speak
and, as far as I noticed, with a slight accent which was familiar to me
and immediately marked the man as coming from the place I had left
a considerable time ago.

I do remember the name the man said and the way he said that
name, which was what made me look up for a moment at the man
who was standing before me. There was something about the way he
said the name, something almost tentative and tremulous, which took
me by surprise; it did not seem to match the rest of the man.

Even then I glanced at him for only a second and went on doing
whatever it was I had been doing before: just gazing or reading my
book or sipping tea. The name, though I recognized it vaguely, meant
nothing to me, and the man actually interested me even less, of course.

I do not have a clear recollection of the man's face. All I remember was that there was something vaguely dark about his presence: either it was the hair or the eyebrows, or even the eyes or the skin, or perhaps even the fact that the fellow was not particularly well shaven; whatever it was, there was some impression of darkness to the man, that's all I can say, never having bothered, then or later, to peruse his countenance with much interest. He had on a white, not absolutely clean shirt, open at the neck, with no tie but the hint of some sort of vulgar gold chain around the neck, and beneath that what I imagined might be one of those hirsute chests; a shiny jacket, rather too broad at the shoulders and too narrow at the waist for my liking; a pair of dark tight trousers which might have been navy or black or even dark green, which showed far more than I wished to see of the man's masculinity; and those shoes which squeaked, went on squeaking, as he shifted his weight.

But even then the chap did not remove himself but continued to hover there beside me, blocking my afternoon light and view of the lawns and the trees.

To get the man's shadow out of my way, or because I could not really do otherwise and remain within the bounds of common courtesy, or finally, because of the name, or the way the man said the name, I motioned him to the chair opposite. It was all the invitation the fellow required. He sat down with his back to the lake. As he sat down, something about the way he seated himself, or perhaps it was more something not a little familiar about the way he held his head or leaned forward across the table, I can't quite pinpoint what it was about the chap as, naturally, I was not really paying him any sort of attention at all, but still, something did give me the impression that this was not the first time I had seen the man on the terrace; the fellow might have been there before; I might have seen him before.

As far as I remember, the chap launched into the conversation by asking me if I knew what had happened to the woman whose name he had already mentioned.

"What happened to whom?" I suppose I must have asked him, and

gone on watching the boats coming back to the land, after a day on the
water, with their sails folded around their booms.

At times I liked to watch the way the boats slid through the water
at the end of the day, coming silently into the shelter of the harbor.
There was something slow and peaceful about the way the hull of the
boat cut cleanly through the calm surface of the water which satisfied
me and distracted me from the presence of those mountains, which I
felt hung over the place so somberly, like some sort of warning of
disaster.

By that time of evening the water was a steel-blue; the mountains
were already dark. They loomed above us, I felt.

I suppose I must have been talking about the boats while the fellow
was going on about this woman, whom he called Claire Richdale—
one of those conversations one engages in so frequently, you know
what I mean, the kind which runs along parallel lines.

I made a vague attempt to fit the name to a face, but I didn't exert
myself overmuch. I was still under the impression the man was using
some trumped-up and rather unimaginative excuse to come over to
my table and strike up some sort of conversation with me, which I
presumed he would relinquish—the conversation, that is—without
much persuasion, to take up other, more promising prospects. I suppose I attempted to keep the conversation, as the fellow seemed to feel
obliged to converse, as anodyne as possible. I think I said, "We've been
lucky this month with the weather, haven't we?" or some such remark
about the weather, thinking the fellow would be glad to follow my
lead.

The pink rambling roses which grew along the wall of the terrace
had already been covered over to protect them from the cold of the
night. I remember wondering whether this protection was absolutely
necessary and why it was the hotel gardener felt these roses needed
this particular type of covering during the night.

However, the fellow did nothing to improve his position by going on
to apologize at length and, as far as I can recollect, in the most unorig-
inal tiring way, for this intrusion. He kept insisting that he had no
desire to disturb me, that he was not accustomed to disturbing solitary
women, particularly attractive women, or perhaps he said elegant

women, something of that sort, that he was aware it was really quite
rash of him, etc., etc., none of which I believed for a moment, naturally, and all of which did more than a little to add to my growing
annoyance. He continued to maintain, with exasperating insistence,
despite the fact that I gave him no encouragement whatsoever, that he
was quite certain he had seen me with this woman, or that I was
related in some way to this woman, or had even been close friends
with this woman he called Claire Richdale. Not only did the chap's
words annoy me, but for a reason which was not yet apparent, they
began to make me not a little uneasy, although I scarcely knew with
what.

However, I let him run on for a while, rather as one does a horse
which has bolted, you know, hoping he would eventually tire and
come to a stop of his own volition.

I have often found this an excellent means of coping with bores, and
how many people are there who are not bores? The world, of course, is
peopled mainly with bores, isn't it? I find it not unpleasant, though, to
just sit back and relax, awash in a murmur of half-heard words, letting
them ebb and flow like waves around me, my attention wandering
where it will, while the other, the speaker, goes on, sails forth quite
contentedly onward; it is quite amazing how long people will go on
quite contentedly without requiring any sort of encouragement. One
can generally pick up the thread at some crucial point, or simply add a
nod or a grunt here or there, and no one is the wiser. I have always
asked myself how people can possibly believe anyone would want to
listen to all of that.

So I sat there, as I often do, hardly listening, or only listening
sufficiently to follow the gist of what the fellow was saying—going on
with my tea, I believe, or perhaps I had already moved from tea to a
gin-and-tonic with lime, and only conscious, really, to tell you the
truth, of the fact that the light was fading rapidly, the sun was sinking,
the mountains were black above us, and that the fellow had somehow
shifted his weight as he talked so that he was leaning rather uncomfortably close to me, breathing almost directly into my face.

It was not, I realized afterward, only his closeness that made me
uncomfortable.

"Hardly that," I said finally, in reference to this supposed close friendship or relation that he was so certain had linked me to this woman called Claire. I unzippered my inhalator, pumped a couple of times, and repeated, "It could hardly have been that," in a somewhat exasperated tone at that point, wishing then to rid myself of this importunate fellow. "That could only be a gross overstatement," I said, and began, I must say, at that point, to wonder vaguely why the man kept on going on about this business, whatever it was, and how I was going to get rid of him. I didn't imagine that a man of this sort had anything of interest to tell me about anyone, and least of all about this woman, whoever she was.

I said, "Actually, I don't think I could really say I was close friends with anyone, for that matter."

As far as I remember, that remark silenced him for a while, but still he did not move. We went on sitting there, on the terrace, under the geraniums—I've never particularly liked geraniums: too bright, too stiff, the sort of flowers one finds in the window boxes of Swiss banks —the fellow leaning half across the table with his shiny sleeve brushing my arm.

But even then the chap did not give up. After a pause, he renewed his attack. He asked me to try to consider where I might have met this woman, if I might not have been at school with this woman, or have met her, perhaps, at some party, even as a child. Would I not, he begged me, with an urgency in his voice which struck me then as nothing but tiresome, because I was beginning to realize that the fellow was going to be not a little difficult to ignore, was not going to simply get up and dissolve into the darkening sky, nor was he going to settle, even, for what it was that I had originally thought he was after, which after all would have been something I could have handled, could have understood, which I could have taken or left as I wished— would I not, he asked me, reflect carefully and make absolutely certain that I had not even been at school with this woman. Could boarding school have been the place where we had met?

In an attempt to sum up, to conclude the matter in some way that might be satisfactory to this man and thus shake the fellow off, I did, perhaps, make some sort of an effort to place the name. I said, "Perhaps we were at school together. Maybe that's it. I suppose we might have been. The name is vaguely familiar. We might even have been in the same class at some point. I rather think we were. Perhaps she failed down into my class or they put me up into hers. I really don't remember. It was a long time ago," and pulled my shawl—the black wool one with the red flowers embroidered around the edge—around my shoulders and snapped the flap of my handbag in preparation for a move. I added, still hoping to change the subject and thus rid myself of the fellow or at least this tiresome conversation, "The light is fading fast. Odd how it lingers and then suddenly gets dark, isn't it?" or something of that sort.

But the man refused to be put off. He still wanted to know if I knew what had happened to this woman, as though it were possible that, not even remembering who she was, I could possibly have known or wanted to know what had happened to her.

"No idea. Whoever she is, I certainly haven't seen the woman for years," I said.

But even that reasonable statement did not satisfy the chap. He could not believe I had not read something about the matter in the papers somewhere or had not spoken to someone who would have told me what had happened to the woman.

I tried, summarily, to explain that I had left all of that far behind me, that my life out there might almost have belonged to someone else. I believe I said something like: "I haven't been back there for years. I move around a lot, you know. Never stay anywhere for very long. Quite lost touch with all of that. Always found that place killingly boring, myself. I prefer Europe these days. I have a place in the Cotswolds where I keep my things. This is rather a pretty spot, don't you think?"

It seems to me that it was at that point in the conversation—but I may, of course, not be remembering all of this in the order in which it actually happened, particularly as I was hardly listening to the chap, was paying much more attention to the water and the mountains and even the geraniums than to what the man was trying to say to me— that the fellow said he was sure he had seen me with this woman he called Claire Richdale at her house. He said something about my having spent a day with the woman at her house. I remember this clearly, as the chap repeated this supposition more than a couple of times. The fellow, as I remember, was the sort who repeated himself continuously, whether it was because the topic excited him particularly or because this was his habit, I did not know, but I did know that his propensity to repetition added not a little to the general dreariness of his conversation.

The man said something to the effect that he thought I might have visited at this Claire's home, spent a day with the woman, and that he might have seen me there at that particular moment. I suppose I answered something along the lines of: "It is possible I visited her home once. I was often invited to the homes of my school friends and sometimes I went. I might have visited these people you are talking about. I do have a vague recollection of some dreary house, now that you mention it, and even some relatives who might have been hers: a mother, perhaps, or an aunt, perhaps more than one aunt, something like that. So I suppose it's possible you saw me there."

Then I made another, last-ditch effort to shut the fellow up—I was deadly bored by that point, reduced to plucking off the petals from a geranium and crushing the stem between finger and thumb to keep myself occupied—you can imagine. I attempted to get rid of the chap entirely by assuring him that, despite all my efforts, I could honestly not remember another thing about this woman. I believe I told him, what was certainly the case, that I really didn't have a very good memory for that sort of thing. I said, "Curiously, I tend to remember things more than people. Anyway, one always remembers the most insignificant, the most useless of details, and forgets the essentials, don't you think?"

This remark, however apt, and surely it was, in this case, particularly apt, seemed to have little or no effect on the man. I remember how he sat there: by then the man's face was so close to me I could hear the sound of his breathing. He breathed audibly, with his lips open on the dark of his mouth. I was left no recourse but my inhalator, which I pulled out once again and pumped.

I said, still trying to be courteous—I believe good manners are probably the most useful of all the virtues—but by then almost ready to get up and leave the fellow sitting there in his shiny jacket and his squeaking shoes: "You know, it really is getting rather late. I remember so little about this woman. I am honestly trying to tell you everything I know, but I don't think I can help you at all. I may have spent a day with her, it's quite possible, I do remember something about that house. She may have asked me to come and spend the day with her and she may even have talked to me, told me the story of her life, told me . . . heaven knows what she might have told me. But I really have no recollection of what she said or what I might have said or what I might have done. It was a long time ago, and besides, none of us listens much to one another, do we? In my experience people just don't listen. They may even ask questions, but they don't listen to the answers."

But even this had apparently little effect. The man's tenacity was beyond my comprehension. I could in no way grasp what it was the chap was after, with his incessant questions and his continuous flow of words. Of course, I had no idea, nor did I particularly care what the man was after with me, I had only one thought at that point, which was, as it is with a fly which buzzes against one's face in the night, to get rid of the fellow.

Unbelievably, the chap went on talking, though I can hardly tell you what it was he said to me at that point. I believe there was some question of a name. The fellow seemed not a little anxious to know if this Claire had mentioned the name of someone, perhaps some man she might have been involved with or something of that sort. All of this was interspersed in a most confused and irrational way with various odd bits of information about the man himself; I believe he actually tried to tell me something about his own life, his mother, his father, a house he had once rented, a straw mattress, his profession or his lack of a profession, what he was doing up there in the mountains, but naturally, I paid no attention at all to any of that at the time.

As far as the name was concerned—the name the man thought this woman might have mentioned to me—I told the man I had never been very good with names. I said, "My goodness, I even have difficulty introducing my own mother."

Finally, I told the fellow that it was the time that, in the normal course of things, I went in for dinner, that I found it wiser not to eat too late and that the hors d'oeuvres were much better before anyone else attacked them. On Sunday nights the hotel always served a buffet dinner and I presume this must have been a Sunday evening.

At that point I almost forgot the chap, who had slumped again into silence, sitting in the rapidly fading light. I was thinking about the amazing quantities of food people took from buffet tables; the way they piled up their plates and how they managed to eat all of that and remain so thin. Perhaps I told the chap that personally I found the whole business of eating rather a bore. I could never decide what to eat, particularly in that place where the choice was generally between a *bifteck aux pommes frites* and a *bifteck aux pommes frites*.

He said suddenly—I suppose he may have been staring at me or what he could see of me in that dim light—I remember this clearly: "You know, you look like her. You really do. There's definitely something about you that makes me think of her. There's some resemblance."

I had lost the thread of his conversation to the point that I replied, "I look like whom?" When he had made it evident that he was still talking about the same woman, I suppose I replied that I couldn't imagine why he thought I looked like this Claire Richdale, though to tell you the truth, I had great difficulty conjuring up her features at all. The only impression I had of the woman's face was that it was quite probably a most ordinary one, a face, as far as I could remember, without any sort of distinction at all.

To which I believe he replied, "You have the same fair skin which burns easily."

I said abruptly, with the desire that this would close our discussion, "It starts to get cool at around this hour. It is really rather chilly this evening, don't you find? It is definitely time for me to go into dinner. Please excuse me now."

But the fellow's expansive presence did not undergo any sort of contraction. He could not let me go. He only crushed the book of matches he held in his hand and went on sitting there; I was beginning to feel the chap was as immovable as the mountains above us. He begged for just a minute more of my time. He was still certain that I might be able to remember something. He seemed quite unable to let the matter lie and to get up and leave me to go in for my dinner.

After that I hardly listened to what the man said. I heard but barely registered what the man was saying. At the time I was only aware that he became most insistent, and that a flood of words came from him. Afterward, I was able to recollect some of what the man said to me, but at the time, I paid little attention to his words. Afterward, I was to remember more than I wanted to remember of the man's words, but that was later.

Finally, as I was about to simply get up while the man was rambling on in this almost incoherent way about the night he had spent with this woman and how young and foolish he had been at the time, about the importance of my recollecting or the importance of his knowing or even the importance to the general public of my remembering whatever it was he was begging me to remember: what this woman had said, or some name this woman might have said, or something of that sort, the fellow put his hand on my arm, I suspect in his eagerness to retain me, as he told me, what I actually knew by then, anyway, that someone must have done away with this woman in mysterious circumstances.

It was not possible for me to get up at that point; all I could do was to pull my shawl about my shoulders and cross my arms and watch the rambling roses along the wall, lit by the light from the dining room within, under the netting which covered them over against the cold of the night. I was obliged to sit there for a moment at least; it would hardly have been appropriate to leave right then.

I sat for a while in silence staring at the flowers and then, my eyes drawn upward despite myself, staring at the mountains, whose darkness had almost completely merged with the dark of the night. Though even the outlines of the mountains had gone, could only be imagined, felt, the night was full of their ominous form. I sensed their presence huddled over us; the sense of foreboding they inspired conglomerated, gathered force in their physical absence.

I was suddenly quite overcome with hunger and tiredness, worn out suddenly by this man's insistence, the boredom his presence provoked, or simply by the length of time I had been sitting in the same place. I

had been exposed for too long. The night had grown cool, the mist had
risen from the lake, and for a moment I shivered. I was afraid I might
have caught cold sitting out in the damp evening air.

At that point, too, something else happened, which I think I should
mention: I realized that the man had moved, had somehow taken my
wrist, had his hand on my wrist, was holding, gripping, not my hand,
but my wrist. His face, as far as I could see in the dim light, was quite
red and he appeared to me to be sweating slightly, beads of sweat
clung to his forehead, and his dark hair was not a little damp around
the hairline.

I let my arm lie in his hand. I looked down at the man's hand. He
had long, fine, blunt-tipped fingers; deft hands; strong, agile hands;
hands that were very clean, the nails carefully manicured; he wore a
diamond ring set in gold on the little finger. The ring looked too small
for him. His hands, like the way he said the woman's, Claire
Richdale's, name, surprised me; they didn't seem to fit the man.

It crossed my mind then that one might sleep with this man or not
sleep with this man and that it would come to exactly the same thing.

I rose then and left the man sitting there.

The dining room seemed particularly lugubrious to me that evening.
It was a large room which led off one of the lounges and looked over
the lake. At that hour, though, the heavy green-velvet curtains were
drawn across the windows and billowed gently in the evening breeze.
The whole room, for some reason, I thought that evening, resembled
some underwater region.

The lime-green walls seemed to me to cast a sickly glow, accentu-
ated by the discreet lighting of the small shaded table lamps, so that
even the white tablecloths and the limp pink carnations in their silver
vases, reflecting the green, glowed, seemingly phosphorescent. The
potted palms in the corners of the room, I observed, appeared to fold
and unfold the fingers of their leaves in the slight breeze, like sea
anemones.

There was no one in the room except a few guests who sat wrapped
in the anonymity of their age and wealth, huddled over their soup.

There was almost no sound in the room, as though, I imagined, the pervading gloom had silenced the guests. Besides the waiter's discreet murmuring and the scrape of silver on porcelain, there was nothing to be heard.

I sat at my table wondering why on earth the walls had been painted such a ghastly green. I am not a little sensitive to colors, and the green jarred on my nerves particularly that evening. The duck which I had ordered was definitely a mistake, and even the bottle of wine I had chosen, a not inexpensive bottle of Dole, was not enough to muffle my mood.

My encounter with the importunate man on the terrace and the fate of the barely remembered woman he had spoken of had almost entirely slipped my mind, I was certainly not thinking of either of them, but something about the man's words must have unsettled me. The stillness of the room, which generally went by unnoticed, or was welcomed, troubled my nerves.

I looked around at the room, suddenly struck by the absurdity of it all: the silver shining, the ridiculous tubular flower bowls on each table, the half-dead, drooping carnations, each object in its well-chosen place, all the apparent solidity of a supposedly well-organized world. For a moment the whole room seemed to shift slightly, to tremble, and an absurd thought crossed my mind: I thought I heard the sound of the fellow's crepe-soled shoes on the parquet floor.

I was even drawn, for some unaccountable reason, to exchange a few pleasantries with my neighbor in the lounge after the meal over a cup of coffee, something I had naturally never done before, a ridiculous elderly woman whom I had always avoided, who dined alone and wore the same absurd black taffeta hat every night to dinner and generally tucked a couple of oranges into her knitting bag before retiring.

In my room I lay on my bed and actually smoked a cigarette. I gave it up—cigarette smoking, that is—years ago, naturally, with my complaint, but I always keep a pack of filter-tipped Dunhills handy for emergencies such as this one.

I lay there with only the bedside lamp lit, inhaling, drawing the smoke deep into my lungs, savoring the nicotine and the thought of what it was doing to my lungs, voluptuously—it was, of course, strictly against doctor's orders—I even washed the cigarette down with a stiff neat whiskey. A bottle of that, too, I keep in my room for medicinal purposes. I remember thinking that I had no wish, anyway, to live on for as long as these same doctors would have liked me to go on living and to go on paying their bills.

I stubbed out my half-finished cigarette and tried to read, but with little success. I was unable to concentrate. What I was thinking of as I lay there was the dormitory at school, the light in the dormitory at school.

I could see then that, in the dormitory, the light was silver. The moon lit the room. The mosquito nets, which hung from the row of narrow beds, were drawn back, gathered into thick coils at the head of the beds.

There was a smell of oranges, someone had smuggled an orange into the room from dinner and the orange, or rather the skin of the orange, perfumed the air. It was very hot, although the windows were wide open.

I do not know what season it was. The seasons out there are hardly seasons, they change fast, with no twilight pauses: no melancholy autumnal moments or gauzy spring promises; summer slips into winter almost imperceptibly. It is always more or less hot and more or less humid.

The girls stood on the beds and threw a pillow from bed to bed, giggling, bouncing, waving their arms wildly, their hair flying, bending over to clutch their hollow stomachs in silent laughter, whispering in loud hoarse whispers. The penalty for dropping the pillow was the removal of an article of clothing. That was the rule of the game.

The girl was wearing little clothing at the start of the game. She jumped up and down on the bed, her half-formed breasts naked, her puerile body tight in her moist skin and silver in the light of the moon. I threw the pillow high and hard, so that she reached for it, her arms flailing the air; she fumbled; she teetered, and almost fell.

It was somewhere around ten o'clock, I think, when the telephone rang. I was not really surprised, I suppose, to hear the man's voice.

As I remember it, he began once again by apologizing, but I cut him short this time and simply asked him what he wanted. There was a pause.

Finally the chap asked if he might see me again.

I hesitated a moment, considering. I stood with the receiver in my hand, staring at the bowl of red roses on the dressing table: twelve red roses sent by an admirer; their heads drooped and a fine coating of slime lined their stems. I'm not quite sure why I then said what I did, but it may have had something to do with the flowers.

I told the man I had met on the terrace that if he wanted to see me to obtain information about the woman he had been talking about all that afternoon, there was no point in his coming.

He then made his intentions sufficiently clear.

To be absolutely certain there would be no mistake, I told him he might come to my room then, but that I would not expect him to stay long. I told him I always went to sleep early, which was not actually a lie—I often do go to bed early with a book, not even answering my phone after a certain hour. In this way, I thought, I would avoid any other lengthy conversations. As it turned out, I did avoid any lengthy conversations—the man said hardly more than a dozen sentences—but I was not prepared for what I actually got.

By the time the man arrived in my room I had bathed, perfumed, and powdered my body and was already partly undressed. This was not particularly for the man's benefit but simply a ritual I always performed before any such encounter. Such rituals I find are what enable one to get through life, though there are times when they seem almost too much effort. I had perfunctorily brushed out my hair and let it lie loose around my shoulders—not out of any sort of coquetry, but so that the hairpins I use for my chignon would not dig into the back of my neck. I was already feeling worn out with the effort of all this activity and beginning, as is so often the case, to regret ever having told the man to come to my room, when he rang my doorbell.

I cursorily inspected myself in the full-length mirror in the bathroom. I was attired, I believe, in nothing much more than my short pink silk shift—not the black one—and my black sandals.

As an adolescent I always felt I was too tall and too thin—all arms and legs and eyes. My stepfather, a military man, who finally received his just deserts, kicked in the head by a horse—though there were moments when I thought that even this end was too quick and pain-less for the man and that I might have enjoyed seeing him lie and suffer for a while—spent his time telling me, among other things of this sort, that I was too tall and that, above all, my feet were too large.

However, the advantage of such a figure—I'm talking about my figure, of course—is that with the years—I'm not, of course, going to commit the indiscretion of telling you my age, but leave you to come to some reasonable conclusion on your own—there is not much flesh to sag or fall. I think I can say, without much vanity, that I have retained a deceptively youthful appearance, in certain kind lights—I always say, past a certain age, women should come out only at night. At any rate, what I saw in the mirror that night, while the man was knocking on my door—I let him cool his heels out there for a while—did not entirely displease me.

I noticed, too, with some relief, that the man, when I finally opened the door to him and he stepped into my room, had changed his shirt to a clean one of some rather more attractive transparent material and he smelled of some not unpleasant eau de cologne. He was, however, wearing the same shoes, though I noticed he must have given, or had them given, a polish, but that they continued to squeak as mournfully as ever as I led him across to the bed.

The maid had removed the bedcover, and I had lit the bedside lamp —I like to see whom I'm making love to, naturally. I let the man commence with the proceedings without any further preliminaries.

It was as we were both sprawled across my bed, and were already somewhat in disarray, that the man spoke of the fly. The fellow, as I remember, was reclining beside me, or rather against me, hardly even as clothed as I was. I believe he had on nothing more than the gold chain which he wore around his neck and which dangled back and forth in the hair on his chest. He had risen up on one elbow, so as to

look down at me, or rather to watch both his hand, I suppose, and my
body, while all the while touching my body.

He was not unschooled in the art. I allowed him to work his way
freely from my upper extremities to the lower, which he accomplished
with not a little ease, his hand maneuvering craftily with the straps of
my shift so as to expose as much flesh as he could, going on deftly with
some method and some skill, lingering in the appropriate places, doing
nothing in too hurried a fashion, nor did he stall for too long, his
touch sufficiently strong without being rough—I remember thinking
that the fellow would have known how to shampoo hair excellently,
that his touch would have been just the thing for a really good shampoo, that it was a pity that I couldn't think of some way to have him
give me a shampoo; as he touched me, I let him press his own swollen
member against me or, rather, against the remaining thin silk of my
shift, which was all that still divided us and which I had allowed him
to work down and up, to cover nothing much more than my waist and
buttocks.

I lay there with my hands folded under my head and my gaze on the
ceiling—there was quite a pretty molding on the ceiling of that room
—letting him touch me—his caresses were not unpleasant, after all—
but with not a little disinterest, letting him go through the motions; I
was certainly in no way excited by his hands or his body—there was
nothing exciting about the fellow, I felt.

There was nothing actually wrong with the body, which was tanned
for that time of year, broad-chested and slim-hipped, and the legs were
really not bad at all, but rather too short it seemed to me—he was
probably an inch or so shorter than I am—and I've never been one,
though I know there are some who do, to go for that much dark hair
on the chest.

At this point in the lovemaking, if you could call it that, when I was
beginning to wonder whether it would be worth my while to go
through with the whole business or if it would not be wiser to end the
proceedings with some trumped-up excuse—a sudden stomach cramp
or nausea, or even a qualm of conscience, a husband I had not mentioned, perhaps, who could be dragged in at the last minute to get me
out of the final act—without any apparent reason, and without slow-

ing down in any way the movement of his hand or stopping stroking, whatever it was he was stroking at that moment, the fellow made that remark about the fly. I think what he said was: "But she would never have hurt a fly." I'm not absolutely certain of his words, but what I do know is what happened as he said those words.

I remembered something about the woman he was talking about, the woman he called Claire Richdale. A vivid image of this woman came to me.

The woman was in a large sunlit room with two or perhaps three beds. I saw her, this Claire Richdale, from behind, bending down, squatting on her haunches at first and then actually getting down onto her hands and knees and scooping at a small spider, a button spider, I believe they are called—a tiny black spider—pushing a stiff piece of white paper against the carpet, chasing the spider with a piece of white paper, chasing it along the edge of the mauve carpet onto the parquet floor, again and again, turning the paper as it ran one way and then the other, until she caught it on the edge of the page and ran to the window to set the creature free.

She threw open the window with one arm and the spider out into the creeper with the other, and then she turned to face me. The bay window which gave onto the garden was open and the wind whipped the loose sleeves of the woman's dress against her arms. I saw her sleeves flapping against her arms in the wind from the open window. That was what I saw more clearly than anything else in that initial image which came to me: the wide, loose sleeves of her dress; that was what I noticed more than anything else and certainly I noticed that more than her face or even her body, though I cannot tell you exactly of what material the sleeve was made: something soft like shantung or crepe de chine or silk of some sort, something almost transparent flapping, beating against her arms.

While I let the man go on touching my body, his hands descending into the inner recesses of my body, I was thinking of this woman he called Claire Richdale standing in the early-morning sunlight with the bay window open behind her. I could see her quite clearly, almost as though magnified by memory: her arms and the sleeves of her dress flapping gently against her skin; I could see the blond hair on her plump rounded arms and the pale freckles on her honey-colored skin. For some reason the image was exciting to me.

And I was enjoying the man.

It was only when the man had gone that it occurred to me that he had never mentioned his name. All that evening he had been saying the name of this Claire Richdale, but he had never mentioned his own name.

When the man had gone, I rose from the rumpled bed and walked around tidying up the room: remaking the bed carefully, emptying the ashtray and putting the glass away, actually wiping the trace of his shoes from the parquet floor—I cannot abide any sort of disorder—and touching my things: my books: the Austen, the Henry James, the Naipaul, and the Virginia Woolf; the silver brush-and-comb set; the photo of Mother, as a young woman, in its silver frame; the cut-glass bowl; the petit-point cushion; my rings; the cameo brooch; the creams for my face; the clothes in my closet; my suitcases and the straw bag I used on my walks. Somehow the room looked bare to me, as though something was missing. It even occurred to me that the man might have taken something from me, but when I checked, nothing was actually gone.

I took a long shower and scrubbed my skin with a loofah, dusted and perfumed my body, creamed my face. I felt a sudden need for air. I went over and opened the window and stood there gasping for a while, taking in great deep gulps of night air. I realized, as I stood there, that a light rain was falling. I could hear the sound of the water dripping into the gutters and smell the damp earth. The weather had changed.

I stood looking up at what I knew were the mountains, trying to make out their shape in the mist and the dark of the night. There was no moon visible over Gerzett, not even a lone star in the sky. The heavy presence of the mountains, unseen, was suddenly quite unbearable to me. I felt an attack of my complaint coming on; a sudden breathlessness overwhelmed me; I reached for my inhalator. I shivered and began to cough. I was certain I was feverish. I had caught cold. I had been rash remaining so long on the terrace that evening talking to a stranger, and then standing before the window in the damp night air after a hot shower. I knew all too well how dangerous a cold could be for someone with my illness. I wrapped myself hurriedly in a gown and climbed into bed, but I was unable to sleep. As I lay there tossing back and forth, alternately hot and then cold, through what remained of the night, that absurd thought came to me again.

It seemed to me that I could still hear, would go on hearing, in the rustlings and heavings, in the creaks and the muffled cries, in all the anonymous sounds of the night, the man's crepe-soled shoes squeaking.

Long Distance

•

——————— JANE SMILEY ———————

"Long Distance" is included in Jane Smiley's short story collection
The Age of Grief, *published by Knopf in 1987. Her fourth novel,* The
Greenlanders, *is being published by Knopf in 1988.*

Kirby Christianson is standing under the shower, fiddling with the
hot-water spigot and thinking four apparently simultaneous thoughts:
that there is never enough hot water in this apartment, that there was
always plenty of hot water in Japan, that Mieko will be here in four
days, and that he is unable to control Mieko's expectations of him in
any way. The thoughts of Mieko are accompanied by a feeling of
anxiety as strong as the sensation of the hot water, and he would like
the water to flow through him and wash it away. He turns from the
shower head and bends backward, so that the stream can pour over
his face.

When he shuts off the shower, the phone is ringing. A sense that it
has been ringing for a long time—can a mechanical noise have a quality of desperation?—propels him naked and dripping into the living
room. He picks up the phone and his caller, as he has suspected, is
Mieko. Perhaps he is psychic; perhaps this is only a coincidence, or
perhaps no one else has called him in the past week or so.

The connection has a crystalline clarity that tricks him into not
allowing for the satellite delay. He is already annoyed after the first
hello. Mieko's voice is sharp, high, very Japanese, although she speaks
superb English. He says, "Hello, Mieko," and he *sounds* annoyed, as if
she called him too much, although she has only called once to give

him her airline information and once to change it. Uncannily attuned to the nuances of his voice, she says, "Oh, Kirby," and falls silent.

Now there will be a flurry of tedious apologies, on both sides. He is tempted to hang up on her, call her back, and blame his telephone— faulty American technology. But he can't be certain that she is at home. So he says, "Hello, Mieko? Hello, Mieko? Hello, Mieko?" more and more loudly, as if her voice were fading. His strategy works. She shouts, "Can you hear me, Kirby? I can hear you, Kirby."

He holds the phone away from his ear. He says, "That's better. Yes, I can hear you now."

"Kirby, I cannot come. I cannot go through with my plan. My father has lung cancer, we learned this morning."

He has never met the father, has seen the mother and the sister only from a distance, at a department store.

"Can you hear me, Kirby?"

"Yes, Mieko. I don't know what to say."

"You don't have to say anything. I have said to my mother that I am happy to stay with her. She is considerably relieved."

"Can you come later, in the spring?"

"My lie was that this Melville seminar I was supposed to attend would be offered just this one time, which was why I had to go now."

"I'm sorry."

"I know that I am only giving up pleasure. I know that my father might die."

As she says this, Kirby is looking out his front window at the snowy roof of the house across the street, and he understands at once from the hopeless tone of her voice that to give up the pleasure that Mieko has promised herself is harder than to die. He understands that in his whole life he has never given up a pleasure that he cherished as much as Mieko cherished this one. He understands that in a just universe the father would rather die alone than steal such a pleasure from his daughter. All these thoughts occur simultaneously, and are accompanied by a lifting of the anxiety he felt in the shower. She isn't coming. She is never coming. He is off the hook. He says, "But it's hard for you to give it up, Mieko. It is for me, too. I'm sorry."

The sympathetic tones in his voice wreck her self-control, and she begins to weep. In the five months that Kirby knew Mieko in Japan, and in the calls between them since, she has never shed a tear, hardly ever let herself be caught in a low moment, but now she weeps with absolute abandon, in long, heaving sobs, saying, "Oh, oh, oh," every so often. Once the sounds fade, as if she has put down the phone, but he does not dare hang up, does not even dare move the phone from one ear to the other. This attentive listening is what he owes to her grief, isn't it? If she had come, and he had disappointed her, as he would have, this is how she would have wept in solitude after swallowing her disappointment in front of him. But her father has done it, not him. He can give her a little company after all. He presses the phone so hard to his ear that it hurts. The weeping goes on for a long time and he is afraid to speak and interfere with what will certainly be her only opportunity to give way to her feelings. She gives one final wailing "Ohhh" and begins to cough and choke. Finally she quiets, and then sighs. After a moment of silence she says, "Kirby, you should not have listened."

"How could I hang up?"

"A Japanese man would have."

"You sound better, if you are back to comparing me with Japanese men."

"I am going to hang up now, Kirby. I am sorry not to come. Good-bye."

"Don't hang up."

"Good-bye."

"Mieko?"

"Good-bye, Kirby."

"Call me! Call me again!" He is not sure that she hears him. He looks at the phone and then puts it on the cradle.

Two hours later he is on the highway. This is, after all, two days before Christmas, and he is on his way to spend the holidays with his two brothers and their wives and children, whom he hasn't seen in years. He has thought little about this visit, beyond buying a few presents. Mieko's coming loomed, imposing and problematic. They had planned to drive out west together—she had paid extra so that she

could land in Minneapolis and return from San Francisco—and he
had looked forward to seeing the mountains again. They had made
reservations on a bus that carries tourists into Yellowstone Park in the
winter, to look at the smoky geysers and the wildlife and the snow.
The trip would have seemed very American to her—buffalo and men
in cowboy boots and hats. But it seemed very Japanese to him—deep
snow, dark pines, sharp mountains.

The storm rolls in suddenly, the way it sometimes does on I-35 in
Iowa, startling him out of every thought except alertness. Snow swirls
everywhere, blotting out the road, the other cars, sometimes even his
own front end. The white of his headlights reflects back at him, so that
he seems to be driving into a wall. He can hardly force himself to
maintain thirty-five miles an hour, although he knows he must. To
stop would be to invite a rear-end collision. And the shoulder of the
road is invisible. Only the white line, just beside the left front corner of
the car, reveals itself intermittently as the wind blows the snow off the
pavement. He ejects the tape he is playing and turns on the radio, to
the state weather station. He notices that his hand is shaking. He
could be killed. The utter blankness of the snowy whirl gives him a
way of imagining what it would be like to be dead. He doesn't like the
feeling.

He remembers reading two winters ago about an elderly woman
whose son dropped her off at her apartment. She discovered that she
had forgotten her key, and with the wind-chill factor at eighty below
zero, she froze before she got to the manager's office. The winter
before that a kid who broke his legs in a snowmobile accident crawled
three miles to the nearest farmhouse, no gloves, only a feed cap on his
head.

Twenty below, thirty below—the papers always make a big deal of
the temperature. Including wind chill, seventy, a hundred below.
Kirby carries a flashlight, a down sleeping bag, a sweatshirt that reads
UNIVERSITY OF NEBRASKA, gloves and mittens. His car has new tires,
front-wheel drive, and plenty of antifreeze. He has a thermos of coffee.
But the horror stories roll through his mind anyway. A family without
boots or mittens struggles two miles to a McDonald's through high
winds, blowing snow, thirty below. *Why would they travel in that*

weather? Kirby always thinks when he reads the papers, but of course they do. He does. Always has.

A gust takes the car, just for a second, and Kirby grips the wheel more tightly. The same gust twists the enveloping snow aloft and reveals the Clear Lake rest stop. Kirby is tempted to stop, tempted not to. He has, after all, never died before, and he has driven through worse than this. He passes the rest stop. Lots of cars are huddled there; but then, lots of cars are still on the highway. Maybe the storm is letting up.

As soon as he is past the rest stop, he thinks of Mieko, her weeping. She might never weep like that again, even if she heard of his death. The connection in her mind between the two of them, the connection that she allowed to stretch into the future despite all his admonitions and all her resolutions, is broken now. Her weeping was the sound of its breaking. And if he died here, in the next ten minutes, how would she learn of it? His brothers wouldn't call her, not even if she were still coming, because they didn't know she had planned to come. And if she were ever to call him back, she would get only a disconnect message and would assume that he had moved. He can think of no way that she could hear of his death, even though no one would care more than she would. These thoughts fill him with self-pity, but at least they drive out the catalogue of horror: station wagon skids into bridge abutment, two people are killed, two paralyzed from the neck down, mother survives unharmed, walks to nearby farmhouse. Kirby weighs the boredom and good fellowship he will encounter sitting out the storm at a truck stop against possible tragedy. Fewer cars are on the road; more are scattered on the median strip. Inertia carries him onward. He is almost to Minnesota, after all, where they really know how to take care of the roads. He will stop at the tourist center and ask about conditions.

But he drives past the tourist center by mistake, lost in thought. He decides to stop in Faribault. But by then the snow seems to be tapering off. Considering the distance he has traveled, Minneapolis isn't far now. He checks the odometer. Only fifty miles or so. An hour and a half away, at this speed. His mind eases over the numbers with customary superhighway confidence, but at once he imagines himself re-

duced to walking, walking in this storm, with only a flashlight, a
thermos of coffee, a University of Nebraska sweatshirt—and the distance swells to infinity. Were he reduced to his own body, his own
power, it might be too far to walk just to find a telephone.

For comfort he calls up images of Japan and southern China, something he often does. That he produces these images is the one tangible
change that his travels have made in him. So many human eyes have
looked upon every scene there for so many eons that every sight has
an arranged quality: a flowering branch in the foreground, a precipi-
tous mountainside in the background, a small bridge between. A path,
with two women in red kimonos, that winds up a hillside. A white
room with pearly rice-paper walls and a futon on the mat-covered
floor, branches of cherry blossoms in a vase in the corner. They seem
like pictures, but they are scenes he has actually looked upon: on a
three-day trip out of Hong Kong into southern China, with some
other teachers from his school on a trip to Kyoto, and at Akira's
house. Akira was a fellow teacher at his school who befriended him.
His house had four rooms, two Japanese style and two Western style.

He remembers, of course, other scenes of Japan—acres of buses,
faces staring at his Westernness, the polite but bored rows of students
in his classroom—when he is trying to decide whether to go back
there. But these are not fixed, have no power; they are just memories,
like memories of bars in Lincoln or the pig houses on his grandfather's
farm.

And so, he survives the storm. He pulls into the driveway of Harold's
new house, one he has not seen, though it is in a neighborhood he
remembers from junior high school. The storm is over. Harold has his
snowblower out and is making a path from the driveway to his front
door. With the noise and because his back is turned, he is unaware of
Kirby's arrival. Kirby stops the car, stretches, and looks at his watch.
Seven hours for a four-hour trip. Kirby lifts his shoulders and rotates
his head but does not beep his horn just yet. The fact is that he has
frightened himself with the blinding snow, the miles of slick and fea-
tureless landscape, thoughts of Japan, and the thousands and thousands of miles between here and there. His car might be a marble that

has rolled, only by luck, into a safe corner. He presses his fingers against his eyes and stills his breathing.

Harold turns around, grins, and shuts off the snowblower. It is a Harold identical to the Harold that Kirby has always known. Same bright snowflake ski hat, same bright ski clothing. Harold has spent his whole life skiing and ski-jumping. His bushy beard grows up to the hollows of his eyes, and when he leans into the car his moustache is, as always, crusted with ice.

"Hey!" he says. He backs away, and Kirby opens the car door.

"Made it!" Kirby says. That is all he will say about the trip. The last thing he wants to do is start a discussion about near misses. Compared with some of Harold's near misses, this is nothing. In fact, near misses on the highway aren't worth mentioning unless a lot of damage has been done to the car. Kirby knows of near misses that Harold has never dared to describe to anyone besides him, because they show a pure stupidity that even Harold has the sense to be ashamed of.

Over dinner, sweet and savory Nordic fare that Kirby is used to but doesn't much like, he begins to react to his day. The people around the table, his relatives, waver in the smoky candlelight, and Kirby imagines that he can feel the heat of the flames on his face. The other people at the table seem unfamiliar. Leanne, Harold's wife, he has seen only once, at their wedding. She is handsome and self-possessed-look-ing, but she sits at the corner of the table, like a guest in her own house. Eric sits at the head, and Mary Beth, his wife, jumps up and down to replenish the food. This assumption of primogeniture is a peculiarity of Eric's that has always annoyed Kirby, but even aside from that they have never gotten along. Eric does his best—earnest handshake and smile each time they meet, two newsy letters every year, pictures of the children (known between Harold and Kirby as "the little victims"). Eric has a Ph.D. from Columbia in American history, but he does not teach. He writes for a conservative think tank —articles that appear on the op-ed pages of newspapers and in the think tank's own publications. He specializes in "the family." Kirby and Harold have made countless jokes at Eric's expense. Kirby knows that more will be made this trip, if only in the form of conspiratorial looks, rolling eyes. Eric's hobby—Mary Beth's, too, for they share everything—is developing each nuance of his Norwegian heritage into a fully realized ostentation. Mary Beth is always busy, usually baking. That's all Kirby knows about her, and all he cares to know.

Across the table Anna, their older daughter, pale, blue-eyed, cool, seems to be staring at him, but Kirby can hardly see her. He is thinking about Mieko. Kirby looks at his watch. It is very early morning in Osaka. She is probably about to wake up. Her disappointment will have receded hardly a particle, will suck her down as soon as she thuds into consciousness. "Oh, oh, oh": he can hear her cries as clearly as if they were vibrating in the air. He is amazed at having heard such a thing, and he looks carefully at the women around the table. Mieko would be too eager to please here, always looking after Mary Beth and Leanne, trying to divine how she might be helpful. Finally, Mary Beth would speak to her with just a hint of sharpness, and Mieko would be crushed. Her eyes would seek Kirby's for reassurance, and he would have none to give. She would be too little, smaller even than Anna, and her voice would be too high and quick. These thoughts give him such pain that he stares for relief at Kristin, Eric's youngest, age three, who is humming over her dinner. She is round-faced and paunchy, with dark hair cut straight across her forehead and straight around her collar. From time to time she and Leanne exchange merry glances.

Harold is beside him; that, at least, is familiar and good, and it touches Kirby with a pleasant sense of expectation, as if Harold, at any moment, might pass him a comic book or a stick of gum. In fact, Harold does pass him something—an icy cold beer, which cuts the sweetness of the food and seems to adjust all the figures around the table so that they stop wavering.

Of course his eyes open well before daylight, but he dares not move. He is sharing a room with Harold the younger, Eric's son, whose bed is between his and the door. He worries that if he gets up he will stumble around and crash into walls and wake Harold. The digits on the clock beside Harold's bed read 5:37, but when Kirby is quiet, he can hear movement elsewhere in the house. When he closes his eyes, the footsteps present themselves as a needle and thread, stitching a line through his thoughts. He has just been driving. His arms ache from gripping the wheel. The car slides diagonally across the road, toward the median. It slides and slides, through streams of cars, toward a familiar exit, the Marshalltown exit, off to the left, upward. His eyes open again. The door of the room is open, and Anna is looking in. After a moment she turns and goes away. It is 6:02. Sometime later Leanne passes with Isaac, the baby, in her arms.

Kirby cannot bear to get up and face his brothers and their families. As always, despair presents itself aesthetically. The image of Harold's and Leanne's living room, matching plaid wing chairs and couch, a triple row of wooden pegs by the maple front door, seems to Kirby the image of the interior of a coffin. The idea of spending five years, ten years, a lifetime, with such furniture makes him gasp. But his own apartment, armchair facing the television, which sits on a spindly coffee table, is worse. Mary Beth and Eric's place, where he has been twice, is the worst, because it's pretentious; they have antique wooden trunks and high-backed benches painted blue with stenciled flowers in red and white. Everything, everything, they own is blue and white, or white and blue, and Nordic primatif. Now even the Japanese images he calls up are painful. The pearly white Japanese-style room in Akira's house was bitterly cold in the winter, and he spent one night there only half-sleeping, his thighs drawn to his chest, the perimeters of the bed too cold even to touch. His head throbbing, Kirby lies pinned to the bed by impossibility. He literally can't summon up a room, a stick of furniture, that he can bear to think of. Harold the younger rolls over and groans, turning his twelve-year-old face toward Kirby's. His mouth opens and he breathes noisily. It is 6:27.

Not until breakfast, when Leanne sets a bowl of raisin bran before him on the table, does he recall the appearance of Anna in the door to his room, and then it seems odd, especially when, ten minutes later, she enters the kitchen in her bathrobe, yawning. Fifth grade. Only fifth grade. He can see that now, but the night before, and in the predawn darkness, she had seemed older, more threatening, the way girls get at fourteen and fifteen. "Cereal, sweetie?" Leanne says, and Anna nods, scratching. She sits down without a word and focuses on the back of the Cheerios box. Kirby decides that he was dreaming and puts the incident out of his mind.

Harold, of course, is at his store, managing the Christmas rush, and the house is less festive in his absence. Eric has sequestered himself in Leanne's sewing room, with his computer, and as soon as Anna stands up from breakfast, Mary Beth begins to arrange the day's kitchen schedule. Kirby rinses his cup and goes into the living room. It is nine in the morning, and the day stretches before him, empty. He walks through the plaid living room to the window, where he regards the outdoor thermometer. It reads four degrees below zero. Moments later it is five degrees below zero. Moments after that he is standing beside Harold's bar, pouring himself a glass of bourbon. He has already drunk it when Anna appears in the doorway, dressed now, and staring at him again. She makes him think of Mieko again—though the child is blonde and self-contained, she is Mieko's size. Last evening, when he was thinking of Mieko, he was looking at Anna. He says, attempting jovial warmth, "Good morning, Anna. Why do you keep staring at me?"

She is startled. "I don't. I was looking at the bookshelves."

"But you stared at me last night, at dinner. And you came to the door of my room early this morning. I know because I was awake."

"No, I didn't." But then she softens, and says with eager curiosity, "Are you a socialist?"

While Kirby is trying not to laugh, he hears Mary Beth sing from the kitchen. "Anna? Your brother is going sledding. You want to go?"

Anna turns away before Kirby can answer, and mounts the stairs. A "No!" floats, glassy and definite, from the second floor.

Kirby sits down in one of the plaid armchairs and gazes at an arrangement of greenery and shiny red balls and candles that sits on a table behind the couch. He gazes and gazes, contemplating the notion of Eric and Mary Beth discussing his politics and his life. He is offended. He knows that if he were to get up and do something he would stop being offended, but he gets up only to pour himself another drink. It is nearly ten. Books are around everywhere, and Kirby picks one up.

People keep opening doors and coming in, having been elsewhere.

Harold comes home for lunch; Leanne and Isaac return from the grocery store and the hardware store; Harold the younger stomps in, covered with snow from sledding, eats a sandwich, and stomps out again. Eric opens the sewing-room door, takes a turn through the house, goes back in again. He does this three times, each time failing to speak to Kirby, who is sitting quietly. Perhaps he does not see him. He is an old man, Kirby thinks, and his rear has spread considerably in the past four years; he is thirty-six going on fifty, round-shouldered, wearing slacks rather than jeans. What a jerk.

But then Kirby's bad mood twists into him, and he lets his head drop on the back of his chair. What is a man? Kirby thinks. What is a man, what is a man? It is someone, Eric would say, who votes, owns property, has a wife, worries. It is someone, Harold would say, who can chop wood all day and make love all night, who can lift his twenty-five-pound son above his head on the palm of his hand.

After lunch the men all vanish again, even Isaac, who is taking a nap. In various rooms the women do things. They make no noise. Harold's house is the house of a wealthy man, Kirby realizes. It is large enough to be silent and neat most of the time, the sort of house Kirby will never own. It is Harold and Eric who are alike now. Only Kirby's being does not extend past his fingertips and toes to family, real estate, reputation.

Sometime in the afternoon, when Kirby is still sitting quietly and his part of the room is shadowed by the movement of the sun to the other side of the house, Kristin comes in from the kitchen, goes straight to the sofa, pulls off one of the cushions, and begins to jump repeatedly from the cushion to the floor. When he says, "Kristin, what are you doing?" she is not startled. She says, "Jumping."

"Do you like to jump?"

She says, "It's a beautiful thing to do," in her matter-of-fact, deep, three-year-old voice. Kirby can't believe she knows what she is saying. She jumps three or four more times and then runs out again.

At dinner she is tired and tiresome. When Eric tells her to eat a bite of her meat (ham cooked with apricots), she looks him right in the face and says, "No."

"One bite," he says. "I mean it."

"No. I mean it." She looks up at him. He puts his napkin on the table and pushes back his chair. In a moment he has swept her through the doorway and up the stairs. She is screaming. A door slams and the screaming is muffled. When he comes down and seats himself, carefully laying his napkin over his slacks, Anna says, "It's her body."

The table quiets. Eric says, "What?"

"It's her body."

"What does that mean?"

"She should have control over her own body. Food. Other stuff. I don't know." She has started strong but weakens in the face of her father's glare. Eric inhales sharply, and Kirby cannot restrain himself. He says, "How can you disagree with that? It sounds self-evident to me."

"Does it? The child is three years old. How can she have control over her own body when she doesn't know anything about it? Does she go out without a coat if it's twenty below zero? Does she eat only cookies for three days? Does she wear a diaper until she's five? This is one of those phrases they are using these days. They all mean the same thing."

"What do they mean?" As Kirby speaks, Leanne and Mary Beth look up, no doubt wishing that he had a wife or a girlfriend here to restrain him. Harold looks up too. He is grinning.

Eric shifts in his chair, uncomfortable, Kirby suddenly realizes, at being predictably stuffy once again. Eric says, "It's Christmas. Let's enjoy it."

Harold says, "Principles are principles, any day of the year."

Eric takes the bait and lets himself say, "The family is constituted for a purpose, which is the sometimes difficult socialization of children. For a certain period of their lives others control them. In early childhood others control their bodies. They are taught to control themselves. Even Freud says that the young barbarian has to be taught to relinquish his feces, sometimes by force."

"Good Lord, Eric," Leanne says.

Eric is red in the face. "Authority is a principle I believe in." He

looks around the table and then at Anna, openly angry that she has
gotten him into this. Across Anna's face flits a look that Kirby has
seen before, has seen on Mieko's face, a combination of self-doubt and
resentment molded into composure.

"Patriarchy is what you mean," Kirby says, realizing from the tone
of his own voice that rage has replaced sympathy and, moreover, is
about to get the better of him.

"Why not? It works."

"For some people, at a great cost. Why should daughters be sacri-
ficed to the whims of the father?" He should stop now. He doesn't.
"Just because he put his dick somewhere once or twice." The result of
too many bourbons too early in the day.

"In my opinion—" Eric seems not to notice the vulgarity, but Harold, beside Kirby, snorts with pleasure.

"I don't want to talk about this," Leanne says. Kirby blushes and
falls silent, knowing that he has offended her. It is one of those long
holiday meals, and by the time they get up from the table, Kirby feels
as if he has been sitting in a dim, candlelit corner most of his life.

There is another ritual—the Christmas Eve unwrapping of presents
—and by that time Kirby realizes that he is actively intoxicated and
had better watch his tone of voice and his movements. Anna hands
out the gifts with a kind of rude bashfulness, and Kirby is surprised at
the richness of the array: from Harold he has gotten a cotton turtle-
neck and a wool sweater, in bright, stylish colors; from Leanne a pair
of very fancy gloves; from Isaac three pairs of ragg wool socks; from
Eric's family, as a group, a blue terrycloth robe and sheepskin slippers.
When they open his gifts, he is curious to see what the wrappings
reveal: he has bought it all so long before. Almost everything is some
gadget available in Japan but not yet in the States. Everyone peers and
oohs and aahs. It gives Kirby a headache and a sense of his eyeballs
expanding and contracting. Tomorrow night he will be on his way
home again, and though he cannot bear to stay here after all, he
cannot bear to go, either.

He drifts toward the stairs, intending to go to bed, but Harold
looms before him, grinning and commanding. "Your brain needs some
oxygen, brother," he says. Then they are putting on their parkas, and

then they are outside, in a cold so sharp that Kirby's nose, the only exposed part of him, stings. Harold strides down the driveway, slightly ahead of him, and Kirby expects him to speak, either for or against Eric, but he doesn't. He only walks. The deep snow is so solidly frozen that it squeaks beneath their boots. The only thing Harold says the whole time they are walking is, "Twenty-two below, not counting the wind chill. Feels good, doesn't it?"

"Feels dangerous," Kirby says.

"It is," Harold says.

The neighborhood is brightly decorated, and the colored lights have their effect on Kirby. For the first time in three Christmases he feels a touch of the mystery that he thinks of as the Christmas spirit. Or maybe it is love for Harold.

Back at the house, everyone has gone to bed except Leanne and Mary Beth, who are drying dishes and putting them away. They are also, Kirby realizes—after Harold strides through the kitchen and up the stairs—arguing, although with smiles and in polite tones. Kirby goes to a cabinet and lingers over getting himself a glass for milk. Mary Beth says, "Kristin will make the connection. She's old enough."

"I can't believe that."

"She saw all the presents being handed out and unwrapped. And Anna will certainly make the connection."

"Anna surely doesn't believe in Santa Claus anymore."

"Unofficially, probably not."

"It's Isaac's first Christmas," Leanne says. "He'll like all the wrappings."

"I wish you'd thought of that before you wrapped the family presents and his Santa presents in the same paper."

"That's a point too. They're his presents. I don't think Kristin will notice them."

"If they're the only wrapped presents, she will. She notices everything."

Now Leanne turns and gazes at Mary Beth, her hands on her hips. A long silence follows. Leanne flicks a glance at Kirby, who pretends not to notice. Finally she says, "All right, Mary Beth. I'll unwrap them."

"Thank you," Mary Beth says. "I'll finish this, if you want." Kirby goes out of the kitchen and up to his bedroom. The light is already off, and Harold the younger is on his back, snoring.

When he gets up an hour later, too drunk to sleep, Kirby sees Leanne arranging the last of Santa's gifts under the tree. She turns the flash of her glance upon him as he passes through the living room to the kitchen. "Mmm," he says, uncomfortable, "can't sleep."

"Want some cocoa? I always make some before I go to bed."

He stops. "Yeah. Why not? Am I mistaken, or have you been up since about six A.M.?"

"About that. But I'm always wired at midnight, no matter what."

He follows her into the kitchen, remembering now that they have never conversed, and wishing that he had stayed in bed. He has drunk himself stupid. Whatever words he has in him have to be summoned from very far down. He sits at the table. After a minute he puts his chin in his hand. After a long, blank, rather pleasant time, the cocoa is before him, marshmallow and all. He looks at it. When Leanne speaks, Kirby is startled, as if he had forgotten that she was there.

"Tired?" she says.

"Too much to drink."

"I noticed."

"I don't have anything more to say about it."

"I'm not asking."

He takes a sip of his cocoa. He says, "Do you all see much of Eric and family?"

"They came last Christmas. He came by himself in the summer. To a conference on the future of the family."

"And so you have to put up with him, right?"

"Harold has a three-day limit. I don't care."

"I noticed you unwrapped all Isaac's presents."

She shrugs, picks at the sole of her boot. She yawns without covering her mouth, and then says, "Oh, I'm sorry." She smiles warmly, looking right at him. "I am crazy about Kristin. Crazy enough to not chance messing up Christmas for her."

"Today she told me that jumping off a cushion was a beautiful thing to do."

Leanne smiles. "Yesterday she said that it was wonderful of me to give her a napkin. You know, I don't agree with Eric about that body stuff. I think they naturally do what is healthy for them. Somebody did an experiment with one-year-olds, gave them a range of foods to choose from, and they always chose a balanced diet. They also want to be toilet trained sooner or later. I think it's weird the way Eric thinks that every little thing is learned rather than realized."

"That's a nice phrase." He turns his cup handle so that it points away and then back in his direction. Finally he says, "Can I tell you about something?"

"Sure."

"Yesterday a friend of mine called me from Japan, a woman, to say that she couldn't come visit me. Her father has cancer. She had planned to arrive here the day after tomorrow, and we were going to take a trip out west. It isn't important, exactly. I don't know."

Leanne is silent but attentive, picking at the sole of her boot. Now that he has mentioned it, the memory of Mieko's anguish returns to him like a glaring light or a thundering noise, so enormous that he is nearly robbed of the power to speak. He pushes it out. "She can't come now, ever. She probably won't ever call or write me again. And really, this has saved her. She had all sorts of expectations that I couldn't have . . . well, wouldn't have fulfilled, and if she had come she would have been permanently compromised."

"Did you have some kind of affair when you were there?"

"For a few months. She's very pretty. I think she's the prettiest woman I've ever seen. She teaches mathematics at the school where I was teaching. After I had been with Mieko for a few weeks, I realized that no one, maybe in her whole adult life, had asked her how she was, or had put his arm around her shoulders, or had taken care of her in any way. The slightest affection was like a drug she couldn't get enough of."

"What did you feel?"

"I liked her. I really did. I was happy to see her when she came by. But she longed for me more than I have ever longed for anything."

"You were glad to leave."

"I was glad to leave."

"So what's the problem?"

"When she called yesterday, she broke down completely. I listened. I thought it was the least I could do, but now I think that she is compromised. Japanese people are very private. It scares me how much I must have embarrassed her. I look back on the spring and the summer and yesterday's call, and I see that, one by one, I broke down every single one of her strengths, everything she had equipped herself with to live in a Japanese way. I was so careful for a year and a half. I didn't date Japanese women, and I was very distant—but then I was so lonely, and she was so pretty, and I thought, well, she's twenty-seven, and she lives in this sophisticated city, Osaka. But mostly I was lonely."

Leanne gazes across the table in that way of hers, calm and considering. Finally she says, "Eric comes in for a lot of criticism around here. His style's all wrong, for one thing. And he drives Harold the younger and Anna crazy. But I've noticed something about him. He never tries to get something for nothing. I admire that."

Now Kirby looks around the room, at the plants on the windowsill, the hoarfrost on the windowpanes, the fluorescent light harsh on the stainless-steel sink, and it seems to him that all at once, now that he realizes it, his life and Mieko's have taken their final form. She is nearly too old to marry, and by the end of her father's cancer and his life she will be much too old. And himself. Himself. Leanne's cool remark has revealed his permanent smallness. He looks at his hands, first his knuckles, then his palms. He says, "It seems so dramatic to say that I will never get over this."

"Does it? To me it seems like saying that what people do is important." And though he looks at her intently, seeking some sort of pardon, she says nothing more, only picks at her boot for a moment or two, and then gets up and puts their cups in the sink. He follows her out of the kitchen, through the living room. She turns out all the lights, so that the house is utterly dark. At the bottom of the stairs, unable to see anything, he stumbles against her and excuses himself. There, soft and fleeting, he feels a disembodied kiss on his cheek, and her voice, nearly a whisper, says, "Merry Christmas, Kirby. I'm glad you're here."

Arcola Girls

•

====== PHILIP F. DEAVER ======

*Philip F. Deaver lives in Longwood, Florida, with his wife, Cyndie,
and three children. He was raised in Tuscola, Illinois, seven miles
north of Arcola. His collection of stories* Silent Retreats *won the Flan-
nery O'Connor Award for Short Fiction and is due out this spring
from the University of Georgia Press.*

On Saturday night, Arcola girls would come north on the two-lane for
the dance. The road, Route 45, was flat, and the grass grew right up to
the edge, crowding in on them, narrowing the alley of their headlight
beam. With their windows open they could smell the warm, damp
night air and the cornfields as they came. They could hear everywhere
the swarms of crickets. Sometimes grasshoppers would land right on
the windshield or thump onto the hood. Crows would sweep from the
wires, stay on the road until the last moment, picking at run-over barn
cats and field mice. The car tires would thump on the seams of the
concrete road. It was a seven-mile drive.

By eight in the evening their white Chevys and green Mustangs and
burgundy Corvairs would be cruising through the drive-in and making
the Webster Park loop. They would glide through the downtown, past
the community building where the dance was just getting started.
Sometimes you'd hear their tires screech as they stopped, or they'd
peel out at the intersection, showing off. You could hear them laughing.

One of them, named Kelly, had beautiful blond hair, long like that
of Mary Travers. There was one named Karen who was famous for

singing like Connie Francis, and sometimes at the dance she'd join the
band and sing "Where the Boys Are," just for fun. Another, Sandra,
was very tall, and her hair was ratted in a bubble after the fashion. She
had odd eye-habits, always seeming to observe. Sometimes, playing in
the park, she'd be running—her strides were long and confident like a
boy's.

They all wore shorts and colorful sweatshirts, white tennis shoes. At
the dance they would huddle together in a corner, doing committee
work on the latest rumor, the latest dirty joke. Sandra, alert in the
corners of her eyes, would look over her shoulder in case anyone was
coming.

"I think you love those girls," my girlfriend said to me on the phone
one night, "the way you watch them."

There were two bad S curves in the road from Arcola. They were
where the highway was rerouted fifty yards west of itself for a certain
short stretch because it would always flood in a heavy rain and people
would get killed. So, instead, people got killed in the curves. Late one
night in that particular summer, early June, Karen, with another
Arcola girl named Marie, ran off the road at high speed on their way
home. They went over the ditch and deep into the weeds, through a
fence, flipped into a field. They weren't found until morning.

The crumpled ghost of their Chevy rusted most of the summer and
part of the fall where the wrecker let it down, half a block from the
Dairy Queen in the wreck lot of Ford Motor Sales. I don't know what
the fascination was, but sometimes I'd go by there. Through the
crunched, blue-tinted windows, in the folds of the damp, bent seats, I
could see a Beatles album and a soggy package of Kools. There were
stains of blood in the driver's seat. One of their shoes was decomposing in the gravel next to the car. I'd find myself staring. This was
before Vietnam really got going. Back then, the whole idea of people
dying who were about my age was a rare and somehow fascinating
thing. The Arcola girls, Karen and Marie, they were the first I remember.

There was one Arcola girl named Rhonda Hart, a wild girl with
dark brown hair and strange, blue catlike eyes. Each Saturday night,
late, when the dance was almost over and the room was humid and

warm like hot breath, a group would gather around Rhonda, who was by then dancing alone, doing, if the chaperones weren't looking, a pantomime of taking her clothes off to a grinding-on-and-on rendition of "Louie, Louie" that the local bands had turned into the theme of the summer.

I remember that her legs were skinny, but she was round and ample under a pure-white sweatshirt, and her menacing cat eyes stared into the group around her, mostly boys, her lips pouting like a bad girl. She'd make-believe unzip her candy-colored red shorts at the back, make-believe slip her panties off her hips and slide them down the skinny legs to the cold cork-looking floor of the West Ridge community building. A little kick at the last and, imaginary pale pink, they sailed through the imaginary air. And on she danced, her arms out to you. She was pretty good.

You're going to film this?!

At Webster Park there was an old bandstand the Arcola girls used to gather at on summer nights. They would park their cars in the deep shadows. The local high school boys would go there, too, and in the black shade of the park maples they would all play, smoke, make out, the Lord knew what else (there were always whisperings, strange rumors going around). These were country girls. Maybe some of them might not have gotten a second look from the boys in Arcola, but in West Ridge they were exotic and different, from a place that, to us, then, seemed far away. They made the air palpable with sex and play.

Chevy Chase - v. Lemon

The first time I ever heard a girl say "fuck," it was an Arcola girl, and she didn't say it mean or loud, but it seemed to echo all through Webster Park, down the length of it into the cluster of pine trees, beyond that to the ball diamonds, the deserted playground and city pool, the walking gardens.

"You'd love to go out with one of those girls," my girlfriend would sometimes say.

We'd be at the drive-in and one of their cars might spin through. The curb-hops would jump back to avoid it. I might crane my neck to see who it was.

"Cathy says they're all dumb as posts," she'd say. Cathy was my girlfriend's friend.

frame - narr. + girlfriend

"Cathy should talk," I told her. I'd turn up the radio, the manic, *Another lost allusion* rabble-rousing prattle of Dick Biondi, WLS.

That summer a couple of classmates of mine, Bob Reid and Buzz Talbott, slipped into a slumber party in Arcola. They climbed through a bedroom window, bringing with them their sleeping bags and beer. Rumors were it had been some great party. The rumor was that somebody's farmer-dad caught them, though, and there had been a shotgun fired and a quick getaway. Bob Reid, and a kid he paid who was taking shop, had spent an afternoon rubbing out and painting a couple of pockmarks on the white tailgate of his dad's pickup.

would it still happen! Sarah, a buxom little Arcola cheerleader, maybe the prettiest in the whole group, got pregnant that summer and disappeared. They said she went to Texas. It seemed like everything you heard about the Arcola girls was an exotic, strange, wild tale—full of skin and possibilities.

So one Friday afternoon I called up Rhonda Hart to ask her out.

"Tonight?" She seemed real indignant. "Out *where?*" she said. "For chrissake," she added. She was chewing gum. "Give a girl some notice sometime, will ya?" It was her Mae West act. She was laughing.

"Mattoon. A movie. Champaign—I don't know."

"Mattoon a movie Champaign you don't KNOW?"

mystique Shouldn't have called, I thought to myself. Her voice was hard and confident. The Righteous Brothers were playing in the background. I'm different from her, I was thinking. She knows more about the world.

"We could just go talk or something. I don't know," I said. It was all wrong.

"I'm not sure I know who you are even," she said.

"My name's Tom Nichols," I told her. I tried to explain myself to her. Told her I was a friend of Bob Reid and ran cross-country with Talbott. Tried to recall for her times when I was the guy *with* somebody she *did* know when we were all doing something she might remember, such as getting a pizza or buying a Coke at the Sinclair station like a bunch of us did one night and all stood around making wisecracks.

"Well, let's drive around West Ridge—we don't have to go any place special," she said.

"That'd be okay," I said. "I thought a movie maybe."

She was quiet a moment. "So you don't wanna be seen with me or what?"

"Nah. I just want—I don't know—quiet or something, that's all."

"Right." She laughed. She really liked that one. *I've heard of this*

"Wanna go dancing?" she said. "Up at the Chances R? I heard the Artistics are up there. I love their lead singer—he looks exactly like Elvis. Let's go dancing."

Sometimes I'd see her cruising with Bob Reid in his pickup. I knew she occasionally went out with him, and he was never known to dance. So what did they do when *they* went out? Couldn't we just do that, whatever it was?

"Okay," I said. "We'll find a dance or something."

"You don't sound real enthused."

"I'm enthused."

"You don't sound like it."

"Look," I said, "I must be a little enthused, I'm calling you up." *This*

"Down, boy," she said, laughing, chewing her gum. She thought about it for a while.

"Don't make it a gift from the gods or something," I said finally.

"Right," she said. "Hang on." She put the phone against something soft to muffle the sound, and was shouting. Then I heard the phone clank down and she was gone, to ask her mom. You'd always forget that Arcola girls had to ask their moms.

"Yeah, I can go," she said when she came back all breathless. "What time?"

"Eight. Suit yourself," I said.

"Dancing, right?" She seemed to be setting it out as a condition.

"Eight o'clock," I said.

"Seven or eight?" she said.

"Whatever."

After I hung up I went out in the backyard and sat in a lawn chair. I was nervous about this. Rhonda seemed different from my girlfriend,

So why are you going out with her if you have a girlfriend?

rougher and faster. Then my sister yelled from the house that I had a call.

"Hi. This is Rhonda," she said. I didn't say anything. I expected a cancellation. "Remember me?" she said, and laughed. "One more thing. Let's make it around ten-thirty, and you meet me at the bandstand at the park. What do you say?"

"Ten-thirty?"

"Right." She was talking quieter than in the first call.

"No way," I said.

"I got something going I forgot about. I can get loose by ten-thirty."

"No."

"What's wrong?"

"It's too late."

"Look," she said, "I want to introduce you to my friends. I'll ride up with Kelly, and you can bring me home. You know Kelly?" Kelly had the silky, white-blond hair, freckles.

"Yeah, I know her."

"Well, I just talked to her, and she doesn't know you."

"I think I'm losing control of this."

"Ha." She seemed to fade away. Then she was back. "You can handle it. See you at the bandstand. Ten-thirty. Wait if I'm late." She hung up.

At eight I was on the highway to Arcola. I'd decided to try to get to Rhonda before Kelly did. The sun was going down and the Illinois sky was red in the west. The locusts were loud, wheeting in a pulsating rhythm. Much later the moon would rise full and red, blood moon. Jupiter would linger near it all across the sky, stalking. The whole thing was a mistake.

Why does he do this?

I'd never been to Arcola on my own mission, but I found her house, using the phone book in the booth just outside a place downtown called the Youth Center. I parked down the street on the opposite side and watched the house in my mirror. It was dusk. I got out of the car and walked back toward the place, trying to think what to say. I hadn't thought of anything by the time I knocked and Rhonda's

mother came to the door. She was all fixed up, maybe thirty-nine or
forty years old. Her perfume wafted through the screen door.

"Hi," I said. "Is Rhonda home?" I told her my name.

"You're Tom? I thought she was with you," she said.

I turned around to see if she was, a little joke. "Nope."
Rhonda's mother didn't laugh.

"I'm kind of late," I said. "Are you sure she isn't here?"

"God, I'm almost *sure* she's gone," she said, "but I'll check." Her
voice was raspy, had that same worldliness as Rhonda's.

She asked me in and had me sit on the couch. There was what
appeared to be a half-gone seven-and-seven on the coffee table. I heard
her go up the stairs. There was a cat on the couch with me, staring at
me, and there was the tank of fish in the room that I'd been able to see
from the car. The whole room had the fragrance of Rhonda's mom's
perfume.

"Look," she said when she came back in, "I can't find her. I think
she went out already. I thought I heard you come to pick her up half
an hour ago. I'm really sorry, but she's gone."

I sat there on the couch, looking at her.

"There are a couple of places you might find her, is all I can tell
you," she said, sitting down next to the cat and facing me. I looked out
the window into the Arcola night. I noticed that sometimes she herself
was looking out, over my shoulder.

I didn't say anything. I didn't move.

"She might have gone to West Ridge, is all I know. Although if she
did she's in trouble."

Rhonda's mother was wearing a cotton blouse, a tight dark skirt.
Her deeply tanned hand was on the back of the couch near me. Her
fingernails were ruby red. The house was quiet, immaculately clean.
My quietness was giving her some trouble. On the wall was a picture
of Rhonda when she was little. Next to her her father, a truck driver.
They were posing in front of his fancy new semi.

"I'm very sorry about this," she said to me. Her teeth were kind of
crooked.

"Maybe she took off because I was late or something."

"I don't think so. There must have been some misunderstanding.

She was looking forward to this. She really was. She probably told you, I've had her grounded for a couple of weeks because of that drunken slumber party business. She's supposed to be with *you* right now. The condition for this whole thing was that she was going to the movies with you. She's in trouble."

"Well," I said. "It was a misunderstanding maybe."

She was very pretty in a grown-up way, as she shrugged her shoulders and half smiled at me. "Well, she's in trouble." Rhonda's mom was standing up then, my invitation to go. "Good-night, Tom," she said. "I'm sorry about this."

On the way back to the car I looked up at the sky. Moonless, clear as a bell. But a moon was coming—I remembered that from the night before. As I was pulling away, I noticed that a car behind me was passing slowly. I thought it might be Rhonda and Kelly. I drove around the block, and in those few moments Rhonda's mom had turned off the lights and locked up and was darting across the dark yard to the car. It was a white Oldsmobile Starfire with the wide band of stainless steel on the side. I couldn't see the driver before the arching trees and distance intervened.

I imagined that Rhonda had gone north with Kelly and that West Ridge was now aware of my foiled, clandestine date. I decided to drive around the streets of Arcola for a while. West Ridge and Arcola, they were little towns. You could stand in the center of either of them, facing north, and see the bean fields at the city limits to the left and the right; standing there at dawn you could hear the roosters welcome the day out on the farms. In both towns there were the same white clapboard houses with an occasional red brick estate, the same livery stalls down along the Illinois Central railroad where the Amish parked when they came in from the country to shop. There was a grain elevator on the railroad, too, and a lumberyard, and an old hotel downtown. All the themes of West Ridge played out in a variation in Arcola.

I passed the Arcola policeman parked in the shadows up an alley, waiting. I could see the glow from his cigar as I passed. I would turn left at this corner, right at this one, for no reason, but it was a small town and soon I was in front of Rhonda's house again. The lights were

all off, except for a lamp near the fish tank in the living room. I
decided to park and sit a while.

Before long Kelly's car pulled up next to mine. Rhonda looked over
at me. I felt like I'd been caught doing something. Then Kelly pulled
ahead of me and parked. I saw the car door open, and Rhonda was
coming back my way, walking like a curb-hop in her tennis shoes.

"Is it you?" she said. No recognition whatever.

"I thought we could go south from here and catch a movie in
Mattoon," I said.

Now Kelly was coming back, too.

"That's great," Rhonda said, "but it's not the plan. What about my
friend?" She introduced me to Kelly, who did not quite look at me.
She'd been kind of pretty at a distance, cruising by, but close up she
had a hard mouth and a spacey stare. Both girls were chewing gum. I
turned up WLS real loud. "What about my friend?" she said, talking
over it.

"Does Kelly have a date tonight?" I asked Rhonda.

"No."

"You do, I thought."

Rhonda looked at Kelly impatiently, like I was missing the point.

"She can come with us if you want," I said.

"Look," she said. "I've got a problem with this. What are you doing
at my house?"

I looked up beyond the trees, at the ARCOLA in big block letters
on the water tower, lighted from somewhere below. I had once
climbed the West Ridge water tower.

"I mean this is *real* creepy," she said. She looked back up the street,
chewing her gum mouth-open style. "Did you blow this thing with my
mom?"

"Blow what?" I said. "She seemed real nice." Before she could say
anything, I said, "Your mom says you're supposed to be with me.
Let's just have an ordinary date, wha'd'ya say . . ."

"I've got something I've got to do, that's what I say. Don't you
understand that?" She looked at Kelly. "I think he blew it with my
mom." Then back at me. "I've got something I've got to do," she said.

"Yeah, yeah. Do that tomorrow night. Go with me now."

"I'm busy tomorrow night."

We both laughed at that one.

"Look," she said. "Kelly and me talked about this. I was thinking maybe you'd come with us."

I stared ahead. No answer.

Finally she said, "Look. Park the car over at the Youth Center and get in with us—we'll swing by and get it later. You know the center?"

I was thinking about it.

"C'mon! I'm in a big hurry." She walked back to the car. Almost there, she turned around and gestured big. "I'm in a *hurry.*"

I parked my car at the Youth Center and climbed in with them. I sat in the back seat. They paid very little attention to me as we drove around. It was clear they were up to something. Maybe they even went a little out of their way to be mysterious.

"She's supposed to be a good one," I heard Kelly say to Rhonda.

"Right. I can imagine." She hummed the tune they play on *Twilight Zone.*

"Seriously, she's got a certificate from some institute or something. What time is it?"

Kelly reached into a grocery bag in the front seat. She pulled out a jar of kosher dills and handed it back to me. "Open this and you get the first one," she said, keeping her eyes on the street. I opened it, took a pickle, and handed the jar up front. They both chomped pickles for a while.

"What time is it?" Kelly asked again. The radio answered the question.

"Slow down, Nutso," Rhonda said as we approached the alley where the cop was. "Hey, Fat Jack!" she shouted and waved as we went by. He remained where he was.

When the evening train whistle sounded from out north of town, Kelly turned around in an alley and headed back toward the downtown. By the time we got there, the train was through and the Oak Street crossing gates were going back up to let people pass, except nobody was waiting. We drove down a lane along the railroad, a sort of alley. We went alongside the steel quonset-frame warehouses of the local broomcorn factory, passed the railroad depot completely closed down and boarded up, and pulled up in front of an old trailer. Dogs were barking off in the dark.

"Where are we?" I asked them.

"We're at," Kelly said, "a . . . dark . . . old . . . house trailer."

"Wonderful."

She laughed nervously, stared at the place, snapped her gum. Nobody came out. "Looks pretty dark," she said in a loud whisper. The nervous laugh again. "Shall I honk?"

Kelly lightly tapped the horn a couple of times and blinked the lights. The neighborhood dogs intensified their barking. The trailer had burned at some time and had scorch marks above the windows. Several were completely out.

Kelly turned around in her seat and asked me if I would go check in the trailer to see if the woman was in there. She reached down under the dash. "It's worth another pickle to me." She handed me a flashlight.

"What woman?" I asked.

"Jesus! Just go see if anybody's in that trailer. Okay?"

So I went to have a look. The only thing not burned inside the trailer was one overstuffed couch. On it, sure enough, was a woman dressed in black. She was staring straight ahead and the flashlight did not seem to startle her. "Ah. You're here," she said. "Are you Kelly?" she asked.

"No, ma'am. Kelly would be a girl."

"What's that?" she said, coming to the door.

"Kelly would be a girl, ma'am," I said.

"She would, would she? If what?" With my help she stepped down from the trailer to the ground.

"She's in the car, ma'am," I said. She was dressed in a black flowing robe. She smelled like scorched mattresses.

"So. Kelly's a girl is she? Where is she, then?"

"Right, ma'am. She's in the car." I pointed toward the car, and we walked that way. She breathed hard as we went. We had to step over junk.

"Who're you?" she asked.

"I'm a friend of Rhonda's."

"A friend of who?"

"Rhonda." I shined the light ahead so she could see the clear path to the car.

As we were getting there, she asked me, "So how far's this barn?"

"What barn would that be?" I asked.

Kelly heard the question. "Hi," she said. "It's about six miles out."

"Are you Rhonda?"

"Kelly," Kelly and I answered simultaneously.

The woman bent down and looked into the car on Rhonda's side. "Never mind names." Her eyebrows seemed unusually heavy. "I need to be back here in time for the Panama Limited—10:52. Is that going to be a problem, you think?"

"No," said Kelly.

"What's that?"

"No ma'am," I said, for some reason acting as Kelly's interpreter.

The woman sat in the back seat with me. She was maybe sixty and wore a dark paisley bandana in her graying hair. She was very serious. Kelly started the car, and we headed out.

"Did the train thing work okay?" Kelly asked her.

"It worked very well. I thought it would. It's a whistle-stop, real chancy, and sometimes they don't stop and you end up in Carbondale. But I knew they'd stop for an old woman. I come from the age of trains. We speak the same language." She was smiling as she said this. I tried to picture her, all in black like this, attempting to be a typical passenger on the Illinois Central.

Now that we were heading out of town, the woman said, "Girls, I usually am paid in advance."

Kelly looked over at Rhonda, who rummaged in her purse. She came up with a leather bag of change which Kelly reached over and took and started to hand back. No telling how much. Rhonda stopped her.

"You know Kelly's mother, right?" Rhonda asked.

"Yes," the woman said.

"And we don't want her or anyone else to know about this. You know that?" Kelly said.

"Yes."

Rhonda handed over the bag.

It disappeared into the black flowing clothes. "Onward, ladies," she said, satisfied.

After we left the lights of town, there was very little talk in the car for a while. Occasionally Kelly and Rhonda might confer on the right direction. Out on the country road there was a roar of crickets and frogs. The air was almost hot coming in the back window. I slumped down. We were starting to get far enough north that we were in familiar parking territory for West Ridge. We turned, sure enough, onto the Black River Road, crossed the old iron bridge, and went down into the bottoms. We turned onto the predictable tractor path, went along the river and then across the field toward the barn, *the* barn, the great monument in West Ridge parking lore.

We were about two hundred yards from the barn, on a tractor path serving as border between head-high corn and hip-high soybeans, when Kelly and I spotted something at exactly the same moment.

"Oh God, Rhonda, don't look," she said, "don't look," and she actually groped to cover Rhonda's eyes. We were quietly passing the tail end of the white Starfire, partly hidden in the corn. Rhonda stared straight into it as we passed.

"It can't be."

"Don't look," Kelly said.

"What's the deal, ladies?" the old woman said. "You're giving me the heebie-jeebies. What's happening?"

"Nothing," Rhonda said. "We thought we saw somebody, but we didn't."

"Out here?" the woman asked.

"We thought so," Kelly said. "Wrong again, though." She tried to almost sing it.

"Wrong again," Rhonda muttered. "Is that dumb, or what?" she said to Kelly. "Coming here? Is that goddamned stupid, or what?" She was saying this real quietly, her head down almost on her knees. "How could this be happening?"

I sat frozen. I realized something amazing. Just as surely as the summer sky was blue, Rhonda's mom was an Arcola girl, too.

We went on down the tractor path toward the barn, Rhonda staying low in her seat and saying nothing. Once she squirmed up and looked out the back window, but there was nothing to see.

"You wanna forget this?" Kelly said to her, referring to the woman in the back seat. "No big deal."

"Oh *come* now, ladies . . ." the woman said.

We parked the car at the side, and all of us went into the barn. The woman selected a spot on the dirt floor in the middle of the dark, musty space, and Kelly produced six candles from the same bag she'd gotten the pickles from. The woman lit them. Kelly and Rhonda sat and the woman sat next to them, a triangle.

Suddenly the woman looked at me. "He will have to join us or get out," she said.

"Sit down here," Rhonda said to me. She was stricken, very tense. I sat down.

"My boy, this is a seance, what we call a 'circle.' We're here to call forth the spirits, and I'm not kidding, the good spirits of departed friends, Karen Ann Kreitzer and Marie Beth McClain. Can you handle it?" She read the names off a small card in her hand, slipped it back into her robe.

I looked at Rhonda.

"They were our friends," she said to me, her voice actually trembling.

I pictured their car in the wreck lot, the blood in the seat, and the shoe in the white gravel. The woman was bowing forward, toward the ground, staring down, changing postures from moment to moment. The candles made the whole barn jump. Gray webs dangled from the crossbeams.

"What happens if somebody drives up in the middle of this?" I whispered to Rhonda.

"We won't be here real long or anything," Kelly said.

The woman's arms were out, embracing us as a group. "Is there someone who can tell us of Karen and Marie?" she asked the night air. The night air was very quiet. "We wish for only good souls to speak to us, friendly souls and no bad souls. Satan lives and we want none of that. Does anyone know of Karen and Marie? And if you do, can you, will you, join our circle?"

The river-bottom sycamores rustled. I realized I could hear the river.

"We join our hands here to form a circle. We invite you to be with us here. We are all concentrating, thinking toward you, remembering you—your eyes, your smile . . ."

Her arms reached out on both sides, and she took the hands of the girls. Then they took mine.

In the candlelight the woman was alternately very soft and friendly looking, then hard and witchlike. It depended on the candlelight, her movements. I realized there was an old red Farmall not far off behind Kelly, an old red hay baler attached to the back.

"Now, ladies, I want to tell you," the woman said, "that these young girls might well not be ready to talk. It may not be easy for them right now."

Rhonda and Kelly said nothing. I was wondering if they had a money-back guarantee. Rhonda's hand was cool and damp, Kelly's hot as fire.

"I suspect that could be the case," the woman said. "That they aren't ready." Again she bowed forward, her arms out, her hands joined to ours. Again she moved side to side, staring off. "We require the help of a friendly soul, a good soul," she said, "in order to speak with Karen Kreitzer."

"Or with Marie," Kelly said very quietly.

"Marie?" the woman said, suddenly tensing up. She held herself very straight, upright, rigid.

Kelly looked at me and rolled her eyes.

"Marie honey, are you sad?" the woman asked. She held herself rigid for several long moments. Amazingly, the woman's eyes teared up.

In a second Rhonda began to cry also.

"I almost had Marie there," the woman said to Kelly. "She was near. Did you feel it? She was with us in this barn. She passed through here. She passed through us." She looked around. "Marie. Please talk to your friends, to Kelly and . . ." She was stumped.

"Rhonda," the girls said in unison.

"Kelly and Rhonda are here to talk to you, Marie."

Silence. A long way off a private plane was swooping in to land at the West Ridge airfield. I listened to the river, the trees' rustle. I could hear a bird steadily cooing in a tree out there somewhere, peaceful sound, made me feel better. I think I had expected something violent to happen any moment—a barn door to fly open wildly, a ghoul to appear, the old woman's head to do a three-sixty, her eyes to light up like the devil.

"Ladies," the woman said, "this room is full of ghosts—restless souls from this land all around, souls from all ages. There are Indians here and old settlers, pioneers—children and farmers whose bones are buried in this ground. We have made a hole in the firmament and they are crowding to it. Can you sense that they are with us?"

The girls didn't answer.

"Karen? Karen, have you come to speak to us? Will you join our circle? No," she said in just a moment, quietly, "it's Marie who comes near. Marie! Will you speak to your friends? Karen? Are you there, my dear?" The woman's eyes were closed in fierce concentration.

"Karen?" Kelly said quietly into the black.

"What's that?" the woman whispered. "Did you hear that?" She thought Kelly was a spirit talking.

Kelly looked at her. "It was me," she said. Kelly clearly conveyed impatience. This seemed to deflate the woman completely.

"Ladies," she said after a moment, "these are girls who have died very young. Maybe to you your age doesn't seem real young. I believe that they are not yet ready to talk. They are still very sad, I think. There is the sign that they are not happy on the other side. They will be, but they have died young and they aren't happy yet. I'm sorry." She broke hands with Rhonda and Kelly and leaned forward and blew out the candles.

"Or else," she said, "something's distracting you ladies and keeping us from fully communicating."

Abruptly Rhonda went out the door. I suddenly realized where she might be going. Kelly followed me out but ran by me very fast, disappeared on the lane ahead. She wanted to stop Rhonda. I was having a hard time believing Rhonda was really going where it looked like she was. At one point I came around a bend in the path, and could see that Kelly had caught up to her. The two of them were talking, Rhonda waving her arms—she was pretty upset. Kelly had her hands on Rhonda's shoulders—trying to talk sense, it looked like. Then in a moment Rhonda was coming back toward me, and *Kelly* was heading on back toward the car parked in the corn.

"What's going on?" I asked when Rhonda was close enough.

"Kelly's gone bushwhacking," she said. "She's going to get a ride home for her and Ghost-woman." Not knowing I knew what I knew, she lied for my benefit: "I guess Kelly knows those people or something." She looked at me to see if it was going to fly. I let it. "Anyway, I've got Kelly's keys, in case there's a problem," she said. Now she was running back toward the barn with me right behind her. "Give me your keys," she said to me, "so Kelly can get back out here in your car. Then we can go dancing and she can go to West Ridge."

"I don't get this," I said.

"Hang in there," she said.

The windows on Kelly's car had misted up in the night air. The woman was standing next to it. The moon was just up, red and looming low in the east. "The car broke," Rhonda said.

"It what?" the woman said.

"Kelly says it won't start. But you wait here—Kelly's going to get you to the train on time. Him and me . . ." Rhonda indicated me. "We're going to hide from the people in the other car, then stay and guard Kelly's car until Kelly gets back. How's that?"

"You mean she's gone to—er—interrupt those kids parked back yonder?" the woman said.

"Yeah. So you can get to the train. Give these to Kelly," Rhonda said, handing my car keys to the woman.

"Well, what are those kids going to think of me and Kelly out here alone?" she said as the Starfire headlights glanced high off the side of the barn and changed the shadows.

We were retreating into the standing corn. "What are you worried about?" Rhonda shouted. "You've got a whole bag of money."

Later we were near the swimming hole, in a stand of oaks, sycamores, and river willows. Rhonda was munching on a pickle. There

were hedge apples on the ground, and I lobbed a few into the river.
Maybe she seemed a little shorter than I imagined she was. I'd never
stood near her before.

"Pretty strange evening," I said.

She didn't answer. After a while, though, she turned and stood
there looking at me. "We paid her seventy bucks." She kept looking at
me. I did my best not to react.

The moon was up brighter now, and it gave enough light for me to
see the rope I thought I remembered being there, attached high in a
sycamore, for swinging out over the water. The night was muggy and
hot. Rhonda said nothing.

"Try to tell me what was going on back there."

"You mean Ghost-woman? Just something completely insane," she
said. "Kelly gets these great ideas. Kelly's mom knew this nurse up in
Champaign who does this stuff—reads palms, all that. I forgot this
was the night. That's why I messed you over. Forgot."

"Oh. I thought I was the front man. So you could get out of the
house."

She said nothing to that. She was sitting on the riverbank. I sat
down next to her.

"My mom's having an affair with the local veterinarian." She
looked downriver into the dark. "Jesus. I'm coming apart," she said.
She was quiet for a minute. "I feel so sorry for Dad. I can't think
about it," she said. Then she was crying, her head down on her arms,
which were resting on her knees.

I sat next to her. I couldn't think of a thing to tell her.

"I thought we might reach Karen," she said after a while. "I really
loved her. She was my best friend. My best friend. I'm definitely coming apart."

There was nothing to say. I ate a pickle and regretted it. I rolled a
couple of hedge apples down the bank into the water. Finally I stood
up and kicked my shoes off, dropped my wallet on the ground next to
them. I tested the rope to see if the limb would hold me.

"What if Karen had talked tonight?" I said. "What would she say?"

"Don't tease me. It was a nutty idea. Karen would talk to me if she
could. You're going to bust your ass swinging on that thing. I'll tell

you what, that woman was a complete fake." After a while she said, "Didn't you think so?" She didn't move. "Kelly says a medium like this one helped her contact her father."

"Kelly wishes," I said. I swung out over the river, a warm wind in my ears. "One thing I know is that Karen and Marie aren't sad. You are, but they aren't." I grabbed a hedge apple, and I swung out over the river, dropping it straight down. It was hard to tell how far above the water I was. I told Rhonda, "There's not anything to say, is why they didn't talk. They died, and that's all."

Her head was down. "I just don't believe your friends can die like that," she said. "Not your friends." By now it seemed to me like she'd been crying off and on for hours.

"It's a real pretty night, you know it? You ought to try to relax."

"Ha. Relax," she said.

I swung out again and again on the rope. I realized it would have been better if she could have been left to herself. "Lucky I'm here to keep you company," I said. At the far point of the arch, I could see all the way to the iron bridge. Out there, the moon broke through the trees, and I could see the movement of the water downstream. Sometimes I could hear a carp break the surface.

"I didn't want to go dancing anyway," I said. When I swung, I could hear the rope grating on the big limb high above. At one point while I was far out on the rope, I heard Rhonda slip into the water. I swung back to the bank, took a run and swung far out again, trying to spot her in the inky black below. I could hear her swimming.

"It's nice and cool," she said.

At the far point this time I let go of the rope and dropped. En route to the water, in a moment when I was anticipating splashing hard into the Black River, in a turning and falling motion in the dark, I happened to glimpse Rhonda's clothes in a little moonlit pile on the riverbank.

The Dinner Party

•

═══ **JONATHAN BAUMBACH** ═══

Jonathan Baumbach is the author of six novels, including Reruns and Babble, *and two collections of short stories. Mr. Baumbach teaches fiction writing at Brooklyn College and writes about films for various periodicals. This is the third time he has received an O. Henry award. All three of the O. Henry Prize Stories appear in his most recent collection,* The Live and Times of Major Fiction.

I have a rule, one of few—perhaps my only rule—that I never discuss work in progress. To talk about something not fully born is to risk, says my experience, unspeakable loss. So when at a dinner party this youthful gray-haired woman on my right, Isabelle something, some other man's discontented wife, asked me what I was working on, I hedged my answer. This is what I said: I'm working on a novel about a marriage in the process of invisible dissolution. Isabelle gave me an odd, almost censorious look and returned to the business of eating. Had I said the wrong thing? Did she think I was telling her something about her own life? I had said more than I wanted to say, yet perhaps less than she felt it her right to know.

The loss of my audience so early in the proceedings seemed a depressing omen. It provoked me to want to regain her attention. It is a mistake to let yourself get challenged like that in the house of strangers.

For three consecutive nights Joshua Quartz had dreams that included the appearance of his estranged wife, Genevieve. Six months had passed since their separation and he had considered himself free of her until the dreams presented themselves like undiscovered evidence. There was a progression in the dreams as if they were installments in some larger yet undefined unit.

"Isn't there anything else you'd like to know?" I asked, trying to make a joke out of a serious question. She was chewing her food—her chicken or veal—and couldn't find her way clear to making an answer. She held up one finger as if to say, Give me time. I waited, looked around the table and realized there was no one I knew well at the party. The Garretsons, friends of my former wife, had invited me out of some misplaced idea of kindness. For some reason, I was the only one at table—there were fifteen guests in all—who had not been served. Isabelle turned to me and said, "Of course I want to know everything. Do I dare to ask?"

In the first dream, Joshua was in a small bedroom talking to a man —his father? brother? a doctor acquaintance?—about problems he was having with his back. The door to his bedroom was open, offering him a partial view of a long hallway. His wife, Genevieve, was on the phone at the farthest point of his vision. She was talking on the phone to an unnamed man, her current boyfriend, whom she addressed from time to time as darling. He sensed the inappropriateness of the endearment in its present context and was more amused than pained by it. The man in his room continued to talk—something about wrapping the back in Corning's fiberglass—but his attention was on Genevieve. She turned to see if he were there and their eyes met. She seemed to smile at him. As a matter of choice, he declined to smile back. She continued to watch him while she talked on the phone.

I felt a kick under the table and moved my leg away, thinking it an accident. The second kick suggested intention, a statement of presence from the woman on my right. I returned her kick or perhaps kicked someone else, a few heads raised from their plates, a few pained looks here and there. "Consider it a down payment," said the woman, Isabelle something, putting one of her braised potatoes on my plate.

"This is a novel about two people with unrealistic expectations," I said. Then I ate the potato the woman had given me. It created a desire for more and I stared longingly at the three other potatoes on her plate. "Sometimes I just want to scream," Isabelle said. She speared one of her potatoes and held it to her lips, held it suspended in air while she considered its fate. "I don't know how to take you," she whispered. "Much of what you've been telling me is the kind of thing that appears on the dust jacket. Aren't you being just a little bit evasive?"

In the second dream he had come home to his new apartment to discover several radical changes in his absence. For one, the lace curtain on his door had been replaced by a white apron. He knew what it meant, knew instantly that Genevieve was somewhere in the house and that the apron was her calling card. He admired the wit of the apron, though considered its presence inappropriate in a place a man lived in by himself. He planned to take it down at first opportunity. What the hell was going on? His cleaning woman, Jamoon, was in the kitchen preparing a turkey, stuffing it with olives and apricots. The house was pulsing with preparations for some holiday dinner. Thanksgiving or Halloween—it was that time of year. He went back to the vestibule door and removed the apron, intending to replace it with the original curtain, which was not to be found. The door looked naked without a covering, suggested deprivation and loss. He worried that Genevieve would make a fuss about his removing the apron, would take it as a rejection of her gift. When he put it back he couldn't get it straight so he left it hanging at an awkward tilt.

Joshua washed his hands, then went to the bedroom to change his clothes, saw Genevieve in the adjoining room at his desk. Nothing is said. He starts to undress, lifting his shirt over his head. He glances at her to see if she is aware of his presence. It is hard to tell. The book that occupies her, that she is reading or pretending to read, covers her face. The title he notices is *The Curtain Falls*.

The hostess, Kiki Garretson, served me a bowl of shell-shaped pasta in a green sauce. It was not what the others had but certainly an acceptable substitute. I had a reputation when younger for preferring pasta to almost anything. Perhaps the Garretsons had made this separate dinner especially for me. Or, the more likely alternative, they had run out of the main course and this was a leftover from another party. "What the people in your novel love," Isabelle announced, pointing her finger at me, emphasizing each word like a radio announcer, "is the concept of being loved. Isn't that the point?"

I chewed quickly, as quickly as the pasta, which was a touch crisp, allowed, not wanting to lose this audience. Her hand was on my knee, a gentle weight. "Yes and no," I said. I looked around the table to see who if anyone was observing us. "They are both married to others when they fall in love. Their relationship begins in passion and ends in anger and insentience. Ends in the death of feeling." My neighbor nodded her head in acknowledgment, confirmed in some private unhappy truth. "There's nothing worse than the death of feeling," she said, giving me the last and largest of her potatoes. We exchanged sad smiles.

The third dream was the most elaborate. He was with her in an underground parking lot, collecting their car. They were going somewhere together, the destination urgent though obscure. It was as if they were a team of some sort, detectives like Steed and Mrs. Peele or Nick and Nora Charles, a partnership that had survived other disaffections. In this case, they both, he happened to know, knew too much. This too much knowing, this excessive knowledgeability, has put them in a kind of danger, a danger that offers more thrill than anxiety, a danger without menace. The fact is, they are having fun, pursuing and being pursued, each in its turn. Affectionate wisecracks are exchanged. They get into a waiting taxi and Genevieve says to the driver in a perfunctory voice, "Follow that car." In the next moment they are pursuing a black limousine, tearing around corners as in movie chase scenes, going through stop signs, riding on sidewalks. They hear the squeal of brakes as they flash through an intersection, but there is no sign of the car that had skidded to a stop. The canopy of a fruit stand collapses, oranges and apples roll into the street. It's just like a movie, he thinks, which is what he hears himself saying.

"Who's with the children?" she asks him. "I thought you were," he says. Talk of the children deflates his exhilaration. It is too serious a topic, too rueful and painful a topic in light of their present roles. The stretch limo they have been following stops in front of an Italian restaurant called Mafia Pasta. No one emerges from the limousine and they wait expectantly in their cab for some further revelation.

The shells on my plate were not sufficiently cooked, crackled when chewed, though I made no complaint, letting the crunching sound speak for itself, not wanting to seem ungracious. "I've been holding my breath waiting for you to continue," said my neighbor on the right. "I really hope you don't mean to disappoint me." I was reluctant to continue in truth, but having taken her this far I didn't know how to refuse her. "They can't keep apart," I said, rushing the words, "so hate the other for the loss of freedom and self-respect. They agree to stop seeing each other, which only intensifies irrational necessity. It goes on that way for a while, the resolution not to see each other, the breaking of the resolution, false endings, new beginnings, guilt, regret, passion, unforgivable recriminations." When I looked down I noticed another potato on my plate, smaller though more perfectly formed than either of the first two. It was gemlike, this potato, and I had not noticed it on her plate. I ate it slowly, sensuously, holding it on my tongue for a time before letting it ride down my throat. "And what kind of credit does that get me on the literary marketplace?" she said with a corner-of-the-mouth smile.

They tell me my paralysis is a state of mind. I don't move because no matter what I say to the contrary I don't want to move. That is not something I'm willing to believe. They carry me from bed to chair in the morning. How do I start? They bring me my food. Sometimes they —one or the other of them—feed me. Sometimes they leave the food for me on a transparent plastic tray and when they're out of the room I feed myself. I can only move my arms when no one is watching. Not everything I say is true. My memory is short.

Taylor Garretson came by and filled my wine glass, asked if everything was satisfactory. My plate, I noticed, was the only one around the large table that still had food left on it. "I've been talking too much," I said. I studied the food on my plate with apologetic regret, took a small forkful of the brittle shells. My companion on the right, the one who had given me her potatoes, Isabelle something, winked at me. The woman on my left, who had hardly noticed me before, a big-breasted woman with shocking red hair, turned her head in my direction. Everyone at the table, I discovered, was looking at me with apparent curiosity. I held up my wine glass. "To a better year than the last," I said. The others joined me in the toast, all but the red-headed woman on my left, who had returned her attention to the man on her other side.

Joshua departs the cab and enters the restaurant while his estranged wife stays behind. There is no one inside Mafia Pasta that he knows or has even seen before, though they are all undefinably familiar. It is a family restaurant and everyone there is sitting at the same table. Joshua asks to speak to the owner. When the owner, a swarthy type wearing a chef's apron, comes out from the back, Joshua can't remember what it is he is supposed to ask. His wife takes his arm, says this is the wrong place darling, we haven't a moment to lose. Some cliché like that. They run together for a few blocks, Genevieve glancing behind her to check on the distance of some apparent pursuer. It strikes Joshua that the owner of Mafia Pasta was the man in the limo they had been following, that the apron he was wearing had been put on as a disguise. "Who's behind us?" he asks. "Never mind," she says. Joshua is thinking that this experience with his estranged wife requires further definition. "It's been the man in the apron all along," he says, "hasn't it?" The intimacy of them being pursued together touches him. Genevieve makes no comment. They arrive at their former apartment, where he drops her off. "Are you going to be all right?" he asks. "Let's do this again sometime," she says. Joshua is trying to find language for his feelings. Genevieve hesitates at the door, thinks perhaps of inviting him in. They neither embrace nor shake hands. She goes inside.

"I don't have the whole picture," Isabelle was saying in her dramatic way, a knife slicing the air for emphasis. "Something crucial has been left out. I hope you're not one of those writers who leaves out important details in order to be obscure." I was playing with the remainder of my shells, crushing them with my fork into a greenish powder. "Did I tell you how they met?" I asked. "I don't remember if you did," she said. "Of course I'd remember something like that." How did they meet? "They met in a mixed doubles game at the Wall Street Racquet Club," I said. She shook her head, pointed her knife at me. "You know that's not true," she said. I could see the detail was inappropriate and I wondered how I could take it back without giving away that the novel I had been describing had not been written. "The tennis game was in an earlier draft," I said. "In a more recent version, they meet in an analyst's office. She has the appointment before him. They nod to each other for months before they begin to talk. What's important is not how they met but the intuitive sympathy they felt for each other." My plate was removed with the others and I felt a sudden gnawing hunger. "What?" she asked.

Let me start again in a more direct and honest vein. I can stand if I have to. I can walk. I can feed myself as ably as the next person. I walk from bed to door and back again, go the whole route. Most of the time I lie in bed with my hands under my head, thinking about getting up and walking around the room. The door is locked. I am a prisoner in my own room. They bring me my meals on a silver tray three times a day. Perhaps the meals arrive no more than twice a day. I tend to exaggerate for effect. My memory is a string of broken connections.

"One day she was crying when he arrived for his therapy session, shaking with tears and trying without success to slip into her coat. Her grief moved him. He helped her with her coat. She took it as her due, thanked him without saying so. When his own session was over she was still in the waiting room." The salad course was served. The woman on my left with the unreal red hair addressed me directly for the first time. "My husband hates salad," she said. "The children, particularly the older boys, won't touch it with a pole. I think that's sinful, don't you?" I smiled politely, took a forkful of leaves. "I've come to salad late myself," I confessed. "But now I can't get enough of it, particularly when it's good." "You have a good attitude for a man," she said, "but in my unsolicited opinion"—she brought her mouth to my ear—"there's more to salad than leaves no matter how many colors they come in."

I felt a pinch from the other side and turned back to my companion on the right, Isabelle something. "He was helping her on with her coat," she said in an uncharacteristically strident voice. "They were in the waiting room of his shrink. It was the first time they had talked." The woman on my left, the salad partisan, was also saying something, my attention divided. "He invited her for coffee," I heard myself say. "There was a place he knew in the neighborhood that made terrific cappuccino."

Joshua called Genevieve the morning after the third dream. He didn't know what he wanted to say, let the conversation unfold to no purpose. Finally, he mentioned the dream, the first of the three. "I haven't dreamed of you at all," she said with what sounded over the phone like regret, as if she had failed to honor her part of the bargain. "I haven't even thought of you," she said, "though I like hearing your voice over the phone."

The dessert is some kind of berry cobbler—boysenberry is my guess —with a white sauce. As we were waiting to be served, Isabelle said in a somewhat plaintive voice, "What have you and Desirée been chatting about?" Desirée? "You know who I mean," she said, indicating with her eyes the woman on my left. "Nothing of consequence," I said. The salad plates were being retrieved and it came to my attention that I had eaten only two leaves. "In their first few years together, they were obsessively jealous of one another, the woman perhaps more than the man. Because they had started out illicitly, they felt increasingly vulnerable as a legitimate couple, feared betrayal." "Wait just a minute," Isabelle said, "they're still in the therapist's office, they've just begun to talk, he's holding her coat for her." "If I get too specific, there won't be enough time for the whole story." "What's the matter with people?" said Isabelle, aggrieved. "Why must they ruin everything?" My neighbor on the left was saying something about leaving my salad in the lurch. "After what you told me, mister, I was hoping you would set an example for my husband." The hostess had started to serve the cobbler when she realized she had forgotten an intervening course and so collected the plates and returned the dessert to the kitchen. We were crestfallen as a group. The delay seemed intolerable.

The door to my room is not really locked or is only locked from the inside when it suits me to lock it. In truth, my legs are tired. My back is bad. I have no inner life. I sleep half the day. When I leave the room, which is rare, I go directly to the kitchen to get myself something to eat. I go from my room to the kitchen and then from the kitchen directly back to my room. Sometimes I walk into the closet and stand among the shirts and jackets as if I too were something inanimate, something to put on and take off.

"He invites her for coffee after finding her in the waiting room when his own session is finished. She thinks of all the reasons she can't go or shouldn't and offers them with her apology for refusing him. They are only words and once they are out of the way she gladly goes along. They talk for several hours, find themselves of like mind on a number of subjects. It becomes a ritual, this after-therapy assignation, and both look forward to it, both thrive on it. It is the talk that does it. They are both verbal people. Words fly between them like kisses. They are in love before they make love. And then it takes three years for them to disentangle from other relationships." I stopped for breath and Isabelle said, "You don't have to say any more." The host and hostess, I notice, are huddled together in the doorway between kitchen and dining room, planning some new strategy. In a moment, Kiki Garretson goes back into the kitchen and returns again with the cobbler. She wears an apologetic smile. "I'm not what you call a dessert person," Desirée says to me. "I'm going to give you mine if you've no objection." Isabelle, from the other side, says something of the same. New possibilities for my novel float in my head and I long to try them out on Isabelle, though for the moment she is talking to her husband, or somebody else's husband, across the table. "Remember to call my mother," the man says.

I have an antique rocking chair in my room where I take comfort in moments of panic. The rocking of the chair stimulates recollections of sweeter times. I sit and rock until the circulation stops in my left leg, then I get up, force myself to get up. I shake my frozen leg until it un-numbs itself. The shaking of the leg tires me. I am in the business of conserving energy, storing it up like food in wartime for a crisis even more unimaginable than the present one. If for some reason I leave the room, I am filled with uneasiness as if the air that sustains were no longer available.

I have two plates of boysenberry cobbler in front of me. The woman on my right, Desirée, has given me hers after I've already accepted one for myself. When I return her dessert Desirée refuses to accept it, slides it back toward me. "Please," she says. "It makes me happy for you to have it." Meanwhile Isabelle has pushed her plate toward me from the other side. So: I have three plates of boysenberry cobbler with crème anglaise in front of me. "She doted on him in the begin-ning," I said to Isabelle. "It was too much, it was overwhelming. It left no place for their romance to go." "Did she?" said Isabelle in a dreamy voice. "What a coincidence." They were short a dessert on the other side of the table and I gave over one of mine, the one that had been intended for me. I still had the two gift desserts and wasn't sure where to start, not wanting to offend either of my benefactresses. "If you're not going to eat it," Desirée said and reclaimed her cobbler. Isabelle was chipping away at the other one with a spoon. As I took my first bite, her spoon clanked against my fork. "Why didn't you keep yours if you wanted it?" I asked her. "It's irresistible," she said, "and what's more I think sharing is a positive thing to do. If you had taken Desirée's and not mine, I would have been heartbroken." Her husband, or the man I thought was her husband, was watching us from the other side of the table out of the corner of his eye.

I walk a block from the house after breakfast and then, as if invisible chains pull me back, return to my room. In the street, sometimes I pass a woman walking a small terrier and we nod to each other. Sometimes she makes a comment on the weather, an innocuous, impersonal comment. Like: Not so cold today, is it? I share her pleasure in the weather's improvement. I think of things to say to her, variations on our usual exchange. I work up conversations in my hermetic room, rehearse my lines in the mirror before going out. This is what I will say to her.

There is, as it turns out, another course brought belatedly, out of traditional sequence, to the table. A broccoli soufflé with a plum glaze. "This is Bozo's dish," the hostess says. (Taylor's nickname is Bozo.) Taylor stands, bows, shakes a fist in triumph. Desirée whispers, "He's a terrible cook, you can't imagine." I am the only one at table who eats Taylor's dish. Except for the fact that some of the broccoli is still frozen, it is not so bad, not as bad as advertised. Desirée, I notice, has covered her plate with her napkin, apparently unable to bear even the sight of the dish. I said to Isabelle, "In the beginning they talked like angels to each other. After they made love, there seemed nothing else to say." "It makes me sad to think about it," Isabelle said.

There is a cheese course next, followed by coffee, followed by glasses of some green liqueur. During all this, Isabelle and I hold hands under the table. From time to time, I feel compelled to throw out morsels of my novel in her direction, whatever comes to mind. I am aware that the party will be over soon, that someone will get up to leave and that others will follow. An intense sadness overwhelms me.

Genevieve called Joshua in the middle of the night, waking him from a restive sleep. "I want to tell you that I've been dreaming about you," she said. "Look, I'm sleeping," said Joshua. "Why can't you call in the morning like any sane person?"

"My dream," she said, "concerned a dinner party at our old house on Watkins Place." She laughed to herself. "Everyone around the table was naked. You were the only one with clothes on, the only one. I was disappointed in you at first. I thought, how gauche to stand out like that, to not get into the spirit of things. Then I thought, what terrific integrity. You retained your dignity, your propriety, while others had yielded to some pointless fashion."

Joshua thanked her for the compliment.

"That's not the end," she said. "I went upstairs to get dressed to show the others that I was on your side in this. When I got back to the dining room you had gone off with someone else."

"I hate to say good-bye to people I like," Isabelle said. Her husband was waiting for her at the door, tapping his foot impatiently. "Someday you'll have to tell me how your novel ends."

"At this point, Isabelle, you know at least as much about it as I do."

"I don't believe that," she said. "Maybe I'll see it in the window of a bookstore and go in and buy a copy. You can't deny that you haven't really told me all that much."

I had nothing to deny. "You're ungrateful," I said. She seemed to blush, turned her face away. The telling had left out the structure, the formal concerns, the flashes of language, the urgency of experience. The transitions. What had been left out, when I thought of it, was everything. The rest had been devalued by recitation, had slipped away into the smoke.

I held her coat for her. "The next time I see you, I'll tell you the rest," I said. We shook hands in a businesslike way.

"Until then," she said, slipping her hand free—I didn't want to give it up—following her husband out the door into the night.

Leaf Season

•

=========== **JOHN UPDIKE** ===========

John Updike was born in Shillington, Pennsylvania, in 1932. He graduated from Harvard College and worked several years for The New Yorker. *Since 1957 he has lived in Massachusetts as a free-lance writer. This is his eleventh appearance in the* O. Henry Prize Stories.

Off we go! Saturday morning, into our cars, children and dogs and all, driving north to Vermont in leaf season, to the Tremaynes' house on the Columbus Day weekend. It's become a custom, one of the things we all do, the four or five families, a process that can't be stopped without running the risk of breaking a spell. Threading out of greater Boston on its crowded, potholed highways, then smoothly north on 93, and over on 89, across the Connecticut River, into Vermont. At once, there is a difference: things look cleaner, sparser than in New Hampshire. When we leave 89, the villages on the winding state roads, with their white churches and irregular, casually mowed greens and red-painted country stores advertising FUDGE FACTORY or PUMPKIN OUTLET, show a sharp-edged charm, a stagy, calendar-art prettiness that wears at the eyes, after a while, as relentlessly as industrial ugliness. And the leaves, whole valleys and mountains of them—the strident pinks and scarlets of the maples, the clangorous gold of the hickories, the accompanying brasses of birch and beech, on both sides of the road, rise after rise, a heavenly tumult tied to our dull earth only by broad bands of evergreen and outcroppings of granite. We arrive feeling battered by natural glory, by the rush of wind and of small gasoline explosions incessantly hurried one into the next. The dirt driveway—really just ruts that the old wagons and carts wore into the lawn and that modern times have given a dusting of gravel—comes in at right angles off an unmarked macadam road, which came off a numbered state route, which in turn came off a federal highway; so we feel, at last arriving, that we have removed the innermost tissue covering from an ornately wrapped present, or reduced a mathematical problem to its final remainder, or climbed a mountain, or cracked a safe.

The gravel grinds and pops beneath our tires. Marge Tremayne is standing on the porch. She looks pretty good. A little older, a shade overweight, but good.

She and Ralph bought the big wheat-yellow farmhouse with its barn and twenty acres one winter when he had made a killing in oil stocks, the year of the first gas lines, and when their three children were all excited about skiing. Ralph, too, was excited—he grew a Pancho Villa mustache in imitation of the ski instructors and, with his fat cigar in the center of his mouth and his rose-colored goggles and butter-yellow racing suit and clumpy orange step-in boots, was quite a sight on the slopes. Marge, in her tight stretch pants and silver parka and Kelly-green headband and with her hair flying behind, looked rather wonderful, too; her sense of style and her old dance training enabled her to mime the basic moves gracefully enough, and down she would slide, but she wasn't a skier at heart. "I'm too much of a coward," she would say. Or, in another mood, to another listener: "I'm too much of an earth mother." She took to using the Vermont place in the summer (when Ralph had hoped to rent it) and raised vegetables by the bushel and went into canning in a big way, and into spinning wool and mushrooming, and she even began to show a talent for dowsing, serving her apprenticeship with some old mountain man from beyond Montpelier. Ralph was still working in town, and except for Augusts would drive up to his wife on weekends, five hours each way, carting children and their friends back and forth and keeping house in Brookline by himself. So this leaf-season weekend has become a visit to Marge, our chance to see what is going on with her.

Marge and the newly arrived Neusners are standing on the side
porch when the Maloneys pull up. The Maloney children bound or
self-consciously uncoil, depending upon their ages, out of automotive
confinement. There is pleasant confusion and loudly proclaimed ex-
haustion, a swirling of people back and forth; the joy of an adventure
survived animates the families as they piecemeal unload their baggage
and collapse into Marge's care. She has a weary, slangy, factual voice,
slightly nasal as if she has caught a cold. "It's girls' and boys' dormitories again this year. Men at the head of the stairs turn right, women
left. Boys thirteen and older out in the barn, younger than that upstairs with the girls. The Tylers are already here; Linda's taken some
littles for a leaf walk and Andy's helping Ralph load up the wood-
boxes. Ralph says each man's supposed to split his weight in wood.
Each woman is responsible for one lunch or dinner. Breakfasts, it's a
free-for-all as usual, and don't put syrupy knives and forks straight
into the dishwasher, anybody. That means *you,* Teddy Maloney."

The nine-year-old boy, so suddenly singled out, laughs in nervous
fright; he had been preoccupied with trying to coax the family dog,
Ginger, a red-haired setter bitch, out of the car, in spite of the menacing curiosity of Wolf, the Tremaynes' grizzled chow, and Toby
Neusner, an undersized black retriever.

Bernadette Maloney, embracing Marge and kissing her cheek and
thinking how broad her body feels, backs off and asks her, a touch too
solemnly, "How are you doing?"

Marge gazes back as solemnly, her slate-blue eyes muddied by elements of yellow. "The summer's been bliss," she confides, and averts
her gaze with a stoic small shrug. "I don't know. I can't handle people
anymore."

Her headband today is maroon. Her thick long dirty-blond hair
over the years has become indistinguishably mixed with gray, this
subtle dullness intensifying her odd Indian look, not that of blood
Indians but of a paleface maiden captured and raised in their smoky
tepees, in their casually cruel customs; her face up here has turned
harder and more chiselled, her unpainted lips thinner, her eyes more
opaque. She has not so much a tan as a glow, a healthy matte color-
lessness rubbed deep into her skin. Her body has grown wider, but

with her old sense of style she carries the new weight well, in her hip-hugging jeans and a man's checked lumberjack shirt that hangs over her belt like a maternity blouse. Belly, gray hair, and all, she is still our beauty, and Ralph, when he appears—having evidently been hurried from his car straight into service, for his Brooks Brothers shirt is creased and dirtied by the logs he has been lugging and his city shoes are powdered with sawdust—is still a friendly ogre; he exudes fatherly fumes, he emits barks and guffaws of welcome. His eyes are reddened by cigar smoke, he stammers and spits in his greedy hurry to get his jokes out, he laughs aloud before the punch line is quite reached. He appears to have lost some weight. "My d-daughters' awful cooking," he explains. "Th-they're trying to, *ha,* poison the old guy."

How old are we? Scarcely into our forties. Lots of life left to live. The air here is delicious, crisper and drier than air around Boston. We start to breathe it now, and to take in where we are. The sounds are fewer, and those few are different—individual noises: a single car passing on the road, a lone crow scolding above the stubbled side field, a single window sash clicking back and forth in the gentle wind we hadn't noticed when outside unpacking the cars. The smells of the house are country smells—linoleum, ashes, split wood, plaster, a primeval cellar damp that rises through the floorboards and follows us up the steep, wear-rounded stairs to the second floor, where we see the children and their sleeping bags settled in the tangle of middle rooms. The house, like most Vermont farmhouses, has suffered many revisions over the years; they thought nothing, in the old days, of lifting out a staircase and turning it around or of walling in a fireplace to vent a Franklin stove. With our suitcases as claim markers, we stake out bunks in the two large front bedrooms that the Tremaynes, when they were most excited about skiing, had set up as single-sex dormitories.

Deborah Neusner stands by the upstairs-hall window, gazing out at the empty road, at the field across the road, at the woods beyond the field, with all their leaves. Bernadette Maloney joins her, standing so close that the two women feel each other's body warmth as well as the heat from the radiator beneath the window. "The Englehardts are coming, but late. Little Kenneth has a football game."

"Not so little, then," Deborah says dryly, not turning her thoughtful profile, with its long chin and high-bridged nose. When she does face Bernadette, her brown eyes, in the sharp Vermont light, shine on the edge of panic. The Englehardts mean different things to different people, but to all of us they—Lee so bald and earnest and droll, Ruth so skinny and frizzy and nimble and quick-tongued—make things all right, make the whole thing go. Until they arrive, there will be an uneasy question of why we are here, at the top of the map, in this chilly big wheat-yellow farmhouse surrounded by almost vulgarly gorgeous, red-and-gold nature.

The host is under the house! All afternoon, Ralph lies on the cold ground beneath the kitchen wing, wrapping yellow Fiberglas insulation around his pipes. Already there have been frosts, and last winter, when the Tremaynes were renting to skiers, the pipes froze and the people moved to a motel and later sued. He keeps the cigar in his mouth while stretched out grunting in the crawl space; Bill Maloney hopes aloud to Andy Tyler that there is no gas leak under the kitchen. Both men—Bill burly and placid, Andy skinny and slightly hyper— hang there as if to be helpful, now and then passing more insulation, or another roll of duct tape, in to their supine host. Josh Neusner is splitting his weight in wood, an unfamiliar and thus to him somewhat romantic task. The romance intensifies whenever the splitting maul bounces from an especially awkward piece of wood and digs deep into the earth inches from his feet. He is wearing thin black loafers, with tassels. Wood chips and twigs litter the barnyard around him, and white dried dung from the days when Marge tried raising chickens. The barn overhang is loosely battened; upstanding spears of light make sliding patterns as you move your head. It is like an Op Art sculpture in a gallery, but bigger, Josh thinks, and the effect has that coarse broad authority of the actual, of the unintended. This whole milieu and the business of woodchopping is so exotic to him that his awareness flickers like a bad light bulb. Minutes of blankness—rural idiocy, Marx had called it—are abruptly illuminated by the flash of danger when the maul again sinks its murderous edge close to the tips of his city shoes; then the pebbles, the grit, the twigs are superillumined, vivid as the granules of paint in a Dubuffet, and something of this startled radiance is transferred, if he lifts his head quickly enough, to the sky, the fields, the gaudy woods.

Linda Tyler returns from her leaf walk with the children she collected and makes them as a reward for being good some peanut-butter-and-jelly sandwiches. Other children, late arrivals and adolescents too jaded for the walk, slouch in from the long living room, where a fire of green wood is smoking and where they have been dabbling with decks of greasy cards and old board games with pennies and buttons substituted over the years for the correct counters. Though they have been here on other Columbus Day weekends, they are shy of the kitchen. Other years, Mrs. Tremayne was cheerfully in charge, but this year she has withdrawn to her downstairs bedroom and shut the door; from behind it comes the whir and soft clatter of a spinning wheel. At the sound of food being prepared in the kitchen, the children gather like birds at a tray of seeds, and Linda hands out cookies, apples, pretzel sticks. She is petite, with pale freckled skin and kind green eyes, and wears baggy clothes that conceal her oddly good figure. As not only her husband here knows, her body on its modest scale has that voluptuous harmony, that curve of shoulder and swing of hip, which spells urgency to the male eye. She caters to the assembled children, warning them to leave room for the traditional big hot-dog-and-chili dinner tonight, after the Englehardts have arrived.

The children present for this weekend are: Milly, Skip, and Christine Tremayne; Matthew, Mark, Mary, Teddy, and Teresa Maloney; Fritz and Audrey Tyler; and Rebecca, Eve, and Seth and Zebulon (twins) Neusner. The Englehardts will bring Kenneth, Betsey, and their unplanned one-and-a-half-year-old, named in a jocular mood Dorothea—gift of God. The fanciful name would have been a curse had not the child lived up to it—an ethereal little girl with her mother's agility and that milky, abstracted blue-eyed gaze of her father's, set beneath not his bald dome but a head of angelic curls. The pets present are Toby Neusner, Ginger Maloney, Wolf Tremayne, and two cats, a sleepy, vain, long-haired white and a short-haired gray with extra toes who appears throughout the house at the strangest places, in locked rooms and bureau drawers, like an apparition. It is all too much, as the children get bigger. The oldest, Milly Tremayne and

Fritz Tyler, are both seventeen, and embarrassed to be here. They were embarrassed last year as well, but not so keenly.

Ralph emerges at last from underneath the house and announces, spitting smoke and amiably sputtering, that it's way past time for the softball game. "Wh-what are all you young br-bruisers lounging inside for on a gorgeous Saturday like this? Let's c-compete!" He gets down in a football lineman's crouch and, with the cigar stub in the center of his mouth like a rhinoceros horn, looks truly angry.

Softball is organized in the side field. Everyone plays, even Deborah Neusner and Bernadette Maloney, who had been murmuring upstairs for hours. What about? The absent, the present, the recent past, the near future—a liquid soft discourse that leaves, afterward, a scarcely perceptible residue of new information, which yet enhances their sense of who and where they are.

Fritz Tyler bowls Milly Tremayne over, rushing across from short-stop for a pop fly. "You bastard, didn't you hear me calling you off?" she asks him, sprawling in the long dry grass, red-faced and tousled, her upraised legs in their tight jeans looking elegant and thin. Her hair is dark like Ralph's but though not blond has the shape of Marge's, abundant and wiry and loose in a tent shape, before Marge began to braid it and pin it up like a nineteenth-century farmer's wife. Bill Maloney hits a home run, over the heads of Seth and Zebulon—they have been put in right field together, as if two little eight-year-old boys will make one good grownup fielder. Their black, loping dog, Toby, helps them hunt for the ball in the burdock over by the split-rail fence. The sky in the west, above mountains whose blush is turning blue, has begun to develop slant stripes tinged with pink, and the battered hay in the outfield is growing damp, each bent strand throwing a longer and longer shadow. Though the children are encouraged to continue the game until darkness, the grownups drift away, and in the long, narrow living room, with its plaster ceiling drooping in the center like the underside of an old bed, a fresh fire is built, of dry and seasoned logs from the woodbox beneath the stairs (the children had tried to burn freshly split wood, from beneath the barn overhang), and an impressive array of bottles is assembled on the sideboard. Bring your own, the rule is.

Marge, ostentatiously drinking unfermented cider, sits on the sofa, which is faded and plaid and has wide wooden arms, and knits a sweater of undyed wool she has carded and spun herself. Toward seven o'clock Linda and Bernadette go into the kitchen to feed the starving younger children. The older have scattered to their rooms upstairs, or out to the barn. By the time the Englehardts at last arrive, the adults not only are drunk but have gone through two boxes of crackers and a wedge of Vermont cheddar that was bought to last the weekend.

Cheers go up. Roly-poly, sleepy-looking Lee doffs his hunter's cap and reveals the polished dome of his perfectly smooth skull. Tall, frizzy-haired Ruth stands there and surveys the scene through her huge glasses, taking it all in. The temples of her glasses have the shape of a lightning bolt, and the bridge rides so low on her nose as to reduce it to a tiny round tip, a baby's nose. Kenneth and Betsey are lugging knapsacks and suitcases in from the car and up the stairs, including a plastic basket containing little Dorothea. "Who-who won the football game?" the host eagerly asks.

"We won," Ruth tells him, in the complex, challenging tone of a joke on herself, "but Kenny didn't play." The weariness of the long drive is still in her voice. Ruth's words are like glass sandwiches that reflect back an obvious meaning on the first level, a less obvious one on the second, and so on, as deep as you want to look. "The poor child sat on the bench," she adds.

"Oh." Ralph blinks, having evidently been tactless. His eyes slide over to Marge on the sofa, as if to seek support. Her eyes are lowered to the knitting. Wolf, who in his old age has been known to snap, sleeps at her feet. Upstairs, Kenneth and Betsey seek the company and comfort of the other children, as the Englehardts are meshed into the adult group beneath them and the hilarity, the shouting, swells by that increment.

It is hard, afterwards, to remember what was so funny. Their all being here in Vermont, in this old farmhouse with its smells from another century, is in itself funny, and the Saturday-night meal of something so hearty and Western as chili and hot dogs is funny, and the half-gallons of cheap wine that replace themselves at the table, like successive generations of bulbous green dwarfs, are part of the delicate, hallucinatory joke.

They organize two tables of bridge afterwards, and, drunk as they know themselves to be now, this is droll also. "Double," Lee Englehardt keeps saying solemnly, his shinning brow furrowed, the long wisps of hair above his ears grayer than last year in the light of the paper-shaded bridge lamp that, like most of the furnishings of the house, will not be missed if ski tenants destroy it. "Four diamonds," Andy Tyler says, hoping that Deborah Neusner will have the sense to put him back into spades. The Neusners, who spent their time at college less frivolously than the others, rarely play cards of any kind, and Deborah was pressed into service only because Marge pleaded a headache and has gone back into her bedroom. Husbands and wives cannot be partners, and should not be at the same table. "Double," Lee Englehardt says. *Take me out of diamonds,* Andy Tyler thinks intensely, so intensely the message feels engraved on the smoke above his head. "Pass," Deborah Neusner says, weakly. "Four hearts," says Bernadette Maloney, feeling sorry for Deborah, knowing that being so close to Lee upsets her; the two had an affair years ago, a fling that ended up in the air, so in a sense it was never over. That is one of the Englehardts' charms, their ability to leave things up in the air, like jugglers in a freeze-frame. "Four spades," Andy pronounces with great relief, praying that Deborah will now have the wit to pass again. "Five diamonds?" she hesitantly says.

Josh Neusner reads a very old *National Geographic* he found in the woodbox beneath the stairs. It is so old that the photos are mostly black-and-white, and the type is different, and the cultural biases are overt. These bare-breasted women and woolly chiefs with bones through their noses are clearly, cheerfully being condescended to, anthropologically. This would never do now; isn't it one of the tenets of our times that all cultural formations, even cannibalism and foot-binding, make equally good sense? Josh's neck and shoulders ache from splitting his weight in wood. He has taken a glass of dinner wine away from the table and rests it on the broad arm of the corduroy-covered armchair by the dying fire that Ralph built. Suddenly the wine seems an odious, fermented substance, and the hilarious chatter from the bridge tables inane, poisonous. Above his head, on the swaybacked ceiling, footsteps scurry and rustle like those of giant rats. The children; he wants to go upstairs to check on the girls and tuck in the twins, but during these leaf-season weekends the children are invited to make their own society, and exist like a pack of shadows in the corners of the grownup fun. Strange places, strange customs; cannibalism, he reads, is almost never a matter of hunger but of ingesting the enemy's spiritual virtues. He wonders why liquor is called spirits. The cheap wine tastes dead. The thumping and scurrying overhead slowly weakens, loses its grip. He himself, when at midnight both tables loudly announce another rubber, goes upstairs and puts himself into one of the upper bunk beds in the men's dormitory. The window in the upstairs hall where Deborah and Bernadette met and talked this afternoon now displays white, scratchy, many-tentacled frost ferns above the radiator.

The bunk isn't quite long enough for him to stretch out in. He thinks of Marge alone in her room below him, her sulky mystery, her beautiful dancer's body. She was the queen of all this and now is trying to withdraw. He could sneak down the back stairs and they could spin together. Josh cannot sleep. The noise from below, the sound of rampant spirits, is too great. And when at last the bridge concludes and people begin to clatter up the stairs, he still cannot sleep. Andy underneath him, Lee and Bill across the room in the other double bunk, all fall asleep swiftly, and snore. Lee is the most spectacular—nasal arpeggios that encompass octaves, up and down the scale —but Bill plugs steadily away, his rhythmic wheeze like a rusty engine that will not die, and Andy demonstrates, a few feet below Josh's face, the odd talent of coughing in his sleep, coughing prolongedly without waking himself. Josh feels trapped. A broadsword of light falls diagonally across the floor, and there are faint, halting footsteps. One of the Tremaynes' cats has pushed open the door and is nosing about. Josh strains his eyes and sees it is the gray one with extra toes. He reaches out from the upper bunk with his foot and nudges the door shut again.

The house's huge content of protoplasm ebbs in little stages into quiet, into sleep: twenty-six other human beings—he counts them up, including the boys in the barn—soaking up restorative dreams, leaving him stranded, high and listening, his ears staring into the tense, circumambient wilderness. Never again. This is the last time he and his family are going to come for this weekend to Vermont. This is torture.

Bacon! The crisp, illicit, life-enhancing smell of it penetrates the room, his nostrils, his brain. Josh sees that the three other bunks are empty, the day is well advanced. He must have fallen asleep after all. He remembers, as the wee hours became larger and lighter, conducting mental negotiations, amid the brouhaha of the other men's snoring, with the gray cat, who seemed to be here, and then there, in the room. Now the animal is nowhere to be seen, and Josh must have dropped off for an hour or two.

The house, like a ship under way, is shaking, trembling, with the passage of feet, with activity. A maul and wedge ring: Lee Englehardt is splitting his weight in wood. Car doors slam: the Maloneys, all seven of them, are going off to Mass. They'll bring back Sunday papers and a whole list of staples—crackers, orange juice, cheddar cheese, tonic water—that Marge has pressed upon them. She seems in a better mood. She is wearing, instead of the sullen peasant skirt and sweater and shawl of last night, tight shiny red pants that make her legs look almost as thin and sexy as her daughter Milly's. Her hair is done up in a fat blond-gray pigtail that bounces on her back as she friskily, bossily prepares breakfast, wave after wave, flipping six pieces of bacon at a time with a long aluminum spatula. "Three pieces per person, and that includes you, Fritz Tyler," she says severely. "Those who like their scrambled eggs runny, come serve yourselves right now. Those who don't, get at the end of the line. We don't believe in Sugar Pops in this household, Seth Neusner. Up here in the mountains it's all bran and granola and yucky fiber. Betsey, go out to the woodpile and tell your father the baby's just spit up all over herself and your mother's in the bathroom."

Ralph comes sleepily into the kitchen, the first cigar of the day in his mouth, its lit end making a triangle with his two red eyes. He is barefoot—pathetic white feet, with ingrown yellow toenails and long toes crushed together—and is coming from the wrong direction, if we assume he slept in the master bedroom, at the front of the downstairs. He hasn't slept in the master bedroom. Beyond the kitchen lies a small room with a few cots in it, for an overflow ski crowd. Ralph slept in there. He did not sleep with Marge! The knowledge runs silently through the mingled families, chastening them. For this weekend Marge and Ralph are like the mother and father, even of the other adults. We want them to love each other. For if they do not love each other, how can they love and take care of us?

Marge seems intent on showing that she can do it all. She ruffles Ralph's head as he sits groggily at the breakfast table. Grownups eat at the long dining-room table, where one of the bridge groups played last night, and children at the round butcher-block table in the center of the kitchen. "Achey, achey?" Marge asks, cooingly.

"T-too much grape juice, Mother," Ralph says.

They are trying to make up. We all feel better, bolder. Josh Neusner describes his terrible night, quite comically as he relives his mental negotiations with the mysterious cat, but Lee Englehardt, having come in from wood-splitting to care for Dorothea, without smiling states, "Jews make poor campers." We are shocked. It is the sort of thing that can be said only among intimate friends or confirmed enemies. And why would they be enemies?

Josh, remembering Lee's aggressive unconscious arpeggios, and his position at the card table next to Deborah, chooses to accept the remark as a piece of ethnology, arrived at innocently: Lee is an insurance salesman whose father was a professor of history, and as if in compensation for a lesser career he collects such small pedantic conclusions as that Jews make poor campers. Lee's charm really rests on his insecurity. Josh chooses to keep playing the clown. He covers his forehead with one hand and moans, "I can't sleep without a woman. Men are *hide*ous."

Deborah, a little later, when they meet on the stair landing, says, "Baby, I'm sorry you had such a poor night; you should have played bridge."

"I wasn't asked."

"You didn't want to be asked. I would have given you my seat. Andy Tyler kept wanting to kill me, I could tell."

"The only person I like here is Linda," Josh petulantly volunteers. "And Dorothea," he adds, to soften it.

This reminds her: "Ruth didn't sleep in the girls' dormitory last night. Marge set her up in the living room with the baby after everybody else had gone to bed, in case Dorothea yelled. So the bunk above me is empty if you really want it. Linda and Bernadette wouldn't care."

"It would make me look like a sissy." He goes on, "And then yesterday I kept nearly cutting off my foot splitting their idiotic wood."

"Come on, honey, try to get into the spirit of things."

"It's all barbaric," he says, so lightheaded with lack of sleep that every perception has a translucent, revelatory quality. Suddenly, he is having a very good time. He goes down and has some more coffee and bacon and discusses Boston-area private schools with Linda and Lee, who are disenchanted with highly touted Brookline High.

The Maloneys return laden with the Sunday New York *Times,* the Boston *Globe,* and the Burlington *Free Press.* The children fight over the funnies, the men over the sports and financial pages. The day proceeds with that unreality peculiar to Sunday; one hour seems as long as two, and the next goes by in ten minutes. A great deal of the conversation concerns where various other people are. Marge is in the car, with her son, Skip, and her dog, Wolf, performing some errands having to do with quantities of natural fleece—uncarded, greasy-wet with lanolin—to be found at a farm fifteen miles away. It turns out that Andy Tyler has gone along for the ride. Bernadette Maloney is in Marge's garden salvaging tomatoes and zucchini from last night's frost; Mark and Mary and Teddy are helping her, by holding the paper bags with bored expressions and then by throwing the rotten vegetables at one another. Linda Tyler, having been told that her husband has disappeared with Marge, announces that she will go on a mushrooming walk in the woods; her daughter, Audrey, and Betsey Englehardt and the two Neusner girls come with her, like a procession of little witches in training. Christine Tremayne—who has inherited Marge's dull complexion and Ralph's stocky build, unfortunately—is showing Teresa Maloney the barn, and the Neusner twins tag along. The interior is awesome; some high small windows and the gaps between the slats admit shafts of light as if in a cathedral. They have all seen slides of cathedrals at school. The light reveals an atmosphere glittering with dust, dust from the hay still stacked in staircases of bales at one end, a dust that thickens the air, that makes light visible while lessening it. The children feel deep in the sea of time. Elements of old farm machinery rust in corners here and there, with pieces of lumber, ten-gallon milk cans, strawberry boxes, and glass eggs. They find an old rope-quoit set, and the four of them play until a dispute between Seth and Zebulon makes it no fun.

Milly Tremayne and Fritz Tyler—who knows where they have gone to? Mary Maloney, having left the garden party in tearful disgust when Mark caught her right on the mouth with a rotten zucchini, has come into the house; the television set gets only one channel, and that one full of ghosts from the hills and valleys between here and the station, but she is happily watching some man with big eyebrows and a Southern accent give a sermon, and a lot of fat ladies in glitzy dresses sing hymns, until her father comes and tells her she should be outdoors in the sunshine.

What sunshine? A cloud has just passed across the sun, not a little cloud but a large dark one, with a wide leaden center and agitated, straggling edges—a cloud it seems the surrounding mountains have given birth to.

Bill Maloney and Lee Englehardt find a shovel and refresh the holes that take the posts for the volleyball net. Nature fills in the holes from one leaf season to the next. Then they find and unwind the two-by-fours and the net and the guy ropes and pegs where they have reposed all wound and tangled up in the barn since last October. As they move slowly, in the quickly moving cloud shadows, through the tedious ritual of setting up the net, Lee asks Bill, "How was Mass?"

Bill, who has a moonface and delicate pink Irish skin, looks at Lee cockeyed and says, "Like it always is. That's the beauty of it, Mr. Eng."

Lee makes a rueful nod, concluding to himself that this is the essence of male companionship: cards close to the chest.

Inside the kitchen, Bernadette and Deborah are making lunch—a cauldron of clam chowder Bernadette has lugged up from Boston; and a tuna salad Deborah is whipping up out of four cans plus chopped celery, scallions, mayonnaise, lemon juice, and a head of lettuce; and a tinned ham for those who, like most of the children, hate fish. As the two women slide and bump past each other between Marge's old-fashioned black soapstone sink and the wooden countertops on either side, they quietly talk about the situation between Marge and Ralph, which seems far gone, and that between Andy and Linda, which seems to be heading for trouble.

Ruth Englehardt comes into the kitchen with her curly-headed toddler propped on her hip and a cigarette tilting at an opposite angle out of her mouth. "So the Queen of Sheba has eloped with the handyman," she says, "the Queen of Sheba" referring to Marge and "the handyman" to Andy, not just because of his name but because of his tendency, well known to all the women, to reach out under the table and touch. "If you two were about to discuss Lee and me, I'll leave," she adds; then she begins to cough, and one eye cries from the smoke. She sets down the heavy child and watches her stagger across the worn linoleum to one of the low old mahogany counters, where Dorothea quicker than thought reaches up and flips a sharp knife down past her own ear. Ruth deftly retrieves the knife and her daughter; the little girl, as she feels herself being lifted, reflexively spreads her legs to sit astride her mother's hip. The three women talk, touching their friends with their tongues not to harm them but to give themselves pleasure; little new can be offered, mere pinches or slivers added to the salad, tiny, almost meaningless remarks or glimpses that yet do enhance the flavor. The conversation, too, serves a purpose of location, of locating the others on a continuum of happiness or its opposite, of satisfying the speakers that the others are within hailing distance in this our dark passage through life, with its mating and birthing, its getting and spending, its gathering and scattering. Some, indeed, are even closer than hailing distance, for from underneath the floor there comes a sudden grumbling and scraping: their host wrapping more insulation.

Lunch is served, then volleyball. Let's not do the volleyball. Let's just say that once there were five on a side and now the children have grown so that three eight-person teams must be fielded, and some of the boys lunge and swagger and swat as lustily as their fathers. More lustily, since these powers are new to them. Matthew Maloney knocks Audrey Tyler flat on her back, and Fritz Tyler comes down from a spike right on Deborah Neusner's toe, so that she thinks it might be broken. She thinks she heard it snap, at the still center of the swelling red cloud of pain. She hops off the court. "This hasn't been their weekend," Ruth Englehardt says *sotto voce* to Marge, who has returned from her drive to buy the wool.

"I just can't get excited about any of it," Marge confides to Ruth, under the net, while Bill Maloney, with much drolly elaborate ceremony, is winding up to serve. For all of his elaboration, the ball flies too high and sails out. The other side hoots. The sight of such a throng, in suburban shorts and halters and stencilled sweatshirts, is so unusual here in Vermont this time of year that cars and pickup trucks slow down on the little quiet unnumbered road. One truck (passing, everybody later agrees, for about the fourth time) fails to brake when the ball, hit wild by Eve Neusner, bounces under his chassis and, with a sound as sickening as that of a box turtle being crushed beneath the wheels, bursts. Then the truck brakes. Ralph slightly knows the driver, and a pleasant and apologetic palaver takes place by the fence, though the red-bearded, red-hatted face of the truck driver doesn't look apologetic. Mark Maloney has brought his soccer ball, and that is substituted, though it is enough heavier that a number of the females complain of stinging hands and sprained wrists.

So we have done the volleyball after all. The sun, momentarily appearing between the ridge of a mountain and the edge of another great cloud, throws the shadows of the poles right to the edge of the road. The smallest children—Teddy and Teri Maloney, Seth and Zebulon Neusner, even little Dorothea Englehardt, the knees of whose bib overalls are filthy and whose lips drool from sucking on a milk-

weed pod—scrimmage in the trampled grass and try to heave the
heavy soccer ball, cunningly stitched together of pentagons, over the
sagging net. The clouds have thickened and darkened so as to form a
continuous ragged canopy. A cool wind blows as if through a hole in a
tent.

The exercise has left the adults feeling contentious, vigorous, and
thirsty. They rush to the bottles. They go upstairs one by one to take
showers in the only bathroom on the second floor. Josh Neusner by
now is feeling quite delirious with fatigue and is experiencing small,
flashlike epiphanies of love for each of his friends as they move in and
out of the living room, up the stairs, out of doors, and back in. They
all look very tall to him, even the children, from where he lies on the
plaid couch, fighting off the sleep that refused to come last night. He
shuts his eyes a moment and when he opens them, Bill Maloney, his
oldest son, Matthew, Lee Englehardt, and Josh's own wife, Deborah,
are over by the far wall, where the wallpaper has been scorched and
curled by the pipes of an old woodstove that was taken away when
Ralph installed the new heating system whose pipes he has been so
desperately, patiently insulating. The four people over there are engaged in a contest of endurance—seeing how long each can sit against
the wall, posed as if on a chair that is not there, before the muscle pain
in their thighs forces them to surrender and stand. Bill Maloney times
each contestant with a watch; his own son seems to be winning, until
Lee Englehardt, exposing that something fanatic and needy he keeps
hidden behind his mild eyes, continues to hold the pose—straight back
flat on the wall, thighs at a ninety-degree angle—for the number of
seconds needed to win. Bill counts off the seconds. Lee's bald head fills
with blood like the bulb of a thermometer. Deborah is visibly impressed, even moved, by Lee's macho effort. Her long jaw has dropped
as if she might swoon. In women, Josh thinks, admiration and pity are
faces of one emotion.

Other games are introduced, other feats are performed. Andy Tyler,
it turns out, slim and flexible as he is, can hold a broom in both hands
and jump over it without letting go. He can then, the broom now held
behind him, reverse the trick, hopping up like a handkerchief pulled
through a ring. Others try, and kick the broom to the floor with a

smack, or else themselves fall to the floor like misfired cannon balls.
Ralph Tremayne demonstrates his ability to set a coin on his uplifted
elbow and with the same hand grab it in midair. He can even do it
with a small stack of quarters. Now coins are flying all over the room,
and scatter into the corners. Ralph, encouraged, revives an old drill
from his college football years; you squat, he eagerly explains, and fall
backwards, and push off with your hands at your shoulders so that
you land back on your feet. Every time he tries it, Marge's collection
of stippled milk glass on the mantel trembles, and Ralph, after a tanta-
lizing, teetering moment of near-success, drops with a plaster-cracking
thud onto his back. Others also fail. Josh, amid much noisy skepti-
cism, gets up off the sofa and succeeds at his first try. He startles
himself, too. He used to be good at gym, a talent he had thought
unusable in real life. In the aftermath of his exertion the roomful of
people lurches slightly, like the first hesitant movement of a carrousel
when all the rides are sold.

   Linda Tyler introduces a contest whereby a box of matches is set on
the floor a forearm's length from the kneeling person's knees. She
demonstrates. Then, her hands clasped behind her, she explains that
she will attempt to knock the matchbox over with her nose. She does
this easily. But when Bill Maloney tries, he falls forward onto his thin-
skinned moonface. Even Lee's stubborn determination fails; his nose,
grimace though he will, comes up a millimeter short. Bernadette, however, performs the trick without effort, and Deborah also. There is
something affecting in the position of abasement the women assume
on the floor, their hair falling forward, their hands behind them like a
manacled slave's, their hips broad and round in the crouching position, their feet—bare or in little ballerina slippers—soles up beneath
their hips. It's all in the hips, Linda explains, patting her nicely convex
own: weight distribution. Almost no man can knock the matchbox
over, and almost every woman can. Even Ruth, long and lanky as she
is, condescending to try it, illustrates this sexist truth: though there is
a precarious moment of balance striven for, the matchbox falls. Everybody cheers, and Dorothea, put to sleep in Marge's bedroom, cries at
the sudden loud noise.

   And then there is leg wrestling, man against man and man against woman, if the woman is wearing slacks. How strangely sweet and clarifying it is to be lying hip to hip, face to feet, with someone of the opposite sex while the circle of excited faces above counts, "One! Two! Three!" On the count of three, the inside legs, lifted on each count, are joined and a brief struggle ensues, brief as the mating of animals, and ends with a moment's exhausted repose side by side. And then there are ways in which a woman can lift a man, by standing back to back and hooking arms at the elbows, and ways in which two people, holding tight to each other's ankles, can somersault the length of a carpet. There seems no end to what bodies can do, but at last Bill Maloney complains that if he has another drink he will fall down and why the hell isn't there any food?

The Englehardts remember the beef casserole they were going to heat. Milly Tremayne, fortunately, with the help of Fritz Tyler, Becky Neusner, Betsey Englehardt, and Mark Maloney, has got the meal started in the oven and fed the younger, ravenous children on baloney sandwiches, chili, and tuna salad left over from other meals. The television set has been rescued from the living room and plugged in upstairs, its rabbit ears augmented with Reynolds Wrap that the Neusner twins, who are clever about such things, took from a kitchen drawer. The children also have fed the three dogs and two cats, even though, unbeknownst to all except the animals (who didn't tell), Marge had fed them earlier. She disappeared into her bedroom when little Dorothea began to cry and never, come to think of it, returned. Worn out with their drinking and wrestling, the grownups in sudden spurts of familial conscience now scold the children for being so addicted to television (some dreadful car-chase thing, totally unsuitable) and pack them into their bunk beds and cots and sleeping bags.

Dinner, served at ten o'clock, feels anticlimactic; angels of awkward silence keep passing overhead, and Linda Tyler, quite prettily, keeps yawning, showing the velvety red lining of her mouth, her tense tongue, the horseshoe arc of her lower teeth. Deborah Neusner is sure she has broken her toe; she reinjured it when the corduroy armchair tipped over while she was trying to do a headstand on it. Ruth Englehardt says, "There's a hospital in Barre," which might mean that they should drive her to it, or that it is too far to drive anyone to, or that

Deborah is being ridiculous to think she has a broken toe. Ruth has
not been blind to the frequency with which, in the night's tumbling,
Deborah and Lee bumped or rubbed against each other. Bernadette
Maloney says she just can't keep her eyes open another minute; it
must be the Vermont air.

Only one table for bridge can be mustered. Bill and Lee are keen to
play, and it seems Ruth might be willing but that something during
the evening has offended her—perhaps being the last woman invited to
knock the matchbox over, perhaps Marge's somehow taking over little
Dorothea, perhaps feeling that as the mother of a child much younger
than anyone else's she is not as free as they, as frivolous—and she says
no, she thinks she'll put a load of dishes into the washer and then go to
bed. Bernadette and Linda help her. Even Andy Tyler makes a move
for the kitchen, his slim hands lifted as if to pat something agreeably
yielding, but the other men coarsely, in voices that grind together like
gears and gravel, insist he play bridge with them. Ralph, who at the
dinner table, without warning, while plucking at his mustache, seemed
to turn green and wiggly like the elephant king in *Babar*, has disappeared into the dismal room, beyond the kitchen, where he slept last
night. Ruth's helpers at the dishwasher have taken from her the cue
that the time has come in the weekend to say no, and they, at first
coquettishly and then quite firmly, resist the men's importunities to
make the fourth. This leaves Deborah, who has been sitting on the
living-room floor sorrowfully inspecting her bare foot. Her feet and
legs have a certain chunkiness, a bit like that of children; the mis-
match of her doughy, low-waisted figure with the fineness of her face
—the tapering long chin, the moist brown eyes, the pensive dents at
the corners of her mouth, a hint of haughtiness in the high bridge of
her nose—forms the secret of her charm, her vulnerability. She says
that with the pain in her toe she wouldn't be able to sleep anyway, so
why not? The men cheer. She turns and explains to someone behind
her, rolling her eyes so the whites seem to leap from a Biblical tableau,
"Sweetie, these men are crazy to have me play bridge with them!"

But Josh is no longer standing there, solicitously. He has crept
upstairs. Fleeing the scene of last night's horror, so bone-weary he

seems to be floating, he crosses the hall in his pajamas and looks into the girls' dormitory, where Deborah had said there was an extra bunk. All four beds are empty; he tries to imagine which one his wife sleeps in and, silent and light as last night's cat, climbs into the bunk above it. A low-watt light bulb under a brown shade patterned in pinholes is burning across the room; he pulls the covers over his head and wishes himself invisible and very small. There is a soft sound around him, distinct from the conversation and scraping of chairs downstairs. A sound with its own life, with subtle pauses and renewals and changes of mind. Of course. Rain. Those huge clouds this afternoon.

He is not conscious of falling asleep. He is awakened by some small noise, a delicate alteration, in the room. He opens one eye, frightened that if he opens two he will be ousted from this haven. Linda Tyler has entered, in a white nightgown. Her shadowy nipples tap the cloth from within. Her entire slender body appears angelic, lifted at all its points by a lightness that leaves her preoccupied face behind, sullen and even ugly, unaware of being watched. This impassive sad face looms close to his eye, and vanishes. She has put herself into the bunk beneath him. The lamp with its bright pinholes has been switched off. Josh can just barely make out across the room, by the hall light that slides itself like a huge yellow letter under the door, that Bernadette Maloney, with her splash of black hair, is asleep in the lower bunk and some other woman, unseeable, in the top. The rain continues its purring, its caressing of the roof shingles, its leisurely debate with itself, drowning out the gentle breathing of the women. This is lovely. This is bliss.

When Monday morning arrives, everyone is irritable, though the rain has stopped. Only Josh, it would seem, slept well. Evidently, Marge emerged from her bedroom when Ruth, after kibitzing at bridge for an hour, went in, to transfer Dorothea to the living room, and Marge suggested to Deborah that she switch beds with her, so the other women wouldn't be disturbed when the bridge at last was over. Also, there was something mysterious about her not being there in case Ralph "got ideas." So Marge herself must have been the unseeable woman in the other top bunk. The bridge had lasted until three.

Deborah has taken so much aspirin her stomach burns and she got hardly an hour's worth of sleep, in Marge's bed, but this morning she does doubt that the toe is actually broken. If it was broken, she couldn't take a step; she demonstrates, on the kitchen floor, some limping strides, and Josh thinks of how lightly Linda moved into his vision last night, her breasts uplifted behind their veil, and how he slept all night with her beneath him, awakening once or twice with an erection but listening to the rain intermingled with the women's gentle breathing and sinking with his steely burden deep into sweet sleep again.

He volunteers, so full of energy, to go out and split some more wood. Ralph, who looks only half sick today, but with a curious pinkness around his eyes as if he were wearing his old rosy ski goggles, says one of the boys broke off the maul, up at the neck, by swinging and missing the wedge. The boy, unnamed, is Matthew Maloney, and Mark and Mary were leaders in this morning's plot to make French toast for the children's breakfast, which has left everything in the kitchen sticky with syrup. So the Maloneys as a family are in bad odor, and Bill and Bernadette go out on the porch to fight about something—his staying up till three, perhaps, or her failure to supervise the making of the French toast.

She has been gossiping, actually, over coffee in the living room with Andy Tyler. As the weekend wears on the sex distinctions wear down, as limestone statues turn androgynous in the weather. Bill's drinking, Bernadette confided to Andy, really has passed well beyond the social stage, and she is afraid it's beginning to hurt him at work. As for herself, as soon as Teresa hits kindergarten, she's going back to nursing and complete her R.N.; once you have your cap, you're ready for anything. A woman has to think that way these days, no matter what the Church says—these ridiculous old men, who have never known love or had families, telling us how to behave. Seeing her wince as she moved her head for emphasis, Andy offered to massage her neck, and she let him, not stretching out on the sofa—that would have been too much, at least at this stage—but perching on the edge of the corduroy armchair so he could get at her shoulder muscles with his thumbs. She groaned, "That feels so good. It's sleeping with a strange pillow does

me in every time. My doctor says I have a very delicate cervical area.
Up top, of course."

Perhaps this massage is what she and Bill were fighting about. It
hasn't been a very good weekend for Bernadette, what with Deborah
and Ruth between them getting such a lock on Lee. The Maloneys, at
any rate, are the first to pack up and leave, though it takes them all
morning. They have all sorts of yard work at home to do, and they
want to beat that terrible rush, it happens every Columbus Day, on 89
and 93, especially at the Hooksett tollbooth. The Neusners wave good-
bye from the porch and wonder if they, too, shouldn't be thinking
about going. They are tender with each other, each having endured a
night without sleep, and each having fallen more deeply in love with a
person outside the marriage—with Lee, with Linda. Also, the twins
have a Cub Scout party in Newton they had hoped to get to. The
father of one of the pack leaders knows a linebacker for the Patriots
and he's supposed to come and give the kids an inspirational message.

As for Marge and Ralph, they seem pleased to have gotten through
the weekend with no more showing than did. They beg the Englehardts and Tylers not to go. The six of them, the hard core, sit
around in the living room lunching on leftovers and finishing a bottle
of red wine found at the back of the refrigerator. There are few leftovers, and the supply of wood also appears to have been exhausted, for
what is in the fireplace smokes and fails to catch, in spite of repeated
kindlings by muttering, grunting Ralph. Even the cigar in the center
of his face has gone out. Every motion he makes, up or down, seems to
give him pain: old football injuries. "Y-you young fellas, w-w-wait till
you get to be my age," he says to Andy and Lee, though he is only a
year or two older.

They are sleepily at ease, these six, the two other couples gone. They
sit sprawled in a kind of spiritual deshabille, open to inspection, their
dismissive remarks about the Maloneys and Neusners desultory and
not unfond, their inventory of one another's failings and wounds
mostly silent, an unspoken ticking-off. "I asked Bill how Mass had
been," Lee complains, "and he nearly bit my head off." Andy contrib-
utes, "Bernadette gave me quite an earful, how she hates the Church. I
think she's fixing to bust out of the whole shmeer." "And oh my

goodness, I don't mean to be the complaining type," Ruth says, "but wasn't our little Debbie absolutely insufferable, a cat in with the catnip with all that bridge?" "They're very quick learners," Lee says, leaving who "they" are up in the air, and trusting Andy to keep silent about how little time he, Lee, spent in the boys' dormitory last night. His mild big blue eyes are still a baby's beneath his bald dome; Ruth's frizzy crown of honey-blond hair seems avid, as do her sharp nose and flexible quick mouth and the pockets of emaciated shadow beneath her cheekbones. She and Andy do most of the talking, Lee and Marge most of the appreciative laughing. Marge's good humor is striking; as the pressure of being a hostess lifts, she expands, and in her loose-hanging man's shirt distinctly shows middle-aged spread, the fleshly generosity of a beauty who has fulfilled her duties and knows herself to be, whatever shape the future will bring, basically beautiful. Her head-band today is turquoise. Ralph squints at her and appears both puz-zled and wise, a bloodshot old owl who can still swoop down from a branch and carry off in his claws a piping, furry treasure.

After an hour and a half of this, this complacent torpor, Linda can't stand it. She jumps up and announces she is going on another leaf walk. Do any of the littles want to go with her? Surprisingly, a few do, again all girls—Christine, Audrey, and Betsey. Also, Wolf comes; he misses Ginger and Toby. They file diagonally across the trampled softball field, leaving the barn behind them on the right, into the long strip of woods along the creek, which has grown up thick since the remote days when all this difficult land was cleared for farming. Bits of old stone wall and tumbled-in cellar holes hide in the woods. The sound of the cars on the road can barely be heard.

Linda gestures up and around her. "The bright colors we've all come all the way up here to admire are, above all, the turning leaves of the maple tree, especially the sugar maple, from which we get—?"

"Maple syrup," says Christine Tremayne, who knows she is homely, but will make up for it in life by being dutiful.

"But all the trees contribute, from the stately beech, which you can recognize by its smooth gray bark, and the birch family, of which you especially know the white, or paper, birch, from which the Indians used to make—?"

"Canoes," says Betsey Englehardt. She misses the Neusner twins, even though Zebulon did take the rope quoits and throw them down the well so nobody could play the game anymore. When she cried about it, her father explained to her at length why Jewish children are spoiled.

"The last trees to let go of their leaves are the oaks," Linda tells the children. She picks up an oak leaf and holds it out to impress upon them its lobed, deeply indented shape. "Even in the winter snows, the oak will cling to its old brown leaves. The *first* tree to let go tends to be another giant of the forest—the ash. Its leaves, the only opposite feather-compound leaves in the American forest, turn an unusual purplish-blue color, unlike anything else, and then suddenly, one day, are gone. Girls, look up and around you. Those who went walking with me Saturday, do you notice any difference?"

"More sky," says Audrey, her own daughter, who knows what answer she wants.

"That's right," Linda says, intensely grateful. "And yet, standing here, who can see a leaf fall?"

No one speaks. A minute passes. No leaf falls.

"Oh, if we stood here long enough," Linda concedes, "or if there were a wind, or a hard rain like we had last night; but normally it happens unobserved, the moment when the root of the stem, where the bud once was, decides the time has come to let go. But it happens." She looks upward and lifts her arms. The widened light falls upon her face and palms, and the little girls grow still, feeling threatened by something within the woman that she is pulling from the air, from the reds and golds trembling around them. "Nobody sees it happen, but it does. For suddenly, it seems, the woods are bare."

Magazines
Consulted

Agada, 2020 Essex Street, Berkeley, Calif. 94703

The Agni Review, P.O. Box 229, Cambridge, Mass. 02238

Alaska Quarterly Review, Dept. of English, 3221 Providence Drive, Anchorage, Alaska 99508

American Book Review, P.O. Box 188, Cooper Station, New York, N.Y. 10003

The American Voice, The Kentucky Foundation for Women, Inc., Heyburn Bldg., Suite 1215, Broadway at 4th Avenue, Louisville, Ky. 40202

Antaeus, Ecco Press, 26 West 17th Street, New York, N.Y. 10011

Antietam Review, 33 West Washington Street, Hagerstown, Md. 21740

The Antioch Review, P.O. Box 148, Yellow Springs, Ohio 45387

The Apalachee Quarterly, P.O. Box 20106, Tallahassee, Fla. 32304

Arizona Quarterly, University of Arizona, Tucson, Ariz. 85721

Arrival, 48 Shattuck Square, Suite 194, Berkeley, Calif. 94704

Ascent, Department of English, University of Illinois, Urbana, Ill. 61801

Asimov's Science Fiction Magazine, Davis Publications, 380 Lexington Avenue, New York, N.Y. 10017

The Atlantic, 8 Arlington Street, Boston, Mass. 02116

Aura, P.O. Box 76, University Center, The University of Alabama at Birmingham, Birmingham, Ala. 35294

Backbone, P.O. Box 95315, Seattle, Wash. 98145

Black Ice, 571 Howell Avenue, Cincinnati, Ohio 45220

The Black Warrior Review, P.O. Box 2936, University, Ala. 34586

The Bloomsbury Review, 2933 Wyandot Street, Denver, Colo. 80211

Boston Review, 991 Massachusetts Avenue, Cambridge, Mass. 02138

Buffalo Spree, 4511 Harlem Road, P.O. Box 38, Buffalo, N.Y. 14226

California Quarterly, 100 Sproul Hall, University of California, Davis, Calif. 95616

Canadian Fiction Magazine, P.O. Box 46422, Station G, Vancouver, B.C., Canada V6R 4G7

Carolina Quarterly, Greenlaw Hall 066-A, University of North Carolina, Chapel Hill, N.C. 27514

The Chariton Review, The Division of Language and Literature, Northeast Missouri State University, Kirksville, Mo. 63501

Chelsea, P.O. Box 5880, Grand Central Station, New York, N.Y. 10163

Chicago, WFMT, Inc. 3 Illinois Center, 303 E. Wacker Drive, Chicago, Ill. 60601

Chicago Review, 970 East 58th Street, Box C, University of Chicago, Chicago, Ill. 60637

Cimarron Review, 208 Life Sciences East, Oklahoma State University, Stillwater, Okla. 74078 - 0273

Clinton St. Quarterly, P.O. Box 3588, Portland, Oregon 97208

Clockwatch Review, 737 Penbrook Way, Hartland, Wisc. 53021

Colorado Review, Department of English, Colorado State University, Fort Collins, Colo. 80523

Columbia, 404 Dodge Hall, Columbia University, New York, N.Y. 10027

Confrontation, Department of English, C. W. Post of Long Island University, Greenvale, N.Y. 11548

Cosmopolitan, 224 West 57th Street, New York, N.Y. 10019

Crosscurrents, 2200 Glastonbury Rd., Westlake, Calif. 92361

Cutbank, c/o Dept. of English, University of Montana, Missoula, Mont. 59812

Denver Quarterly, Department of English, University of Denver, Denver, Colo. 80210

Descant, Department of English, Texas Christian University, Fort Worth, Tex. 76129

Epoch, 254 Goldwyn Smith Hall, Cornell University, Ithaca, N.Y. 14853

Esquire, 2 Park Avenue, New York, N.Y. 10016

Farmer's Market, P.O. Box 1272, Galesburg, Illinois 61402

The Fessenden Review, Box 7272, San Diego, Calif. 92107

Fiction, Dept. of English, The City College of New York, N.Y. 10031

Fiction 86, Exile Press, P.O. Box 1768, Novato, Calif. 94948

Fiction/86, The Paycock Press, P.O. Box 30906, Bethesda, Maryland 20814

Fiction International, Department of English, St. Lawrence University, Canton, N.Y. 13617

Fiction Network, P.O. Box 5651, San Francisco, Calif. 94101

The Fiction Review, P.O. Box 1508, Tempe, Arizona 85281

The Fiddlehead, The Observatory, University of New Brunswick, P.O. Box 4400, Fredericton, N.B., Canada E3B 5A3

Five Fingers Review, 100 Valencia Street, Suite #303, San Francisco, Calif. 94103

The Florida Review, Dept. of English, University of Central Florida, Orlando, Florida 32816

FM. Five, P.O. Box 882108, San Francisco, Calif. 94188

Formations, 832 Chilton Lane, Wilmette, Illinois 60091

Forum, Ball State University, Muncie, Ind. 47306

Four Quarters, La Salle College, Philadelphia, Pa. 19141

Frank, Mixed General Delivery, APO, New York, N.Y. 09777

Gargoyle, P.O. Box 3567, Washington, D.C. 20007

Gentlemen's Quarterly, 350 Madison Avenue, New York, N.Y. 10017

The Georgia Review, University of Georgia, Athens, Ga. 30602

Grain, Box 1154, Regina, Saskatchewan, Canada S4P 3B4

Grand Street, 50 Riverside Drive, New York, N.Y. 10024

Granta, 13 White Street, New York, N.Y. 10013

Gray's Sporting Journal, 205 Willow Street, P.O. Box 2549, South Hamilton, Mass. 01982

Great River Review, 211 West 7th, Winona, Minn. 55987

The Greensboro Review, University of North Carolina, Greensboro, N.C. 27412

Hard Copies, Dept. of English and Foreign Languages, California State Polytechnic University, Pomona, Calif. 91768

Harper's Magazine, 2 Park Avenue, New York, N.Y. 10016

Hawaii Review, Hemenway Hall, University of Hawaii, Honolulu, Hawaii 96822

High Plains Literary Review, 180 Adams Street, Suite 250, Denver, Colorado 80206

The Hoboken Terminal, P.O. Box 841, Hoboken, N.J. 07030

The Hudson Review, 684 Park Avenue, New York, N.Y. 10021

Image—The Magazine of Northern California, 110 Fifth Street, San Francisco, Calif. 94103

Indiana Review, 316 North Jordan Avenue, Bloomington, Ind. 47405

Iowa Review, EPB 453, University of Iowa, Iowa City, Iowa 52240

The Journal, The Ohio State University, Department of English, 164 West 17th Avenue, Columbus, Ohio 43210

Kairos, Hermes House Press, 900 West End Avenue, #10-D, New York, N.Y. 10025

Kansas Quarterly, Department of English, Kansas State University, Manhattan, Kansas 66506

The Kenyon Review, Kenyon College, Gambier, Ohio 43022

Ladies' Home Journal, 641 Lexington Avenue, New York, N.Y. 10022

The Literary Review, Fairleigh Dickinson University, Teaneck, N.J. 07666

Mademoiselle, 350 Madison Avenue, New York, N.Y. 10017

The Magazine of Fantasy and Science Fiction, Box 56, Cornwall, Conn. 06753

Magical Blend, P.O. Box 11303, San Francisco, Calif. 94101

Malahat Review, University of Victoria, Victoria, B.C., Canada V8W 2Y2

The Massachusetts Review, Memorial Hall, University of Massachusetts, Amherst, Mass. 01002

McCall's, 230 Park Avenue, New York, N.Y. 10017

Medical Heritage, Georgetown University Hospital, 3800 Reservoir Road, N.W., Washington, D.C. 20007

Memphis, 460 Tennessee St., P.O. Box 256, Memphis, Tenn. 38101

Memphis State Review, Department of English, Memphis State University, Memphis, Tenn. 38152

Michigan Quarterly Review, 3032 Rackham Building, University of Michigan, Ann Arbor, Mich. 48109

Mid-American Review, 106 Hanna Hall, Bowling Green State University, Bowling Green, Ohio 43403

Midstream, 515 Park Avenue, New York, N.Y. 10022

The Missouri Review, Department of English, 231 Arts and Sciences, University of Missouri, Columbia, Mo. 65211

Mother Jones, 1663 Mission Street, San Francisco, Calif. 94103

MSS, Box 530, Department of English, SUNY-Binghamton, Binghamton, N.Y. 13901

The Nantucket Review, P.O. Box 1234, Nantucket, Mass. 02554

The Nassau Review, Nassau Community College, Garden City, N.Y. 11530

The Nebraska Review, The Creative Writing Program, University of Nebraska-Omaha, Omaha, Neb. 68182-0324

New America, Dept. of English Language and Literature, Humanities Bldg. 217, Albuquerque, N.M. 87131

The New Black Mask, 2006 Sumter Street, Columbia, S.C. 29201

New Directions, 80 Eighth Avenue, New York, N.Y. 10011

New England Review and Breadloaf Quarterly, Middlebury College, Middlebury, Vt. 05753

New Letters, University of Missouri-Kansas City, Kansas City, Mo. 64110

New Mexico Humanities Review, The Editors, Box A, New Mexico Tech., Socorro, N.M. 57801

The New Renaissance, 9 Heath Road, Arlington, Mass. 02174

New Virginia Review, 1306 East Cary Street, 2-A, Richmond, Virginia 23219

The New Yorker, 25 West 43rd, New York, N.Y. 10036

The North American Review, University of Northern Iowa, 1222 West 27th Street, Cedar Falls, Iowa 50613

North Dakota Quarterly, University of North Dakota, Box 8237, Grand Forks, N.D. 58202

Northwest Review, 129 French Hall, University of Oregon, Eugene, Ore. 97403

The Ohio Review, Ellis Hall, Ohio University, Athens, Ohio 45701

Omni, 1965 Broadway, New York, N.Y. 10067

The Ontario Review, 9 Honey Brook Drive, Princeton, N.J. 08540

Orim, Box 1904A, Yale Station, New Haven, Conn. 06520

Other Voices, 820 Ridge Road, Highland Park, Ill. 60035

The Paris Review, 541 East 72nd Street, New York, N.Y. 10021

The Partisan Review, 128 Bay State Road, Boston, Mass. 02215/552 Fifth Avenue, New York, N.Y. 10036

Passages North, William Bonifas Fine Arts Center, 7th Street and 1st Avenue South, Escanaba, Mich. 49829

The Pennsylvania Review, University of Pittsburgh, Department of English, 526 C.L., Pittsburgh, Penn. 15260

Phylon, 223 Chestnut Street, S.W., Atlanta, Ga. 30314

Playboy, 919 North Michigan Avenue, Chicago, Ill. 60611

Playgirl, 801 Second Ave., New York, N.Y. 10017

Ploughshares, Box 529, Cambridge, Mass. 02139

Prairie Schooner, Andrews Hall, University of Nebraska, Lincoln, Neb. 68588

Puerto Del Sol, English Dept., New Mexico State University, Box 3E, Las Cruces, N.M. 88003

The Quarterly, 201 East 50th Street, New York, N.Y. 10022

Quarterly West, 312 Olpin Union, University of Utah, Salt Lake City, Utah 84112

Quarto, 608 Lewisohn Hall, Columbia Univ., New York, N.Y. 10027

Raritan, 165 College Avenue, New Brunswick, N.J. 08903

RE:Artes Liberales, School of Liberal Arts, Stephen F. Austin St. Univ., Nacogdoches, Texas 75962

Reconstructionist, Church Road and Greenwood Avenue, Wyncote, Penn. 19095

Redbook, 230 Park Avenue, New York, N.Y. 10017

River City Review, P.O. Box 34275, Louisville, Ky. 40232

Sailing, 125 E. Main St., P.O. Box 248, Port Washington, Wisc. 53074

Salamagundi, Skidmore College, Saratoga Springs, N.Y. 12866

The Seneca Review, P.O. Box 115, Hobart and William Smith College, Geneva, N.Y. 14456

Sequoia, Storke Student Publications Building, Stanford, Calif. 94305

Seventeen, 850 Third Avenue, New York, N.Y. 10022

The Sewanee Review, University of the South, Sewanee, Tenn. 37375

Shenandoah: The Washington and Lee University Review, Box 722, Lexington, Virginia 24450

The Short Story Review, P.O. Box 882108, San Francisco, Calif. 94188

Sinister Wisdom, P.O. Box 1023, Rockland, Maine 04841

Sojourner: The Women's Forum, 143 Albany Street, Cambridge, Mass. 02139

Sonora Review, Dept. of English, University of Arizona, Tucson, Ariz. 85721

The South Carolina Review, Department of English, Clemson University, Clemson, S.C. 29631

South Dakota Review, Box 111, University Exchange, Vermillion, S.D. 57069

Southern Humanities Review, Auburn University, Auburn, Ala. 36830

The Southern Review, Drawer D, University Station, Baton Rouge, La. 70803

Southwest Review, Southern Methodist University Press, Dallas, Tex. 75275

Stone Drum, P.O. Box 233, Valley View, Texas 76272-0233

Stories, 14 Beacon Street, Boston, Mass. 02108

StoryQuarterly, P.O. Box 1416, Northbrook, Ill. 60062

St. Andrews Review, St. Andrews Presbyterian College, Laurinburg, N.C. 28352

St. Anthony Messenger, 1615 Republic Street, Cincinnati, Ohio 45210-1298

Studia Mystica, California State University, Sacramento, Calif. 95819

The Texas Review, English Dept., Sam Houston University, Huntsville, Texas 77341

This World, San Francisco Chronicle, 901 Mission Street, San Francisco, Calif. 94103

The Threepenny Review, P.O. Box 9131, Berkeley, Calif. 94709

Tikkun, Institute of Labor and Mental Health, 5100 Leona Street, Oakland, Calif. 94619

Trillium, Jackson Community College, 2111 Emmons Road, Jackson, Michigan 49201

TriQuarterly, 2020 Ridge Avenue, Evanston, Ill. 60208

Twilight Zone, 800 Second Avenue, New York, N.Y. 10017

Twin Cities, 7834 East Bush Lake Road, Minneapolis, Minn. 55435

University of Windsor Review, Department of English, University of Windsor, Windsor, Ont., Canada N9B 3P4

U.S. Catholic, 221 West Madison Street, Chicago, Ill. 60606

Vanity Fair, 350 Madison Avenue, New York, N.Y. 10017

The Virginia Quarterly Review, University of Virginia, 1 West Range, Charlottesville, Va. 22903

Vogue, 350 Madison Avenue, New York, N.Y. 10017

Washington Review, Box 50132, Washington, D.C. 20004

Webster Review, Webster College, Webster Groves, Mo. 63119

West Coast Review, Simon Fraser University, Burnaby, B.C., Canada V5A 1S6

Western Humanities Review, Building 41, University of Utah, Salt Lake City, Utah 84112

Wind, RFD Route 1, Box 809, Pikeville, Ky. 41501

Woman's Day, 1515 Broadway, New York, N.Y. 10036

Women's Sports and Fitness, 501 Second Street, Suite 400, San Francisco, Calif. 94107

Writer's Forum, University of Colorado, Colorado Springs, Colo. 80907

Yale Review, 250 Church Street, 1902A Yale Station, New Haven, Conn. 06520

Yankee, Dublin, N.H. 03444

Zyzzyva, 55 Sutter Street, Suite 400, San Francisco, Calif. 94104